THE MORTAL INSTRUMENTS

Book Two

# City of Ashes

Also by Cassandra Clare

THE MORTAL INSTRUMENTS

*City of Bones*

*City of Glass*

*City of Fallen Angels*

*City of Lost Souls*

THE INFERNAL DEVICES

*Clockwork Angel*

*Clockwork Prince*

*Clockwork Princess*

THE MORTAL INSTRUMENTS

Book Two

# City of Ashes

CASSANDRA CLARE

Margaret K. McElderry Books
NEW YORK LONDON TORONTO SYDNEY

MARGARET K. McELDERRY BOOKS
An imprint of Simon & Schuster Children's Publishing Division
1230 Avenue of the Americas, New York, NY 10020

Also available in a hardcover edition.
Book design by Mike Rosamilia
The text for this book is set in Dolly.
Manufactured in the United States of America
First paperback edition March 2009
32 34 36 38 40 39 37 35 33 31
The Library of Congress has cataloged the hardcover edition as follows:
Clare, Cassandra.
City of ashes / Cassandra Clare.
p. cm.— (The mortal instruments ; bk. two)
Summary: Sixteen-year-old Clary continues trying to make sense of the swiftly changing events and relationships in her life as she becomes further involved with the Shadowhunters and their pursuit of demons and discovers some terrifying truths about her parents, her brother Jace, and her boyfriend Simon.
ISBN 978-1-4169-1429-7 (hc)
[1. Supernatural—Fiction. 2. Demonology—Ficiton. 3. Magic—Fiction.
4. New York (N.Y.)—Fiction.] I. Title.
PZ7.C5265Cga 2008
[Fic]—dc22
2007014714
ISBN 978-1-4169-7224-2 (pbk)

For my father,
who is not evil.
Well, maybe a little bit.

# Acknowledgments

The writing of this book would not have been possible without the support and encouragement of my writing group: Holly Black, Kelly Link, Ellen Kushner, Delia Sherman, Gavin Grant, and Sarah Smith. I also couldn't do without the NB Team: Justine Larbalestier, Maureen Johnson, Margaret Crocker, Libba Bray, Cecil Castellucci, Jaida Jones, Diana Peterfreund, and Marissa Edelman. Thanks also go to Eve Sinaiko and Emily Lauer for their help (and snarky commentary), and to Sarah Rees Brennan, for loving Simon more than anyone else on earth. My gratitude goes out to everyone at Simon & Schuster and Walker Books for believing in these books. Special thanks to my editor, Karen Wojtyla, for all the purple pencil marks, Sarah Payne for making changes way past the deadline, Bara MacNeill for keeping track of Jace's weaponry stash, and my agent, Barry Goldblatt, for telling me I'm being an idiot when I'm being an idiot. To my family as well: my mother, my father, Kate Conner, Jim Hill, my aunt Naomi, and my cousin Joyce for their encouragement. And for Josh, who is less than three.

This Bitter Language

*I know your streets, sweet city,*
*I know the demons and angels that flock*
*and roost in your boughs like birds.*
*I know you, river, as if you flowed through my heart.*
*I am your warrior daughter.*
*There are letters made of your body*
*as a fountain is made of water.*
*There are languages*
*of which you are the blueprint*
*and as we speak them*
*the city rises.*

—Elka Cloke

# Prologue
## Smoke and Diamonds

**The formidable glass-and-steel structure rose from its** position on Front Street like a glittering needle threading the sky. There were fifty-seven floors to the Metropole, Manhattan's most expensive new downtown condominium tower. The topmost floor, the fifty-seventh, contained the most luxurious apartment of all: the Metropole penthouse, a masterpiece of sleek black-and-white design. Too new to have gathered dust yet, its bare marble floors reflected back the stars visible through the enormous floor-to-ceiling windows. The window glass was perfectly translucent, providing such a complete illusion that there was nothing between the viewer and the view that it had been known to induce vertigo even in those unafraid of heights.

Far below ran the silver ribbon of the East River, braceleted by shining bridges, flecked by boats as small as flyspecks, splitting the shining banks of light that were Manhattan and Brooklyn on either side. On a clear night the illuminated Statue of Liberty was just visible to the south—but there was fog tonight, and Liberty Island was hidden behind a white bank of mist.

However spectacular the view, the man standing in front of the window didn't look particularly impressed by it. There was a frown on his narrow, ascetic face as he turned away from the glass and strode across the floor, the heels of his boots echoing against the marble floor. "Aren't you ready *yet?*" he demanded, raking a hand through his salt-white hair. "We've been here nearly an hour."

The boy kneeling on the floor looked up at him, nervous and petulant. "It's the marble. It's more solid than I thought. It's making it hard to draw the pentagram."

"So skip the pentagram." Up close it was easier to see that despite his white hair, the man wasn't old. His hard face was severe but unlined, his eyes clear and steady.

The boy swallowed hard and the membranous black wings protruding from his narrow shoulder blades (he had cut slits in the back of his denim jacket to accommodate them) flapped nervously. "The pentagram is a necessary part of any demon-raising ritual. You know that, sir. Without it . . ."

"We're not protected. I know that, young Elias. But get on with it. I've known warlocks who could raise a demon, chat him up, and dispatch him back to hell in the time it's taken you to draw half a five-pointed star."

The boy said nothing, only attacked the marble again, this time with renewed urgency. Sweat dripped from his forehead and he pushed his hair back with a hand whose fingers were connected with delicate weblike membranes. "Done," he said at last, sitting back on his heels with a gasp. "It's done."

"Good." The man sounded pleased. "Let's get started."

"My money—"

"I told you. You'll get your money *after* I talk to Agramon, not before."

Elias got to his feet and shrugged his jacket off. Despite the holes he'd cut in it, it still compressed his wings uncomfortably; freed, they stretched and expanded themselves, wafting a breeze through the unventilated room. His wings were the color of an oil slick: black threaded with a rainbow of dizzying colors. The man looked away from him, as if the wings displeased him, but Elias didn't seem to notice. He began circling the pentagram he'd drawn, circling it counterclockwise and chanting in a demon language that sounded like the crackle of flames.

With a sound like air being sucked from a tire, the outline of the pentagram suddenly burst into flames. The dozen huge windows cast back a dozen burning reflected five-pointed stars.

Something was moving inside the pentagram, something formless and black. Elias was chanting more quickly now, raising his webbed hands, tracing delicate outlines on the air with his fingers. Where they passed, blue fire crackled. The man couldn't speak Chthonian, the warlock language, with any fluency, but he recognized enough of the words to understand Elias's repeated chant: *Agramon, I summon thee. Out of the spaces between the worlds, I summon thee.*

The man slid a hand into his pocket. Something hard and cold and metallic met the touch of his fingers. He smiled.

Elias had stopped walking. He was standing in front of the pentagram now, his voice rising and falling in a steady chant, blue fire crackling around him like lightning. Suddenly a plume of black smoke rose inside the pentagram; it spiraled upward, spreading and solidifying. Two eyes hung in the shadow like jewels caught in a spider's web.

*"Who has called me here across the worlds?"* Agramon demanded in a voice like shattering glass. *"Who summons me?"*

Elias had stopped chanting. He was standing still in front of the pentagram—still except for his wings, which beat the air slowly. The air stank of corrosion and burning.

"Agramon," the warlock said. "I am the warlock Elias. I am the one who has summoned you."

For a moment there was silence. Then the demon laughed, if smoke can be said to laugh. The laugh itself was caustic as acid. *"Foolish warlock,"* Agramon wheezed. *"Foolish boy."*

"You are the foolish one, if you think you can threaten me," Elias said, but his voice trembled like his wings. "You will be a prisoner of that pentagram, Agramon, until I release you."

*"Will I?"* The smoke surged forward, forming and re-forming itself. A tendril took the shape of a human hand and stroked the edge of the burning pentagram that contained it. Then, with a surge, the smoke seethed past the edge of the star, poured over the border like a wave breaching a levee. The flames guttered and died as Elias, screaming, stumbled backward. He was chanting now, in rapid Chthonian, spells of containment and banishment. Nothing happened; the black smoke-mass came on inexorably, and now it was starting to have something of a shape—a malformed, enormous, hideous shape, its glowing eyes altering, rounding to the size of saucers, spilling a dreadful light.

The man watched with impassive interest as Elias screamed again and turned to run. He never reached the door. Agramon surged forward, his dark mass crashing down over the warlock like a surge of boiling black tar. Elias struggled feebly for a moment under the onslaught—and then was still.

The black shape withdrew, leaving the warlock lying contorted on the marble floor.

"I do hope," said the man, who had taken the cold metal object out of his pocket and was toying with it idly, "that you haven't done anything to him that will render him useless to me. I need his blood, you see."

Agramon turned, a black pillar with deadly diamond eyes. They took in the man in the expensive suit, his narrow, unconcerned face, the black Marks covering his skin, and the glowing object in his hand. *"You paid the warlock child to summon me? And you did not tell him what I could do?"*

"You guess correctly," said the man.

Agramon spoke with grudging admiration. *"That was clever."*

The man took a step toward the demon. "I *am* very clever. And I'm also your master now. I hold the Mortal Cup. You must obey me, or face the consequences."

The demon was silent a moment. Then it slid to the ground in a mockery of obeisance—the closest a creature with no real body could come to kneeling. *"I am at your service, my Lord . . . ?"*

The sentence ended politely, on a question.

The man smiled. "You may call me Valentine."

# Part One
# A Season in Hell

*I believe I am in Hell, therefore I am.*
—Arthur Rimbaud

# 1

# Valentine's Arrow

**"Are you still mad?"**

Alec, leaning against the wall of the elevator, glared across the small space at Jace. "I'm not mad."

"Oh, yes you are." Jace gestured accusingly at his stepbrother, then yelped as pain shot up his arm. Every part of him hurt from the thumping he'd taken that afternoon when he'd dropped three floors through rotted wood onto a pile of scrap metal. Even his fingers were bruised. Alec, who'd only recently put away the crutches he'd had to use after his fight with Abbadon, didn't look much better than Jace felt. His clothes were covered in mud and his hair hung down in lank, sweaty strips. There was a long cut down the side of his cheek.

"I am not," Alec said, through his teeth. "Just because you said dragon demons were extinct—"

"I said mostly extinct."

Alec jabbed a finger toward him. "Mostly extinct," he said, his voice trembling with rage, "is NOT EXTINCT ENOUGH."

"I see," said Jace. "I'll just have them change the entry in the demonology textbook from 'almost extinct' to 'not extinct enough for Alec. He prefers his monsters really, really extinct.' Will *that* make you happy?"

"Boys, boys," said Isabelle, who'd been examining her face in the elevator's mirrored wall. "Don't fight." She turned away from the glass with a sunny smile. "All right, so it was a little more action than we were expecting, but I thought it was fun."

Alec looked at her and shook his head. "How do you manage *never* to get mud on you?"

Isabelle shrugged philosophically. "I'm pure at heart. It repels the dirt."

Jace snorted so loudly that she turned on him with a frown. He wiggled his mud-caked fingers at her. His nails were black crescents. "Filthy inside and out."

Isabelle was about to reply when the elevator ground to a halt with the sound of screeching brakes. "Time to get this thing fixed," she said, yanking the door open. Jace followed her out into the entryway, already looking forward to shucking his armor and weapons and stepping into a hot shower. He'd convinced his stepsiblings to come hunting with him despite the fact that neither of them was entirely comfortable going out on their own now that Hodge wasn't there to give them instructions. But Jace had wanted the oblivion of fighting, the harsh diversion of killing, and the distraction of injuries. And knowing he wanted it, they'd gone along with it, crawling through filthy deserted subway tunnels until they'd found the Draconidae demon and killed it. The three of them working together in perfect unison, the way they always had. Like family.

He unzipped his jacket and slung it over one of the pegs hanging on the wall. Alec was sitting on the low wooden bench next to him, kicking off his muck-covered boots. He was humming tunelessly under his breath, letting Jace know he wasn't *that* annoyed. Isabelle was pulling the pins out of her long dark hair, allowing it to shower down around her. "Now I'm hungry," she said. "I wish Mom were here to cook us something."

"Better that she isn't," said Jace, unbuckling his weapons belt. "She'd already be shrieking about the rugs."

"You're right about that," said a cool voice, and Jace swung around, his hands still at his belt, and saw Maryse Lightwood, her arms folded, standing in the doorway. She wore a stiff black traveling suit and her hair, black as Isabelle's, was drawn back into a thick rope that hung halfway down her back. Her eyes, a glacial blue, swept over the three of them like a tracking searchlight.

"Mom!" Isabelle, recovering her composure, ran to her mother for a hug. Alec got to his feet and joined them, trying to hide the fact that he was still limping.

Jace stood where he was. There had been something in Maryse's eyes as her gaze had passed over him that froze him in place. Surely what he had said wasn't *that* bad. They joked about her obsession with the antique rugs all the time—

"Where's Dad?" Isabelle asked, stepping back from her mother. "And Max?"

There was an almost imperceptible pause. Then Maryse said, "Max is in his room. And your father, unfortunately, is still in Alicante. There was some business there that required his attention."

Alec, generally more sensitive to moods than his sister, seemed to hesitate. "Is something wrong?"

"I could ask *you* that." His mother's tone was dry. "Are you limping?"

"I . . ."

Alec was a terrible liar. Isabelle picked up for him, smoothly:

"We had a run-in with a Draconidae demon in the subway tunnels. But it was nothing."

"And I suppose that Greater Demon you fought last week, that was nothing too?"

Even Isabelle was silenced by that. She looked to Jace, who wished she hadn't.

"That wasn't planned for." Jace was having a hard time concentrating. Maryse hadn't greeted him yet, hadn't said so much as hello, and she was still looking at him with eyes like blue daggers. There was a hollow feeling in the pit of his stomach that was beginning to spread. She'd never looked at him like this before, no matter what he'd done. "It was a mistake—"

"Jace!" Max, the youngest Lightwood, squeezed his way around Maryse and darted into the room, evading his mother's reaching hand. "You're back! You're all back." He turned in a circle, grinning at Alec and Isabelle in triumph. "I *thought* I heard the elevator."

"And I thought I told you to stay in your room," said Maryse.

"I don't remember that," said Max, with a seriousness that made even Alec smile. Max was small for his age—he looked about seven—but he had a self-contained gravity that, combined with his oversize glasses, gave him the air of someone older. Alec reached over and ruffled his brother's hair, but Max was still looking at Jace, his eyes shining. Jace felt the cold fist clenched in his stomach relax ever so slightly. Max had always hero-worshiped him in a way that he didn't worship his own older brother, probably because Jace was far more tolerant of Max's presence. "I heard you fought a Greater Demon," he said. "Was it awesome?"

"It was . . . different," Jace hedged. "How was Alicante?"

"It was *awesome*. We saw the coolest stuff. There's this huge armory in Alicante and they took me to some of the places where they make the weapons. They showed me a new way to make seraph blades too, so they last longer, and I'm going to try to get Hodge to show me—"

Jace couldn't help it; his eyes flicked instantly to Maryse, his expression incredulous. So Max didn't know about Hodge? Hadn't she *told* him?

Maryse saw his look and her lips thinned into a knifelike line. "That's enough, Max." She took her youngest son by the arm.

He craned his head to look up at her in surprise. "But I'm talking to Jace—"

"I can see that." She pushed him gently toward Isabelle. "Isabelle, Alec, take your brother to his room. Jace,"—there was a tightness in her voice when she spoke his name, as if invisible acid were drying up the syllables in her mouth—"get yourself cleaned up and meet me in the library as soon as you can."

"I don't get it," said Alec, looking from his mother to Jace, and back again. "What's going on?"

Jace could feel cold sweat start up along his spine. "Is this about my father?"

Maryse jerked twice, as if the words "my father" had been two separate slaps. "The *library*," she said, through clenched teeth. "We'll discuss the matter there."

Alec said, "What happened while you were gone wasn't Jace's fault. We were all in on it. And Hodge said—"

"We'll discuss Hodge later as well." Maryse's eyes were on Max, her tone warning.

"But, Mother," Isabelle protested. "If you're going to punish Jace, you should punish us as well. It would only be fair. We all did exactly the same things."

"No," said Maryse, after a pause so long that Jace thought perhaps she wasn't going to say anything at all. "You didn't."

"Rule number one of anime," Simon said. He sat propped up against a pile of pillows at the foot of his bed, a bag of potato chips in one hand and the TV remote in the other. He was wearing a black T-shirt that said I BLOGGED YOUR MOM and a pair of jeans with a hole ripped in one knee. "Never screw with a blind monk."

"I know," Clary said, taking a potato chip and dunking it into the can of dip balanced on the TV tray between them. "For some reason they're always way better fighters than monks who can see." She peered at the screen. "Are those guys dancing?"

"That's not dancing. They're trying to kill each other. This is the guy who's the mortal enemy of the other guy, remember? He killed his dad. Why would they be dancing?"

Clary crunched at her chip and stared meditatively at the screen, where animated swirls of pink and yellow clouds rippled between the figures of two winged men, who floated around each other, each clutching a glowing spear. Every once in a while one of them would speak, but since it was all in Japanese with Chinese subtitles, it didn't clarify much. "The guy with the hat," she said. "He was the evil guy?"

"No, the hat guy was the dad. He was the magical emperor, and that was his hat of power. The evil guy was the one with the mechanical hand that talks."

The telephone rang. Simon set the bag of chips down and made as if to get up and answer it. Clary put her hand on his wrist. "Don't. Just leave it."

"But it might be Luke. He could be calling from the hospital."

"It's not Luke," Clary said, sounding more sure than she felt. "He'd call my cell, not your house."

Simon looked at her a long moment before sinking back down on the rug beside her. "If you say so." She could hear the doubt in his voice, but also the unspoken assurance, *I just want you to be happy.* She wasn't sure "happy" was anything she was likely to be right now, not with her mother in the hospital hooked up to tubes and bleeping machines, and Luke like a zombie, slumped in the hard plastic chair next to her bed. Not with worrying about Jace all the time and picking up the phone a dozen times to call the Institute before setting it back down, the number still undialed. If Jace wanted to talk to her, *he* could call.

Maybe it had been a mistake to take him to see Jocelyn. She'd been so sure that if her mother could just hear the voice of her son, her firstborn, she'd wake up. But she hadn't. Jace had stood stiff and awkward by the bed, his face like a painted angel's, with blank indifferent eyes. Clary had finally lost her patience and shouted at him, and he'd shouted back before storming off. Luke had watched him go with a clinical sort of interest on his exhausted face. "That's the first time I've seen you act like sister and brother," he'd remarked.

Clary had said nothing in response. There was no point telling him how badly she wanted Jace *not* to be her brother. You couldn't rip out your own DNA, no matter how much you wished you could. No matter how much it would make you *happy*.

But even if she couldn't quite manage happy, she thought, at least here in Simon's house, in his bedroom, she felt comfortable and at home. She'd known him long enough to remember when he had a bed shaped like a fire truck and LEGOs piled in a corner of the room. Now the bed was a futon with a brightly striped quilt that had been a present from his sister, and the walls were plastered with posters of bands like Rock Solid Panda and Stepping Razor. There was a drum set wedged into the corner of the room where the LEGOs had been, and a computer in the other corner, the screen still frozen on an image from World of Warcraft. It was almost as familiar as being in her own bedroom at home—which no longer existed, so at least this was the next best thing.

"More chibis," said Simon gloomily. All the characters on-screen had turned into inch-high baby versions of themselves and were chasing each other around waving pots and pans. "I'm changing the channel," Simon announced, seizing the remote. "I'm tired of this anime. I can't tell what the plot is and no one ever has sex."

"Of course they don't," Clary said, taking another chip. "Anime is wholesome family entertainment."

"If you're in the mood for less wholesome entertainment, we could try the porn channels," Simon observed. "Would you rather watch *The Witches of Breastwick* or *As I Lay Dianne*?"

"Give me that!" Clary grabbed for the remote, but Simon, chortling, had already switched the TV to another channel.

His laughter broke off abruptly. Clary looked up in surprise and saw him staring blankly at the TV. An old black-and-white movie was playing—*Dracula*. She'd seen it before, with her mother. Bela Lugosi, thin and white-faced, was on-screen, wrapped in the familiar high-collared cloak, his lips curled back from his pointed teeth. "I never drink . . . wine," he intoned in his thick Hungarian accent.

"I love how the spiderwebs are made out of rubber," Clary said, trying to sound light. "You can totally tell."

But Simon was already on his feet, dropping the remote onto the bed. "I'll be right back," he muttered. His face was the color of winter sky just before it rained. Clary watched him go, biting her lip hard—it was the first time since her mother had gone to the hospital that she'd realized maybe Simon wasn't too *happy* either.

Toweling off his hair, Jace regarded his reflection in the mirror with a quizzical scowl. A healing rune had taken care of the worst of his bruises, but it hadn't helped the shadows under his eyes or the tight lines at the corners of his mouth. His head ached and he felt slightly dizzy. He knew he should have eaten something that morning, but he'd woken up nauseated and panting from nightmares, not wanting to pause to eat, just wanting the release of physical activity, to burn out his dreams in bruises and sweat.

Tossing the towel aside, he thought longingly of the sweet black tea Hodge used to brew from the night-blooming flowers in the greenhouse. The tea had taken away hunger pangs and brought a swift surge of energy. Since Hodge's disappearance, Jace had tried boiling the plants' leaves in water to see if he could produce the same effect, but the only result was a bitter, ashy-tasting liquid that made him gag and spit.

Barefoot, he padded into the bedroom and threw on jeans and a clean shirt. He pushed back his wet blond hair, frowning. It was too long at the moment, falling into his eyes—something Maryse would be sure to chide him about. She always did. He might not be the Lightwoods' biological son, but they'd treated him like it since they'd adopted him at age ten, after the death of his own father. The *supposed* death, Jace reminded himself, that hollow feeling in his guts resurfacing again. He'd felt like a jack-o'-lantern for the past few days, as if his guts had been yanked out with a fork and dumped in a heap while a grinning smile stayed plastered on his face. He often wondered if anything he'd believed about his life, or himself, had ever been true. He'd thought he was an orphan—he wasn't. He'd thought he was an only child—he had a sister.

*Clary*. The pain came again, stronger. He pushed it down. His eyes fell on the bit of broken mirror that lay atop his dresser, still reflecting green boughs and a diamond of blue sky. It was nearly twilight now in Idris: The sky was dark as cobalt. Choking on hollowness, Jace yanked his boots on and headed downstairs to the library.

He wondered as he clattered down the stone steps just what it was that Maryse wanted to say to him alone. She'd looked like she'd wanted to haul off and smack him. He couldn't remember the last time she'd laid a hand on him. The Lightwoods weren't given to corporal punishment—quite a change from being brought up by Valentine, who'd concocted all sorts of painful castigations to encourage obedience. Jace's Shadowhunter skin always healed, covering all but the worst of the evidence. In the days and weeks after his father died Jace could remember searching his body for scars, for some mark that would be a token, a remembrance to tie him physically to his father's memory.

He reached the library and knocked once before pushing the door open. Maryse was there, sitting in Hodge's old chair by the fire. Light streamed down through the high windows and Jace could see the touches of gray in her hair. She was holding a glass of red wine; there was a cut-glass decanter on the table beside her.

"Maryse," he said.

She jumped a little, spilling some of the wine. "Jace. I didn't hear you come in."

He didn't move. "Do you remember that song you used to sing to Isabelle and Alec—when they were little and afraid of the dark—to get them to fall asleep?"

Maryse appeared taken aback. "What are you talking about?"

"I used to hear you through the walls," he said. "Alec's bedroom was next to mine then."

She said nothing.

"It was in French," Jace said. "The song."

"I don't know why you'd remember something like that." She looked at him as if he'd accused her of something.

"You never sang to me."

There was a barely perceptible pause. Then, "Oh, you," she said. "You were never afraid of the dark."

"What kind of ten-year-old is never afraid of the dark?"

Her eyebrows went up. "Sit down, Jonathan," she said. "Now."

He went, just slowly enough to annoy her, across the room, and threw himself into one of the wing-back chairs beside the desk. "I'd rather you didn't call me Jonathan."

"Why not? It's your name." She looked at him consideringly. "How long have you known?"

"Known what?"

"Don't be stupid. You know exactly what I'm asking you." She turned her glass in her fingers. "How long have you known that Valentine is your father?"

Jace considered and discarded several responses. Usually he could get his way with Maryse by making her laugh. He was one of the only people in the world who *could* make her laugh. "About as long as you have."

Maryse shook her head slowly. "I don't believe that."

Jace sat up straight. His hands were in fists where they rested on the chair arms. He could see a slight tremor in his fingers, wondered if he'd ever had it before. He didn't think so. His hands had always been as steady as his heartbeat. "You don't *believe* me?"

He heard the incredulity in his own voice and winced inwardly. Of course she didn't believe him. That had been obvious from the moment she had arrived home.

"It doesn't make sense, Jace. How could you not know who your own father is?"

"He told me he was Michael Wayland. We lived in the Wayland country house—"

"A nice touch," said Maryse, "that. And your name? What's your real name?"

"You know my real name."

"Jonathan. I knew that was Valentine's son's name. I knew Michael had a son named Jonathan too. It's a common enough Shadowhunter name—I never thought it was strange they shared it, and as for Michael's boy's middle name, I never inquired. But now I can't help wondering. How long had Valentine been planning what he was going to do? How long did he know he was going to murder Jonathan Wayland—?" She broke off, her eyes fixed on Jace. "You never looked like Michael, you know," she said. "But sometimes children don't look like their parents. I didn't think about it before. But now I can see Valentine in you. The way you're looking at me. That defiance. You don't care what I say, do you?"

But he did care. All he was good at was making sure she couldn't see it. "Would it make a difference if I did?"

She set the glass down on the table beside her. It was empty. "And you answer questions with questions to throw me off, just like Valentine always did. Maybe I should have known."

"Maybe nothing. I'm still exactly the same person I've been for the past seven years. Nothing's changed about me. If I didn't remind you of Valentine before, I don't see why I would now."

Her glance moved over him and away as if she couldn't bear to look directly at him. "Surely when we talked about Michael, you must have known we couldn't possibly have meant your father. The things we said about him could never have applied to Valentine."

"You said he was a good man." Anger twisted inside him. "A brave Shadowhunter. A loving father. I thought that seemed accurate enough."

"What about photographs? You must have seen photographs of Michael Wayland and realized he wasn't the man you called your father." She bit her lip. "Help me out here, Jace."

"All the photographs were destroyed in the Uprising. That's what *you* told me. Now I wonder if it wasn't because Valentine had them all burned so nobody would know who was in the Circle. I never had a photograph of my father," Jace said, and wondered if he sounded as bitter as he felt.

Maryse put a hand to her temple and massaged it as if her head were aching. "I can't believe this," she said, as if to herself. "It's insane."

"So don't believe it. Believe *me*," Jace said, and felt the tremor in his hands increase.

She dropped her hand. "Don't you think I *want* to?" she demanded, and for a moment he heard the echo in her voice of the Maryse who'd come into his bedroom at night when he was ten years old and staring dry-eyed at the ceiling, thinking of his father—and she'd sat by the bed with him until he'd fallen asleep just before dawn.

"I didn't know," Jace said again. "And when he asked me to come with him back to Idris, I said no. I'm still here. Doesn't that count for anything?"

She turned to look back at the decanter, as if considering another drink, then seemed to discard the idea. "I wish it did," she said. "But there are so many reasons your father might want you to remain at the Institute. Where Valentine is concerned, I can't afford to trust anyone his influence has touched."

"His influence touched you," Jace said, and instantly regretted it at the look that flashed across her face.

"And *I* repudiated him," said Maryse. "Have you? *Could* you?" Her blue eyes were the same color as Alec's, but Alec had never looked at him like this. "Tell me you hate him, Jace. Tell me you hate that man and everything he stands for."

A moment passed, and another, and Jace, looking down, saw that his hands were so tightly fisted that the knuckles stood out white and hard like the bones in a fish's spine. "I can't say that."

Maryse sucked in her breath. "*Why not?*"

"Why can't you say that you trust me? I've lived with you almost half my life. Surely you must know me better than that?"

"You sound so honest, Jonathan. You always have, even when you were a little boy trying to pin the blame for something you'd done wrong on Isabelle or Alec. I've only ever met one person who could sound as persuasive as you."

Jace tasted copper in his mouth. "You mean my father."

"There were only ever two kinds of people in the world for Valentine," she said. "Those who were for the Circle and those who were against it. The latter were enemies, and the former were weapons in his arsenal. I saw him try to turn each of his friends, even his own wife, into a weapon for the Cause—and you want me to believe he wouldn't have done the same with his own son?" She shook her head. "I knew him better than that." For the first time, Maryse looked at him with more sadness than anger. "You are an arrow shot directly into the heart of the Clave, Jace. You are Valentine's arrow. Whether you know it or not."

* * *

Clary shut the bedroom door on the blaring TV and went to look for Simon. She found him in the kitchen, bent over the sink with the water running. His hands were braced on the draining board.

"Simon?" The kitchen was a bright, cheerful yellow, the walls decorated with framed chalk and pencil sketches Simon and Rebecca had done in grade school. Rebecca had some drawing talent, you could tell, but Simon's sketches of people all looked like parking meters with tufts of hair.

He didn't look up now, though she could tell by the tightening of his shoulder muscles that he'd heard her. She went over to the sink, laying a hand lightly on his back. She felt the sharp nubs of his spine through the thin cotton T-shirt and wondered if he'd lost weight. She couldn't tell by looking at him, but looking at Simon was like looking in a mirror—when you saw someone every day, you didn't always notice small changes in their outward appearance. "Are you okay?"

He turned the water off with a hard jerk of his wrist. "Sure. I'm fine."

She laid a finger against the side of his chin and turned his face toward her. He was sweating, the dark hair that lay across his forehead stuck to his skin, though the air coming through the half-open kitchen window was cool. "You don't look fine. Was it the movie?"

He didn't answer.

"I'm sorry. I shouldn't have laughed, it's just—"

"You don't remember?" His voice sounded hoarse.

"I . . ." Clary trailed off. That night, looking back, seemed a long haze of running, of blood and sweat, of shadows glimpsed in doorways, of falling through space. She remembered the white faces of the vampires, like paper cutouts against the darkness, and remembered Jace holding her, shouting hoarsely into her ear. "Not really. It's a blur."

His gaze flicked past her and then back. "Do I seem different to you?" he asked.

She raised her eyes to his. His were the color of black coffee—not really black, but a rich brown without a touch of gray or hazel. Did he seem different? There might have been an extra touch of confidence in the way he held himself since the day he'd killed Abbadon, the Greater Demon; but there was also a wariness about him, as if he were waiting or watching for something. It was something she had noticed about Jace as well. Perhaps it was only the awareness of mortality. "You're still Simon."

He half-closed his eyes as if in relief, and as his eyelashes lowered, she saw how angular his cheekbones looked. He *had* lost weight, she thought, and was about to say so when he leaned down and kissed her.

She was so surprised at the feel of his mouth on hers that she went rigid all over, grabbing for the edge of the draining board to support herself. She did not, however, push him away, and clearly taking this as a sign of encouragement, Simon slid his hand behind her head and deepened the kiss, parting her lips with his. His mouth was soft, softer than Jace's had been, and the hand that cupped her neck was warm and gentle. He tasted like salt.

She let her eyes fall shut and for a moment floated dizzily in the darkness and the heat, the feel of his fingers moving through her hair. When the harsh ring of the telephone cut through her daze, she jumped back as if he'd pushed her away, though he hadn't moved. They stared at each other for a moment, in wild confusion, like two people finding themselves suddenly transported to a strange landscape where nothing was familiar.

Simon turned away first, reaching for the phone that hung on the wall beside the spice rack. "Hello?" He sounded normal, but his chest was rising and falling fast. He held the receiver out to Clary. "It's for you."

Clary took the phone. She could still feel the pounding of her heart in her throat, like the fluttering wings of an insect trapped under her skin. *It's Luke, calling from the hospital. Something's happened to my mother.*

She swallowed. "Luke? Is it you?"

"No. It's Isabelle."

"Isabelle?" Clary looked up and saw Simon watching her, leaning against the sink. The flush on his cheeks had faded. "Why are you—I mean, what's up?"

There was a hitch in the other girl's voice, as if she'd been crying. "Is Jace there?"

Clary actually held out the phone so she could stare at it before bringing the receiver back to her ear. "Jace? No. Why would he be here?"

Isabelle's answering breath echoed down the phone line like a gasp. "The thing is . . . he's *gone*."

# 2
# The Hunter's Moon

**Maia Roberts had never trusted beautiful boys, which was why** she hated Jace Wayland the first time she ever laid eyes on him.

Her older brother, Daniel, had been born with her mother's honey-colored skin and huge dark eyes, and he'd turned out to be the sort of person who lit the wings of butterflies on fire to watch them burn and die as they flew. He'd tormented her as well, in small and petty ways at first, pinching her where the bruises wouldn't show, switching the shampoo in her bottle for bleach. She'd gone to her parents but they hadn't believed her. No one had, looking at Daniel; they'd confused beauty with innocence and harmlessness. When he broke her arm in ninth grade, she ran away from home, but her parents brought her back. In tenth grade, Daniel was knocked down in the street by a hit-and-run driver and killed instantly. Standing next to her parents at the graveside, Maia had been ashamed by her own overwhelming sense of relief. God, she thought, would surely punish her for being glad that her brother was dead.

The next year, He did. She met Jordan. Long dark hair, slim hips in worn jeans, indie-boy rocker shirts and lashes like a girl's. She never thought he'd go for her—his type usually preferred skinny, pale girls in hipster glasses—but he seemed to like her rounded shape. He told her she was beautiful in between kisses. The first few months were like a dream; the last few months like a nightmare. He became possessive, controlling. When he was angry with her, he'd snarl and whip the back of his hand across her cheek, leaving a mark like too much blusher. When she tried to break up with him, he pushed her, knocked her down in her own front yard before she ran inside and slammed the door.

Later, she let him see her kissing another boy, just to get the point across that it was over. She didn't even remember that boy's name anymore. What she did remember was walking home that night, the rain misting her hair in fine droplets, mud splattering up the legs of her jeans as she took a shortcut through the park near her house. She remembered the dark shape exploding out from behind the metal merry-go-round, the huge wet wolf body knocking her into the mud, the savage pain as its jaws clamped down on her throat. She'd screamed and thrashed, tasting her own hot blood in her mouth, her brain screaming: *This is impossible. Impossible.* There weren't wolves in New Jersey, not in her ordinary suburban neighborhood, not in the twenty-first century.

Her cries brought lights on in the nearby houses, one after

another of the windows lighting up like struck matches. The wolf let her go, its jaws trailing ribbons of blood and torn flesh.

Twenty-four stitches later, she was back in her pink bedroom, her mother hovering anxiously. The emergency room doctor had said the bite looked like a large dog's, but Maia knew better. Before the wolf had turned to race away, she'd heard a hot, familiar whispered voice in her ear, "You're mine now. You'll always be mine."

She never saw Jordan again—he and his parents packed up their apartment and moved, and none of his friends knew where he'd gone, or would admit they did. She was only half-surprised the next full moon when the pains started: tearing pains that ripped up and down her legs, forcing her to the ground, bending her spine the way a magician might bend a spoon. When her teeth burst out of her gums and rattled to the floor like spilled Chiclets, she fainted. Or thought she did. She woke up miles away from her house, naked and covered in blood, the scar on her throat pulsing like a heartbeat. That night she hopped the train to Manhattan. It wasn't a hard decision. It was bad enough being biracial in her conservative suburban neighborhood. God knew what they'd do to a werewolf.

It hadn't been that hard to find a pack to fall in with. There were several of them in Manhattan alone. She wound up with the downtown pack, the ones who slept in the old police station in Chinatown.

Pack leaders were mutable. There'd been Kito first, then Véronique, then Gabriel, and now Luke. She'd liked Gabriel all right, but Luke was better. He had a trustworthy look and kind blue eyes and wasn't too handsome, so she didn't dislike him on the spot. She was comfortable enough here with the pack, sleeping in the old police station, playing cards and eating Chinese food on nights when the moon wasn't full, hunting through the park when it was, and the next day drinking off the hangover of the Change at the Hunter's Moon, one of the city's better underground werewolf bars. There was ale by the yard, and nobody ever carded you to see if you were under twenty-one. Being a lycanthrope made you grow up fast, and as long as you sprouted hair and fangs once a month, you were good to drink at the Moon, no matter how old you were in mundane years.

These days she hardly thought of her family at all, but when the blond boy in the long black coat stalked his way into the bar, Maia stiffened all over. He didn't look like Daniel, not exactly—Daniel had had dark hair that curled close to the nape of his neck and honey skin, and this boy was all white and gold. But they had the same lean bodies, the same way of walking, like a panther on the lookout for prey, and the same total confidence in their own attraction. Her hand tightened convulsively around the stem of her glass and she had to remind herself: *He's dead. Daniel's dead.*

A rush of murmurs swept through the bar on the heels of the boy's arrival, like the froth of a wave spreading out from the stern of a boat. The boy acted as if he didn't notice anything, hooking a bar stool toward himself with a booted foot and settling onto it with his elbows on the bar. Maia heard him order a shot of single malt in the quiet that followed the murmurs. He downed half the drink with a neat flip of his wrist. The liquor was the same dark gold color as his hair. When he lifted his hand to set the glass back down on the bar, Maia saw the thick coiling black Marks on his wrists and the backs of his hands.

Bat, the guy sitting next to her—she'd dated him once, but they were friends now—muttered something under his breath that sounded like "Nephilim."

*So that's it.* The boy wasn't a werewolf at all. He was a Shadowhunter, a member of the arcane world's secret police force. They upheld the Law, backed by the Covenant, and you couldn't become one of them: You had to be born into it. Blood made them what they were. There were a lot of rumors about them, most unflattering: They were haughty, proud, cruel; they looked down on and despised Downworlders. There were few things a lycanthrope liked less than a Shadowhunter—except maybe a vampire.

People also said that the Shadowhunters killed demons. Maia remembered when she'd first heard that demons existed and had been told about what they did. It had given her a headache. Vampires and werewolves were just people with a disease, that much she understood, but expecting her to believe in all that heaven and hell crap, demons and angels, and still nobody could tell her for sure if there was a God or not, or where you went after you died? It wasn't fair. She believed in demons now—she'd seen enough of what they did that she wasn't able to deny it—but she wished she didn't have to.

"I take it," the boy said, leaning his elbows onto the bar, "that you don't serve Silver Bullet here. Too many bad associations?" His eyes gleamed, narrow and shining like the moon at a quarter full.

The bartender, Freaky Pete, just looked at the boy and shook his head in disgust. If the boy hadn't been a Shadowhunter, Maia guessed, Pete would have tossed him out of the Moon, but instead he just walked to the other end of the bar and busied himself polishing glasses.

"Actually," said Bat, who was unable to stay out of anything, "we don't serve it because it's really crappy beer."

The boy turned his narrow, shining gaze on Bat, and smiled delightedly. Most people didn't smile delightedly when Bat looked at them funny: Bat was six and a half feet tall, with a thick scar that disfigured half his face where silver powder had burned his skin. Bat wasn't one of the overnighters, the pack who lived in the police station, sleeping in the old cells. He had his own apartment, even a job. He'd been a pretty good boyfriend, right up until he dumped Maia for a redheaded witch named Eve who lived in Yonkers and ran a palmistry shop out of her garage.

"And what are *you* drinking?" the boy inquired, leaning so close to Bat that it was like an insult. "A little hair of the dog that bit—well, everyone?"

"You really think you're pretty funny." By this point the rest of the pack was leaning in to hear them, ready to back up Bat if he decided to knock this obnoxious brat into the middle of next week. "Don't you?"

"Bat," Maia said. She wondered if she were the only pack member in the bar who doubted Bat's *ability* to knock the boy into next week. It wasn't that she doubted Bat. It was something about the boy's eyes. "Don't."

Bat ignored her. "*Don't* you?"

"Who am I to deny the obvious?" The boy's eyes slid over Maia as if she were invisible and went back to Bat. "I don't suppose you'd like to tell me what happened to your face? It looks like—" And here he leaned forward and said something to Bat so quietly that Maia didn't hear it. The next thing she knew, Bat was swinging a blow at the boy that should have shattered his jaw, only the boy was no longer there. He was standing a good five feet away, laughing, as Bat's fist connected with his abandoned glass and sent it soaring across the bar to strike the opposite wall in a shower of shattering glass.

Freaky Pete was around the side of the bar, his big fist knotted in Bat's shirt, before Maia could blink an eye. "That's enough," he said. "Bat, why don't you take a walk and cool down."

Bat twisted in Pete's grasp. "Take a *walk?* Did you hear—"

"I heard." Pete's voice was low. "He's a Shadowhunter. Walk it off, cub."

Bat swore and pulled away from the bartender. He stalked toward the exit, his shoulders stiff with rage. The door banged shut behind him.

The boy had stopped smiling and was looking at Freaky Pete with a sort of dark resentment, as if the bartender had taken away a toy he'd intended to play with. "That wasn't necessary," he said. "I can handle myself."

Pete regarded the Shadowhunter. "It's my bar I'm worried about," he said finally. "You might want to take your business elsewhere, Shadowhunter, if you don't want any trouble."

"I didn't say I didn't want trouble." The boy sat back down on his stool. "Besides, I didn't get to finish my drink."

Maia glanced behind her, where the wall of the bar was soaked with alcohol. "Looks like you finished it to me."

For a second the boy just looked blank; then a curious spark of amusement lit in his golden eyes. He looked so much like Daniel in that moment that Maia wanted to back away.

Pete slid another glass of amber liquid across the bar before the boy could reply to her. "Here you go," he said. His eyes drifted to Maia. She thought she saw some admonishment in them.

"Pete—," she began. She didn't get to finish. The door to the bar flew open. Bat was standing there in the doorway. It took a moment for Maia to realize that the front of his shirt and his sleeves were soaked with blood.

She slid off her stool and ran to him. "Bat! Are you hurt?"

His face was gray, his silvery scar standing out on his cheek like a piece of twisted wire. "An attack," he said. "There's a body in the alley. A dead kid. Blood—everywhere." He shook his head, looked down at himself. "Not my blood. I'm fine."

"A body? But who—"

Bat's reply was swallowed in the commotion. Seats were abandoned as the pack rushed to the door. Pete came out from behind his counter and pushed his way through the mob. Only the Shadowhunter boy stayed where he was, his head bent over his drink.

Through gaps in the crowd around the door, Maia caught a glimpse of the gray paving of the alley, splashed with blood. It was still wet and had run between the cracks in the paving like the tendrils of a red plant. "His *throat* cut?" Pete was saying to Bat, whose color had come back. "How—"

"There was someone in the alley. Someone kneeling over him," Bat said. His voice was tight. "Not like a person—like a shadow. They ran off when they saw me. He was still alive. A little. I bent down over him, but—" Bat shrugged. It was a casual movement, but the cords in his neck were standing out like thick roots wrapping a tree trunk. "He died without saying anything."

"Vampires," said a buxom female lycanthrope—her name was Amabel, Maia thought—who was standing by the door. "The Night Children. It can't have been anything else."

Bat looked at her, then turned and stalked across the room toward the bar. He grabbed the Shadowhunter by the back of the jacket—or reached out as if he meant to, but the boy was already on his feet, turning fluidly. "What's your problem, werewolf?"

Bat's hand was still outstretched. "Are you deaf, Nephilim?" he snarled. "There's a dead boy in the alley. One of ours."

"Do you mean a lycanthrope or some other sort of Downworlder?" The boy arched his light eyebrows. "You all blend together to me."

There was a low growl—from Freaky Pete, Maia noted with some surprise. He had come back into the bar and was surrounded by the rest of the pack, their eyes fixed on the Shadowhunter. "He was only a cub," said Pete. "His name was Joseph."

The name didn't ring any bells for Maia, but she saw the tight set of Pete's jaw and felt a flutter in her stomach. The pack was on the warpath now and if the Shadowhunter had any sense, he'd be backpedaling like crazy. He wasn't, though. He was just standing there looking at them with those gold eyes and that funny smile on his face. "A lycanthrope boy?" he said.

"He was one of the pack," said Pete. "He was only fifteen."

"And what exactly do you expect me to do about it?" said the boy.

Pete was staring incredulously. "You're Nephilim," he said. "The Clave owes us protection in these circumstances."

The boy looked around the bar, slowly and with such a look of insolence that a flush spread over Pete's face.

"I don't see anything you need protecting from here," said the boy. "Except some bad décor and a possible mold problem. But you can usually clear that up with bleach."

"There's a *dead body* outside this bar's front door," said Bat, enunciating carefully. "Don't you think—"

"I think it's a little too late for him to need protection," said the boy, "if he's already dead."

Pete was still staring. His ears had grown pointed, and when he spoke, his voice was muffled by his thickening canine teeth. "You want to be careful, Nephilim," he said. "You want to be very careful."

The boy looked at him with opaque eyes. "Do I?"

"So you're going to do nothing?" Bat said. "Is that it?"

"I'm going to finish my drink," said the boy, eyeing his half-empty glass, still on the counter, "if you'll let me."

"So that's the attitude of the Clave, a week after the Accords?" said Pete with disgust. "The death of Downworlders is nothing to you?"

The boy smiled, and Maia's spine prickled. He looked exactly like Daniel just before Daniel reached out and yanked the wings off a ladybug. "How like Downworlders," he said, "expecting the Clave to clean your mess up for you. As if we could be bothered just because some stupid cub decided to splatter-paint himself all over your alley—"

And he used a word, a word for weres that they never used themselves, a filthily unpleasant word that implied an improper relationship between wolves and human women.

Before anyone else could move, Bat flung himself at the Shadowhunter—but the boy was gone. Bat stumbled and whirled around, staring. The pack gasped.

Maia's mouth dropped open. The Shadowhunter boy was standing on the bar, feet planted wide apart. He really did look like an avenging angel getting ready to dispatch divine justice from on high, as the Shadowhunters were meant to do. Then he reached out a hand and curled his fingers toward himself, quickly, a gesture familiar to her from the playground as *Come and get me*—and the pack rushed at him.

Bat and Amabel swarmed up onto the bar; the boy spun, so quickly that his reflection in the mirror behind the bar seemed to blur. Maia saw him kick out, and then the two were groaning on the floor in a flurry of smashed glass. She could hear the boy laughing even as someone else reached up and pulled him down; he sank into the crowd with an ease that spoke of willingness, and then she couldn't see him at all, just a welter of flailing arms and legs. Still, she thought she could hear him laughing, even as metal flashed—the edge of a knife—and she heard herself suck in her breath.

"That's enough."

It was Luke's voice, quiet, steady as a heartbeat. It was strange how you always knew your pack leader's voice. Maia turned and saw him standing just at the entrance to the bar, one hand against the wall. He looked not just tired, but *ravaged*, as if something were tearing him down from the inside; still, his voice was calm as he said again, "That's enough. Leave the boy alone."

The pack melted away from the Shadowhunter, leaving just Bat still standing there, defiant, one hand still gripping the back of the Shadowhunter's shirt, the other holding a short-bladed knife. The boy himself was bloody-faced but hardly looked like someone who needed saving; he was grinning a grin as dangerous-looking as the broken glass that littered the floor. "He's not a boy," Bat said. "He's a Shadowhunter."

"They're welcome enough here," said Luke, his tone neutral. "They are our allies."

"He said it didn't matter," said Bat angrily. "About Joseph—"

"I know," Luke said quietly. His eyes shifted to the blond boy. "Did you come in here just to pick a fight, Jace Wayland?"

The boy—Jace—smiled, stretching his split lip so that a thin trickle of blood ran down his chin. "Luke."

Bat, startled to hear their pack leader's first name come out of the Shadowhunter's mouth, let go of the back of Jace's shirt. "I didn't know—"

"There's nothing *to* know," said Luke, the tiredness in his eyes creeping into his voice.

Freaky Pete spoke, his voice a bass rumble. "He said the Clave wouldn't care about the death of a single lycanthrope, even a child. And it's a week after the Accords, Luke."

"Jace doesn't speak for the Clave," said Luke, "and there's nothing he could have done even if he'd wanted to. Isn't that right?"

He looked at Jace, who was very pale. "How do you—"

"I know what happened," said Luke. "With Maryse."

Jace stiffened, and for a moment Maia saw through the Daniel-like savage amusement to what was underneath, and it was dark and agonized and reminded her more of her own eyes in the mirror than of her brother's. "Who told you? Clary?"

"Not Clary." Maia had never heard Luke speak that name before, but he said it with a tone that implied that this was someone special to him, and to the Shadowhunter boy as well.

"I'm the pack leader, Jace. I hear things. Now come on. Let's go to Pete's office and talk."

Jace hesitated for a moment before shrugging. "Fine," he said, "but you owe me for the Scotch I didn't drink."

"That was my last guess," Clary said with a defeated sigh, sinking down onto the steps outside the Metropolitan Museum of Art and staring disconsolately down Fifth Avenue.

"It was a good one." Simon sat down beside her, long legs sprawled out in front of him. "I mean, he's a guy who likes weapons and killing, so why not the biggest collection of weapons in the whole city? And I'm always up for a visit to Arms and Armor, anyway. Gives me ideas for my campaign."

She looked at him in surprise. "You still gaming with Eric and Kirk and Matt?"

"Sure. Why wouldn't I be?"

"I thought gaming might have lost some of its appeal for you since . . ." *Since our real lives started to resemble one of your campaigns.* Complete with good guys, bad guys, really nasty magic, and important enchanted objects you had to find if you wanted to win the game.

Except in a game, the good guys always won, defeated the bad guys and came home with the treasure. Whereas in real life, they'd lost the treasure, and sometimes Clary still wasn't clear on who the bad and good guys actually were.

She looked at Simon and felt a wave of sadness. If he did give up gaming, it would be her fault, just like everything that had happened to him in the past weeks had been her fault. She remembered his white face at the sink that morning, just before he'd kissed her.

"Simon—," she began.

"Right now I'm playing a half-troll cleric who wants revenge on the Orcs who killed his family," he said cheerfully. "It's awesome."

She laughed just as her cell phone rang. She dug it out of her pocket and flipped it open; it was Luke. "We didn't find him," she said, before he could say hello.

"No. But I did."

She sat up straight. "You're kidding. Is he there? Can I talk to him?" She caught sight of Simon looking at her sharply and dropped her voice. "Is he all right?"

"Mostly."

"What do you mean, mostly?"

"He picked a fight with a werewolf pack. He's got some cuts and bruises."

Clary half-closed her eyes. Why, oh why, had Jace picked a fight with a pack of wolves? What had possessed him? Then again, it was Jace. He'd pick a fight with a Mack truck if the urge took him.

"I think you should come down here," Luke said. "Someone has to reason with him and I'm not having much luck."

"Where are you?" Clary asked.

He told her. A bar called the Hunter's Moon on Hester Street. She wondered if it was glamoured. Flipping her phone shut, she turned to Simon, who was staring at her with raised eyebrows.

"The prodigal returns?"

"Sort of." She scrambled to her feet and stretched her tired legs, mentally calculating how long it would take them to get to Chinatown on the train and whether it was worth shelling out the pocket money Luke had given her for a cab. Probably not, she decided—if they got stuck in traffic, it would take longer than the subway.

"... come with you?" Simon finished, standing up. He was on the step below her, which made them almost the same height. "What do you think?"

She opened her mouth, then closed it again quickly. "Er ..."

He sounded resigned. "You haven't heard a word I said these past two minutes, have you?"

"No," she admitted. "I was thinking about Jace. It sounded like he was in bad shape. Sorry."

His brown eyes darkened. "I take it you're rushing off to bind up his wounds?"

"Luke asked me to come down," she said. "I was hoping you'd come with me."

Simon kicked at the step above his with a booted foot. "I will, but—why? Can't Luke return Jace to the Institute without your help?"

"Probably. But he thinks Jace might be willing to talk to me about what's going on first."

"I thought maybe we could do something tonight," Simon said. "Something fun. See a movie. Get dinner downtown."

She looked at him. In the distance, she could hear water splashing into a museum fountain. She thought of the kitchen at his house, his damp hands in her hair, but it all seemed very far away, even though she could picture it—the way you might remember the photograph of an incident without really remembering the incident itself any longer.

"He's my brother," she said. "I have to go."

Simon looked as if he were too weary to even sigh. "Then I'll go with you."

* * *

The back office of Hunter's Moon was down a narrow corridor strewn with sawdust. Here and there the sawdust was churned up by footsteps and spotted with a dark liquid that didn't look like beer. The whole place smelled smoky and gamy, a little like—Clary had to admit it, though she wouldn't have said so to Luke—wet dog.

"He's not in a very good mood," said Luke, pausing in front of a closed door. "I shut him up in Freaky Pete's office after he nearly killed half my pack with his bare hands. He wouldn't talk to me, so"—Luke shrugged—"I thought of you." He looked from Clary's baffled face to Simon's. "What?"

"I can't believe he came *here*," Clary said.

"I can't believe you know someone named Freaky Pete," said Simon.

"I know a lot of people," said Luke. "Not that Freaky Pete is strictly *people*, but I'm hardly one to talk." He swung the office door wide. Inside was a plain room, windowless, the walls hung with sports pennants. There was a paper-strewn desk weighted down with a small TV set, and behind it, in a chair whose leather was so cracked it looked like veined marble, was Jace.

The moment the door opened, Jace seized up a yellow pencil lying on the desk and threw it. It sailed through the air and struck the wall just next to Luke's head, where it stuck, vibrating. Luke's eyes widened.

Jace smiled faintly. "Sorry, I didn't realize it was you."

Clary felt her heart contract. She hadn't seen Jace in days, and he looked different somehow—not just the bloody face and bruises, which were clearly new, but the skin on his face seemed tighter, the bones more prominent.

Luke indicated Simon and Clary with a wave of his hand. "I brought some people to see you."

Jace's eyes moved to them. They were as blank as if they had been painted on. "Unfortunately," he said, "I only had the one pencil."

"Jace—," Luke started.

"I don't want him in here." Jace jerked his chin toward Simon.

"That's hardly fair." Clary was indignant. Had he forgotten that Simon had saved Alec's life, possibly all their lives?

"Out, mundane," said Jace, pointing to the door.

Simon waved a hand. "It's fine. I'll wait in the hallway." He left, refraining from banging the door shut behind him, though Clary could tell he wanted to.

She turned back to Jace. "Do you have to be so—," she began, but stopped when she saw his face. It looked stripped down, oddly vulnerable.

"Unpleasant?" he finished for her. "Only on days when my adoptive mother tosses me out of the house with instructions never to darken her door again. Usually, I'm remarkably good-natured. Try me on any day that doesn't end in *y*."

Luke frowned. "Maryse and Robert Lightwood are not my favorite people, but I can't believe Maryse would do that."

Jace looked surprised. "You know them? The Lightwoods?"

"They were in the Circle with me," said Luke. "I was surprised when I heard they were heading the Institute here. It seems they made a deal with the Clave, after the Uprising, to ensure some kind of lenient treatment for themselves, while Hodge—well, we know what happened to him." He was silent a moment. "Did Maryse say why she was exiling you, so to speak?"

"She doesn't believe that I thought I was Michael Wayland's son. She accused me of being in it with Valentine all along—saying I helped him get away with the Mortal Cup."

"Then why would you still be here?" Clary asked. "Why wouldn't you have fled with him?"

"She wouldn't say, but I suspect she thinks I stayed to be a spy. A viper in their bosoms. Not that she used the word 'bosoms,' but the thought was there."

"A spy for Valentine?" Luke sounded dismayed.

"She thinks Valentine assumed that because of their affection for me, she and Robert would believe whatever I said. So Maryse has decided that the solution to that is not to have any affection for me."

"Affection doesn't work like that." Luke shook his head. "You can't turn it off, like a tap. Especially if you're a parent."

"They're not really my parents."

"There's more to parentage than blood. They've been your parents for seven years in all the ways that matter. Maryse is just hurt."

"Hurt?" Jace sounded incredulous. "*She's* hurt?"

"She loved Valentine, remember," said Luke. "As we all did. He hurt her badly. She doesn't want his son to do the same. She worries you've lied to them. That the person she thought you were all these years was a ruse, a trick. You have to reassure her."

Jace's expression was a perfect mixture of stubbornness and astonishment. "Maryse is an adult! She shouldn't need reassurance from me."

"Oh, come *on*, Jace," Clary said. "You can't wait for perfect behavior from everyone. Adults screw up too. Go back to the Institute and talk to her rationally. Be a man."

"I don't want to be a man," said Jace. "I want to be an angst-ridden teenager who can't confront his own inner demons and takes it out verbally on other people instead."

"Well," said Luke, "you're doing a fantastic job."

"Jace," Clary said hastily, before they could start fighting in earnest, "you have to go back to the Institute. Think about Alec and Izzy, think what this will do to them."

"Maryse will make something up to calm them down. Maybe she'll say I ran off."

"That won't work," said Clary. "Isabelle sounded frantic on the phone."

"Isabelle always sounds frantic," said Jace, but he looked pleased. He leaned back in the chair. The bruises along his jaw and cheekbone stood out like dark, shapeless Marks against his skin. "I won't go back to a place where I'm not trusted. I'm not ten years old anymore. I can take care of myself."

Luke looked as if he weren't sure about that. "Where will you go? How will you live?"

Jace's eyes glittered. "I'm seventeen. Practically an adult. Any adult Shadowhunter is entitled to—"

"Any *adult*. But you're not one. You can't draw a salary from the Clave because you're too young, and in fact the Lightwoods are bound by the Law to care for you. If they won't, someone else would be appointed or—"

"Or what?" Jace sprang up from the chair. "I'll go to an orphanage in Idris? Be dumped on some family I've never met? I can get a job in the mundane world for a year, live like one of *them*—"

"No, you can't," Clary said. "I ought to know, Jace, I *was* one of them. You're too young for any job you'd want and besides, the skills you have—well, most professional killers are older than you. And they're criminals."

"I'm not a killer."

"If you lived in the mundane world," said Luke, "that's all you'd be."

Jace stiffened, his mouth tightening, and Clary knew Luke's words had hit him where it hurt. "You don't get it," he said, a sudden desperation in his voice. "I can't go back. Maryse wants me to say I hate Valentine. And I can't do that."

Jace raised his chin, his jaw set, his eyes on Luke as if he half-expected the older man to respond with derision or even horror. After all, Luke had more reason to hate Valentine than almost anyone else in the world.

"I know," said Luke. "I loved him once too."

Jace exhaled, almost a sound of relief, and Clary thought suddenly, *This is why he came here, to this place. Not just to start a fight, but to get to Luke. Because Luke would understand.* Not everything Jace did was insane and suicidal, she reminded herself. It just seemed that way.

"You shouldn't have to claim you hate your father," said Luke. "Not even to reassure Maryse. She ought to understand."

Clary looked at Jace closely, trying to read his face. It was like a book written in a foreign language she'd studied all too briefly. "Did she really say she never wanted you to come back?" Clary asked. "Or did you just assume that was what she meant, so you left?"

"She told me it would probably be better if I found somewhere else to be for a while," Jace said. "She didn't say where."

"Did you give her a chance to?" Luke said. "Look, Jace.

You're absolutely welcome to stay with me as long as you need to. I want you to know that."

Clary's stomach flipped. The thought of Jace in the same house she lived in, always nearby, filled her with a mixture of exultation and horror.

"Thanks," said Jace. His voice was even, but his eyes had gone instantly, helplessly, to Clary, and she could see in them the same awful mixture of emotions she felt herself. *Luke*, she thought. *Sometimes I wish you weren't quite so generous. Or so blind.*

"But," Luke went on, "I think you should at least go back to the Institute long enough to talk to Maryse and find out what's really going on. It sounds like there's more to this than she's telling you. More, maybe, than you were willing to hear."

Jace tore his gaze from Clary's. "All right." His voice was rough. "But on one condition. I don't want to go by myself."

"I'll go with you," Clary said quickly.

"I know." Jace's voice was low. "And I want you to. But I want Luke to come too."

Luke looked startled. "Jace—I've lived here fifteen years and I've never gone to the Institute. Not once. I doubt Maryse is any fonder of me—"

"Please," Jace said, and though his voice was flat and he spoke quietly, Clary could almost feel, like a palpable thing, the pride he'd had to fight down to say that single word.

"All right." Luke nodded, the nod of a pack leader used to doing what he had to do, whether he wanted to or not. "Then I'll come with you."

Simon leaned against the wall in the corridor outside Pete's office and tried not to feel sorry for himself.

The day had started off well. Fairly well, anyway. First there'd been that bad episode with the Dracula film on television making him feel sick and faint, bringing up all the emotions, the longings, he'd been trying to push down and forget about. Then somehow the sickness had knocked the edge off his nerves and he'd found himself kissing Clary the way he'd wanted to for so many years. People always said that things never turned out the way you imagined they would. People were wrong.

And she'd kissed him *back*. . . .

But now she was in there with Jace, and Simon had a knotting, twisting feeling in his stomach, like he'd swallowed a bowl full of worms. It was a sick feeling he'd grown used to lately. It hadn't always been like this, even after he'd realized how he felt about Clary. He'd never pressed her, never pushed his feelings on her. He'd always been sure that one day she would wake up out of her dreams of animated princes and kung fu heroes and realize what was staring them both in the face: They belonged together. And if she hadn't seemed interested in Simon, at least she hadn't seemed interested in anyone else either.

Until Jace. He remembered sitting on the porch steps of Luke's house, watching Clary as she explained to him who Jace was, what he did, while Jace examined his nails and looked superior. Simon had barely heard her. He'd been too busy noticing how she *looked* at the blond boy with the strange tattoos and the angular, pretty face. Too pretty, Simon had thought, but Clary clearly hadn't thought so: She'd looked at him as though he were one of her animated heroes come to life. He had never seen her look at anyone that way before, and had always thought that if she ever did, it would be him. But it wasn't, and that hurt more than he'd ever imagined anything could hurt.

Finding out that Jace was Clary's brother was like being marched up in front of a firing squad and then being handed a reprieve at the last minute. Suddenly the world seemed full of possibilities again.

Now he wasn't so sure.

"Hey, there." Someone was coming along the corridor, a not-very-tall someone picking their way gingerly among the blood spatters. "Are you waiting to see Luke? Is he in there?"

"Not exactly." Simon moved away from the door. "I mean, sort of. He's in there with a friend of mine."

The person, who had just reached him, stopped and stared. Simon could see that she was a girl, about sixteen years old, with smooth light brown skin. Her brown-gold hair was braided close to her head in dozens of small braids, and her face was nearly the exact shape of a heart. She had a compact, curvy body, wide hips flaring out from a smaller waist. "That guy from the bar? The Shadowhunter?"

Simon shrugged.

"Well, I hate to tell you this," she said, "but your friend is an asshole."

"He's not my friend," said Simon. "And I couldn't agree with you more, actually."

"But I thought you said—"

"I'm waiting for his sister," said Simon. "She's my best friend."

"And she's in there with him right now?" The girl jerked her thumb toward the door. She wore rings on each of her fingers, primitive-looking bands hammered out of bronze and gold. Her jeans were worn but clean and when she turned her head, he saw the scar that ran along her neck, just above the collar of her T-shirt. "Well," she said grudgingly, "I know about asshole brothers. I guess it's not her fault."

"It's not," said Simon. "But she's maybe the only person he might listen to."

"He didn't strike me as the listening type," said the girl, and caught his sidelong look with a look of her own. Amusement flickered across her face. "You're looking at my scar. It's where I was bitten."

"Bitten? You mean you're a—"

"A werewolf," said the girl. "Like everyone else here. Except you, and the asshole. And the asshole's sister."

"But you weren't always a werewolf. I mean, you weren't born one."

"Most of us aren't," said the girl. "That's what makes us different than your Shadowhunter buddies."

"What?"

She smiled fleetingly. "We were human once."

Simon said nothing to that. After a moment the girl held her hand out. "I'm Maia."

"Simon." He shook her hand. It was dry and soft. She looked up at him through golden-brown eyelashes, the color of buttered toast. "How do you know Jace is an asshole?" he said. "Or maybe I should say, how did you find out?"

She took her hand back. "He tore up the bar. Punched out my friend Bat. Even knocked a couple of the pack unconscious."

"Are they all right?" Simon was alarmed. Jace hadn't seemed perturbed, but knowing him, Simon had no doubt he could kill several people in a single morning and go out for waffles afterward. "Did they get to a doctor?"

"A warlock," said the girl. "We don't have much to do with mundane doctors, our kind."

"Downworlders?"

Her eyebrows went up. "Someone taught you all the lingo, didn't they?"

Simon was nettled. "How do you know I'm not one of them? Or you? A Shadowhunter or a Downworlder, or—"

She shook her head until her braids bounced. "It just shines out of you," she said, a little bitterly, "your *humanity*."

The intensity in her voice almost made him shiver. "I could knock on the door," he suggested, feeling suddenly lame. "If you want to talk to Luke."

She shrugged. "Just tell him Magnus is here, checking out the scene in the alley." He must have looked startled, because she said, "Magnus Bane. He's a warlock."

*I know*, Simon wanted to say, but didn't. The whole conversation had been weird enough already. "Okay."

Maia turned as if to go, but paused partway down the hall, one hand on the doorjamb. "You think she'll be able to talk sense into him?" she asked. "His sister?"

"If he listens to anyone, it would be her."

"That's sweet," said Maia. "That he loves his sister like that."

"Yeah," Simon said. "It's precious."

# 3

# The Inquisitor

**The first time Clary had ever seen the Institute, it had** looked like a dilapidated church, its roof broken in, stained yellow police tape holding the door closed. Now she didn't have to concentrate to dispel the illusion. Even from across the street she could see it exactly as it was, a towering Gothic cathedral whose spires seemed to pierce the dark blue sky like knives.

Luke fell silent. It was clear from the look on his face that some kind of struggle was taking place inside him. As they mounted the steps, Jace reached inside his shirt as if from habit, but when he drew his hand out, it was empty. He laughed without any mirth. "I forgot. Maryse took my keys from me before I left."

"Of course she did." Luke was standing directly in front of the Institute's doors. He gently touched the symbols carved into the wood, just below the architrave. "These doors are just like the ones at the Council Hall in Idris. I never thought I would see their like again."

Clary almost felt guilty interrupting Luke's reverie, but there were practical matters to attend to. "If we don't have a key—"

"One shouldn't be necessary. An Institute should be open to any of the Nephilim who mean no harm to the inhabitants."

"What if they mean harm to us?" Jace muttered.

Luke's mouth quirked at the corner. "I don't think that makes a difference."

"Yeah, the Clave always stacks the deck its way." Jace's voice sounded muffled—his lower lip was swelling, his left eyelid turning purple.

*Why didn't he heal himself?* Clary wondered. "Did she take your stele, too?"

"I didn't take anything when I left," Jace said. "I didn't want to take anything the Lightwoods got for me."

Luke looked at him with some concern. "Every Shadowhunter must have a stele."

"So I'll get another one," said Jace, and put his hand to the Institute's door. "In the name of the Clave," he said, "I ask entry to this holy place. And in the name of the Angel Raziel, I ask your blessings upon my mission against—"

The doors swung open. Clary could see the cathedral's interior through them, the shadowy darkness illuminated here and there by candles in tall iron candelabras.

"Well, that's convenient," said Jace. "I guess blessings are easier to come by than I thought. Maybe I should ask for blessings on my mission against all those who wear white after Labor Day."

"The Angel knows what your mission is," said Luke. "You don't have to say the words aloud, Jonathan."

For a moment Clary thought she saw something flicker across Jace's face—uncertainty, surprise—and maybe even relief? But all he said was, "Don't call me that. It's not my name."

They made their way through the ground floor of the cathedral, past the empty pews and the light burning forever on the altar. Luke looked around him curiously, and even seemed surprised when the elevator, like a gilded birdcage, arrived to carry them up. "This must have been Maryse's idea," he said as they stepped into it. "It's entirely her taste."

"It's been here as long as I have," said Jace, as the door clanged shut behind them. The ride up was brief, and none of them spoke. Clary played nervously with the fringe of her scarf. She felt a little guilty about having told Simon to go home and wait for her to call him later. She had seen from the annoyed set of his shoulders as he stalked off down Canal Street that he'd felt summarily dismissed. Still, she couldn't imagine having him—a mundane—here while Luke petitioned Maryse Lightwood on Jace's behalf; it would just make everything awkward.

The elevator came to a clanging stop and they stepped out to find Church waiting for them in the entryway, a slightly dilapidated red bow around his neck. Jace bent to rub the back of his hand along the cat's head. "Where's Maryse?"

Church made a noise in his throat, halfway between a purr and a growl, and headed off down the corridor. They followed,

Jace silent, Luke glancing around with evident curiosity. "I never thought I'd see the inside of this place."

Clary asked, "Does it look like you thought it would?"

"I've been to the Institutes in London and Paris; this is not unlike those, no. Though somehow—"

"Somehow what?" Jace was several strides ahead.

"Colder," said Luke.

Jace said nothing. They had reached the library. Church sat down as if to indicate that he planned to go no farther. Voices were faintly audible through the thick wooden door, but Jace pushed it open without knocking and strode inside.

Clary heard a voice exclaim in surprise. For a moment her heart contracted as she thought of Hodge, who had all but lived in this room. Hodge, with his gravelly voice, and Hugin, the raven who was his almost constant companion—and who had, at Hodge's orders, nearly ripped out her eyes.

It wasn't Hodge, of course. Behind the enormous plank desk that balanced on the backs of two kneeling angels sat a middle-aged woman with Isabelle's ink black hair and Alec's thin, wiry build. She wore a neat black suit, very plain, in contrast to the multiple brightly colored rings that burned on her fingers.

Beside her stood another figure: a slender teenage boy, slightly built, with curling dark hair and honey-colored skin. As he turned to look at them, Clary couldn't hold back an exclamation of surprise. "Raphael?"

For a moment the boy looked taken aback. Then he smiled, his teeth very white and sharp—not surprising, considering that he was a vampire. *"Dios,"* he said, addressing himself to Jace. "What happened to you, brother? You look as if a pack of wolves tried to tear you apart."

"That's either a shockingly good guess," said Jace, "or you heard about what happened."

Raphael's smile turned into a grin. "I hear things."

The woman behind the desk rose to her feet. "Jace," she said, her voice full of anxiety. "Did something happen? Why are you back so soon? I thought you were going to stay with—" Her gaze moved past him to Luke and Clary. "And who are you?"

"Jace's sister," Clary said.

Maryse's eyes rested on Clary. "Yes, I can see it. You look like Valentine." She turned back to Jace. "You brought your sister with you? And a mundane, as well? It's not safe for any of you here right now. And *especially* a mundane—"

Luke, smiling faintly, said, "But I'm not a mundane."

Maryse's expression changed slowly from bewilderment to shock as she looked at Luke—*really* looked at him—for the first time. "*Lucian?*"

"Hello, Maryse," said Luke. "It's been a long time."

Maryse's face was very still, and in that moment she looked suddenly much older, older even than Luke. She sat down carefully. "Lucian," she said again, her hands flat on the desk. "Lucian Graymark."

Raphael, who had been watching the proceedings with the bright, curious gaze of a bird, turned to Luke. "You killed Gabriel."

*Who was Gabriel?* Clary stared at Luke, puzzled. He gave a slight shrug. "I did, yes, just like he killed the pack leader before him. That's how it works with lycanthropes."

Maryse looked up at that. "The pack leader?"

"If you lead the pack now, it's time for us to talk," said Raphael, inclining his head graciously in Luke's direction, though his eyes were wary. "Though not at this exact moment, perhaps."

"I'll send someone over to arrange it," said Luke. "Things have been busy lately. I might be behind on the niceties."

"You might," was all that Raphael said. He turned back to Maryse. "Is our business here concluded?"

Maryse spoke with an effort. "If you say the Night Children aren't involved in these killings, then I'll take you at your word. I'm required to, unless other evidence comes to light."

Raphael frowned. "To light?" he said. "That is not a phrase I like." He turned then, and Clary saw with a start that she could see *through* the edges of him, as if he were a photograph that had blurred around the margins. His left hand was transparent, and through it she could see the big metal globe Hodge had always kept on the desk. She heard herself make a little noise of surprise as the transparency spread up his arms from his hands—and down his chest from his shoulders, and in a moment he was gone, like a figure erased from a sketch. Maryse exhaled a sigh of relief.

Clary gaped. "Is he *dead?*"

"What, Raphael?" said Jace. "Not likely. That was just a projection of him. He can't come into the Institute in his corporeal body."

"Why not?"

"Because this is hallowed ground," said Maryse. "And he is damned." Her wintry eyes lost none of their coldness when she turned her glance on Luke. "You, head of the pack here?" she asked. "I suppose I should hardly be surprised. It does seem to be your method, doesn't it?"

Luke ignored the bitterness in her tone. "Was Raphael here about the cub who was killed today?"

"That, and a dead warlock," Maryse said. "Found murdered downtown, two days apart."

"But why was Raphael here?"

"The warlock was drained of blood," said Maryse. "It seems that whoever murdered the werewolf was interrupted before the blood could be taken, but suspicion naturally fell on the Night Children. The vampire came here to assure me his folk had nothing to do with it."

"Do you believe him?" Jace said.

"I don't care to talk about Clave business with you right now, Jace—especially not in front of Lucian Graymark."

"I'm just called Luke now," Luke said placidly. "Luke Garroway."

Maryse shook her head. "I hardly recognized you. You look like a mundane."

"That's the idea, yes."

"We all thought you were dead."

"Hoped," said Luke, still placidly. "Hoped I was dead."

Maryse looked as if she'd swallowed something sharp. "You might as well sit down," she said finally, pointing toward the chairs in front of the desk. "Now," said Maryse, once they'd taken their seats, "perhaps you might tell me why you're here."

"Jace," said Luke, without preamble, "wants a trial before the Clave. I'm willing to vouch for him. I was there that night at Renwick's, when Valentine revealed himself. I fought him and we nearly killed each other. I can confirm that everything Jace says happened is the truth."

"I'm not sure," countered Maryse, "what *your* word is worth."

"I may be a lycanthrope," said Luke, "but I'm also a Shadowhunter. I'm willing to be tried by the Sword, if that will help."

*By the Sword?* That sounded bad. Clary looked over at Jace. He was outwardly calm, his fingers laced together in his lap, but there was a shuddering tension about him, as if he were a hairsbreadth from exploding. He caught her look and said, "The Soul-Sword. The second of the Mortal Instruments. It's used in trials to determine if a Shadowhunter is lying."

"You're not a Shadowhunter," said Maryse to Luke, as if Jace hadn't spoken. "You haven't lived by the Law of the Clave in a long, long time."

"There was a time when you didn't live by it either," said Luke. High color flooded Maryse's cheeks. "I would have thought," he went on, "that by now you would have gotten past not being able to trust anyone, Maryse."

"Some things you never forget," she said. Her voice held a dangerous softness. "You think pretending his own death was the biggest lie Valentine ever told us? You think charm is the same as honesty? I used to think so. I was wrong." She stood up and leaned on the table with her thin hands. "He told us he would lay down his life for the Circle and that he expected us to do the same. And we would have—all of us—I know it. I nearly *did* it." Her gaze swept over Jace and Clary and her eyes locked with Luke's. "You remember," she said, "the way he told us that the Uprising would be nothing, hardly a battle, a few unarmed ambassadors against the full might of the Circle. I was so confident in our swift victory that when I rode out to Alicante, I left Alec at home. I asked Jocelyn to watch him while I was away. She refused. I know why now. She *knew*—and so did you. And you didn't warn us."

"I'd tried to warn you about Valentine," said Luke. "You didn't listen."

"I don't mean about Valentine. I mean about the Uprising! There were fifty of us against five hundred Downworlders—"

"You'd been willing to slaughter them unarmed when you thought there would be only five of them," said Luke quietly.

Maryse's hands clenched on the desk. "*We* were slaughtered," she said. "In the midst of the carnage, we looked to Valentine to lead us. But he wasn't there. By that time the Clave had surrounded the Hall of Accords. We thought Valentine had been killed, were ready to give our own lives in a final desperate rush. Then I remembered Alec—if I died, what would happen to my little boy?" Her voice caught. "So I laid my arms down and gave myself up to the Clave."

"You did the right thing, Maryse," said Luke.

She turned on him, eyes blazing. "Don't *patronize* me, werewolf. If it weren't for you—"

"Don't yell at him!" Clary cut in, almost rising to her feet herself. "It's your fault for believing Valentine in the first place—"

"You think I don't know that?" There was a ragged edge to Maryse's voice now. "Oh, the Clave made that point nicely when they questioned us—they had the Soul-Sword and they knew when we were lying, but they couldn't *make* us talk—nothing could make us talk, until—"

"Until what?" It was Luke who spoke. "I've never known. I always wondered what they told you to make you turn on him."

"Just the truth," Maryse said, sounding suddenly tired. "That Valentine hadn't died there in the Hall. He'd fled—left us there to die without him. He'd died later, we were told, burned to death in his house. The Inquisitor showed us his bones, the charred bones of his family. Of course, that was another lie. . . ." Her voice trailed off, and then she rallied again, her words crisp: "It was all coming apart by then, anyway. We were finally talking to one another, those of us in the Circle. Before the battle, Valentine had drawn me aside, told me that out of all the Circle, I was the one he trusted most, his closest lieutenant. When the Clave questioned us I found out he'd said the same thing to everyone."

"Hell hath no fury," Jace muttered, so quietly that only Clary heard him.

"He lied not just to the Clave but to us. He used our loyalty and our affection. Just as he did when he sent you to us," Maryse said, looking directly at Jace now. "And now he's back, and he has the Mortal Cup. He's been planning all this for years, all along, all of it. I can't afford to trust you, Jace. I'm sorry."

Jace said nothing. His face was expressionless, but he'd gone paler as Maryse spoke, his new bruises standing out livid on his jaw and cheek.

"Then what?" Luke said. "What is it you expect him to do? Where is he supposed to go?"

Her eyes rested for a moment on Clary. "Why not to his sister?" she said. "Family—"

"*Isabelle* is Jace's sister," interrupted Clary. "Alec and Max are his brothers. What are you going to tell them? They'll hate you forever if you throw Jace out of your house."

Maryse's eyes rested on her. "What do *you* know about it?"

"I know Alec and Isabelle," said Clary. The thought of Valentine came, unwelcome; she pushed it away. "Family is more than blood. Valentine isn't my father. Luke is. Just like Alec and Max and Isabelle are Jace's family. If you try to tear him out of your family, you'll leave a wound that won't ever heal."

Luke was looking at her with a sort of surprised respect. Something flickered in Maryse's eyes—uncertainty?

"Clary," Jace said softly. "Enough." He sounded defeated. Clary turned on Maryse.

"What about the Sword?" she demanded.

Maryse looked at her for a moment with genuine puzzlement. "The Sword?"

"The Soul-Sword," said Clary. "The one you can use to tell if a Shadowhunter is lying or not. You can use it on Jace."

"That's a good idea." There was a spark of animation in Jace's voice.

"Clary, you mean well, but you don't know what the Sword entails," Luke said. "The only one who can use it is the Inquisitor."

Jace sat forward. "Then call on her. Call the Inquisitor. I want to end this."

"*No,*" Luke said, but Maryse was looking at Jace.

"The Inquisitor," she said reluctantly, "is already on her way—"

"Maryse." Luke's voice cracked. "Tell me you haven't called her into this!"

"I didn't! Did you think the Clave wouldn't involve itself in this wild tale of Forsaken warriors and Portals and staged deaths? After what Hodge did? We're all under investigation now, thanks to Valentine," she finished, seeing Jace's white and stunned expression. "The Inquisitor could put Jace in prison. She could strip his Marks. I thought it would be better . . ."

"If Jace were gone when she arrived," said Luke. "No wonder you've been so eager to send him away."

"Who is the Inquisitor?" Clary demanded. The word conjured up images of the Spanish Inquisition, of torture, the whip and the rack. "What does she *do*?"

"She investigates Shadowhunters for the Clave," said Luke. "She ensures the Law hasn't been broken by Nephilim. She investigated all the Circle members after the Uprising."

"She cursed Hodge?" Jace said. "She sent you here?"

"She chose our exile and his punishment. She has no love for us, and hates your father."

"I'm not leaving," said Jace, still very pale. "What will she do to you if she gets here and I'm gone? She'll think you conspired to hide me. She'll punish *you*—you and Alec and Isabelle and Max."

Maryse said nothing.

"Maryse, don't be a fool," Luke said. "She'll blame you more if you let Jace go. Keeping him here and allowing the trial by Sword would be a sign of good faith."

"Keeping Jace—you can't be serious, Luke!" Clary said. She knew using the Sword had been her idea, but she was beginning to regret ever having brought it up. "She sounds awful."

"But if Jace leaves," said Luke, "he can never come back. He'll never be a Shadowhunter again. Like it or not, the Inquisitor is the Law's right hand. If Jace wants to stay a part of the Clave, he has to cooperate with her. He does have something on his side, something the members of the Circle did not have after the Uprising."

"And what's that?" Maryse asked.

Luke smiled faintly. "Unlike you," he said, "Jace is telling the truth."

Maryse took a hard breath, then turned to Jace. "Ultimately, it's your decision," she said. "If you want the trial, you can stay here until the Inquisitor comes."

"I'll stay," Jace said. There was a firmness in his tone, devoid of anger, that surprised Clary. He seemed to be looking past Maryse, a light flickering in his eyes, as if of reflected fire. In that moment Clary couldn't help but think that he looked very like his father.

# 4

# The Cuckoo in the Nest

**"Orange juice, molasses, eggs—weeks past their sell-by** date, though—and something that looks kind of like lettuce."

"Lettuce?" Clary peered over Simon's shoulder into the fridge. "Oh. That's some mozzarella."

Simon shuddered and kicked Luke's fridge door shut. "Order pizza?"

"I already did," said Luke, coming into the kitchen with the cordless phone in hand. "One large veggie pie, three Cokes. And I called the hospital," he added, hanging the phone up. "There's been no change with Jocelyn."

"Oh," Clary said. She sat down at the wooden table in Luke's kitchen. Usually Luke was pretty neat, but at the moment the table was covered in unopened mail and stacks of dirty plates.

Luke's green duffel hung across the back of a chair. She knew she should be helping with the cleaning up, but lately she just hadn't had the energy. Luke's kitchen was small and a little dingy at the best of times—he wasn't much of a cook, as evidenced by the fact that the spice rack that hung over the old-fashioned gas stove was empty of spices. Instead, he used it to hold boxes of coffee and tea.

Simon sat down next to her as Luke cleared the dirty dishes off the table and dumped them into the sink. "Are you okay?" he asked in a low voice.

"I'm all right." Clary managed a smile. "I didn't expect my mom to wake up today, Simon. I have this feeling she's—waiting for something."

"Do you know what?"

"No. Just that something's missing." She looked up at Luke, but he was involved in vigorously scrubbing the plates clean in the sink. "Or someone."

Simon looked quizzically at her, then shrugged. "So it sounds like the scene at the Institute was pretty intense."

Clary shuddered. "Alec and Isabelle's mom is scary."

"What's her name again?"

"May-ris," said Clary, copying Luke's pronunciation.

"It's an old Shadowhunter name." Luke dried his hands on a dishcloth.

"And Jace decided to stay there and deal with this Inquisitor person? He didn't want to leave?" Simon said.

"It's what he has to do if he ever wants to have a life as a Shadowhunter," said Luke. "And being that—one of the Nephilim—means everything to him. I knew other Shadowhunters like him, back in Idris. If you took that away from him—"

The familiar buzz of the doorbell sounded. Luke tossed the dishcloth onto the counter. "I'll be right back."

As soon as he was out of the kitchen, Simon said, "It's really weird thinking of Luke as someone who was once a Shadowhunter. Weirder than it is thinking of him as a werewolf."

"Really? Why?"

Simon shrugged. "I've heard of werewolves before. They're sort of a known element. So he turns into a wolf once a month, so what. But the Shadowhunter thing—they're like a cult."

"They're not like a cult."

"Sure they are. Shadowhunting is their whole lives. And they look down on everyone else. They call us mundanes. Like they're not human beings. They're not friends with ordinary people, they don't go to the same places, they don't know the same jokes, they think they're above us." Simon pulled one gangly leg up and twisted the frayed edge of the hole in the knee of his jeans. "I met another werewolf today."

"Don't tell me you were hanging out with Freaky Pete at the Hunter's Moon." There was an uneasy feeling in the pit of her stomach, but she couldn't have said exactly what was causing it. Probably free-floating stress.

"No. It was a girl," Simon said. "About our age. Named Maia."

"Maia?" Luke was back in the kitchen carrying a square white pizza box. He dropped it onto the table and Clary reached over to pop it open. The smell of hot dough, tomato sauce, and cheese reminded her how starved she was. She tore off a slice, not waiting for Luke to slide a plate across the table to her. He sat down with a grin, shaking his head.

"Maia's one of the pack, right?" Simon asked, taking a slice himself.

Luke nodded. "Sure. She's a good kid. I've had her over here a few times looking out for the bookstore while I've been at the hospital. She lets me pay her in books."

Simon looked at Luke over his pizza. "Are you low on money?"

Luke shrugged. "Money's never been important to me, and the pack looks after its own."

Clary said, "My mom always said that when we ran low on money she'd sell one of my dad's stocks. But since the guy I thought was my dad wasn't my dad, and I doubt Valentine has any stocks—"

"Your mother was selling her jewelry off bit by bit," said Luke. "Valentine had given her some of his family's pieces, jewelry that had been with the Morgensterns for generations. Even a small piece would fetch a high price at auction." He sighed. "Those are gone now—though Valentine may have recovered them from the wreckage of your old apartment."

"Well, I hope it gave her some satisfaction, anyway," Simon said. "Selling off his stuff like that." He took a third piece of pizza. It was truly amazing, Clary thought, how much teenage boys were able to eat without ever gaining weight or making themselves sick.

"It must have been weird for you," she said to Luke. "Seeing Maryse Lightwood like that, after such a long time."

"Not precisely weird. Maryse isn't that different now from how she was then—in fact, she's more like herself than ever, if that makes sense."

Clary thought it did. The way that Maryse Lightwood had looked recollected to her the slim dark girl in the photo Hodge had given her, the one with the haughty tilt to her chin. "How do you think she feels about you?" she asked. "Do you really think they hoped you were dead?"

Luke smiled. "Maybe not out of hatred, no, but it would have been more convenient and less messy for them if I had died, certainly. That I'm not just alive but am leading the downtown pack can't be something they'd hoped for. It's their job, after all, to keep the peace between Downworlders—and here I come, with a history with them and plenty of reason to want revenge. They'll be worried I'm a wild card."

"Are you?" asked Simon. They were out of pizza, so he reached over without looking and took one of Clary's nibbled crusts. He knew she hated crust. "A wild card, I mean."

"There's nothing wild about me. I'm stolid. Middle-aged."

"Except that once a month you turn into a wolf and go tearing around slaughtering things," Clary said.

"It could be worse," Luke said. "Men my age have been known to purchase expensive sports cars and sleep with supermodels."

"You're only thirty-eight," Simon pointed out. "That's not middle-aged."

"Thank you, Simon, I appreciate that." Luke opened the pizza box and, finding it empty, shut it with a sigh. "Though you did eat all the pizza."

"I only had five slices," Simon protested, leaning his chair backward so it balanced precariously on its two back legs.

"How many slices did you think were in a pizza, dork?" Clary wanted to know.

"Less than five slices isn't a meal. It's a snack." Simon looked apprehensively at Luke. "Does this mean you're going to wolf out and eat me?"

"Certainly not." Luke rose to toss the pizza box into the trash. "You would be stringy and hard to digest."

"But kosher," Simon pointed out cheerfully.

"I'll be sure to point any Jewish lycanthropes your way." Luke leaned his back against the sink. "But to answer your earlier question, Clary, it was strange seeing Maryse Lightwood, but not because of *her*. It was the surroundings. The Institute reminded me too much of the Hall of Accords in Idris—I could feel the strength of the Gray Book's runes all around me, after fifteen years of trying to forget them."

"Did you?" Clary asked. "Manage to forget them?"

"There are some things you never forget. The runes of the Book are more than illustrations. They become part of you. Part of your skin. Being a Shadowhunter never leaves you. It's a gift that's carried in your blood, and you can no more change it than you can change your blood type."

"I was wondering," Clary said, "if maybe I should get some Marks myself."

Simon dropped the pizza crust he'd been gnawing on. "You're kidding."

"No, I'm not. Why would I joke about something like that? And why *shouldn't* I get Marks? I'm a Shadowhunter. I might as well go for what protection I can get."

"Protection from what?" Simon demanded, leaning forward so that the front legs of his chair hit the floor with a bang. "I thought all this Shadowhunting stuff was over. I thought you were trying to live a normal life."

Luke's tone was mild. "I'm not sure there's such a thing as a normal life."

Clary looked down at her arm, where Jace had drawn the

only Mark she'd ever received. She could still see the lacelike white tracery it had left behind, more a memory than a scar. "Sure, I want to get away from the weirdness. But what if the weirdness comes after me? What if I don't have a choice?"

"Or maybe you don't want to get away from the weirdness that badly," Simon muttered. "Not as long as Jace is still involved with it, anyway."

Luke cleared his throat. "Most Nephilim go through levels of training before they receive their Marks. I wouldn't recommend getting any until you've completed some instruction. And whether you even want to do that is up to you, of course. However, there is something you should have. Something every Shadowhunter should have."

"An obnoxious, arrogant attitude?" Simon said.

"A stele," said Luke. "Every Shadowhunter should have a stele."

"Do *you* have one?" Clary asked, surprised.

Without responding, Luke headed out of the kitchen. He was back in a few moments, holding an object wrapped in black fabric. Setting the object down on the table, he unrolled the cloth, revealing a gleaming wandlike instrument, made of a pale, opaque crystal. A stele.

"Pretty," said Clary.

"I'm glad you think so," said Luke, "because I want you to have it."

"Have it?" She looked at him in astonishment. "But it's yours, isn't it?"

He shook his head. "This was your mother's. She didn't want to keep it at the apartment in case you happened across it, so she asked me to hold on to it for her."

Clary picked the stele up. It felt cool to the touch, though she knew it would heat to a glow when used. It was a strange object, not quite long enough to be a weapon, not quite short enough to be an easily manipulated drawing tool. She supposed the odd size was just something you got used to over time.

"I can have it?"

"Sure. It's an old model, of course, almost twenty years out of date. They may have refined the designs since. Still, it's reliable enough."

Simon watched her as she held the stele like a conductor's baton, tracing invisible patterns lightly on the air between them. "This kind of reminds me of the time my grandfather gave me his old golf clubs."

Clary laughed and lowered her hand. "Yeah, except you never used those."

"And I hope you never have to use that," Simon said, and looked quickly away before she could reply.

*Smoke rose from the Marks in black spirals and he smelled the choking scent of his own skin burning. His father stood over him with the stele, its tip gleaming red like the tip of a poker left too long in the fire.* "Close your eyes, Jonathan," *he said.* "Pain is only what you allow it to be." *But Jace's hand curled in on itself, unwillingly, as if his skin were writhing, twisting to get away from the stele. He heard the snap as one bone in his hand broke, and then another . . .*

Jace opened his eyes and blinked up at the darkness, his father's voice fading away like smoke in rising wind. He tasted pain, metallic on his tongue. He'd bitten the inside of his lip. He sat up, wincing.

The snap came again and involuntarily he glanced down at his hand. It was unmarked. He realized the sound was coming from outside the room. Someone knocking, albeit hesitantly, at the door.

He rolled off the bed, shivering as his bare feet hit the cold floor. He'd fallen asleep in his clothes and he looked down at his wrinkled shirt in distaste. He probably still smelled like wolf. And he ached all over.

The knock came again. Jace strode across the room and threw the door open. He blinked in surprise. "Alec?"

Alec, hands in his jeans pockets, shrugged self-consciously. "Sorry to wake you up. Mom sent me to get you. She wants to see you in the library."

"Right now?" Jace peered at his friend. "I went to your room before, but you weren't there."

"I was out." Alec didn't look eager to give out more information than that.

Jace ran a hand through his tousled hair. "All right. Hang on a second while I change my shirt." Heading to the wardrobe, he rummaged through neatly folded square stacks until he found a dark blue long-sleeved T-shirt. He peeled the shirt he was wearing off carefully—in some places it was stuck to his skin with dried blood.

Alec looked away. "What happened to you?" His voice was oddly constricted.

"Picked a fight with a pack of werewolves." Jace slid the blue shirt over his head. Dressed, he padded after Alec into the hallway. "You have something on your neck," he observed.

Alec's hand flew to his throat. "What?"

"Looks like a bite mark," said Jace. "What have you been doing all day, anyway?"

"Nothing." Beet red, his hand still clamped to his neck, Alec started down the corridor. Jace followed him. "I went walking in the park. Tried to clear my head."

"And ran into a vampire?"

"What? No! I fell."

"On your *neck*?" Alec made a noise, and Jace decided the issue was clearly better dropped. "Fine, whatever. What did you need to clear your head about?"

"You. My parents," Alec said. "My mother came and explained why she was so angry after you left. And she explained about Hodge. Thanks for not telling me that, by the way."

"Sorry." It was Jace's turn to flush. "I couldn't bring myself to do it, somehow."

"Well, it doesn't look good." Alec finally dropped his hand from his neck and turned to look accusingly at Jace. "It looks like you were hiding things. Things about Valentine."

Jace stopped in his tracks. "Do *you* think I was lying? About not knowing Valentine was my father?"

"No!" Alec looked startled, either at the question or at Jace's vehemence in asking it. "And I don't care who your father is either. It doesn't matter to me. You're still the same person."

"Whoever that is." The words came out cold, before he could stop them.

"I'm just saying." Alec's tone was placating. "You can be a little—harsh sometimes. Just think before you talk, that's all I'm asking. No one's your enemy here, Jace."

"Well, thanks for the advice," Jace said. "I can walk myself the rest of the way to the library."

*"Jace—"*

But Jace was already gone, leaving Alec's distress behind. Jace hated it when other people were worried on his behalf. It made him feel like maybe there really was something to worry about.

The library door was half open. Not bothering to knock, Jace went in. It had always been one of his favorite rooms in the Institute—there was something comforting about its old-fashioned mix of wood and brass fittings, the leather- and velvet-bound books ranged along the walls like old friends waiting for him to return. Now a blast of cold air hit him the moment the door swung open. The fire that usually blazed in the huge fireplace all through the fall and winter was a heap of ashes. The lamps had been switched off. The only light came through the narrow louvered windows and the tower's skylight, high above.

Not wanting to, Jace thought of Hodge. If he were here, the fire would be lit, the gas lamps turned up, casting shaded pools of golden light onto the parquet floor. Hodge himself would be slouched in an armchair by the fire, Hugo on one shoulder, a book propped at his side—

But there *was* someone in Hodge's old armchair. A thin, gray someone, who rose from the armchair, fluidly uncoiling like a snake charmer's cobra, and turned toward him with a cool smile.

It was a woman. She wore a long, old-fashioned dark gray cloak that fell to the tops of her boots. Beneath it was a fitted slate-colored suit with a mandarin collar, the stiff points of which pressed into her neck. Her hair was a sort of colorless pale blond, pulled tightly back with combs, and her eyes were flinty gray chips. Jace could feel them, like the touch of freezing water, as her gaze traveled from his filthy, mud-splattered jeans, to his bruised face, to his eyes, and locked there.

For a second something hot flickered in her gaze, like the glow of a flame trapped under ice. Then it vanished. "You are the boy?"

Before Jace could reply, another voice answered: It was Maryse, having come into the library behind him. He wondered why he hadn't heard her approaching and realized she had abandoned her heels for slippers. She wore a long robe of patterned silk and a thin-lipped expression. "Yes, Inquisitor," she said. "This is Jonathan Morgenstern."

The Inquisitor moved toward Jace like drifting gray smoke. She stopped in front of him and held out a hand—long-fingered and white, it reminded him of an albino spider. "Look at me, boy," she said, and suddenly those long fingers were under his chin, forcing his head up. She was incredibly strong. "You will call me Inquisitor. You will not call me anything else." The skin around her eyes was mazed with fine lines like cracks in paint. Two narrow grooves ran from the edges of her mouth to her chin. "Do you understand?"

For most of his life the Inquisitor had been a distant half-mythical figure to Jace. Her identity, even many of her duties, were shrouded in the secrecy of the Clave. He had always imagined she would be like the Silent Brothers, with their self-contained power and hidden mysteries. He had not imagined someone so direct—or so hostile. Her eyes seemed to cut at him, to slice away his armor of confidence and amusement, stripping him down to the bone.

"My name is Jace," he said. "Not boy. Jace Wayland."

"You have no right to the name of Wayland," she said. "You

are Jonathan Morgenstern. To claim the name of Wayland makes you a liar. Just like your father."

"Actually," said Jace, "I prefer to think that I'm a liar in a way that's uniquely my own."

"I see." A small smile curved her pale mouth. It was not a nice smile. "You are intolerant of authority, just as your father was. Like the angel whose name you both bear." Her fingers gripped his chin with a sudden ferocity, her nails digging in painfully. "Lucifer was rewarded for his rebellion when God cast him into the pits of hell." Her breath was sour as vinegar. "If you defy *my* authority, I can promise that you will envy him his fate."

She released Jace and stepped back. He could feel the slow trickle of blood where her nails had cut his face. His hands shook with anger, but he refused to raise one to wipe the blood away.

"Imogen—," began Maryse, then corrected herself. "Inquisitor Herondale. He's agreed to a trial by the Sword. You can find out whether he's telling the truth."

"About his father? Yes. I know I can." Inquisitor Herondale's stiff collar dug into her throat as she turned to look at Maryse. "You know, Maryse, the Clave is not pleased with you. You and Robert are the guardians of the Institute. You're just lucky your record over the years has been relatively clean. Few demonic disturbances until recently, and everything's been quiet the past few days. No reports, even from Idris, so the Clave is feeling lenient. We have sometimes wondered if you'd actually rescinded your allegiance to Valentine. As it is, he set a trap for you and you fell right into it. One might think you'd know better."

"There was no trap," Jace cut in. "My father knew the

Lightwoods would raise me if they thought I was Michael Wayland's son. That's all."

The Inquisitor stared at him as if he were a talking cockroach. "Do you know about the cuckoo bird, Jonathan Morgenstern?"

Jace wondered if perhaps being the Inquisitor—it couldn't be a pleasant job—had left Imogen Herondale a little unhinged. "The what?"

"The cuckoo bird," she said. "You see, cuckoos are parasites. They lay their eggs in other birds' nests. When the egg hatches, the baby cuckoo pushes the other baby birds out of the nest. The poor parent birds work themselves to death trying to find enough food to feed the enormous cuckoo child who has murdered their babies and taken their places."

"Enormous?" said Jace. "Did you just call me fat?"

"It was an analogy."

"I am not fat."

"And I," said Maryse, "don't want your pity, Imogen. I refuse to believe the Clave will punish either myself or my husband for choosing to bring up the son of a dead friend." She squared her shoulders. "It isn't as if we didn't tell them what we were doing."

"And I've never harmed any of the Lightwoods in any way," said Jace. "I've worked hard, and trained hard—say whatever you want about my father, but he made a Shadowhunter out of me. I've earned my place here."

"Don't defend your father to me," the Inquisitor said. "I knew him. He was—is—the vilest of men."

"Vile? Who says 'vile'? What does that even mean?"

The Inquisitor's colorless lashes grazed her cheeks as she narrowed her eyes, her gaze speculative. "You *are* arrogant," she said at last. "As well as intolerant. Did your father teach you to behave this way?"

"Not to him," Jace said shortly.

"Then you're aping him. Valentine was one of the most arrogant and disrespectful men I've ever met. I suppose he brought you up to be just like him."

"Yes," Jace said, unable to help himself, "I was trained to be an evil mastermind from a young age. Pulling the wings off flies, poisoning the earth's water supply—I was covering that stuff in kindergarten. I guess we're all just lucky my father faked his own death before he got to the raping and pillaging part of my education, or no one would be safe."

Maryse let out a sound much like a groan of horror. "Jace—"

But the Inquisitor cut her off. "And just like your father, you can't keep your temper," she said. "The Lightwoods have coddled you and let your worst qualities run rampant. You may look like an angel, Jonathan Morgenstern, but I know exactly what you are."

"He's just a boy," said Maryse. Was she *defending* him? Jace looked at her quickly, but her eyes were averted.

"Valentine was just a boy once. Now before we do any digging around in that blond head of yours to find out the truth, I suggest you cool your temper. And I know just where you can do that best."

Jace blinked. "Are you sending me to my room?"

"I'm sending you to the prisons of the Silent City. After a night there I suspect you'll be a great deal more cooperative."

Maryse gasped. "Imogen—you can't!"

"I certainly can." Her eyes gleamed like razors. "Do you have anything to say to me, Jonathan?"

Jace could only stare. There were levels and levels to the Silent City, and he had seen only the first two, where the archives were kept and where the Brothers sat in council. The prison cells were at the very lowest level of the City, beneath the graveyard levels where thousands of buried Shadowhunter dead rested in silence. The cells were reserved for the worst of criminals: vampires gone rogue, warlocks who broke the Covenant Law, Shadowhunters who spilled each other's blood. Jace was none of those things. How could she even suggest sending him there?

"Very wise, Jonathan. I see you're already learning the best lesson the Silent City has to teach you." The Inquisitor's smile was like a grinning skull's. "How to keep your mouth shut."

Clary was in the middle of helping Luke clean up the remains of dinner when the doorbell rang again. She straightened up, her gaze flicking to Luke. "Expecting someone?"

He frowned, drying his hands on the dish towel. "No. Wait here." She saw him reach up to grab something off one of the shelves as he left the kitchen. Something that glinted.

"Did you see that knife?" Simon whistled, standing up from the table. "Is he expecting trouble?"

"I think he's always expecting trouble," Clary said, "these days." She peered around the side of the kitchen door, saw Luke at the open front door. She could hear his voice, but not what he was saying. He didn't sound upset, though.

Simon's hand on her shoulder pulled her back. "Keep away from the door. What are you, crazy? What if there's some demon thing out there?"

"Then Luke could probably use our help." She looked down at his hand on her shoulder, grinning. "Now you're all protective? That's cute."

"Clary!" Luke called her from the front room. "Come here. I want you to meet someone."

Clary patted Simon's hand and set it aside. "Be right back."

Luke was leaning against the door frame, arms crossed. The knife in his hand had magically disappeared. A girl stood on the front steps of the house, a girl with curling brown hair in multiple braids and a tan corduroy jacket. "This is Maia," Luke said. "Who I was just telling you about."

The girl looked at Clary. Her eyes under the bright porch light were a strange amber green. "You must be Clary."

Clary admitted that this was the case.

"So that kid—the boy with the blond hair who tore up the Hunter's Moon—he's your brother?"

"Jace," Clary said shortly, not liking the girl's intrusive curiosity.

"Maia?" It was Simon, coming up behind Clary, hands thrust into the pockets of his jean jacket.

"Yeah. You're Simon, right? I suck at names, but I remember you." The girl smiled past Clary at him.

"Great," said Clary. "Now we're all friends."

Luke coughed and straightened up. "I wanted you to meet each other because Maia's going to be working around the bookshop for the next few weeks," he said. "If you see her going in and out, don't worry about it. She's got a key."

"And I'll keep an eye out for anything weird," Maia promised. "Demons, vamps, whatever."

"Thanks," said Clary. "I feel so safe now."

Maia blinked. "Are you being sarcastic?"

"We're all a little tense," Simon said. "I for one am happy to know someone will be around here keeping an eye on my girlfriend when no one else is home."

Luke raised his eyebrows, but said nothing. Clary said, "Simon's right. Sorry I snapped at you."

"It's all right." Maia looked sympathetic. "I heard about your mom. I'm sorry."

"Me too," Clary said, turned around, and went back to the kitchen. She sat down at the table and put her face in her hands. A moment later Luke followed her.

"Sorry," he said. "I guess you weren't in the mood to meet anyone."

Clary looked at him through splayed fingers. "Where's Simon?"

"Talking to Maia," Luke said, and indeed Clary could hear their voices, soft as murmurs, from the other end of the house. "I just thought it would be good for you to have a friend right now."

"I have Simon."

Luke pushed his glasses back up his nose. "Did I hear him call you his girlfriend?"

She almost laughed at his bewildered expression. "I guess so."

"Is that something new, or is this something I'm already supposed to know, but forgot?"

"I hadn't heard it before myself." She took her hands away from her face and looked at them. She thought of the rune, the open eye, that decorated the back of the right hand of every Shadowhunter. "Somebody's girlfriend," she said. "Somebody's sister, somebody's daughter. All these things I never knew I was before, and I still don't really know what I am."

"Isn't that always the question," Luke said, and Clary heard the door shut at the other end of the house, and Simon's foot-steps approaching the kitchen. The smell of cold night air came in with him.

"Would it be okay if I crashed here tonight?" he asked. "It's a little late to head home."

"You know you're always welcome." Luke glanced at his watch. "I'm going to get some sleep. Have to be up at five a.m. to get to the hospital by six."

"Why six?" Simon asked, after Luke had left the kitchen.

"That's when hospital visiting hours start," Clary said. "You don't have to sleep on the couch. Not if you don't want to."

"I don't mind staying to keep you company tomorrow," he said, shaking dark hair out of his eyes impatiently. "Not at all."

"I know. I meant you don't have to sleep *on the couch* if you don't want to."

"Then where . . ." His voice trailed off, eyes wide behind his glasses. "Oh."

"It's a double bed," she said. "In the guest room."

Simon took his hands out of his pockets. There was bright color in his cheeks. Jace would have tried to look cool; Simon didn't even try. "Are you *sure?*"

"I'm sure."

He came across the kitchen to her and, bending down, kissed her lightly and clumsily on the mouth. Smiling, she got to her feet. “Enough with the kitchens,” she said. “No more kitchens.” And taking him firmly by the wrists, she pulled him after her, out of the kitchen, toward the guest room where she slept.

# 5

# Sins of the Fathers

**The darkness of the prisons of the Silent City was more** profound than any darkness Jace had ever known. He couldn't see the shape of his own hand in front of his eyes, couldn't see the floor or ceiling of his cell. What he knew of the cell, he knew from the torchlit first glimpse he'd had, guided down here by a contingent of Silent Brothers, who had opened the barred gate of the cell for him and ushered him inside as if he were a common criminal.

Then again, that's probably exactly what they thought he was.

He knew that the cell had a flagged stone floor, that three of the walls were hewn rock, and that the fourth was made of narrowly spaced electrum bars, each end sunk deeply into stone. He knew there was a door set into those bars. He also knew that a long metal bar ran along the east wall, because the Silent Brothers had attached one loop of a pair of silver cuffs to this bar, and the other cuff to his wrist. He could walk up and down the cell a few steps, rattling like Marley's ghost, but that was as far as he could go. He had already rubbed his right wrist raw yanking thoughtlessly at the cuff. At least he was left-handed—a small bright spot in the impenetrable blackness. Not that it mattered much, but it was reassuring to have his better fighting hand free.

He began another slow promenade along the length of his cell, trailing his fingers along the wall as he walked. It was unnerving not to know what time it was. In Idris his father had taught him to tell time by the angle of the sun, the length of afternoon shadows, the position of the stars in the night sky. But there were no stars here. In fact, he had begun to wonder if he would ever see the sky again.

Jace paused. Now, why had he wondered that? Of course he'd see the sky again. The Clave weren't going to *kill* him. The penalty of death was reserved for murderers. But the flutter of fear stayed with him, just under his rib cage, strange as an unexpected twinge of pain. Jace wasn't exactly prone to random fits of panic—Alec would have said he could have benefited from a bit more in the way of constructive cowardice. Fear wasn't something that had ever affected him much.

He thought of Maryse saying, *You were never afraid of the dark.*

It was true. This anxiety was unnatural, not like him at all. There had to be more to it than simple darkness. He took another shallow breath. He just had to get through the night. One night. That was it. He took another step forward, his manacle jingling drearily.

A sound split the air, freezing him in his tracks. It was a high, howling ululation, a sound of pure and mindless terror. It seemed to go on and on like a singing note plucked from a violin, growing higher and thinner and sharper until it was abruptly cut off.

Jace swore. His ears were ringing, and he could taste terror in his mouth, like bitter metal. Who would have thought that fear had a taste? He pressed his back against the wall of the cell, willing himself to calm down.

The sound came again, louder this time, and then there was another scream, and another. Something crashed overhead, and Jace ducked involuntarily before remembering that he was several levels below ground. He heard another crash, and a picture formed in his mind: mausoleum doors smashing open, the corpses of centuries-dead Shadowhunters staggering free, nothing more than skeletons held together by dried tendon, dragging themselves across the white floors of the Silent City with fleshless, bony fingers—

*Enough!* With a gasp of effort, Jace forced the vision away. The dead did not come back. And besides, they were the corpses of Nephilim like himself, his slain brothers and sisters. He had nothing to fear from them. *So why was he so afraid?* He clenched his hands into fists, nails digging into his palms. This panic was unworthy of him. He would master it. He would crush it down. He took a deep breath, filling his lungs, just as another scream sounded, this one very loud. The breath rasped out of his chest as something crashed loudly, very close to him, and he saw a sudden bloom of light, a hot fire-flower stabbing into his eyes.

Brother Jeremiah staggered into view, his right hand

clutching a still-burning torch, his parchment hood fallen back to reveal a face torqued into a grotesque expression of terror. His previously sewn-shut mouth gaped open in a soundless scream, the gory threads of torn stitches dangling from his shredded lips. Blood, black in the torchlight, spattered his light robes. He took a few staggering steps forward, his hands outstretched—and then, as Jace watched in utter disbelief, Jeremiah pitched forward and fell headlong to the floor. Jace heard the shatter of bones as the archivist's body struck the ground and the torch sputtered, rolling out of Jeremiah's hand and toward the shallow stone gutter cut into the floor just outside the barred cell door.

Jace went to his knees instantly, stretching as far as the chain would let him, his fingers reaching for the torch. He couldn't quite touch it. The light was fading rapidly, but by its waning glow he could see Jeremiah's dead face turned toward him, blood still leaking from his open mouth. His teeth were gnarled black stubs.

Jace's chest felt as if something heavy were pressed against it. The Silent Brothers never opened their mouths, never spoke or laughed or screamed. But that had been the sound Jace had heard, he was sure of it now—the screams of men who hadn't cried out in half a century, the sound of a terror more profound and powerful than the ancient Rune of Silence. But how could that be? And where were the other Brothers?

Jace wanted to scream for help, but the weight was still on his chest, pressing down. He couldn't seem to get enough air. He lunged for the torch again and felt one of the small bones in his wrist shatter. Pain shot up his arm, but it gave him the extra inch he needed. He swept the torch into his hand and rose to his feet. As the flame leaped back into life, he heard another noise. A *thick* noise, a sort of ugly, dragging slither. The hair on the back of his neck stood up, sharp as needles. He thrust the torch forward, his shaking hand sending wild flicks of light dancing across the walls, brilliantly illuminating the shadows.

There was nothing there.

Instead of relief, though, he felt his terror intensify. He was now gasping in air in great sucking drafts, as if he'd been underwater. The fear was all the worse because it was so unfamiliar. What had *happened* to him? Had he suddenly become a coward?

He jerked hard against the manacle, hoping the pain would clear his head. It didn't. He heard the noise again, the thumping slither, and now it was close. There was another sound too, behind the slither, a soft, constant whispering. He had never heard any sound quite so evil. Half out of his mind with horror, he staggered back against the wall and raised the torch in his wildly jerking hand.

For a moment, bright as daylight, he saw the whole room: the cell, the barred door, the bare flagstones beyond, and the dead body of Jeremiah huddled against the floor. There was a door just behind Jeremiah. It was opening slowly. Something heaved its way through the door. Something huge and dark and formless. Eyes like burning ice, sunk deep into dark folds, regarded Jace with a snarling amusement. Then the thing lunged forward. A great cloud of roiling vapor rose up in front of Jace's eyes like a wave sweeping across the surface of the ocean. The last thing he saw was the flame of his torch guttering green and blue before it was swallowed up by the darkness.

* * *

Kissing Simon was pleasant. It was a gentle sort of pleasant, like lying in a hammock on a summer day with a book and a glass of lemonade. It was the sort of thing you could keep doing and not feel bored or apprehensive or disconcerted or bothered by much of anything except the fact that the metal bar on the sofa bed was digging into your back.

"Ouch," Clary said, trying to wriggle away from the bar and not succeeding.

"Did I hurt you?" Simon raised himself up on his side, looking concerned. Or maybe it was just that without his glasses his eyes seemed twice as large and dark.

"No, not you—the bed. It's like a torture instrument."

"*I* didn't notice," he said somberly, as she grabbed a pillow from the floor, where it had fallen, and wedged it underneath them.

"You wouldn't." She laughed. "Where were we?"

"Well, my face was approximately where it is now, but your face was a lot closer to mine. That's what I remember, anyway."

"How romantic." She pulled him down on top of her, where he balanced on his elbows. Their bodies lay neatly aligned and she could feel the beat of his heart through both their T-shirts. His lashes, normally hidden behind his glasses, brushed her cheek when he leaned to kiss her. She let out a shaky little laugh. "Is this weird for you?" she whispered.

"No. I think when you imagine something often enough, the reality of it seems—"

"Anticlimactic?"

"No. No!" Simon pulled back, looking at her with nearsighted conviction. "Don't ever think that. This is the opposite of anticlimactic. It's—"

Suppressed giggles bubbled up in her chest. "Okay, maybe you don't want to say *that*, either."

He half-closed his eyes, his mouth curving into a smile. "Okay, now I want to say something smart-ass back at you, but all I can think is . . ."

She grinned up at him. "That you want sex?"

"Stop that." He caught her hands with his, pinned them to the bedspread, and looked down at her gravely. "That I love you."

"So you *don't* want sex?"

He let go of her hands. "I didn't say that."

She laughed and pushed at his chest with both hands. "Let me up."

He looked alarmed. "I didn't mean I *only* want sex . . ."

"It's not that. I want to change into my pajamas. I can't take making out seriously when I still have my socks on." He watched her mournfully while she gathered up her pajamas from the dresser and headed into the bathroom. Pulling the door closed, she made a face at him. "I'll be right back."

Whatever he said in response was lost as she shut the door. She brushed her teeth and then ran the water in the sink for a long time, staring at herself in the medicine cabinet mirror. Her hair was tousled and her cheeks were red. Did that count as glowing, she wondered? People in love were supposed to glow, weren't they? Or maybe that was just pregnant women, she couldn't remember exactly, but surely she was supposed to look a little different. After all, this was the first real long kissing session she'd ever had—and it was nice, she told herself, safe and pleasant and comfortable.

Of course, she'd kissed Jace, on the night of her birthday, and that hadn't been safe and comfortable and pleasant at all. It had been like opening up a vein of something unknown inside her body, something hotter and sweeter and bitterer than blood. *Don't think about Jace,* she told herself fiercely, but looking at herself in the mirror, she saw her eyes darken and knew her body remembered even if her mind didn't want to.

She ran the water cold and splashed it over her face before reaching for her pajamas. Great, she realized, she'd brought her pajama bottoms in with her but not the top. However much Simon might appreciate it, it seemed early to break out the topless sleeping arrangements. She went back into the bedroom, only to discover that Simon was asleep in the center of the bed, clutching the bolster pillow as if it were a human being. She stifled a laugh.

"Simon . . . ," she whispered—then she heard the sharp two-tone beep that signaled that a text message had just arrived on her cell phone. The phone itself was lying folded on the bedside table; Clary picked it up and saw that the message was from Isabelle.

She flipped the phone open and scrolled hastily down to the text. She read it twice, just to make sure she wasn't imagining things. Then she ran to the closet to get her coat.

"Jonathan."

The voice spoke out of the blackness: slow, dark, familiar as pain. Jace blinked his eyes open and saw only darkness. He shivered. He was lying curled on the icy flagstone floor. He must have fainted. He felt a stab of fury at his own weakness, his own frailty.

He rolled onto his side, his torn wrist throbbing in its manacle. "Is anyone there?"

"Surely you recognize your own father, Jonathan." The voice came again, and Jace did know it: its sound of old iron, its smooth near-tonelessness. He tried to scramble to his feet but his boots slipped on a puddle of something and he skidded backward, his shoulders hitting the stone wall hard. His chain rattled like a chorus of steel wind chimes.

"Are you hurt?" A light blazed upward, searing Jace's eyes. He blinked away burning tears and saw Valentine standing on the other side of the bars, beside the corpse of Brother Jeremiah. A glowing witchlight stone in one hand cast a sharp whitish glow over the room. Jace could see the stains of old blood on the walls—and newer blood, a small lake of it, which had spilled from Jeremiah's open mouth. He felt his stomach roil and clench, and thought of the black formless shape he'd seen before with eyes like burning jewels. "That thing," he choked out. "Where is it? What *was* it?"

"You *are* hurt." Valentine moved closer to the bars. "Who ordered you locked up here? Was it the Clave? The Lightwoods?"

"It was the Inquisitor." Jace looked down at himself. There was more blood on his pants legs and on his shirt. He couldn't tell if any of it was his. Blood was seeping slowly from beneath his manacle.

Valentine regarded him thoughtfully through the bars. It was the first time in years Jace had seen his father in real battle dress—the thick leather Shadowhunter clothes that allowed freedom of movement while protecting the skin from most kinds of demon venom; the electrum-plated braces on his arms and legs, each marked with a series of glyphs and runes. There was a wide strap across his chest and the hilt of a sword gleamed above his shoulder. He squatted down then, putting his cool black eyes on a level with Jace's. Jace was surprised to see no anger in them. "The Inquisitor and the Clave are one and the same. And the Lightwoods should never have allowed this to happen. I would never have let anyone do this to you."

Jace pressed his shoulders back against the wall; it was as far as his chain would let him get from his father. "Did you come down here to kill me?"

"*Kill* you? Why would I want to kill you?"

"Well, why did you kill Jeremiah? And don't bother feeding me some story about how you just happened to wander along after he spontaneously died. I know you did this."

For the first time Valentine glanced down at the body of Brother Jeremiah. "I did kill him, and the rest of the Silent Brothers as well. I had to. They had something I needed."

"What? A sense of decency?"

"This," said Valentine, and drew the Sword from his shoulder sheath in one swift movement. "Maellartach."

Jace choked back the gasp of surprise that rose in his throat. He recognized it well enough: The huge, heavy-bladed silver Sword with the hilt in the shape of outspread wings was the one that hung above the Speaking Stars in the Silent Brothers' council room. "You *took* the Silent Brothers' sword?"

"It was never theirs," Valentine said. "It belongs to all Nephilim. This is the blade with which the Angel drove Adam and Eve out of the garden. *And he placed at the east of the garden of Eden Cherubim, and a flaming sword which turned every way,*" he quoted, gazing down at the blade.

Jace licked his dry lips. "What are you going to do with it?"

"I'll tell you that," said Valentine, "when I think I can trust you, and I know that you trust me."

"*Trust* you? After the way you sneaked through the Portal at Renwick's and smashed it so I couldn't come after you? And the way you tried to kill Clary?"

"I would never have hurt your sister," said Valentine, with a flash of anger. "Any more than I would hurt you."

"All you've ever done is hurt me! It was the Lightwoods who protected me!"

"I'm not the one who locked you up here. I'm not the one who threatens and distrusts you. That's the Lightwoods and their friends in the Clave." Valentine paused. "Seeing you like this—how they've treated you, and yet you remain stoic—I'm proud of you."

At that, Jace looked up in surprise, so quickly that he felt a wave of dizziness. His hand gave an insistent throb. He pushed the pain down and back until his breathing eased. "*What?*"

"I realize now what I did wrong at Renwick's," Valentine went on. "I was picturing you as the little boy I left behind in Idris, obedient to my every wish. Instead I found a headstrong young man, independent and courageous, yet I treated you as if you were still a child. No wonder you rebelled against me."

"Rebelled? I—" Jace's throat tightened, cutting off the words he wanted to say. His heart had begun pounding in rhythm with the throbbing in his hand.

Valentine pressed on. "I never had a chance to explain my past to you, to tell you why I've done the things I've done."

"There's nothing to explain. You killed my grandparents. You held my mother prisoner. You slew other Shadowhunters to further your own ends." Every word in Jace's mouth tasted like poison.

"You only know half the facts, Jonathan. I lied to you when you were a child because you were too young to understand. Now you are old enough to be told the truth."

"So *tell* me the truth."

Valentine reached through the bars of the cell and laid his hand on top of Jace's. The rough, callused texture of his fingers felt exactly the way it had when Jace had been ten years old.

"I want to trust you, Jonathan," he said. "Can I?"

Jace wanted to reply, but the words wouldn't come. His chest felt as if an iron band was being slowly tightened around it, cutting off his breath by inches. "I wish . . . ," he whispered.

A noise sounded above them. A noise like the clang of a metal door; then Jace heard footsteps, whispers echoing off the City's stone walls. Valentine started to his feet, closing his hand over the witchlight until it was only a dim glow and he himself was a faintly outlined shadow. "Quicker than I thought," he murmured, and looked down at Jace through the bars.

Jace looked past him, but he could see nothing but blackness beyond the faint illumination of the witchlight. He thought of the roiling dark form he had seen before, crushing out all light before it. "What's coming? What is it?" he demanded, scrabbling forward on his knees.

"I must go," said Valentine. "But we're not done, you and I."

Jace put his hand to the bars. "Unchain me. Whatever it is, I want to be able to fight it."

"Unchaining you would hardly be a kindness now." Valentine closed his hand around the witchlight stone completely. It winked out, plunging the room into darkness. Jace flung himself against the bars of the cell, his broken hand screaming its protest and pain.

"No!" he shouted. "Father, *please.*"

"When you want to find me," Valentine said, "you will find me." And then there was only the sound of his footsteps rapidly receding and Jace's own ragged breathing as he slumped against the bars.

On the subway ride uptown Clary found herself unable to sit down. She paced up and down the near-empty train car, her iPod headphones dangling around her neck. Isabelle hadn't picked up the phone when Clary had called her, and an irrational sense of worry gnawed at Clary's insides.

She thought of Jace at the Hunter's Moon, covered in blood. With his teeth bared in snarling anger, he'd looked more like a werewolf himself than a Shadowhunter charged with protecting humans and keeping Downworlders in line.

She charged up the stairs at the Ninety-sixth Street subway stop, only slowing to a walk as she approached the corner where the Institute hulked like a huge gray shadow. It had been hot down in the tunnels, and the sweat on the back of her neck was prickling coldly as she made her way up the cracked concrete walk to the Institute's front door.

She reached for the enormous iron bellpull that hung from the architrave, then hesitated. She was a Shadowhunter, wasn't she? She had a right to be in the Institute, just as much as the Lightwoods did. With a surge of resolve, she seized the door handle, trying to remember the words Jace had spoken. "In the name of the Angel, I—"

The door swung open onto a darkness starred by the flames of dozens of tiny candles. As she hurried between the pews, the candles flickered as if they were laughing at her. She reached the elevator and clanged the metal door shut behind her, stabbing at the buttons with a shaking finger. She willed her nervousness to subside—was she worried *about* Jace, she wondered, or just worried about *seeing* Jace? Her face, framed by the upturned collar of her coat, looked very white and small, her eyes big and dark green, her lips pale and bitten. Not pretty at all, she thought in dismay, and forced the thought back. What did it matter how she looked? Jace didn't care. Jace *couldn't* care.

The elevator came to a clanging stop and Clary pushed the door open. Church was waiting for her in the foyer. He greeted her with a disgruntled meow.

"What's wrong, Church?" Her voice sounded unnaturally loud in the quiet room. She wondered if anyone were here in the Institute. Maybe it was just her. The thought gave her the creeps. "Is anyone home?"

The blue Persian turned his back and headed down the corridor. They passed the music room and the library, both empty, before Church turned another corner and sat down in front of a closed door. *Right, then. Here we are*, his expression seemed to say.

Before she could knock, the door opened, revealing Isabelle standing on the threshold, barefoot in a pair of jeans and a soft violet sweater. She started when she saw Clary. "I thought I heard someone coming down the hall, but I didn't think it would be *you*," she said. "What are you doing here?"

Clary stared at her. "You sent me that text message. You said the Inquisitor threw Jace in *jail*."

"Clary!" Isabelle glanced up and down the corridor, then bit her lip. "I didn't mean you should race down here right *now*."

Clary was horrified. "Isabelle! *Jail!*"

"Yes, but—" With a defeated sigh, Isabelle stood aside, gesturing for Clary to enter her room. "Look, you might as well come in. And shoo, you," she said, waving a hand at Church. "Go guard the elevator."

Church gave her a horrified look, lay down on his stomach, and went to sleep.

"*Cats*," Isabelle muttered, and slammed the door.

"Hey, Clary." Alec was sitting on Isabelle's unmade bed, his booted feet dangling over the side. "What are you doing here?"

Clary sat down on the padded stool in front of Isabelle's gloriously messy vanity table. "Isabelle texted me. She told me what happened to Jace."

Isabelle and Alec exchanged a meaningful look. "Oh, come on, Alec," Isabelle said. "I thought she should know. I didn't know she'd come racing up here!"

Clary's stomach lurched. "Of course I came! Is he all right? Why on earth did the Inquisitor throw him in prison?"

"It's not prison exactly. He's in the Silent City," said Alec, sitting up straight and pulling one of Isabelle's pillows across his lap. He picked idly at the beaded fringe sewed to its edges.

"In the Silent City? Why?"

Alec hesitated. "There are cells under the Silent City. They keep criminals there sometimes before deporting them to Idris to stand trial before the Council. People who've done really bad things. Murderers, renegade vampires, Shadowhunters who break the Accords. That's where Jace is now."

"Locked up with a bunch of *murderers?*" Clary was on her feet, outraged. "What's wrong with you people? Why aren't you more upset?"

Alec and Isabelle exchanged another look. "It's just for a night," Isabelle said. "And there isn't anyone else down there with him. We asked."

"But why? What did Jace *do?*"

"He mouthed off to the Inquisitor. That was it, as far as I know," said Alec.

Isabelle perched herself on the edge of the vanity table. "It's unbelievable."

"Then the Inquisitor must be insane," said Clary.

"She's not, actually," said Alec. "If Jace were in your mundane army, do you think he'd be allowed to mouth off to his superiors? Absolutely not."

"Well, not during a *war*. But Jace isn't a soldier."

"But we're all soldiers. Jace as much as the rest of us. There's a hierarchy of command and the Inquisitor is near the top. Jace is near the bottom. He should have treated her with more respect."

"If you agree that he ought to be in jail, why did you ask me to come here? Just to get me to agree with you? I don't see the point. What do you want me to do?"

"We didn't say he should be in jail," Isabelle snapped. "Just that he shouldn't have talked back to one of the highest-ranked members of the Clave. Besides," she added in a smaller voice, "I thought that maybe you could help."

"Help? How?"

"I told you before," Alec said, "half the time it seems like Jace is trying to get himself killed. He has to learn to look out for himself, and that includes cooperating with the Inquisitor."

"And you think I can help you make him do that?" Clary said, disbelief coloring her voice.

"I'm not sure anyone can make Jace do anything," said Isabelle. "But I think you can remind him that he has something to live for."

Alec looked down at the pillow in his hand and gave a sudden savage yank to the fringe. Beads rattled down onto Isabelle's blanket like a shower of localized rain.

Isabelle frowned. "Alec, don't."

Clary wanted to tell Isabelle that they were Jace's family, that she wasn't, that their voices carried more weight with him than hers ever would. But she kept hearing Jace's voice in her head, saying, *I never felt like I belonged anywhere. But you make me feel like I belong.* "Can we go to the Silent City and see him?"

"Will you tell him to cooperate with the Inquisitor?" Alec demanded.

Clary considered. "I want to hear what he has to say first."

Alec dropped the denuded pillow onto the bed and stood up, frowning. Before he could say anything, there was a knock at the door. Isabelle unhitched herself from the vanity table and went to answer it.

It was a small, dark-haired boy, his eyes half-hidden by glasses. He wore jeans and an oversize sweatshirt and carried a book in one hand. "Max," Isabelle said, with some surprise, "I thought you were asleep."

"I was in the weapons room," said the boy—who had to be the Lightwoods' youngest son. "But there were noises coming from the library. I think someone might be trying to contact the Institute." He peered around Isabelle at Clary. "Who's that?"

"That's Clary," said Alec. "She's Jace's sister."

Max's eyes rounded. "I thought Jace didn't have any brothers or sisters."

"That's what we all thought," said Alec, picking up the sweater he'd left draped over one of Isabelle's chairs and yanking it on. His hair rayed out around his head like a soft dark halo, crackling with static electricity. He pushed it back impatiently. "I'd better get to the library."

"We'll both go," Isabelle said, taking her gold whip, which was twisted into a shimmering rope, out of a drawer and sliding the handle through her belt. "Maybe something's happened."

"Where are your parents?" Clary asked.

"They got called out a few hours ago. A fey was murdered in Central Park. The Inquisitor went with them," Alec explained.

"You didn't want to go?"

"We weren't invited." Isabelle looped her two dark braids up on top of her head and stuck the coil of hair through with a small glass dagger. "Look after Max, will you? We'll be right back."

"But—," Clary protested.

"We'll be *right back*." Isabelle darted out into the corridor, Alec on her heels. The moment the door shut behind them, Clary sat down on the bed and regarded Max with apprehension. She'd never spent much time around children—her mother had never let her babysit—and she wasn't really sure how to talk to them or what might amuse them. It helped a little that this particular little boy reminded her of Simon at that age, with his skinny arms and legs and glasses that seemed too big for his face.

Max returned her stare with a considering glance of his

own, not shy, but thoughtful and contained. "How old are you?" he said finally.

Clary was taken aback. "How old do I look?"

"Fourteen."

"I'm sixteen, but people always think I'm younger than I am because I'm so short."

Max nodded. "Me too," he said. "I'm nine but people always think I'm seven."

"You look nine to me," said Clary. "What's that you're holding? Is it a book?"

Max brought his hand out from behind his back. He was holding a wide, flat paperback, about the size of one of those small magazines they sold at grocery store counters. This one had a brightly colored cover with Japanese kanji script on it under the English words. Clary laughed. "*Naruto*," she said. "I didn't know you liked manga. Where did you get that?"

"In the airport. I like the pictures but I can't figure out how to read it."

"Here, give it to me." She flipped it open, showing him the pages. "You read it backward, right to left instead of left to right. And you read each page clockwise. Do you know what that means?"

"Of course," said Max. For a moment Clary was worried she'd annoyed him. He seemed pleased enough, though, when he took the book back and flipped to the last page. "This one is number nine," he said. "I think I should get the other eight before I read it."

"That's a good idea. Maybe you can get someone to take you to Midtown Comics or Forbidden Planet."

"Forbidden *Planet*?" Max looked bemused, but before

Clary could explain, Isabelle burst through the door, clearly out of breath.

"It *was* someone trying to contact the Institute," she said, before Clary could ask. "One of the Silent Brothers. Something's happened in the Bone City."

"What kind of something?"

"I don't know. I've never heard of the Silent Brothers asking for help before." Isabelle was clearly distressed. She turned to her brother. "Max, go to your room and stay there, okay?"

Max set his jaw. "Are you and Alec going out?"

"Yes."

"To the Silent City?"

"Max—"

"I want to come."

Isabelle shook her head; the hilt of the dagger at the back of her head glittered like a point of fire. "Absolutely not. You're too young."

"You're not eighteen either!"

Isabelle turned to Clary with a look half of anxiety and half of desperation. "Clary, come here for a second, *please.*"

Clary got up, wonderingly—and Isabelle grabbed her by the arm and yanked her out of the room, slamming the door shut behind her. There was a thump as Max threw himself against it. "Damn it," said Isabelle, holding the knob, "can you grab my stele for me, please? It's in my pocket—"

Hastily, Clary held out the stele Luke had given her earlier that night. "Use mine."

With a few swift strokes, Isabelle had carved a Locking rune onto the door. Clary could still hear Max's protests from the other side as Isabelle stepped away from the door, grimacing, and handed Clary back her stele. "I didn't know you had one of these."

"It was my mother's," said Clary, then she mentally chided herself. *Is my mother's. It is my mother's.*

"Huh." Isabelle thumped on the door with a closed fist. "Max, there's some PowerBars in the nightstand drawer if you get hungry. We'll be back as soon as we can."

There was another outraged yell from behind the door; with a shrug, Isabelle turned and hurried back down the hallway, Clary at her side. "What did the message say?" Clary demanded. "Just that there was trouble?"

"That there was an attack. That's it."

Alec was waiting for them outside the library. He was wearing black leather Shadowhunter armor over his clothes. Gauntlets protected his arms and Marks circled his throat and wrists. Seraph blades, each one named for an angel, gleamed at the belt around his waist. "Are you ready?" he said to his sister. "Is Max taken care of?"

"He's fine." She held out her arms. "Mark me."

As Alec traced the patterns of runes along the backs of Isabelle's hands and the insides of her wrists, he glanced over at Clary. "You should probably head home," he said. "You don't want to be here by yourself when the Inquisitor gets back."

"I want to go with you," Clary said, the words spilling out before she could stop them.

Isabelle took one of her hands back from Alec and blew on the Marked skin as if she were cooling a too-hot cup of coffee. "You sound like Max."

"Max is nine. I'm the same age as you."

"But you haven't got any training," Alec argued. "You'll just be a liability."

"No, I won't. Has either of *you* ever been inside the Silent City?" Clary demanded. "I have. I know how to get in. I know how to find my way around."

Alec straightened up, putting his stele away. "I don't think—"

Isabelle cut in. "She has a point, actually. I think she should come if she wants."

Alec looked taken aback. "Last time we faced a demon, she just cowered and screamed." Seeing Clary's acid glare, he shot her an apologetic glance. "I'm sorry, but it's true."

"I think she needs a chance to learn," Isabelle said. "You know what Jace always says. Sometimes you don't have to search out danger, sometimes danger finds *you*."

"You can't lock me up like you did Max," Clary added, seeing Alec's weakening resolution. "I'm not a child. And I know where the Bone City is. I can find my way there without you."

Alec turned away, shaking his head and muttering something about girls. Isabelle held out a hand to Clary. "Give me your stele," she said. "It's time you got some Marks."

# 6

## City of Ashes

**In the end Isabelle gave Clary only two Marks, one on the** back of each hand. One was the open eye that decorated the hand of every Shadowhunter. The other was like two crossed sickles; Isabelle said it was a Rune of Protection. Both runes burned when the stele first touched skin, but the pain faded as Clary, Isabelle, and Alec headed downtown in a black gypsy cab. By the time they reached Second Avenue and stepped out onto the pavement, Clary's hands and arms felt as light as if she were wearing water wings in a swimming pool.

The three of them were silent as they passed under the wrought iron arch and into the Marble Cemetery. The last time Clary had been in this small courtyard she had been hurrying along after Brother Jeremiah. Now, for the first time, she noticed the names carved into the walls: *Youngblood, Fairchild, Thrushcross, Nightwine, Ravenscar.* There were runes beside them. In Shadowhunter culture each family had their own symbol: The Waylands' was a blacksmith's hammer, the Lightwoods' a torch, and Valentine's a star.

The grass grew tangled over the feet of the Angel statue in the courtyard's center. The Angel's eyes were closed, his slim hands closed over the stem of a stone goblet, a reproduction of the Mortal Cup. His stone face was impassive, streaked with dirt and grime.

Clary said, "Last time I was here, Brother Jeremiah used a rune on the statue to open the door to the City."

"I wouldn't want to use one of the Silent Brothers' runes," Alec said. His face was grim. "They should have sensed our presence before we got this far. Now I'm starting to worry." He took a dagger from his belt and drew the blade of it across his bare palm. Blood welled from the shallow gash. Making a fist over the stone Cup, he let the blood drip into it. "Blood of the Nephilim," he said. "It should work as a key."

The stone Angel's eyelids flew open. For a moment Clary almost expected to see eyes glaring at her from between the folds of stone, but there was only more granite. A second later, the grass at the Angel's feet began to split. A crooked black line, rippling like the back of a snake, curved away from the statue, and Clary jumped back hastily as a dark hole opened at her feet.

She peered down into it. Stairs led away into shadow. Last time she had been here, the darkness had been lit at intervals by torches, illuminating the steps. Now there was only blackness.

"Something's wrong," Clary said. Neither Isabelle nor Alec seemed inclined to argue. Clary took the witchlight stone Jace had given her out of her pocket and raised it overhead. Light burst from it, raying out through her spread fingers. "Let's go."

Alec stepped in front of her. "I'll go first, then you follow me. Isabelle, bring up the rear."

They clambered down slowly, Clary's damp boots slipping on the age-rounded steps. At the foot of the stairs was a short tunnel that opened out into an enormous hall, a stone orchard of white arches inset with semiprecious stones. Rows of mausoleums huddled in the shadows like toadstool houses in a fairy story. The more distant of them disappeared into shadow; the witchlight was not strong enough to light the whole hall.

Alec looked somberly down the rows. "I never thought I would enter the Silent City," he said. "Not even in death."

"I wouldn't sound so sad about it," Clary said. "Brother Jeremiah told me what they do to your dead. They burn them up and use most of the ashes to make the City's marble." *The blood and bone of demon slayers is itself a powerful protection against evil. Even in death, the Clave serves the Cause.*

"Hmph," said Isabelle. "It's considered an honor. Besides, it's not like you mundies don't burn your dead."

*That doesn't make it not creepy*, Clary thought. The smell of ashes and smoke hung heavy on the air, familiar to her from the last time she was here—but there was something else underlying those smells, a heavier, thicker stench, like rotting fruit.

Frowning as if he smelled it too, Alec took one of his angel blades out of his weapons belt. "*Arathiel,*" he whispered, and its glow joined the illumination of Clary's witchlight as they found the second staircase and descended into even denser gloom. The witchlight pulsed in Clary's hand like a dying star—she wondered if they ever ran out of power, witchlight stones, like flashlights ran out of batteries. She hoped not. The idea of being plunged into sightless darkness in this creepy place filled her with a visceral terror.

The smell of rotting fruit grew stronger as they reached the end of the stairs and found themselves in another long tunnel. This one opened out into a pavilion surrounded by spires of carved bone—a pavilion Clary remembered very well. Inlaid silver stars sprinkled the floor like precious confetti. In the center of the pavilion was a black table. Dark fluid had pooled on its slick surface and trickled across the floor in rivulets.

When Clary had stood before the Council of Brothers, there had been a heavy silver sword hanging on the wall behind the table. The Sword was gone now, and in its place, smeared across the wall, was a great fan of scarlet.

"Is that *blood?*" Isabelle whispered. She didn't sound afraid, just stunned.

"Looks like it." Alec's eyes scanned the room. The shadows were as thick as paint, and seemed full of movement. His grip was tight on his seraph blade.

"What could have happened?" Isabelle said. "The Silent Brothers—I thought they were *indestructible*. . . ."

Her voice trailed off as Clary turned, the witchlight in her hand catching strange shadows among the spires. One was more strangely shaped than the others. She willed the witchlight to burn brighter and it did, sending a lancing bolt of brightness into the distance.

Impaled on one of the spires, like a worm on a hook, was the dead body of a Silent Brother. Hands, ribboned in blood, dangled just above the marble floor. His neck looked broken.

Blood had pooled beneath him, clotted and black in the witchlight.

Isabelle gasped. "Alec. Do you see—"

"I see." Alec's voice was grim. "And I've seen worse. It's Jace I'm worried about."

Isabelle went forward and touched the black basalt table, her fingers skimming the surface. "This blood is almost fresh. Whatever happened, it happened not long ago."

Alec moved toward the Brother's impaled corpse. Smeared marks led away from the blood pool on the floor. "Footprints," he said. "Someone running." Alec indicated with a curled hand that the girls should follow him. They did, Isabelle pausing only to wipe her bloody hands off on her soft leather leg guards.

The path of footprints led from the pavilion and down a narrow tunnel, disappearing into darkness. When Alec stopped, looking around him, Clary pushed past him impatiently, letting the witchlight blaze a silvery-white path of light ahead of them. She could see a set of double doors at the end of the tunnel; they were ajar.

Jace. Somehow she sensed him, that he was close. She took off at a half run, her boots clacking loudly against the hard floor. She heard Isabelle call after her, and then Alec and Isabelle were also running, hard on her heels. She burst through the doors at the end of the hall and found herself in a large stone-bound room bisected by a row of metal bars sunk deep into the ground. Clary could just make out a slumped shape on the other side of the bars. Just outside the cell sprawled the limp form of a Silent Brother.

Clary knew immediately that he was dead. It was the way he was lying, like a doll whose joints had been twisted the wrong way until they broke. His parchment-colored robes were half-torn off. His scarred face, contorted into a look of utter terror, was still recognizable. It was Brother Jeremiah.

She pushed past his body to the door of the cell. It was made of bars spaced close together and hinged on one side. There seemed to be no lock or knob that she could pull. She heard Alec, behind her, say her name, but her attention wasn't on him: It was on the door. Of course there was no visible way to open it, she realized; the Brothers didn't deal in what was visible, but rather what wasn't. Holding the witchlight in one hand, she scrabbled for her mother's stele with the other.

From the other side of the bars came a noise. A sort of muffled gasp or whisper; she wasn't sure which, but she recognized the source. *Jace.* She slashed at the cell door with the tip of her stele, trying to hold the rune for Open in her mind even as it appeared, black and jagged against the hard metal. The electrum sizzled where the stele touched it. *Open*, she willed the door, *open*, *open*, *OPEN!*

A noise like ripping cloth tore through the room. Clary heard Isabelle cry out as the door blew off its hinges entirely, crashing into the cell like a drawbridge falling. Clary could hear other noises, metal coming uncoupled from metal, a loud rattle like a handful of tossed pebbles. She ducked into the cell, the fallen door wobbling under her feet.

Witchlight filled the small room, lighting it as bright as day. She barely noticed the rows of manacles—all of different metals: gold, silver, steel, and iron—as they came undone from the bolts in the walls and clattered to the stone floor. Her eyes were on the slumped figure in the corner; she could see the bright hair, the hand outstretched, the loose manacle lying a little distance away. His wrist was bare and bloody, the skin braceleted with ugly bruises.

She went down on her knees, setting her stele aside, and gently turned him over. It *was* Jace. There was another bruise on his cheek, and his face was very white, but she could see the darting movement under his eyelids. A vein pulsed at his throat. He was alive.

Relief went through her like a hot wave, undoing the tight cords of tension that had held her together this long. The witchlight fell to the floor beside her, where it continued to blaze. She stroked Jace's hair back from his forehead with a tenderness that felt foreign to her—she'd never had any brothers or sisters, not even a cousin. She'd never had occasion to bind up wounds or kiss scraped knees or take care of anyone, really. But it was all right to feel tenderness toward Jace like this, she thought, unwilling to draw her hand back even as Jace's eyelids twitched and he groaned. He was her brother; why shouldn't she care what happened to him?

His eyes opened. The pupils were huge, dilated. Maybe he'd banged his head? His eyes fixed on her with a look of dazed bemusement. "*Clary,*" he said. "What are you doing here?"

"I came to find you," she said, because it was the truth.

A spasm went across his face. "You're really here? I'm not—I'm not dead, am I?"

"No," she said, gliding her hand down the side of his face. "You passed out, is all. Probably hit your head too."

His hand came up to cover hers where it lay on his cheek. "Worth it," he said in such a low voice that she wasn't sure it was what he'd said, after all.

"What's going on?" It was Alec, ducking through the low

doorway, Isabelle just behind him. Clary jerked her hand back, then cursed herself silently. She hadn't been doing anything wrong.

Jace struggled into a sitting position. His face was gray, his shirt spotted with blood. Alec's look turned to one of concern. "And are you all right?" he demanded, kneeling down. "What happened? Can you remember?"

Jace held up his uninjured hand. "One question at a time, Alec. My head already feels like it's going to split open."

"Who did this to you?" Isabelle sounded both bewildered and furious.

"No one did anything to me. I did it to myself trying to get the manacles off." Jace looked down at his wrist—it looked as if he'd nearly scraped all the skin off it—and winced.

"Here," said both Clary and Alec at the same time, reaching out for his hand. Their eyes met, and Clary dropped her hand first. Alec took hold of Jace's wrist and drew out his stele; with a few quick flicks of his wrist, he drew an *iratze*—a healing rune—just below the bracelet of bleeding skin.

"Thanks," said Jace, drawing his hand back. The injured part of his wrist was already beginning to knit back together. "Brother Jeremiah—"

"Is dead," said Clary.

"I know." Disdaining Alec's offered assistance, Jace pulled himself up to a standing position, using the wall to hold him up. "He was murdered."

"Did the Silent Brothers kill each other?" Isabelle asked. "I don't understand—I don't understand why they'd *do* that—"

"They didn't," said Jace. "Something killed them. I don't know what." A spasm of pain twisted his face. "My head—"

"Maybe we should go," said Clary nervously. "Before whatever killed them . . ."

"Comes back for us?" said Jace. He looked down at his bloody shirt and bruised hand. "I think it's gone. But I suppose he could still bring it back."

"Who could bring what back?" Alec demanded, but Jace said nothing. His face had gone from gray to paper white. Alec caught him as he began to slide down the wall. "Jace—"

"I'm all right," Jace protested, but his hand gripped Alec's sleeve tightly. "I can stand."

"It looks to me like you're using a wall to prop you up. That's not my definition of 'standing.'"

"It's leaning," Jace told him. "Leaning comes right before standing."

"Stop bickering," said Isabelle, kicking a doused torch out of her way. "We need to get out of here. If there's something out there nasty enough to kill the Silent Brothers, it'll make short work of us."

"Izzy's right. We should go." Clary retrieved the witchlight and stood up. "Jace—are you okay to walk?"

"He can lean on me." Alec drew Jace's arm across his shoulders. Jace leaned heavily against him. "Come on," Alec said gently. "We'll fix you up when we get outside."

Slowly they moved toward the cell door, where Jace paused, staring down at the figure of Brother Jeremiah lying twisted on the paving stones. Isabelle knelt down and drew the Silent Brother's brown wool hood down to cover his contorted face. When she straightened up, all their faces were grave.

"I've never seen a Silent Brother afraid," Alec said. "I didn't think it was possible for them to feel fear."

"Everyone feels fear." Jace was still very pale, and though he was cradling his injured hand against his chest, Clary didn't think it was because of physical pain. He looked distant, as if he had withdrawn into himself, hiding from something.

They retraced their steps through the dark corridors and up the narrow steps that led to the pavilion of the Speaking Stars. When they reached it, Clary noticed the thick scent of blood and burning as she hadn't when she'd passed through it before. Jace, leaning on Alec, looked around with a sort of mingled horror and confusion on his face. Clary saw that he was staring at the far wall where it was splattered thickly with blood, and she said, "Jace. Don't look." Then she felt stupid; he was a demon hunter, after all, he'd seen worse.

He shook his head. "Something feels wrong—"

"Everything feels wrong here." Alec tilted his head toward the forest of arches that led away from the pavilion. "That's the fastest way out of here. Let's go."

They didn't talk much as they made their way back through the Bone City. Every shadow seemed to surge with movement, as if the darkness concealed creatures waiting to jump out at them. Isabelle was whispering something under her breath. Though Clary couldn't hear the words themselves, it sounded like another language, something old—Latin, maybe.

When they reached the stairs that led up out of the City, Clary breathed a silent sigh of relief. The Bone City might have been beautiful once, but it was terrifying now. As they reached the last flight of steps, light stabbed into her eyes, making her cry out in surprise. She could faintly see the Angel statue that stood at the head of the stairs, backlit with brilliant golden light, bright as day. She glanced around at the others; they looked as confused as she felt.

"The sun couldn't have risen yet—could it?" Isabelle murmured. "How long were we down here?"

Alec checked his watch. "Not that long."

Jace muttered something, too low for anyone else to hear him. Alec craned his ear down. "What did you say?"

"Witchlight," Jace said, more loudly this time.

Isabelle hurried up the stairs, Clary behind her, Alec just behind them, struggling to half-carry Jace up the steps. At the head of the stairs Isabelle stopped suddenly as if frozen. Clary called out to her, but she didn't move. A moment later Clary was standing beside her and it was her turn to stare around in amazement.

The garden was full of Shadowhunters—twenty, maybe thirty, of them in dark hunting regalia, inked with Marks, each holding a blazing witchlight stone.

At the front of the group stood Maryse, in black Shadowhunter armor and a cloak, her hood thrown back. Behind her ranged dozens of strangers, men and women Clary had never seen, but who bore the Marks of the Nephilim on their arms and faces. One of them, a handsome ebony-skinned man, turned to stare at Clary and Isabelle—and beside her, at Jace and Alec, who had come up from the steps and stood blinking in the unexpected light.

"By the Angel," the man said. "Maryse—there was already someone down there."

Maryse's mouth opened in a silent gasp when she saw Isabelle. Then she closed it, her lips tightening into a thin white line, like a slash drawn in chalk across her face.

"I know, Malik," she said. "These are my children."

# 7

# The Mortal Sword

**A muttering gasp went through the crowd. The ones who** were hooded threw their hoods back, and Clary could see from the looks on the faces of Jace, Alec, and Isabelle that many of the Shadowhunters in the courtyard were familiar to them.

"By the Angel." Maryse's incredulous gaze swept from Alec to Jace, passed over Clary, and returned to her daughter. Jace had moved away from Alec the moment Maryse spoke, and he stood a little way away from the other three, his hands in his pockets as Isabelle nervously twisted her golden-white whip in her hands. Alec, meanwhile, seemed to be fidgeting with his cell phone, though Clary couldn't imagine who he might be calling. "What are you doing here, Alec? Isabelle? There was a distress call from the Silent City—"

"We answered it," Alec said. His gaze moved anxiously over the gathered crowd. Clary could hardly blame him for his nerves. This was the largest crowd of adult Shadowhunters—of Shadowhunters in general—that she herself had ever seen. She kept looking from face to face, marking the differences between them—they varied widely in age and race and overall appearance, and yet they all gave the same impression of immense, contained power. She could sense their subtle gazes on her, examining her, evaluating. One of them, a woman with rippling silver hair, was staring at her so fiercely that there was nothing subtle about it. Clary blinked and looked away as Alec continued, "You weren't at the Institute—and we couldn't raise anyone—so we came ourselves."

"Alec—"

"It doesn't matter, anyway," Alec said. "They're dead. The Silent Brothers. They're all dead. They've been murdered."

This time there was no sound from the assembled crowd. Instead they seemed to go still, the way a pride of lions might go still when it spotted a gazelle.

*"Dead?"* Maryse repeated. "What do you mean, they're dead?"

"I think it's quite clear what he means." A woman in a long gray coat had appeared suddenly at Maryse's side. In the flickering light she looked to Clary like a sort of Edward Gorey caricature, all sharp angles and pulled-back hair and eyes like black pits scraped out of her face. She held a glimmering chunk of witchlight on a long silver chain, looped through the skinniest fingers Clary had ever seen. "They are all dead?" she asked, addressing herself to Alec. "You found no one alive in the City?"

Alec shook his head. "Not that we saw, Inquisitor."

So *that* was the Inquisitor, Clary realized. She certainly looked like someone capable of tossing teenage boys into dungeon cells for no reason other than that she didn't like their attitude.

"That you *saw*," repeated the Inquisitor, her eyes like hard, glittering beads. She turned to Maryse. "There may yet be survivors. I would send your people into the City for a thorough check."

Maryse's lips tightened. From what very little Clary had learned about Maryse, she knew that Jace's adoptive mother didn't like being told what to do. "Very well."

She turned to the rest of the Shadowhunters—there were not as many, Clary was coming to realize, as she had initially thought, closer to twenty than thirty, though the shock of their appearance had made them seem like a teeming crowd.

Maryse spoke to Malik in a low voice. He nodded. Taking the arm of the silver-haired woman, he led the Shadowhunters toward the entrance to the Bone City. As one after another descended the stairs, taking their witchlight with them, the glow in the courtyard began to fade. The last one in line was the woman with the silver hair. Halfway down the stairs she paused, turned, and looked back—directly at Clary. Her eyes were full of a terrible yearning, as if she longed desperately to tell Clary something. After a moment she drew her hood back up over her face and vanished into the shadows.

Maryse broke the silence. "Why would anyone murder the Silent Brothers? They're not warriors, they don't carry battle Marks—"

"Don't be naive, Maryse," said the Inquisitor. "This was no

random attack. The Silent Brothers may not be warriors, but they are primarily guardians, and very good at their jobs. Not to mention hard to kill. Someone wanted something from the Bone City and was willing to kill the Silent Brothers to get it. This was premeditated."

"What makes you so sure?"

"That wild goose chase that called us all out to Central Park? The dead fey child?"

"I wouldn't call that a wild goose chase. The fey child was drained of blood, like the others. These killings could cause serious trouble between the Night Children and other Downworlders—"

"Distractions," said the Inquisitor dismissively. "He wanted us gone from the Institute so that no one would respond to the Brothers when they called for aid. Ingenious, really. But then he always was ingenious."

"He?" It was Isabelle who spoke, her face very pale between the black wings of her hair. "You mean—"

Jace's next words sent a shock through Clary, as if she'd touched a live current. "Valentine," he said. "Valentine took the Mortal Sword. That's why he killed the Silent Brothers."

A thin, sudden smile curved on the Inquisitor's face, as if Jace had said something that pleased her very much.

Alec started and turned to stare at Jace. "*Valentine?* But you didn't say he was here."

"Nobody asked."

"He couldn't have killed the Brothers. They were torn *apart*. No one person could have done all that."

"He probably had demonic help," said the Inquisitor. "He's used demons to aid him before. And with the protection of the

Cup on him, he could summon some very dangerous creatures. More dangerous than Raveners," she added with a curl of her lip, and though she didn't look at Clary when she said it, the words felt somehow like a verbal slap. Clary's faint hope that the Inquisitor hadn't noticed or recognized her vanished. "Or the pathetic Forsaken."

"I don't know about that." Jace was very pale, with hectic spots like fever on his cheekbones. "But it was Valentine. I saw him. In fact, he had the Sword with him when he came down to the cells and taunted me through the bars. It was like a bad movie, except he didn't actually twirl his mustache."

Clary looked at him worriedly. He was talking too fast, she thought, and looked unsteady on his feet.

The Inquisitor didn't seem to notice. "So you're saying that Valentine *told* you all this? He told you he killed the Silent Brothers because he wanted the Angel's Sword?"

"What else did he tell you? Did he tell you where he was going? What he plans to do with the two Mortal Instruments?" Maryse asked quickly.

Jace shook his head.

The Inquisitor moved toward him, her coat swirling around her like drifting smoke. Her gray eyes and gray mouth were drawn into tight horizontal lines. "I don't believe you."

Jace just looked at her. "I didn't think you would."

"I doubt the Clave will believe you either."

Alec said hotly, "Jace isn't a liar—"

"Use your brain, Alexander," said the Inquisitor, not taking her eyes off Jace. "Leave aside your loyalty to your friend for a moment. What's the likelihood that Valentine stopped by his son's cell for a paternal chat about the Soul-Sword, and didn't mention what he planned to do with it, or even where he was going?"

*"S'io credesse che mia risposta fosse,"* Jace said in a language Clary didn't know, *"a persona che mai tornasse al mondo . . ."*

"Dante." The Inquisitor looked dryly amused. "The *Inferno*. You're not in hell yet, Jonathan Morgenstern, though if you insist on lying to the Clave, you'll wish you were." She turned back to the others. "And doesn't it seem odd to anyone that the Soul-Sword should disappear the night before Jonathan Morgenstern is supposed to stand trial by its blade—and that his father is the one who took it?"

Jace looked shocked at that, his lips parting slightly in surprise, as if this had never occurred to him. "My father didn't take the Sword for *me*. He took it for *him*. I doubt he even knew about the trial."

"How awfully convenient for you, regardless. And for him. He won't have to worry about you spilling his secrets."

"Yeah," Jace said, "he's terrified I'll tell everyone that he's always really wanted to be a ballerina." The Inquisitor simply stared at him. "I don't *know* any of my father's secrets," he said, less sharply. "He never told me anything."

The Inquisitor regarded him with something close to boredom. "If your father didn't take the Sword to protect you, then why *did* he take it?"

"It's a Mortal Instrument," said Clary. "It's powerful. Like the Cup. Valentine likes power."

"The Cup has an immediate use," said the Inquisitor. "He can use it to make an army. The Sword is used in trials. I can't see how that would interest him."

"He might have done it to destabilize the Clave," suggested

Maryse. "To sap our morale. To say that there is nothing we can protect from him if he wants it badly enough." It was a surprisingly good argument, Clary thought, but Maryse didn't sound very convinced. "The fact is—"

But they never got to hear what the fact was, because at that moment Jace raised his hand as if he meant to ask a question, looked startled, and sat down on the grass suddenly, as if his legs had given out. Alec knelt down next to him, but Jace waved away his concern. "Leave me alone. I'm fine."

"You're not fine." Clary joined Alec on the grass, Jace watching her with eyes whose pupils were huge and dark, despite the witchlight illuminating the night. She glanced down at his wrist, where Alec had drawn the *iratze*. The Mark was gone, not even a faint white scar left behind to show that it had worked. Her eyes met Alec's and she saw her own anxiety reflected there. "Something's wrong with him," she said. "Something serious."

"He probably needs a healing rune." The Inquisitor looked as if she were exquisitely annoyed at Jace for being injured during events of such importance. "An *iratze*, or—"

"We tried that," said Alec. "It isn't working. I think there's something of demonic origin going on here."

"Like demon poison?" Maryse moved as if she meant to go to Jace, but the Inquisitor held her back.

"He's shamming," she said. "He ought to be in the Silent City's cells right now."

Alec rose to his feet at that. "You can't say that—*look* at him!" He gestured at Jace, who had slumped back on the grass, his eyes closed. "He can't even stand up. He needs doctors, he needs—"

"The Silent Brothers are dead," said the Inquisitor. "Are you suggesting a mundane hospital?"

"No." Alec's voice was tight. "I thought he could go to Magnus."

Isabelle made a sound somewhere between a sneeze and a cough. She turned away as the Inquisitor looked at Alec blankly. "Magnus?"

"He's a warlock," said Alec. "Actually, he's the High Warlock of Brooklyn."

"You mean Magnus Bane," said Maryse. "He has a reputation—"

"He healed me after I fought a Greater Demon," said Alec. "The Silent Brothers couldn't do anything, but Magnus . . ."

"It's ridiculous," said the Inquisitor. "What you want is to help Jonathan escape."

"He's not well enough to escape," Isabelle said. "Can't you see that?"

"Magnus would never let that happen," Alec said, with a quelling glance at his sister. "He's not interested in crossing the Clave."

"And how would he propose preventing it?" The Inquisitor's voice dripped acid sarcasm. "Jonathan *is* a Shadowhunter; we're not so easy to keep under lock and key."

"Maybe you should ask him," Alec suggested.

The Inquisitor smiled her razor smile. "By all means. Where is he?"

Alec glanced down at the phone in his hand and then back at the thin gray figure in front of him. "He's here," he said. He raised his voice. "Magnus! Magnus, come on out."

Even the Inquisitor's eyebrows shot up when Magnus

strode through the gate. The High Warlock was wearing black leather pants, a belt with a buckle in the shape of a jeweled *M*, and a cobalt-blue Prussian military jacket open over a white lace shirt. He shimmered with layers of glitter. His gaze rested for a moment on Alec's face with amusement and a hint of something else before moving on to Jace, prone on the grass. "Is he dead?" he inquired. "He looks dead."

"No," snapped Maryse. "He's not dead."

"Have you checked? I could kick him if you want." Magnus moved toward Jace.

"Stop that!" the Inquisitor snapped, sounding like Clary's third-grade teacher demanding that she stop doodling on her desk with a marker. "He's not dead, but he's injured," she added, almost grudgingly. "Your medical skills are required. Jonathan needs to be well enough for the interrogation."

"Fine, but it'll cost you."

"I'll pay it," said Maryse.

The Inquisitor didn't even blink. "Very well. But he can't remain at the Institute. Just because the Sword is gone doesn't mean the interrogation won't proceed as planned. And in the meantime, the boy must be held under observation. He's clearly a flight risk."

"A flight risk?" Isabelle demanded. "You act as if he tried to escape from the Silent City—"

"Well," the Inquisitor said. "He's no longer in his cell now, is he?"

"That's not fair! You couldn't have expected him to stay down there surrounded by dead people!"

"Not fair? Not *fair*? Do you honestly expect me to believe that you and your brother were motivated to come to the Bone

City because of a distress call, and not because you wanted to free Jonathan from what you clearly consider unnecessary confinement? And do you expect me to believe you won't try to free him again if he's allowed to remain at the Institute? Do you think you can fool me as easily as you fool your parents, Isabelle Lightwood?"

Isabelle turned scarlet. Magnus cut in before she could reply:

"Look, it's not a problem," he said. "I can keep Jace at my place easily enough."

The Inquisitor turned to Alec. "Your warlock does realize," she said, "that Jonathan is a witness of utmost importance to the Clave?"

"He's not *my* warlock." The tops of Alec's angular cheekbones flared a dark red.

"I've held prisoners for the Clave before," Magnus said. The joking edge had left his voice. "I think you'll find I have an excellent record in that department. My contract is one of the best."

Was it Clary's imagination, or did his eyes seem to linger on Maryse when he said that? She didn't have time to wonder; the Inquisitor made a sharp noise that might have been amusement or disgust, and said, "It's settled, then. Let me know when he's well enough to talk, warlock. I've still got plenty of questions for him."

"Of course," Magnus said, but Clary got the sense that he wasn't really listening to her. He crossed the lawn gracefully and came to stand over Jace; he was as tall as he was thin, and when Clary glanced up to look at him, she was surprised how many stars he blotted out. "Can he talk?" Magnus asked Clary, indicating Jace.

Before Clary could respond, Jace's eyes slid open. He looked up at the warlock, dazed and dizzy. "What are you doing here?"

Magnus grinned down at Jace, and his teeth sparkled like sharpened diamonds.

"Hey, roommate," he said.

# Part Two
# The Gates of Hell

*Before me things created were none, save things*
*Eternal, and eternal I endure.*
*All hope abandon, ye who enter here.*
—Dante, *Inferno*

# 8

# The Seelie Court

***In the dream Clary was a child again, walking down the*** *narrow strip of beach near the boardwalk at Coney Island. The air was thick with the smell of hot dogs and roasting peanuts, and with the shouts of children. The sea surged in the distance, its blue-gray surface alive with sunlight.*

*She could see herself as if from a distance, wearing oversize child's pajamas. The hems of the pajama bottoms dragged along the beach. Damp sand grated between her toes, and her hair hung heavily against the nape of her neck. There were no clouds and the sky was blue and clear, but she shivered as she walked along the perimeter of the water toward a figure she could see only dimly in the distance.*

*As she approached, the figure became suddenly clear, as if Clary had focused the lens of a camera. It was her mother, kneeling in the ruins of a half-built sand castle. She wore the same white dress Valentine had put her in at Renwick's. In her hand was a twisted bit of driftwood, silvery from long exposure to salt and wind.*

"Have you come to help me?" *her mother said, raising her head. Jocelyn's hair was undone and it blew free in the wind, making her look younger than she was.* "There's so much to do and so little time."

*Clary swallowed against the hard lump in her throat.* "Mom—I've missed you, Mom."

*Jocelyn smiled.* "I've missed you, too, honey. But I'm not gone, you know. I'm only sleeping."

"Then how do I wake you up?" *Clary cried, but her mother was looking out to sea, her face troubled. The sky had turned a twilight iron gray and the black clouds looked like heavy stones.*

"Come here," *said Jocelyn, and when Clary came to her, she said,* "Hold out your arm."

*Clary did. Jocelyn moved the driftwood over her skin. The touch stung like the burning of a stele, and left the same thick black line behind. The rune Jocelyn drew was a shape Clary had never seen before, but she found it instinctively soothing to her eye.* "What does this do?"

"It should protect you." *Clary's mother released her.*

"Against what?"

*Jocelyn didn't answer, just looked out toward the sea. Clary turned and saw that the ocean had drawn far out, leaving brackish piles of garbage, heaps of seaweed and flopping, desperate fish in its wake. The water had gathered itself into a huge wave, rising like the side of a mountain, like an avalanche ready to fall. The shouts of children from the boardwalk had turned into screams. As Clary stared in horror, she saw that the side of the wave was as transparent as a membrane, and through it she could see* things *that seemed to move under the surface of the sea, huge dark shapeless things pushing against the skin of the water. She threw up her hands—*

And woke up, gasping, her heart slamming painfully against her ribs. She was in her bed in the spare room in Luke's house, and afternoon light was filtering in through the curtains. Her hair was plastered to her neck with sweat, and her arm burned and ached. When she sat up and flipped on the bedside light, she saw without surprise the black Mark that ran the length of her forearm.

When she went into the kitchen, she found Luke had left breakfast for her in the form of a Danish in a grease-spotted cardboard box. He'd also left a note stuck to the fridge. *Gone to the hospital.*

Clary ate the Danish on the way to meet Simon. He was supposed to be on the corner of Bedford by the L train stop at five, but he wasn't. She felt a faint tug of anxiety before she remembered the used record store on the corner of Sixth. Sure enough, he was sorting through the CDs in the new arrivals section. He wore a rust-colored corduroy jacket with a torn sleeve and a blue T-shirt bearing the logo of a headphone-wearing boy dancing with a chicken. He grinned when he saw her. "Eric thinks we should change the name of our band to Mojo Pie," he said, by way of greeting.

"What is it now? I forgot."

"Champagne Enema," he said, selecting a Yo La Tengo CD.

"Change it," Clary said. "By the way, I know what your T-shirt means."

"No you don't." He headed up to the front of the store to buy his CD. "You're a good girl."

Outside, the wind was cold and brisk. Clary drew her striped scarf up around her chin. "I was worried when I didn't see you at the L stop."

Simon pulled his knit cap down, wincing as if the sunlight hurt his eyes. "Sorry. I remembered I wanted this CD, and I thought—"

"It's fine." She waved a hand at him. "It's me. I panic way too easily these days."

"Well, after what you've been through, no one could blame you." Simon sounded contrite. "I still can't believe what happened to the Silent City. I can't believe you were *there*."

"Neither could Luke. He freaked out completely."

"I bet." They were walking through McCarren Park, the grass underfoot turning winter brown, the air full of golden light. Dogs were running off their leashes among the trees. *Everything changes in my life, and the world stays the same,* Clary thought. "Have you talked to Jace since it happened?" Simon asked, keeping his voice neutral.

"No, but I checked in with Isabelle and Alec a few times. Apparently he's fine."

"Did he ask to see you? Is that why we're going?"

"He doesn't *have* to ask." Clary tried to keep the irritation out of her voice as they turned onto Magnus's street. It was lined with low warehouse buildings that had been converted into lofts and studios for artistic—and wealthy—residents. Most of the cars parked along the shallow curb were expensive.

As they neared Magnus's building, Clary saw a lanky figure unfurl itself from where it had been sitting on the stoop. Alec.

He was wearing a long black coat made of the tough, slightly shiny material Shadowhunters liked to use for their gear. His hands and throat were marked with runes, and it was evident from the faint shimmer in the air around him that he was glamoured into invisibility.

"I didn't know you were bringing the mundane." His blue eyes flicked uneasily over Simon.

"That's what I like about you people," said Simon. "You always make me feel so welcome."

"Oh, come on, Alec," said Clary. "What's the big deal? It's not like Simon hasn't been here before."

Alec heaved a theatrical sigh, shrugged, and led the way up the stairs. He unlocked the door to Magnus's apartment using a thin silver key, which he tucked back into the breast pocket of his jacket the moment he'd finished, as if he hoped to keep his companions from seeing it.

In daylight the apartment looked the way an empty nightclub might look during off hours: dark, dirty, and unexpectedly small. The walls were bare, spackled here and there with glitter paint, and the floorboards where faeries had danced a week ago were warped and shiny with age.

"Hello, hello." Magnus swept toward them. He was wearing a floor-length green silk dressing gown open over a silver mesh shirt and black jeans. A glittering red stone winked in his left ear. "Alec, my darling. Clary. And rat-boy." He swept a bow toward Simon, who looked annoyed. "To what do I owe the pleasure?"

"We came to see Jace," Clary said. "Is he all right?"

"I don't know," Magnus said. "Does he normally just lie on the floor like that without moving?"

"What—," Alec began, and broke off as Magnus laughed. "That's not funny."

"You're so easy to tease. And yes, your friend is just fine. Well, except that he keeps putting all my things away and trying to clean up. Now I can't find anything. He's compulsive."

"Jace does like things neat," Clary said, thinking of his monklike room at the Institute.

"Well, I don't." Magnus was watching Alec out of the corner of his eye while Alec stared off into the middle distance, scowling. "Jace is in there if you want to see him." He pointed toward a door at the end of the room.

"In there" turned out to be a medium-size den—surprisingly cozy, with smudged walls, velvet curtains drawn across the windows, and cloth-draped armchairs marooned like fat, colorful icebergs in a sea of nubbly beige carpeting. A hot-pink couch was made up with sheets and a blanket. Next to it was a duffel bag stuffed full of clothes. No light came through the heavy curtains; the only source of illumination was a flickering television screen, which glowed brightly despite the fact that the television itself was not plugged in.

"What's on?" Magnus inquired.

"*What Not to Wear,*" came a familiar drawling voice, emanating from a sprawled figure in one of the armchairs. He sat forward and for a moment Clary thought Jace might get up and greet them. Instead, he shook his head at the screen. "High-waisted khaki pants? Who *wears* those?" He turned and glared at Magnus. "Nearly unlimited supernatural power," he said, "and all you do is use it to watch reruns. What a waste."

"Also, TiVo accomplishes much the same thing," pointed out Simon.

"My way is cheaper." Magnus clapped his hands together and the room was suddenly flooded with light. Jace, slumped in the chair, raised an arm to cover his face. "Can you do *that* without magic?"

"Actually," said Simon, "yes. If you watched infomercials, you'd know that."

Clary sensed the mood in the room was deteriorating. "That's enough," she said. She looked at Jace, who had lowered his arm and was blinking resentfully into the light. "We need to talk," she said. "All of us. About what we're going to do now."

"I was going to watch *Project Runway*," said Jace. "It's on next."

"No you're not," said Magnus. He snapped his fingers and the TV went off, releasing a small puff of smoke as the picture died. "You need to deal with this."

"Suddenly you're interested in solving my problems?"

"I'm interested in getting my apartment back. I'm tired of you cleaning all the time." Magnus snapped his fingers again, menacingly. "Get up."

"Or you'll be the next one to go up in smoke," said Simon with relish.

"There's no need to clarify my finger snap," said Magnus. "The implication was clear in the snap itself."

"Fine." Jace got up out of the chair. He was barefoot and there was a line of purplish silver skin around his wrist where his injuries were still healing. He looked tired, but not as if he were still in pain. "You want a round table meeting, we can have a round table meeting."

"I love round tables," said Magnus brightly. "They suit me so much better than square."

In the living room Magnus conjured up an enormous circular table surrounded by five high-backed wooden chairs. "That's amazing," Clary said, sliding into a chair. It was surprisingly comfortable. "How can you create something out of nothing like that?"

"You can't," said Magnus. "Everything comes from somewhere. These come from an antiques reproduction store on Fifth Avenue, for instance. And these"—suddenly five white waxed paper cups appeared on the table, steam rising gently from the holes in their plastic lids—"come from Dean & DeLuca on Broadway."

"That seems like stealing, doesn't it?" Simon pulled a cup toward him. He drew the lid back. "Ooh. Mochaccino." He looked at Magnus. "Did you pay for these?"

"Sure," said Magnus, while Jace and Alec snickered. "I make dollar bills magically appear in their cash register."

"Really?"

"No." Magnus popped the lid off his own coffee. "But you can pretend I did if it makes you feel better. So, first order of business is what?"

Clary put her hands around her own coffee cup. Maybe it was stolen, but it was also hot and full of caffeine. She could stop by Dean & DeLuca and drop a dollar in their tip jar some other time. "Figuring out what's going on would be a start," she said, blowing on her foam. "Jace, you said what happened in the Silent City was Valentine's fault?"

Jace stared down at his coffee. "Yes."

Alec put his hand on Jace's arm. "What happened? Did you see him?"

"I was in the cell," said Jace, his voice dead. "I heard the

Silent Brothers screaming. Then Valentine came downstairs with—with something. I don't know what it was. Like smoke, with glowing eyes. A demon, but not like any I've ever seen before. He came up to the bars and he told me . . ."

"Told you what?" Alec's hand slid up Jace's arm to his shoulder. Magnus cleared his throat. Alec dropped his hand, red-faced, while Simon grinned into his undrunk coffee.

"Maellartach," Jace said. "He wanted the Soul-Sword and he killed the Silent Brothers to get it."

Magnus was frowning. "Alec, last night, when the Silent Brothers called for your help, where was the Conclave? Why was no one at the Institute?"

Alec looked surprised to be asked. "There was a Downworlder murder in Central Park last night. A faerie child was killed. The body was drained of blood."

"I bet the Inquisitor thinks I did that, too," said Jace. "My reign of terror continues."

Magnus stood up and went to the window. He pushed the curtain back, letting in just enough light to silhouette his hawklike profile. "Blood," he said, half to himself. "I had a dream two nights ago. I saw a city all of blood, with towers made of bone, and blood ran in the streets like water."

Simon slewed his eyes over to Jace. "Is standing by the window muttering about blood something he does all the time?"

"No," said Jace, "sometimes he sits on the couch and does it."

Alec shot them both a sharp glance. "Magnus, what's wrong?"

"The blood," said Magnus again. "It can't be a coincidence." He seemed to be looking down at the street. Sunset was coming on fast over the silhouette of the city in the distance: The sky was striped with bars of aluminum and rosy gold. "There have been several murders this week," he said, "of Downworlders. A warlock, killed in an apartment tower down by the South Street Seaport. His neck and wrists were cut and the body drained of blood. And a werewolf was killed at the Hunter's Moon a few days ago. The throat was cut in that case as well."

"It sounds like vampires," said Simon, suddenly very pale.

"I don't think so," Jace said. "At least, Raphael said it wasn't the Night Children's work. He seemed adamant about it."

"Yeah, 'cause *he's* trustworthy," muttered Simon.

"In this case I think he was telling the truth," said Magnus, drawing the curtain closed. His face was angular, shadowed. As he came back to the table, Clary saw that he was carrying a heavy book bound in green cloth. She didn't think he'd been holding it a few moments ago. "There was a strong demonic presence at both locations. I think someone else was responsible for all three deaths. Not Raphael and his tribe, but Valentine."

Clary's eyes went to Jace. His mouth was a thin line, but "Why do you say that?" was all he asked.

"The Inquisitor thought the faerie murder was a diversion," she said quickly. "So that he could plunder the Silent City without worrying about the Conclave."

"There are easier ways to create a diversion," said Jace, "and it is unwise to antagonize the Fair Folk. He wouldn't have murdered one of the clan of faerie if he didn't have a reason."

"He had a reason," said Magnus. "There was something he wanted from the faerie child, just as there was something he wanted from the warlock and the werewolf he killed."

"What's that?" asked Alec.

"Their blood," said Magnus, and opened the green book. The thin parchment pages had words written on them that glowed like fire. "Ah," he said, "here." He looked up, tapping the page with a sharp fingernail. Alec leaned forward. "You won't be able to read it," Magnus warned him. "It's written in a demon language. Purgatic."

"I can recognize the drawing, though. That's Maellartach. I've seen it before in books." Alec pointed at an illustration of a silver sword, familiar to Clary—it was the one she'd noticed was missing from the wall of the Silent City.

"The Ritual of Infernal Conversion," Magnus said. "That's what Valentine's trying to do."

"The what of what?" Clary frowned.

"Every magical object has an alliance," Magnus explained. "The alliance of the Soul-Sword is seraphic—like those angel knives you Shadowhunters use, but a thousand times more so, because its power was drawn from the Angel himself, not simply from the invocation of an angelic name. What Valentine wants to do is reverse its alliance—make it an object of demonic rather than angelic power."

"Lawful good to lawful evil!" said Simon, pleased.

"He's quoting Dungeons and Dragons," said Clary. "Ignore him."

"As the Angel's Sword, Maellartach's use to Valentine would be limited," said Magnus. "But as a sword whose demonic power is equal to the angelic power it once possessed—well, there is much it could offer him. Power over demons, for one. Not just the limited protection the Cup might offer, but power to call demons to him, to force them to do his bidding."

"A demon army?" said Alec.

"This guy is big on armies," observed Simon.

"Power even to bring them into Idris, perhaps," Magnus finished.

"I don't know why he'd want to go there," Simon said. "That's where all the demon hunters are, aren't they? Wouldn't they just *annihilate* the demon guys?"

"Demons come from other dimensions," said Jace. "We don't know how many of them there are. Their numbers could be infinite. The wardings keep most of them back, but if they all came through at once . . ."

*Infinite*, Clary thought. She remembered the Greater Demon, Abbadon, and tried to imagine hundreds more of it. Or thousands. Her skin felt cold and exposed.

"I don't get it," said Alec. "What does the ritual have to do with dead Downworlders?"

"To perform the Ritual of Conversion, you need to seethe the Sword until it's red-hot, then cool it four times, each time in the blood of a Downworld child. Once in the blood of a child of Lilith, once in the blood of a child of the moon, once in the blood of a child of the night, and once in the blood of a child of faerie," Magnus explained.

"Oh my God," said Clary. "So he's not done killing? There's still one more child to go?"

"Two more. He didn't succeed with the werewolf child. He was interrupted before he could get all the blood he needed." Magnus shut the book, dust puffing out from its pages. "Whatever Valentine's ultimate goal is, he's already more than halfway to reversing the Sword. He's probably able to garner some power from it already. He could already be calling on demons—"

"But you'd think if he were doing that, there'd be reports of disturbances, excess demon activity," Jace said. "But the Inquisitor said the opposite is true—that everything's been quiet."

"And so it might be," said Magnus, "if Valentine were calling *all the demons to him.* No wonder it's quiet."

The group stared at one another. Before anyone could think of a single thing to say, a sharp noise cut through the room, making Clary start. Hot coffee spilled onto her wrist and she gasped at the sudden pain.

"It's my mother," said Alec, checking his phone. "I'll be right back." He went over to the window, head down, voice too low to overhear.

"Let me see," said Simon, taking Clary's hand. There was an angry red blotch on her wrist where the hot liquid had scalded her.

"It's okay," she said. "No big deal."

Simon lifted her hand and kissed the injury. "All better now."

Clary made a startled noise. He had never done anything like that before. Then again, that was the sort of thing boyfriends did, didn't they? Drawing her wrist back, she looked across the table and saw Jace staring at them, his golden eyes blazing. "You're a Shadowhunter," he said. "You know how to deal with injuries." He slid his stele across the table toward her. "Use it."

"No," Clary said, and pushed the stele back across the table at him.

Jace slammed his hand down on the stele. "Clary—"

"She said she doesn't want it," said Simon. "Ha-ha."

"Ha-ha?" Jace looked incredulous. "*That's* your comeback?"

Alec, folding his phone, approached the table with a puzzled look. "What's going on?"

"We seem to be trapped in an episode of *One Life to Waste*," Magnus observed. "It's all very dull."

Alec flicked a strand of hair out of his eyes. "I told my mother about the Infernal Conversion."

"Let me guess," said Jace. "She didn't believe you. Plus, she blamed everything on me."

Alec frowned. "Not exactly. She said she'd bring it up with the Conclave, but that she didn't have the Inquisitor's ear right now. I get the feeling the Inquisitor has pushed Mom out of the way and taken over. She sounded angry." The phone in his hand rang again. He held up a finger. "Sorry. It's Isabelle. One sec." He wandered to the window, phone in hand.

Jace glanced over at Magnus. "I think you're right about the werewolf at the Hunter's Moon. The guy who found his body said someone else was in the alley with him. Someone who ran off."

Magnus nodded. "It sounds to me like Valentine was interrupted in the middle of doing whatever it is he does to get the blood he needs. He'll probably try again with a different lycanthrope child."

"I ought to warn Luke," Clary said, half-rising out of her chair.

"Wait." Alec was back, phone in hand, a peculiar expression on his face.

"What did Isabelle want?" Jace asked.

Alec hesitated. "Isabelle says the Queen of the Seelie Court has requested an audience with us."

"Sure," said Magnus. "And Madonna wants me as a backup dancer on her next world tour."

Alec looked puzzled. "Who's Madonna?"

"Who's the Queen of the Seelie Court?" said Clary.

"She is the Queen of Faerie," said Magnus. "Well, the local one, anyway."

Jace put his head in his hands. "Tell Isabelle no."

"But she thinks it's a good idea," Alec protested.

"Then tell her no *twice*."

Alec frowned. "What's that supposed to mean?"

"Oh, just that some of Isabelle's ideas are world-beaters and some are total disasters. Remember that idea she had about using abandoned subway tunnels to get around under the city? Talk about giant rats—"

"Let's not," said Simon. "I'd rather not talk about rats at all, in fact."

"This is different," said Alec. "She wants us to go to the Seelie Court."

"You're right, this is different," said Jace. "This is her worst idea *ever*."

"She knows a knight in the Court," said Alec. "He told her that the Seelie Queen is interested in meeting with us. Isabelle overheard my conversation with our mother—and she thought if we could explain our theory about Valentine and the Soul-Sword to the Queen, the Seelie Court would side with us, maybe even ally with us against Valentine."

"Is it safe to go there?" Clary asked.

"Of course it's not *safe*," Jace said, as if she'd asked the stupidest question he'd ever heard.

She shot a glare at him. "I don't know anything about the Seelie Court. Vampires and werewolves I get. There are enough movies about them. But faeries are little-kid stuff. I dressed up as a faerie for Halloween when I was eight. My mom made me a hat shaped like a buttercup."

"I remember that." Simon had leaned back in his chair, arms crossed over his chest. "I was a Transformer. Actually, I was a Decepticon."

"Can we get back to the point?" Magnus asked.

"Fine," Alec said. "Isabelle thinks—and I *agree*—that it's not a good idea to ignore the Fair Folk. If they want to talk, what harm can it do? Besides, if the Seelie Court were on our side, the Clave would *have* to listen to what we have to say."

Jace laughed without any humor. "The Fair Folk don't help *humans*."

"Shadowhunters are not human," Clary said. "Not really."

"We are not much better to them," said Jace.

"They can't be worse than vampires," Simon muttered. "And you did all right with them."

Jace looked at Simon as if he were something he'd found growing under the sink. "Did *all right with them*? By which I take it you mean we survived?"

"Well . . ."

"Faeries," Jace went on, as if Simon hadn't spoken, "are the offspring of demons and angels, with the beauty of angels and the viciousness of demons. A vampire might attack you, if you entered its domain, but a faerie could make you dance until you died with your legs ground down into stumps, trick you into a midnight swim and drag you screaming underwater until your lungs burst, fill your eyes with faerie dust until you gouged them out at the roots—"

"Jace!" Clary snapped, cutting him off mid-rant. "Shut up. Jesus. That's enough."

"Look, it's easy to outsmart a werewolf or a vampire," Jace said. "They're no smarter than anyone else. But faeries live for hundreds of years and they're as cunning as snakes. They can't lie, but they love to engage in creative truth-telling. They'll find out whatever it is you want most in the world and give it to you—with a sting in the tail of the gift that will make you regret you ever wanted it in the first place." He sighed. "They're not really about helping people. More about harm disguised as help."

"And you don't think we're smart enough to know the difference?" asked Simon.

"I don't think you're smart enough not to get turned into a rat by accident."

Simon glared at him. "I don't see that it matters what you think we should do," he said. "Considering that you can't go with us in the first place. You can't go anywhere."

Jace stood up, knocking his chair back violently. "You are not taking Clary to the Seelie Court without me and *that is final*!"

Clary stared at him with her mouth open. He was flushed with anger, teeth gritted, veins corded in his neck. He was also avoiding looking at her.

"I can take care of Clary," Alec said, and there was hurt in his voice—whether because Jace had doubted his abilities or because of something else, Clary wasn't sure.

"Alec," said Jace, his eyes locked with his friend's. "No. You can't."

Alec swallowed. "We're going," he said. He spoke the words like an apology. "Jace—a request from the Seelie Court—it would be stupid to ignore it. Besides, Isabelle's probably already told them we're coming."

"There is no chance I'm going to let you do this, Alec," Jace said in a dangerous voice. "I'll wrestle you to the ground if I have to."

"While that does sound tempting," said Magnus, flipping his long silk sleeves back, "there is another way."

"What other way? This is a directive from the Clave. I can't just weasel out of it."

"But I can." Magnus grinned. "Never doubt my weaseling abilities, Shadowhunter, for they are epic and memorable in their scope. I specifically enchanted the contract with the Inquisitor so that I could let you go for a short time if I desired, as long as another of the Nephilim was willing to take your place."

"Where are we going to find another—Oh," Alec said meekly. "You mean me."

Jace's eyebrows shot up. "Oh, now you don't *want* to go to the Seelie Court?"

Alec flushed. "I think it's more important for you to go than me. You're Valentine's son, I'm sure you're the one the Queen really wants to see. Besides, you're charming."

Jace glared at him.

"Maybe not at the moment," Alec amended. "But you're *usually* charming. And faeries are very susceptible to charm."

"Plus, if you stay here, I've got the whole first season of *Gilligan's Island* on DVD," Magnus said.

"No one could turn *that* down," said Jace. He still wouldn't look at Clary.

"Isabelle can meet you in the park by Turtle Pond," said Alec. "She knows the secret entrance to the Court. She'll be waiting."

"And one last thing," Magnus said, jabbing a ringed finger at Jace. "Try not to get yourself killed in the Seelie Court. If you die, I'll have a lot of explaining to do."

At that, Jace broke into a grin. It was an unsettling grin, less a flash of amusement than the gleam of an unsheathed blade. "You know," he said, "I have a feeling that that's going to be the case whether I get myself killed or not."

Thick tendrils of moss and plants surrounded the rim of Turtle Pond like a bordering of green lace. The surface of the water was still, rippled here and there in the wake of drifting ducks, or dimpled by the silvery flick of a fish's tail.

There was a small wooden gazebo built out over the water; Isabelle was sitting in it, staring out across the lake. She looked like a princess in a fairy tale, waiting at the top of her tower for someone to ride up and rescue her.

Not that traditional princess behavior was like Isabelle at all. Isabelle with her whip and boots and knives would chop anyone who tried to pen her up in a tower into pieces, build a bridge out of the remains, and walk carelessly to freedom, her hair looking fabulous the *entire time*. This made Isabelle a hard person to like, though Clary was trying.

"Izzy," said Jace, as they neared the pond, and she jumped up and spun around. Her smile was dazzling.

"Jace!" She flew at him and hugged him. Now that was the

way sisters were supposed to act, Clary thought. Not all stiff and weird and peculiar, but happy and loving. Watching Jace hug Isabelle, she tried to school her features into a happy and loving expression.

"Are you all right?" Simon asked, with some concern. "Your eyes are crossing."

"I'm fine." Clary abandoned the attempt.

"Are you sure? You looked sort of . . . *contorted.*"

"Something I ate."

Isabelle drifted over, Jace a pace behind her. She was wearing a long black dress with boots and an even longer cutaway coat of soft green velvet, the color of moss. "I can't believe you did it!" she exclaimed. "How did you get Magnus to let Jace leave?"

"Traded him for Alec," Clary said.

Isabelle looked mildly alarmed. "Not *permanently?*"

"No," said Jace. "Just for a few hours. Unless I don't come back," he added thoughtfully. "In which case, maybe he does get to keep Alec. Think of it as a lease with an option to buy."

Isabelle looked dubious. "Mom and Dad won't be pleased if they find out."

"That you freed a possible criminal by trading away your brother to a warlock who looks like a gay Sonic the Hedgehog and dresses like the Child Catcher from *Chitty Chitty Bang Bang*?" Simon inquired. "No, probably not."

Jace looked at him thoughtfully. "Is there some particular reason that you're here? I'm not so sure we should be bringing you to the Seelie Court. They hate mundanes."

Simon rolled his eyes upward. "Not this again."

"Not what again?" said Clary.

"Every time I annoy him, he retreats into his No Mundanes Allowed tree house." Simon pointed at Jace. "Let me remind you, the last time you wanted to leave me behind, I saved all your lives."

"Sure," said Jace. "One time—"

"The faerie courts *are* dangerous," cut in Isabelle. "Even your skill with the bow won't help you. It's not that kind of danger."

"I can take care of myself," said Simon. A sharp wind had come up. It blew drying leaves across the gravel at their feet and made Simon shiver. He dug his hands into the wool-lined pockets of his jacket.

"You don't have to come," Clary said.

He looked at her, a steady, measured look. She remembered him back at Luke's, calling her *my girlfriend* with no measure of doubt or indecision. Whatever else you could say about Simon, he knew what he wanted. "Yeah," he said. "I do."

Jace made a noise under his breath. "Then I suppose we're ready," he said. "Don't expect any special consideration, mundane."

"Look on the bright side," said Simon. "If they need a human sacrifice, you can always offer me. I'm not sure the rest of you qualify anyway."

Jace brightened. "It's always nice when someone volunteers to be the first up against the wall."

"Come on," Isabelle said. "The door is about to open."

Clary glanced around. The sun had set completely and the moon was up, a wedge of creamy white casting its reflection onto the pond. It wasn't quite full, but shadowed at one edge, giving it the look of a half-lidded eye. Night wind rattled the tree branches, knocking them against one another with a sound like hollow bones.

"Where do we go?" Clary asked. "Where's the door?"

Isabelle's smile was like a whispered secret. "Follow me."

She moved down to the edge of the water, her boots leaving deep impressions in the wet mud. Clary followed, glad she was wearing jeans and not a skirt as Isabelle hiked her coat and dress up over her knees, leaving her slim white legs bare above her boots. Her skin was covered in Marks like licks of black fire.

Simon, behind her, swore as he slipped in the mud; Jace moved automatically to steady him as they all turned. Simon jerked his arm back. "I don't need your help."

"Stop it." Isabelle tapped a booted foot in the shallow water at the lake's edge. "Both of you. In fact, all three of you. If we don't stick together in the Seelie Court, we're dead."

"But I haven't—," Clary started.

"Maybe *you* haven't, but the way you let those two act . . ." Isabelle indicated the boys with a disdainful wave of her hand.

"I can't tell them what to do!"

"Why not?" the other girl demanded. "Honestly, Clary, if you don't start utilizing a bit of your natural feminine superiority, I just don't know what I'll do with you." She turned toward the pond, then spun around again. "And lest I forget," she added sternly, "for the love of the Angel, *don't* eat or drink anything while we're underground, any of you. Okay?"

"Underground?" said Simon worriedly. "Nobody said anything about underground."

Isabelle threw up her hands and splashed out into the

pond. Her green velvet coat swirled out around her like an enormous lily pad. "Come on. We only have until the moon moves."

The moon *what*? Shaking her head, Clary stepped out into the pond. The water was shallow and clear; in the bright starlight, she could see the black shapes of tiny darting fish moving past her ankles. She gritted her teeth as she waded farther out into the pond. The cold was intense.

Behind her, Jace moved out into the water with a contained grace that barely rippled the surface. Simon, behind him, was splashing and cursing. Isabelle, having reached the center of the pond, paused there, up to her rib cage in water. She held out her hand toward Clary. "Stop."

Clary stopped. Just in front of her, the reflection of the moon glimmered atop the water like a huge silvery dinner plate. Some part of her knew that it didn't work like this; the moon was supposed to move away from you as you approached, ever receding. But here it was, hovering just on the surface of the water as if it were anchored in place.

"Jace, you go first," Isabelle said, and beckoned him. "Come on."

He brushed past Clary, smelling of wet leather and char. She saw him smile as he turned, and then he stepped backward into the reflection of the moon—and vanished.

"Okay," said Simon unhappily. "Okay, that was weird."

Clary glanced back at him. He was only hip-deep in water, but he was shivering, his hands hugging his elbows. She smiled at him and took a step backward, feeling a shock of icier cold when she moved into the shimmering silver reflection. She teetered for a moment, as if she'd lost her balance on the highest rung of a ladder—and then fell backward into darkness as the moon swallowed her up.

She hit packed earth, stumbled, and felt a hand on her arm, steadying her. It was Jace. "Easy does it," he said, and let her go.

She was soaking wet, rivulets of cold water running down the back of her shirt, her damp hair clinging to her face. Her drenched clothes felt as if they weighed a ton.

They were in a hollowed-out dirt corridor, illuminated by faintly glowing moss. A tangle of dangling vines formed a curtain at one end of the corridor and long, hairy tendrils hung like dead snakes from the ceiling. Tree roots, Clary realized. They were underground. And it was cold down here, cold enough to make her breath puff out in an icy mist when she exhaled.

"Cold?" Jace was soaking wet too, his light hair almost colorless where it stuck to his cheeks and forehead. Water ran from his wet jeans and jacket, and made the white shirt he was wearing transparent. She could see the dark lines of his permanent Marks through it and the faint scar on his shoulder.

She looked away quickly. Water clung to her lashes, blurring her vision like tears. "I'm fine."

"You don't look fine." He moved closer, and she could feel the warmth of him even through his wet clothes and hers, thawing her icy skin.

A dark shape hurtled by, just out of the corner of her eye, and hit the ground with a thud. It was Simon, also soaking wet. He rolled onto his knees and looked around frantically. "My glasses—"

"I've got them." Clary was used to retrieving Simon's

glasses for him during soccer games. They always seemed to fall just under his feet, where they were inevitably stepped on. "Here you go."

He slid them on, scraping dirt off the lenses. "Thanks."

Clary could feel Jace watching them, feel his gaze like a weight on her shoulders. She wondered if Simon could too. He stood up with a frown, just as Isabelle dropped out of the heavens, landing gracefully on her feet. Water ran from her long, streaming hair and weighed down her heavy velvet coat, but she barely seemed to notice. "Oooh, that was fun."

"That does it," said Jace. "I'm going to get you a dictionary for Christmas this year."

"Why?" Isabelle said.

"So you can look up 'fun.' I'm not sure you know what it means."

Isabelle pulled the long heavy mass of her wet hair forward and wrung it out as if it were wet washing. "You're raining on my parade."

"It's a pretty wet parade already, if you hadn't noticed." Jace glanced around. "Now what? Which way do we go?"

"Neither way," said Isabelle. "We wait here, and they come and get us."

Clary was not impressed by this suggestion. "How do they know we're here? Is there a doorbell we have to ring or something?"

"The Court knows all that happens in their lands. Our presence won't go unnoticed."

Simon looked at her with suspicion. "And how do you know so much about faeries and the Seelie Court, anyway?"

Isabelle, to everyone's surprise, blushed. A moment later

the curtain of vines was drawn aside and a faerie stepped through it, shaking back his long hair. Clary had seen some of the fey before at Magnus's party and had been struck by both their cold beauty and a certain wild unearthliness they possessed even when they were dancing and drinking. This faerie was no exception: His hair fell in blue-black sheets around a cool, sharp, lovely face; his eyes were green as vines or moss and there was the shape of a leaf, either a birthmark or tattoo, across one of his cheekbones. He wore an armor of a silvery brown like the bark of trees in winter, and when he moved, the armor flashed a multitude of colors: peat black, moss green, ash gray, sky blue.

Isabelle gave a cry and jumped into his arms. "Meliorn!"

"Ah," said Simon, quietly and not without amusement, "so *that's* how she knows."

The faerie—Meliorn—looked down at her gravely, then detached her and set her gently aside. "This is not a time for affection," he said. "The Queen of the Seelie Court has requested an audience with the three Nephilim among you. Will you come?"

Clary put a protective hand on Simon's shoulder. "What about our friend?"

Meliorn looked impassive. "Mundane humans are not permitted in the Court."

"I wish someone had mentioned that earlier," said Simon, to no one in particular. "I take it I'm just supposed to wait out here until vines start growing on me?"

Meliorn considered. "That might offer significant amusement."

"Simon's not an ordinary mundane. He can be trusted," Jace said, startling them all, and Simon more than the rest.

Clary could tell Simon was surprised because he stared at Jace without offering a single smart remark. "He has fought many battles with us."

"By which you mean one battle," muttered Simon. "Two if you count the one where I was a rat."

"We will not enter the Seelie Court without Simon," Clary said, her hand still on Simon's shoulder. "Your Queen requested this audience with us, remember? It wasn't our idea to come here."

There was a spark of dark amusement in Meliorn's green eyes. "As you wish," he said. "Let it not be said that the Seelie Court does not respect the desires of its guests." He spun on a perfectly booted heel and began to lead them down the corridor without pausing to see if they were following him. Isabelle hurried to walk alongside him, leaving Jace, Clary, and Simon to follow the two of them in silence.

"Are you *allowed* to date faeries?" Clary asked finally. "Would your—would the Lightwoods be cool with Isabelle and whatshisname—"

"Meliorn," put in Simon.

"—Meliorn going out?"

"I'm not sure they're *going out*," Jace said, weighting the last two words with a heavy irony. "I'd guess they mostly stay in. Or in this case, under."

"You sound like you disapprove." Simon pushed a tree root aside. They had moved from a dirt-walled corridor to one lined with smooth stones, only the occasional root snaking down between the stones from above. The floor was some kind of polished hard stuff, not marble but stone veined and flaked with lines of shimmering material like powdered jewels.

"I don't disapprove exactly," said Jace. "The faeries are known to dally with the occasional mortal, but they always end in abandoning them, usually the worse for wear."

His words sent a shiver down Clary's spine. At that moment Isabelle laughed, and Clary could see now why Jace had dropped his voice, because the stone walls threw Isabelle's voice back to them amplified and echoing so that Isabelle's laughter seemed to bounce off the walls.

"You're so funny!" She tripped as the heel of her boot caught between two stones, and Meliorn caught and righted her without changing expression.

"I do not understand how you humans can walk in shoes that are that tall."

"It's my motto," said Isabelle, with a sultry smile. "'Nothing less than seven inches.'"

Meliorn gazed at her stonily.

"I'm talking about my *heels*," she said. "It's a pun. You know? A play on—"

"Come," the faerie knight said. "The Queen will be growing impatient." He headed down the corridor without giving Isabelle a second glance.

"I forgot," Isabelle muttered as the rest of them caught up to her. "Faeries have no sense of humor."

"Oh, I wouldn't say that," said Jace. "There's a pixie night-club downtown called Hot Wings. Not," he added, "that I have ever been there."

Simon looked at Jace, opened his mouth as if he intended to ask him a question, then seemed to think better of it. He closed his mouth with a snap just as the corridor opened out into a wide room whose floor was packed dirt and whose walls were lined with high stone pillars twined all over with vines and bright flowers bursting with color. Thin cloths were hung between the pillars, dyed a soft blue that was almost the exact hue of the sky. The room was filled with light, though Clary could see no torches, and the overall effect was of a summer pavilion in bright sunshine rather than a dirt and stone room underground.

Clary's first impression was that she was outside; her second was that the room was full of people. There was a strange sweet music playing, flawed with sweet-sour notes, a sort of aural equivalent of honey mixed with lemon juice, and there was a circle of faeries dancing to the music, their feet barely seeming to skim the floor. Their hair—blue, black, brown and scarlet, metal gold and ice white—flew like banners.

She could see why they were called the Fair Folk, for they were fair indeed with their pale lovely faces, their wings of lilac and gold and blue—how could she have believed Jace that they meant to harm her? The music that had jarred her ears at first now sounded only sweet. She felt the urge to toss her own hair and to move her own feet in the dance. The music told her that if she did that, she too would be so light that her feet would barely touch the earth. She took a step forward—

And was jerked back by a hand on her arm. Jace was glaring at her, his golden eyes bright as a cat's. "If you dance with them," he said in a low voice, "you'll dance until you die."

Clary blinked at him. She felt as if she'd been pulled out of a dream, groggy and half-awake. Her voice slurred when she spoke. "Whaaat?"

Jace made an impatient noise. He had his stele in his hand;

she hadn't seen him take it out. He gripped her wrist and inscribed a quick, stinging Mark onto the skin of her inner arm. "Now look."

She looked again—and froze. The faces that had seemed so lovely to her were *still* lovely, yet behind them lurked something vulpine, almost feral. The girl with the pink and blue wings beckoned, and Clary saw that her fingers were made of twigs, budded with closed leaves. Her eyes were entirely black, without iris or pupil. The boy dancing next to her had poison green skin and curling horns twisting from his temples. When he turned in the dance, his coat fell open and Clary saw that beneath it, his chest was an empty rib cage. Ribbons were woven through his bare rib bones, possibly to make him look more festive. Clary's stomach lurched.

"Come *on*." Jace pushed her and she stumbled forward. When she regained her balance, she looked around anxiously for Simon. He was up ahead and she saw that Isabelle had a firm grip on him. This once, she didn't mind. She doubted Simon would have made it through the room on his own.

Skirting the circle of dancers, they made their way to the far end of the room and through a parted curtain of blue silk. It was a relief to be out of the room and into another corridor, this one carved from a glossy brown material like the outside of a nut. Isabelle let go of Simon and he stopped walking immediately; when Clary caught up to him, she saw that this was because Isabelle had tied her scarf across his eyes. He was fiddling with the knot when Clary reached him. "Let me get it," she said, and he went still while she untied him and handed the scarf back to Isabelle with a nod of thanks.

Simon pushed his hair back; it was damp where the scarf

had held it down. "That was some music," he observed. "A little bit country, a little bit rock and roll."

Meliorn, who had paused to wait for them, frowned. "You didn't care for it?"

"I cared for it a little too much," Clary said. "What was that supposed to be, some kind of test? Or a joke?"

He shrugged. "I am used to mortals who are easily swayed by our faerie glamours; not so the Nephilim. I thought you had protections."

"She does," Jace said, meeting Meliorn's jade green gaze with his own.

Meliorn only shrugged and began walking again. Simon kept pace beside Clary for a few moments without speaking before he said, "So what did I miss? Naked dancing ladies?"

Clary thought of the male faerie's torn-open ribs and shuddered. "Nothing that pleasant."

"There are ways for a human to join the faerie revels," Isabelle, who had been eavesdropping, put in. "If they give you a token—like a leaf or a flower—to hold on to, and you keep it through the night, you'll be fine in the morning. Or if you go with a faerie for a companion . . ." She shot a glance at Meliorn, but he had reached a leafy screen set into the wall and paused there.

"These are the Queen's chambers," he said. "She's come from her Court in the north to see about the child's death. If there's to be war, she wants to be the one declaring it."

Up close, Clary could see that the screen was made of thickly woven vines, budded with amber droplets. He drew the vines apart and ushered them into the chamber on the other side.

Jace ducked through first, followed by Clary. She straightened up, looking around her curiously.

The room itself was plain, the earthen walls hung with pale fabric. Will-o'-the-wisps glowed in glass jars. A lovely woman reclined on a low couch surrounded by what must have been her courtiers—a motley assortment of faeries, from tiny sprites to what looked like lovely human girls with long hair . . . if you discounted their black, pupil-less eyes.

"My Queen," said Meliorn, bowing low. "I have brought the Nephilim to you."

The Queen sat up straight. She had long scarlet hair that seemed to float around her like autumn leaves in a breeze. Her eyes were clear blue as glass, her gaze sharp as a razor. "Three of these are Nephilim," she said. "The other is a mundane."

Meliorn seemed to shrink back, but the Queen didn't even look at him. Her gaze was on the Shadowhunters. Clary could feel the weight of it, like a touch. Despite her loveliness, there was nothing fragile about the Queen. She was as bright and hard to look at as a burning star.

"Our apologies, my lady." Jace stepped forward, putting himself between the Queen and his companions. His voice had changed its tone—there was something in the way he spoke now, something careful and delicate. "The mundane is our responsibility. We owe him protection. Therefore we keep him with us."

The Queen tilted her head to the side, like an interested bird. All her attention was on Jace now. "A blood debt?" she murmured. "To a mundane?"

"He saved my life," Jace said. Clary felt Simon stiffen beside her in surprise. She willed him not to show it. Faeries couldn't lie, Jace had said, and Jace wasn't lying, either—Simon *had* saved his life. That just wasn't why they'd brought him with them. Clary began to appreciate what Jace had meant by creative truth-telling. "Please, my lady. We had hoped you would understand. We had heard you were as kind as you were beautiful, and in that case—well," Jace said, "your kindness must be extreme indeed."

The Queen smirked and leaned forward, gleaming hair falling to shadow her face. "You are as charming as your father, Jonathan Morgenstern," she said, and gestured at the cushions scattered around the floor. "Come, sit beside me. Eat something. Drink. Rest yourselves. Talk is better with wet lips."

For a moment Jace looked thrown. He hesitated. Meliorn leaned over to him and spoke softly. "It would be unwise to refuse the bounty of the Queen of the Seelie Court."

Isabelle's eyes flicked toward him. Then she shrugged. "It won't hurt us just to sit down."

Meliorn led them over to a pile of silky cushions near the Queen's divan. Clary sat down cautiously, half-expecting there to be some kind of big sharp root just waiting to poke her in the behind. It seemed like the sort of thing the Queen would find amusing. But nothing happened. The cushions were very comfortable; she settled back with the others around her.

A pixie with bluish skin came toward them carrying a platter with four silver cups on it. They each took a cup of the gold-toned liquid. There were rose petals floating on the top.

Simon set his cup down beside him.

"Don't you want any?" the pixie asked.

"The last faerie drink I had didn't agree with me," he muttered.

Clary barely heard him. The drink had a heady, intoxicating scent, richer and more delicious than roses. She picked a petal out of the liquid and crushed it between her thumb and fore-finger, releasing more of the scent.

Jace jostled her arm. "Don't drink any of it," he said under his breath.

"But—"

"Just don't."

She set the cup down, as Simon had done. Her finger and thumb were stained pink.

"Now," said the Queen. "Meliorn tells me you claim to know who killed our child in the park last night. Though I tell you now, it seems no mystery to me. A faerie child, drained of blood? Is it that you bring me the name of a single vampire? But all vampires are at fault here, for the breaking of the Law, and should be punished accordingly. Despite what may seem, we are not such a particular people."

"Oh, come on," said Isabelle. "It isn't vampires."

Jace shot her a look. "What Isabelle means to say is that we're almost certain that the murderer is someone else. We think he may be trying to throw suspicion on the vampires to shield himself."

"Have you proof of that?"

Jace's tone was calm, but the shoulder that brushed Clary's was tight with tension. "Last night the Silent Brothers were slaughtered as well, and none of them were drained of blood."

"And this has to do with our child, how? Dead Nephilim are a tragedy to Nephilim, but nothing to me."

Clary felt a sharp sting at her left hand. Looking down, she saw the tiny shape of a sprite darting away between the pillows. A red bead of blood had risen on her finger. She put the finger into her mouth with a wince. The sprites were cute, but they had a mean bite.

"The Soul-Sword was stolen as well," said Jace. "You know of Maellartach?"

"The sword that makes Shadowhunters tell the truth," said the Queen, with dark amusement. "We fey have no need of such an object."

"It was taken by Valentine Morgenstern," said Jace. "He killed the Silent Brothers to get it, and we think he killed the faerie as well. He needed the blood of a faerie child to effect a transformation on the Sword. To make it a tool he could use."

"And he won't stop," Isabelle added. "He needs more blood after that."

The Queen's high eyebrows were arched even higher. "More blood of the Folk?"

"No," Jace said, shooting a look at Isabelle that Clary couldn't quite interpret. "More Downworlder blood. He needs the blood of a werewolf, and a vampire—"

The Queen's eyes shone with reflected light. "That seems hardly our concern."

"He killed one of *yours*," Isabelle said. "Don't you want revenge?"

The Queen's gaze brushed her like a moth's wing. "Not immediately," she said. "We are a patient folk, for we have all the time in the world. Valentine Morgenstern is an old enemy of ours—but we have enemies older still. We are content to wait and watch."

"He's summoning demons to him," Jace said. "Creating an army—"

"Demons," said the Queen lightly, as her courtiers chattered behind her. "Demons are your charge, are they not, Shadowhunter? Is that not why you hold authority over us all? Because you are the ones who *slay demons?*"

"I'm not here to give you orders on behalf of the Clave. We came when you asked us because we thought that if you knew the truth, you'd help us."

"Is that what you thought?" The Queen sat forward in her chair, her long hair rippling and alive. "Remember, Shadowhunter, there are those of us who chafe under the rule of the Clave. Perhaps we are tired of fighting your wars for you."

"But it isn't our war alone," said Jace. "Valentine hates Downworlders more than he hates demons. If he defeats us, he'll go after you next."

The Queen's eyes bored into him.

"And when he does," said Jace, "remember that it was a Shadowhunter who warned you what was coming."

There was silence. Even the Court had fallen silent, watching their Lady. At last, the Queen leaned back on her cushions and took a swallow from a silver chalice. "Warning me about your own parent," she said. "I had thought you mortals capable of filial affection, at least, and yet you seem to feel no loyalty toward Valentine your father."

Jace said nothing. He seemed, for a change, lost for words.

Sweetly, the Queen went on, "Or perhaps this hostility of yours is the pretense. Love does make liars out of your kind."

"But we don't love our father," said Clary, as Jace remained frighteningly silent. "We hate him."

"*Do* you?" The Queen looked almost bored.

"You know how the bonds of family are, my lady," said Jace, recovering his voice. "They cling as tightly as vines. And sometimes, like vines, they cling tightly enough to kill."

The Queen's lashes fluttered. "You would betray your own father for the sake of the Clave?"

"Even so, Lady."

She laughed, a sound as bright and cold as icicles. "Who would have thought," she said, "that Valentine's little experiments would turn on him?"

Clary looked at Jace, but she could see by the expression on his face that he had no idea what the Queen meant.

It was Isabelle who spoke. "*Experiments?*"

The Queen didn't even glance at her. Her gaze, a luminous blue, was fixed on Jace. "The Fair Folk are a people of secrets," she said. "Our own, and others'. Ask your father, when next you see him, what blood runs in your veins, Jonathan."

"I hadn't planned on asking him anything next time I see him," Jace said. "But if you desire it, my lady, it will be done."

The Queen's lips curved into a smile. "I think you are a liar. But what a charming one. Charming enough that I will swear you this: Ask your father that question, and I will promise you what aid is in my power, should you strike against Valentine."

Jace smiled. "Your generosity is as remarkable as your loveliness, Lady."

Clary made a gagging noise, but the Queen looked pleased.

"And I think we're done here now," Jace added, rising from the cushions. He'd set his untouched drink down earlier, beside Isabelle's. They all rose after him. Isabelle was already talking to Meliorn in the corner, by the vine door. He looked slightly hunted.

"A moment." The Queen rose. "One of you must remain."

Jace paused halfway to the door, and turned to face her. "What do you mean?"

She stretched out one hand to indicate Clary. "Once our food or drink passes mortal lips, the mortal is ours. You know that, Shadowhunter."

Clary was stunned. "But I didn't drink any of it!" She turned to Jace. "She's lying."

"Faeries don't lie," he said, confusion and dawning anxiety chasing each other across his face. He turned back to the Queen. "I'm afraid you're mistaken, Lady."

"Look to her fingers and tell me she didn't lick them clean."

Simon and Isabelle were staring now. Clary glanced down at her hand. "Of blood," she said. "One of the sprites bit my finger—it was bleeding—" She remembered the sweet taste of the blood, mixed with the juice on her finger. Panicked, she moved toward the vine door, and stopped as what felt like invisible hands shoved her back into the room. She turned to Jace, stricken. "It's true."

Jace's face was flushed. "I suppose I should have expected a trick like that," he said to the Queen, his previous flirtatiousness gone. "Why are you doing this? What do you want from us?"

The Queen's voice was soft as spider's fur. "Perhaps I am only curious," she said. "It is not often I have young Shadowhunters so close within my purview. Like us, you trace your ancestry to heaven; that intrigues me."

"But unlike you," said Jace, "there is nothing of hell in us."

"You are mortal; you age; you die," the Queen said dismissively. "If that is not hell, pray tell me, what is?"

"If you just want to study a Shadowhunter, I won't be much use to you," Clary cut in. Her hand ached where the sprite had bitten it, and she fought the urge to scream or burst into tears. "I don't know anything about Shadowhunting. I hardly have any training. I'm the wrong person to pick." *On*, she added silently.

For the first time the Queen looked directly at her. Clary wanted to shrink back. "In truth, Clarissa Morgenstern, you are precisely the right person." Her eyes gleamed as she took in Clary's discomfiture. "Thanks to the changes your father worked in you, you are not like other Shadowhunters. Your gifts are different."

"My *gifts?*" Clary was bewildered.

"Yours is the gift of words that cannot be spoken," the Queen said to her, "and your brother's is the Angel's own gift. Your father made sure of it, when your brother was a child and before you were ever born."

"My father never gave me anything," Clary said. "He didn't even give me a name."

Jace looked as blank as Clary felt. "While the Fair Folk do not lie," he said, "they can be lied *to*. I think you have been the victim of a trick or joke, my lady. There is nothing special about myself or my sister."

"How deftly you downplay your charms," said the Queen with a laugh. "Though you must know you are not of the usual sort of human boy, Jonathan. . . ." She looked from Clary to Jace to Isabelle—Isabelle closed her mouth, which had been wide open, with a snap—and back at Jace again. "Could it be that you do not know?" she murmured.

"I know that I will not leave my sister here in your Court," said Jace, "and since there is nothing to be learned from either her or myself, perhaps you could do us the favor of releasing her?" *Now that you've had your fun?* his eyes said, though his voice was polite and cool as water.

The Queen's smile was wide and terrible. "What if I told you she could be freed by a kiss?"

"You want Jace to *kiss* you?" Clary said, bewildered.

The Queen burst out laughing, and immediately, the courtiers copied her mirth. The laughter was a bizarre and inhuman mix of hoots, squeaks, and cackles, like the high shrieking of animals in pain.

"Despite his charms," the Queen said, "that kiss will not free the girl."

The four looked at each other, startled. "I could kiss Meliorn," suggested Isabelle.

"Nor that. Nor any one of my Court."

Meliorn moved away from Isabelle, who looked at her companions and threw up her hands. "I'm not kissing *any* of you," she said firmly. "Just so it's official."

"That hardly seems necessary," Simon said. "If a kiss is all . . ."

He moved toward Clary, who was frozen in surprise. When he took her by the elbows, she had to fight the urge to push him away. Not that she hadn't kissed Simon before, but this would have been a peculiar situation even if kissing him were something she was entirely comfortable doing, which it wasn't. And yet it was the logical answer, wasn't it? Without being able to help it, she cast a quick look over her shoulder at Jace and saw him scowl.

"No," said the Queen, in a voice like tinkling crystal. "That is not what I want either."

Isabelle rolled her eyes. "Oh, for the Angel's sake. Look, if there's no other way of getting out of this, *I'll* kiss Simon. I've done it before, it wasn't that bad."

"Thanks," said Simon. "That's very flattering."

"Alas," said the Queen of the Seelie Court. Her expression was sharp with a sort of cruel delight, and Clary wondered if it weren't a kiss she wanted so much as simply to watch them all squirm in discomfort. "I'm afraid that won't do either."

"Well, I'm not kissing the mundane," said Jace. "I'd rather stay down here and rot."

"Forever?" said Simon. "Forever's an awfully long time."

Jace raised his eyebrows. "I knew it," he said. "You want to kiss me, don't you?"

Simon threw up his hands in exasperation. "Of course not. But if—"

"I guess it's true what they say," observed Jace. "There are no straight men in the trenches."

"That's *atheists*, jackass," said Simon furiously. "There are no *atheists* in the trenches."

"While this is all very amusing," said the Queen coolly, leaning forward, "the kiss that will free the girl is the kiss that she most desires." The cruel delight in her face and voice had sharpened, and her words seemed to stab into Clary's ears like needles. "Only that and nothing more."

Simon looked as if she had hit him. Clary wanted to reach out to him, but she stood frozen to the spot, too horrified to move.

"Why are you doing this?" Jace demanded.

"I rather thought I was offering *you* a boon."

Jace flushed, but said nothing. He avoided looking at Clary.

Simon said, "That's ridiculous. They're brother and sister."

The Queen shrugged, a delicate twitch of her shoulders. "Desire is not always lessened by disgust. Nor can it be bestowed, like a favor, to those most deserving of it. And as my words bind my magic, so you can know the truth. If she doesn't desire his kiss, she won't be free."

Simon said something angrily, but Clary didn't hear him: Her ears were buzzing, as if a swarm of angry bees were trapped inside her head. Simon whirled around, looking furious, and said, "You *don't* have to do this, Clary, it's a trick—"

"Not a trick," said Jace. "A test."

"Well, I don't know about you, Simon," said Isabelle, her voice edged. "But *I'd* like to get Clary out of here."

"Like you'd kiss Alec," Simon said, "just because the Queen of the Seelie Court asked you to?"

"Sure I would." Isabelle sounded annoyed. "If the other option was being stuck in the Seelie Court forever? Who cares, anyway? It's just a kiss."

"That's right." It was Jace. Clary saw him, at the blurred edge of her vision, as he moved toward her and put a hand on her shoulder, turning her to face him. "It's just a kiss," he said, and though his tone was harsh, his hands were inexplicably gentle. She let him turn her, looked up at him. His eyes were very dark, perhaps because it was so dim down here in the Court, perhaps because of something else. She could see her reflection in each of his dilated pupils, a tiny image of herself inside his eyes. He said, "You can close your eyes and think of England, if you like."

"I've never even been to England," she said, but she shut her eyelids. She could feel the dank heaviness of her clothes, cold and itchy against her skin, and the cloying sweet air of the cave, colder yet, and the weight of Jace's hands on her shoulders, the only things that were warm. And then he kissed her.

She felt the brush of his lips, light at first, and her own opened automatically beneath the pressure. Almost against her will she felt herself go fluid and pliant, stretching upward to twine her arms around his neck the way that a sunflower twists toward light. His arms slid around her, his hands knotting in her hair, and the kiss stopped being gentle and became fierce, all in a single moment like tinder flaring into a blaze. Clary heard a sound like a sigh rush through the Court, all around them, a wave of noise, but it meant nothing, was lost in the rush of her blood through her veins, the dizzying sense of weightlessness in her body.

Jace's hands moved from her hair, slid down her spine; she felt the hard press of his palms against her shoulder blades—and then he pulled away, gently disengaging himself, drawing her hands away from his neck and stepping back. For a moment Clary thought she might fall; she felt as if something essential had been torn away from her, an arm or a leg, and she stared at Jace in blank astonishment—what did he feel, did he feel nothing? She didn't think she could bear it if he felt nothing.

He looked back at her, and when she saw the look on his face, she saw his eyes at Renwick's, when he had watched the Portal that separated him from his home shatter into a thousand irretrievable pieces. He held her gaze for a split second, then looked away from her, the muscles in his throat working.

His hands were clenched into fists at his sides. "Was that good enough?" he called, turning to face the Queen and the courtiers behind her. "Did that entertain you?"

The Queen had a hand across her mouth, half-covering a smile. "We are quite entertained," she said. "But not, I think, so much as the both of you."

"I can only assume," said Jace, "that mortal emotions amuse you because you have none of your own."

The smile slipped from her mouth at that.

"Easy, Jace," said Isabelle. She turned to Clary. "Can you leave now? Are you free?"

Clary went to the door and was not surprised to find no resistance barring her way. She stood with her hand among the vines and turned to Simon. He was staring at her as if he'd never seen her before.

"We should go," she said. "Before it's too late."

"It's already too late," he said.

Meliorn led them from the Seelie Court and deposited them back in the park, all without speaking a single word. Clary thought his back looked stiff and disapproving. He turned away after they'd splashed out of the pond, without even a good-bye for Isabelle, and disappeared back into the wavering reflection of the moon.

Isabelle watched him go with a scowl. "He is *so* broken up with."

Jace made a sound like a choked laugh and flipped the collar of his wet jacket up. They were all shivering. The cold night smelled like dirt and plants and human modernity—Clary almost thought she could scent the iron on the air. The ring of city surrounding the park sparked with fierce lights: ice blue, cool green, hot red, and the pond lapped quietly against its dirt shores. The moon's reflection had moved to the pond's far edge and quivered there as if it were afraid of them.

"We'd better get back." Isabelle drew her still-wet coat closer around her shoulders. "Before we freeze to death."

"It's going to take forever to get back to Brooklyn," Clary said. "Maybe we should take a taxi."

"Or we could just go to the Institute," suggested Isabelle. At Jace's look, she said quickly, "No one's there anyway—they're all in the Bone City, looking for clues. It'll just take a second to stop by and grab your clothes, change into something dry. Besides, the Institute is still your home, Jace."

"It's fine," Jace said, to Isabelle's evident surprise. "There's something I need from my room there anyway."

Clary hesitated. "I don't know. I might just grab a cab back with Simon." Maybe if they spent a little time alone together, she could explain to him what had happened down in the Seelie Court, and that it wasn't what he thought.

Jace had been examining his watch for water damage. Now he looked at her, eyebrows raised. "That might be a little difficult," he said, "seeing that he left already."

"He *what*?" Clary whirled around and stared. Simon was gone; the three of them were alone by the pond. She ran a little way up the hill and shouted his name. In the distance, she could just see him, striding purposefully away along the concrete path that led out of the park and onto the avenue. She called out to him again, but he didn't turn around.

# 9

# And Death Shall Have No Dominion

**Isabelle had been telling the truth: The Institute was entirely** deserted. Almost entirely, anyway. Max was asleep on the red couch in the foyer when they came in. His glasses were slightly askew and he clearly hadn't meant to fall asleep: There was a book open on the floor where he'd dropped it and his sneakered feet dangled over the couch's edge in a manner that looked as if it were probably uncomfortable.

Clary's heart went out to him immediately. He reminded her of Simon at the age of nine or ten, all glasses and awkward blinking and *ears*.

"Max is like a cat. He can sleep anywhere." Jace reached down and plucked the glasses from Max's face, setting them down on a squat inlaid table nearby. There was a look on his face Clary had never seen before—a fierce protective gentleness that surprised her.

"Oh, leave his stuff alone—you'll just get mud on it," said Isabelle crossly, unbuttoning her wet coat. Her dress clung to her long torso and water darkened the thick leather belt around her waist. The glitter of her coiled whip was just visible where the handle protruded from the edge of the belt. She was frowning. "I can feel a cold coming on," she said. "I'm going to take a hot shower."

Jace watched her disappear down the corridor with a sort of reluctant admiration. "Sometimes she reminds me of the poem. 'Isabelle, Isabelle, didn't worry. Isabelle didn't scream or scurry—'"

"Do you ever feel like screaming?" Clary asked him.

"Some of the time." Jace shrugged off his wet coat and hung it on the peg next to Isabelle's. "She's right about the hot shower, though. I could certainly use one."

"I don't have anything to change into," Clary said, suddenly wanting a few moments to herself. Her fingers itched to dial Simon's number on her cell phone, find out if he was all right. "I'll just wait for you here."

"Don't be stupid. I'll lend you a T-shirt." His jeans were soaked and hung low on his hipbones, showing a strip of pale, tattooed skin between the denim and the edge of his T-shirt.

Clary looked away. "I don't think—"

"Come on." His tone was firm. "There's something I want to show you, anyway."

Surreptitiously, Clary checked the screen on her phone as she followed Jace down the hall to his room. Simon hadn't tried to call. Ice seemed to crystallize inside her chest. Until two weeks ago, it had been years since she and Simon had had a fight. Now he seemed to be mad at her all the time.

Jace's room was just as she remembered it: neat as a pin and bare as a monk's cell. There was nothing about the room that told you anything about Jace: no posters on the walls, no books stacked on the night table. Even the duvet on the bed was plain white.

He went to the dresser and pulled a folded long-sleeved blue T-shirt out of a drawer. He tossed it to Clary. "That one shrank in the wash," he said. "It'll probably still be big on you, but . . ." He shrugged. "I'm going to shower. Yell if you need anything."

She nodded, holding the shirt across her chest as if it were a shield. He looked as if he were about to say something else, but apparently thought better of it; with another shrug, he disappeared into the bathroom, closing the door firmly behind him.

Clary sank down onto the bed, the shirt across her lap, and pulled her phone out of her pocket. She dialed Simon's number. After four rings, it went to voice mail. "Hi, you've reached Simon. Either I'm away from the phone or I'm avoiding you. Leave me a message and—"

"What are you doing?"

Jace stood in the open doorway of the bathroom. Water ran loudly in the shower behind him and the bathroom was half full of steam. He was shirtless and barefoot, damp jeans riding low on his hips, showing the deep indentations above his hipbones, as if someone had pressed their fingers to the skin there.

Clary snapped her phone closed and dropped it onto the bed. "Nothing. Checking the time."

"There's a clock next to the bed," Jace pointed out. "You were calling the mundane, weren't you?"

"His name is *Simon.*" Clary wadded Jace's shirt into a ball between her fists. "And you don't have to be such a bastard about him all the time. He's helped you out more than once."

Jace's eyes were lidded, thoughtful. The bathroom was rapidly filling with steam, making his hair curl more. He said, "And now you feel guilty because he's run off. I wouldn't bother calling him. I'm sure he's avoiding you."

Clary didn't try to keep the anger out of her voice. "And you know this because you and he are *so close?*"

"I know it because I saw the look on his face before he took off," Jace said. "You didn't. You weren't looking at him. But I was."

Clary raked her still-dank hair out of her eyes. Her clothes itched where they clung to her skin, and she suspected she smelled like the bottom of a pond, and she couldn't stop seeing Simon's face when he'd looked at her in the Seelie Court—as if he hated her. "It's your fault," she said suddenly, rage gathering around her heart. "You shouldn't have kissed me like that."

He had been leaning against the door frame; now he stood up straight. "How should I have kissed you? Is there another way you like it?"

"No." Her hands trembled in her lap. They were cold, white, wrinkled by water. She laced her fingers together to stop the shaking. "I just don't want to be kissed by you."

"It didn't seem to me that either of us had a choice in the matter."

"That's what I don't understand!" Clary burst out. "Why did

she make you kiss me? The Queen, I mean. Why force us to do—that? What pleasure could she possibly have gotten out of it?"

"You heard what the Queen said. She thought she was doing me a favor."

"That's not true."

"It is true. How many times do I have to tell you? The Fair Folk don't lie."

Clary thought of what Jace had said back at Magnus's. *They'll find out whatever it is you want most in the world and give it to you—with a sting in the tail of the gift that will make you regret you ever wanted it in the first place.* "Then she was wrong."

"She wasn't wrong." Jace's tone was bitter. "She saw the way I looked at you, and you at me, and she played us like the instruments we are to her."

"I don't look at you," Clary whispered.

"What?"

"I said, *I don't look at you.*" She released the hands that had been clasped together in her lap. There were red marks where her fingers had gripped each other. "At least I try not to."

His eyes were narrowed, just a glint of gold showing through the lashes, and she remembered the first time she had seen him and how he had reminded her of a lion, golden and deadly. "Why not?"

"Why do you think?" Her words were almost soundless, barely a whisper.

"Then *why?*" His voice shook. "Why all this with Simon, why keep pushing me away, not letting me near you—"

"Because it's *impossible,*" she said, and the last word came out as a sort of wail, despite her efforts at control. "You know that as well as I do!"

"Because you're my sister," Jace said.

She nodded without speaking.

"Possibly," said Jace. "And because of that, you've decided your old friend Simon makes a useful distraction?"

"It's not like that," she said. "I love Simon."

"Like you love Luke," said Jace. "Like you love your mother."

"No." Her voice was as cold and pointed as an icicle. "Don't tell me what I feel."

A small muscle jumped at the side of his mouth. "I don't believe you."

Clary stood up. She couldn't meet his eyes, so instead she fixed her gaze on the thin star-shaped scar on his shoulder, a memory of some old injury. *This life of scars and killing*, Hodge had said once. *You have no part in it*. "Jace," she said. "Why are you doing this to me?"

"Because you're lying to me. And you're lying to yourself." Jace's eyes were blazing, and even though his hands were stuffed into his pockets, she could see that they were knotted into fists.

Something inside Clary cracked and broke, and words came pouring out. "*What do you want me to tell you*? The truth? The truth is that I love Simon like I should love you, and I wish he was my brother and you weren't, but I can't do anything about that and *neither can you*! Or do you have some ideas, since you're so goddamned smart?"

Jace sucked a breath in, and she realized he had never expected her to say what she'd just said, not in a million years. The look on his face said as much.

She scrambled to regain her composure. "Jace, I'm sorry, I didn't mean—"

"No. You're not sorry. Don't be sorry." He moved toward her, almost tripping over his feet—Jace, who never stumbled, never tripped over anything, never made an ungraceful move. His hands came up to cup her face; she felt the warmth of his fingertips, millimeters from her skin; knew she ought to pull away, but stood frozen, staring up at him. "You don't understand," he said. His voice shook. "I've never felt this way about anyone. I didn't think I could. I thought—the way I grew up—my father—"

"To love is to destroy," she said numbly. "I remember."

"I thought that part of my heart was broken," he said, and there was a look on his face as he spoke as if he were surprised to hear himself saying these words, saying *my heart*. "Forever. But you—"

"Jace. Don't." She reached up and covered his hand with hers, folding his fingers into her own. "It's pointless."

"That's not true." There was desperation in his voice. "If we both feel the same way—"

"It doesn't matter what we feel. There's nothing we can do." She heard her voice as if a stranger were speaking: remote, miserable. "Where would we go to be together? How could we live?"

"We could keep it a secret."

"People would find out. And I don't want to lie to my family, do you?"

His reply was bitter. "What family? The Lightwoods hate me anyway."

"No, they don't. And I could never tell Luke. And my mother, what if she woke up, what would we *say* to her? This, what we want, it would be sickening to everyone we care about—"

"*Sickening?*" He dropped his hands from her face as if she'd pushed him away. He sounded stunned. "What we feel—what I feel—it's sickening to you?"

She caught her breath at the look on his face. "Maybe," she said in a whisper. "I don't know."

"Then you should have said that to begin with."

"Jace—"

But he was gone from her, his expression shut and locked like a door. It was hard to believe he'd ever looked at her another way. "I'm sorry I said anything, then." His voice was stiff, formal. "I won't be kissing you again. You can count on that."

Clary's heart did a slow, purposeless somersault as he moved away from her, plucked a towel off the top of the dresser, and headed back toward the bathroom. "But—Jace, what are you doing?"

"Finishing my shower. And if you've made me run through all the hot water, I'll be very annoyed." He stepped into the bathroom, kicking the door shut behind him.

Clary collapsed onto the bed and stared up at the ceiling. It was as blank as Jace's face had been before he turned his back on her. Rolling over, she realized she was lying on top of his blue shirt: It even smelled like him, like soap and smoke and coppery blood. Curling around it like she'd once curled around her favorite blanket when she was very small, she closed her eyes.

*In the dream, she looked down on shimmering water, spread out below her like an endless mirror that reflected the night sky. And like a mirror, it was solid and hard, and she could walk on it. She walked, smelling night air and wet leaves and the smell of the city, glittering in the far distance like a faerie castle wreathed in lights—and where she walked, spiderwebbing cracks fissured out from her footsteps and slivers of glass splashed up like water.*

*The sky began to shine. It was alight with points of fire, like burning match tips. They fell, a rain of hot coals from the sky, and she cowered, throwing up her arms. One fell just in front of her, a hurtling bonfire, but when it struck the ground it became a boy: It was Jace, all in burning gold with his gold eyes and gold hair, and white-gold wings sprouted from his back, wider and more thickly feathered than any bird's.*

*He smiled like a cat and pointed behind her, and Clary turned to see that a dark-haired boy—was it Simon?—was standing there, and wings spread from his back as well, feathered black as midnight, and each feather was tipped with blood.*

Clary woke up gasping, her hands knotted in Jace's shirt. It was dark in the bedroom, the only light streaming from the one narrow window beside the bed. She sat up. Her head felt heavy and the back of her neck ached. She scanned the room slowly and jumped as a bright pinpoint of light, like a cat's eyes in the darkness, shone out at her.

Jace was sitting in an armchair beside the bed. He was wearing jeans and a gray sweater and his hair looked nearly dry. He was holding something in his hand that gleamed like metal. A weapon? Though what he might be guarding against, here in the Institute, Clary couldn't guess.

"Did you sleep well?"

She nodded. Her mouth felt thick. "Why didn't you wake me up?"

"I thought you could use the rest. Besides, you were

sleeping like the dead. You even drooled," he added. "On my shirt."

Clary's hand flew to her mouth. "Sorry."

"It's not often you get to see someone drool," Jace observed. "Especially with such total abandon. Mouth wide open and everything."

"Oh, shut up." She felt around among the bedcovers until she located her phone and checked it again, though she knew what it would say. *No calls.* "It's three in the morning," she noted with dismay. "Do you think Simon's all right?"

"I think he's weird, actually," said Jace. "Though that has little to do with the time."

She shoved the phone into her jeans pocket. "I'm going to change."

Jace's white-painted bathroom was no bigger than Isabelle's, though it was considerably neater. There wasn't much variation among the rooms in the Institute, Clary thought, closing the door behind her, but at least there was privacy. She shucked off her wet shirt and hung it on the towel rack, splashed water over her face, and ran a comb through her wildly curling hair.

Jace's shirt was too big for her, but the material was soft against her skin. She rolled the sleeves up and went back into the bedroom, where she found Jace sitting exactly where he had been before, staring moodily down at the glinting object in his hands. She leaned on the back of the armchair. "What is that?"

Instead of answering, he turned it over so that she could see it properly. It was a jagged piece of broken glass, but instead of reflecting her own face, it held an image of green grass and blue sky and the bare black branches of trees.

"I didn't know you kept that," she said. "That piece of the Portal."

"It's why I wanted to come here," he said. "To get this." Longing and loathing were mixed in his voice. "I keep thinking maybe I'll see my father in a reflection. Figure out what he's up to."

"But he's not there, is he? I thought he was somewhere here. In the city."

Jace shook his head. "Magnus has been looking for him and he doesn't think so."

"Magnus has been looking for him? I didn't know that. How—"

"Magnus didn't get to be High Warlock for nothing. His power extends through the city and beyond. He can sense what's out there, to an extent."

Clary snorted. "He can feel disturbances in the Force?"

Jace slewed around in the chair and frowned at her. "I'm not joking. After that warlock was killed down in TriBeCa, he started looking into it. When I went to stay with him, he asked me for something of my father's to make the tracking easier. I gave him the Morgenstern ring. He said he'd let me know if he senses Valentine anywhere in the city, but so far he hasn't."

"Maybe he just wanted your ring," Clary said. "He sure wears a lot of jewelry."

"He can have it." Jace's hand tightened around the bit of mirror in his grasp; Clary noted with alarm the blood welling up around the jagged edges where they cut into his skin. "It's worthless to me."

"Hey," she said, and leaned down to take the glass out of

his hand. "Easy there." She slid the piece of Portal into the pocket of his jacket where it hung on the wall. The edges of the glass were dark with blood, Jace's palms scored with red lines. "Maybe we should get you back to Magnus's," she said as gently as she could. "Alec's been there a long time, and—"

"I doubt he minds, somehow," Jace said, but he stood up obediently enough and reached for his stele, which was propped against the wall. As he drew a healing rune on the back of his bleeding right hand, he said, "There's something I've been meaning to ask you."

"And what's that?"

"When you got me out of the cell in the Silent City, how did you do it? How did you unlock the door?"

"Oh. I just used a regular Opening rune, and—"

She was interrupted by a harsh, tolling ring, and clapped her hand to her pocket before she realized that the sound she'd heard was much louder and sharper than any sound her phone could make. She looked around in confusion.

"That's the Institute's doorbell," Jace said, grabbing his jacket. "Come on."

They were halfway to the foyer when Isabelle burst out of her own bedroom door, wearing a cotton bathrobe, a pink silk sleep mask pushed up on her forehead, and a semi-dazed expression. "It's three in the morning!" she said to them, in a tone that suggested that this was all Jace's, or possibly Clary's, fault. "Who's ringing our doorbell at three in the morning?"

"Maybe it's the Inquisitor," Clary said, feeling suddenly cold.

"She could get in on her own," said Jace. "Any Shadowhunter could. The Institute is only closed to mundanes and Downworlders."

Clary felt her heart contract. "Simon!" she said. "It must be him!"

"Oh, for goodness' sake," yawned Isabelle, "is he really waking us up at this ungodly hour just to prove his love to you or something? Couldn't he have *called*? Mundane men are such twits." They had reached the foyer, which was empty; Max must have gone to bed on his own. Isabelle stalked across the room and toggled a switch on the far wall. Somewhere inside the cathedral a distant rumbling *thump* was audible. "There," Isabelle said. "Elevator's on its way."

"I can't believe he didn't have the dignity and presence of mind just to get drunk and pass out in some gutter," said Jace. "I must say, I'm disappointed in the little fellow."

Clary barely heard him. A rising sense of fear made her blood slow and thick. She remembered her dream: the angels, the ice, Simon with his bleeding wings. She shivered.

Isabelle looked at her sympathetically. "It *is* cold in here," she observed. She reached up and took down what looked like a blue velvet coat from one of the coat hooks. "Here," she said. "Put this on."

Clary slid the coat on and drew it close around her. It was too long, but it was warm. It had a hood, too, lined with satin. Clary pushed it back so she could see the elevator doors opening.

They opened on a hollow box whose mirrored sides reflected her own pale and startled face. Without a pause for thought, she stepped inside.

Isabelle looked at her in confusion. "What are you doing?"

"It's Simon down there," Clary said. "I know it is."

"But—"

Suddenly, Jace was beside Clary, holding the doors open for

Isabelle. "Come on, Izzy," he said. With a theatrical sigh, she followed.

Clary tried to catch his eye as the three of them rode down in silence—Isabelle pinning up the last long coil of her hair—but Jace wouldn't look at her. He was looking at himself sidelong in the elevator mirror, whistling softly under his breath as he always did when he was nervous. She remembered the slight tremor in his touch as he had taken hold of her in the Seelie Court. She thought of the look on Simon's face—and then of him almost running to get away from her, vanishing into the shadows at the edge of the park. There was a knot of dread inside her chest and she didn't know why.

The elevator doors opened onto the nave of the cathedral, alive with the dancing light of candles. She pushed past Jace in her hurry to get out of the elevator and practically ran down the narrow aisle between the pews. She stumbled on the dragging edge of her coat and bunched it up impatiently in her hand before dashing to the wide double doors. On the inside they were barred with bronze bolts the size of Clary's arms. As she reached for the highest bolt, the bell rang through the church again. She heard Isabelle whisper something to Jace, and then Clary was hauling on the bolt, dragging it back, and she felt Jace's hand over hers, helping her pull the heavy doors open.

Night air swept in, guttering the candles in their brackets. The air smelled of city: of salt and fumes, cooling concrete and garbage, and underneath those familiar smells, the scent of copper, like the tang of a new penny.

At first Clary thought the steps were empty. Then she blinked and saw Raphael standing there, his head of black curls tousled by the night breeze, his white shirt open at the neck to show the scar in the hollow of his throat. In his arms he held a body. That was all Clary saw as she stared at him in bewilderment, a *body*. Someone very dead, arms and legs dangling like limp ropes, head fallen back to expose the mangled throat. She felt Jace's hand tighten around her arm like a vise, and only then did she look more closely and see the familiar corduroy jacket with its torn sleeve, the blue T-shirt underneath now stained and spotted with blood, and she screamed.

The scream made no sound. Clary felt her knees give and would have slid to the ground if Jace hadn't been holding her up. "Don't look," he said in her ear. "For God's sake, don't look." But she couldn't *not* look at the blood matting Simon's brown hair, his torn throat, the gashes along his dangling wrists. Black spots dotted her vision as she fought for breath.

It was Isabelle who snatched one of the empty candelabras from the side of the door and aimed it at Raphael as if it were an enormous three-pointed spear.

"*What have you done to Simon?*" For that moment, her voice clear and commanding, she sounded exactly like her mother.

"*Él no está muerto,*" Raphael said, in a flat and emotionless voice, and laid Simon down on the ground almost at Clary's feet, with a surprising gentleness. She had forgotten how strong he must be—he had a vampire's unnatural strength despite his slightness.

In the light of the candles that spilled through the doorway, Clary could see that Simon's shirt was soaked through at the front with blood.

"Did you say—," she began.

"He isn't dead," Jace said, holding her tighter. "He's not dead."

She pulled away from him with a hard jerk and went to her knees on the concrete. She felt no disgust at touching Simon's bloodied skin as she slid her hands under his head, pulling him up into her lap. She felt only the terrified childish horror she remembered from being five years old and having broken her mother's priceless Liberty lamp. *Nothing*, said a voice in the back of her head, *will put these pieces back together again.*

"Simon," she whispered, touching his face. His glasses were gone. "Simon, it's me."

"He can't hear you," said Raphael. "He's dying."

Her head jerked up. "But you said—"

"I said he was not dead yet," said Raphael. "But in a few minutes—ten, perhaps—his heart will slow and stop. Already he is beyond seeing or hearing anything."

Her arms tightened around him involuntarily. "We have to get him to a hospital—or call Magnus."

"They can't do him any good," said Raphael. "You don't understand."

"No," said Jace, his voice as soft as silk tipped with needle-sharp points. "We don't. And perhaps you should explain yourself. Because otherwise I'm going to assume you're a rogue bloodsucker, and cut your heart out. Like I should have done last time we met."

Raphael smiled at him without amusement. "You swore not to harm me, Shadowhunter. Have you forgotten?"

"I never actually finished the oath," Jace reminded him.

"And I never started," said Isabelle, brandishing the candelabra.

Raphael ignored her. He was still looking at Jace. "I remembered that night you broke into the Dumort looking for your friend. It is why I brought him here"—and he gestured at

Simon—"when I found him in the hotel, instead of letting the others drink him to death. You see, he broke in, without permission, and therefore was fair game for us. But I kept him alive, knowing he was yours. I have no wish for a war with the Nephilim."

"He *broke in*?" Clary said in disbelief. "Simon would never do anything that stupid and crazy."

"But he did," said Raphael, with the faintest trace of a smile, "because he was afraid he was becoming one of us, and he wanted to know if the process could be reversed. You might remember that when he was in the form of a rat, and you came to fetch him from us, he bit me."

"Very enterprising of him," said Jace. "I approved."

"Perhaps," said Raphael. "In any case, he took some of my blood into his mouth when he did it. You know that is how we pass our powers to each other. Through the blood."

Through the blood. Clary remembered Simon jerking away from the vampire film on TV, wincing at the sunlight in McCarren Park. "He thought he was turning into one of you," she said. "He went to the hotel to see if it was true."

"Yes," said Raphael. "The pity of it is that the effects of my blood would probably have faded over time had he done nothing. But now—" He gestured at Simon's limp body expressively.

"Now what?" said Isabelle, with a hard edge to her voice. "Now he'll die?"

"And rise again. Now he will be a vampire."

The candelabra tipped forward as Isabelle's eyes widened in shock. "*What?*"

Jace caught the makeshift weapon before it hit the floor.

When he turned to Raphael, his eyes were bleak. "You're lying."

"He consumed vampire blood," said Raphael. "Therefore he will die and rise as one of the Night Children. That is also why I came. Simon is one of mine now." There was nothing in his voice, no sorrow or pleasure, but Clary could not help but wonder what hidden glee he might feel at having so opportunely lucked into an effective bargaining chip.

"There's nothing that can be done? No way to reverse it?" demanded Isabelle, panic tinging her voice. Clary thought distantly that it was strange that these two, Jace and Isabelle, who did not love Simon the way she did, were the ones doing all the talking. But perhaps they were speaking for her precisely because she couldn't bear to say a word.

"You could cut off his head and burn his heart in a fire, but I doubt that you will do that."

"No!" Clary's arms tightened around Simon. "Don't you dare hurt him."

"I have no need to," said Raphael.

"I wasn't talking to you." Clary didn't look up. "Don't you even think about it, Jace. Don't even think about it."

There was silence. She could hear Isabelle's worried intake of breath, and Raphael of course did not breathe at all. Jace hesitated a moment before he said, "Clary, what would Simon want? Is this what he'd want for himself?"

She jerked her head up. Jace was looking down at her, the three-pronged metal candelabra still in his hand, and suddenly an image flashed across her mental landscape of Jace holding Simon down and plunging the sharp end of it into his chest, making the blood splash up like a fountain. *"Get away from us!"* she screamed suddenly, so loudly that she saw the distant figures walking along the avenue in front of the cathedral turn and look behind them, as if startled at the noise.

Jace went white to the roots of his hair, so white that his wide eyes looked like gold disks, inhuman and weirdly out of place. He said, "Clary, you don't think—"

Simon gasped suddenly, arching upward in Clary's grasp. She screamed again and caught at him, pulling him up toward her. His eyes were wide and blind and terrified. He reached up. She wasn't sure if he was trying to touch her face or claw at her, not knowing who she was.

"It's me," she said, gently pushing his hand down to his chest, lacing their fingers together. "Simon, it's me. It's Clary." Her hands slipped on his; when she looked down, she saw they were wet with blood from his shirt and from the tears that had slid down her face without her noticing. "Simon, I love you," she said.

His hands tightened on hers. He breathed out—a harsh, ratcheting sound—and then did not breathe in again.

*I love you. I love you. I love you.* Her last words to Simon seemed to echo in Clary's ears as he went limp in her grasp. Isabelle was suddenly next to her, saying something in her ear, but Clary couldn't hear her. The sound of rushing water, like an oncoming tidal wave, filled her ears. She watched as Isabelle tried gently to pry her hands away from Simon's, and couldn't. Clary was surprised. She didn't feel like she was holding on to him that tightly.

Giving up, Isabelle got to her feet and turned angrily on Raphael. She was shouting. Halfway through her tirade, Clary's hearing switched back on, like a radio that had finally found a station within range. "—and *now* what are we supposed to do?" Isabelle screamed.

"Bury him," said Raphael.

The candelabra swung up again in Jace's hand. "That's not funny."

"It isn't supposed to be," said the vampire, unfazed. "It is how we are made. We are drained, blooded, and buried. When he digs his own way out of a grave, that is when a vampire is born."

Isabelle made a faint sound of disgust. "I don't think I could do that."

"Some can't," said Raphael. "If no one is there to help them dig out, they stay like that, trapped like rats under the earth."

A sound tore its way out of Clary's throat. A sob that was as raw as a scream. She said, "I won't put him in the ground."

"Then he'll stay like this," said Raphael mercilessly. "Dead but not quite dead. Never waking."

They were all staring down at her. Isabelle and Jace as if they were holding their breaths, waiting on her response. Raphael looked incurious, almost bored.

"You didn't come into the Institute because you can't, isn't that right?" Clary said. "Because it's holy ground and you're unholy."

"That's not exactly—," Jace began, but Raphael cut him off with a gesture.

"I should tell you," said the vampire boy, "that there is not much time. The longer we wait before putting him into the ground, the less likely he'll be able to dig his own way back out of it."

Clary looked down at Simon. He really would look as if he

were sleeping, if it weren't for the long gashes along his bare skin. "We can bury him," she said. "But I want it to be in a Jewish cemetery. And I want to be there when he wakes up."

Raphael's eyes glittered. "It will not be pleasant."

"Nothing ever is." She set her jaw. "Let's get going. We only have a few hours until dawn."

# 10

## A Fine and Private Place

**The cemetery was in the outskirts of Queens, where** apartment buildings gave way to rows of orderly-looking Victorian houses painted gingerbread colors: pink, white, and blue. The streets were wide and mostly deserted, the avenue leading up to the cemetery unlit except by a single streetlight. It took them a short while with their steles to break in through the locked gates, and another while to find a spot hidden enough for Raphael to begin digging. It was at the top of a low hill, sheltered from the road below by a thick line of trees. Clary, Jace, and Isabelle were protected with glamour, but there was no way to hide Raphael, or to hide Simon's body, so the trees provided a welcome cover.

The sides of the hill not facing the road were thickly layered with headstones, many of them bearing a pointed Star of David at the top. They gleamed white and smooth as milk in the moonlight. In the distance was a lake, its surface pleated with glittering ripples. A nice place, Clary thought. A good place to come and lay flowers on someone's grave, to sit awhile and think about their life, what they meant to you. Not a good place to come at night, under cover of darkness, to bury your friend in a shallow dirt grave without the benefit of a coffin or a service.

"Did he suffer?" she asked Raphael.

He looked up from his digging, leaning on the handle of the shovel like the grave digger in *Hamlet*. "What?"

"Simon. Did he suffer? Did the vampires hurt him?"

"No. The blood death is not such a bad way to die," said Raphael, his musical voice soft. "The bite drugs you. It is pleasant, like going to sleep."

A wave of dizziness passed over her, and for a moment she thought she might faint.

"Clary." Jace's voice snapped her out of her reverie. "Come on. You don't have to watch this."

He held out his hand to her. Looking past him, she could see Isabelle standing with her whip in her hand. They had wrapped Simon's body in a blanket and it lay on the ground at her feet, as if she were guarding it. *Not it*, Clary reminded herself fiercely. *Him.* Simon.

"I want to be here when he wakes up."

"I know. We'll come right back." When she didn't move, Jace took her unresisting arm and drew her away from the clearing and down the side of the hill. There were boulders here, just above the first line of graves; he sat down on one, zipping up his jacket. It was surprisingly chilly out. For the first time this season Clary could see her breath when she exhaled.

She sat down on the boulder beside Jace and stared down at the lake. She could hear the rhythmic *thump-thump* of Raphael's spade hitting the dirt and the shoveled dirt hitting the ground. Raphael wasn't human; he worked fast. It wouldn't take that long for him to dig a grave. And Simon wasn't all that big a person; the grave wouldn't have to be that deep.

A stab of pain twisted through her abdomen. She bent forward, hands splayed across her stomach. "I feel sick."

"I know. That's why I brought you out here. You looked like you were going to throw up on Raphael's feet."

She made a soft groaning noise.

"Might have wiped the smirk off his face," Jace observed reflectively. "There's that to consider."

"Shut up." The pain had eased. She tipped her head back, looking up at the moon, a circle of chipped silver polish floating in a sea of stars. "This is my fault."

"It's not your fault."

"You're right. It's *our* fault."

Jace turned toward her, exasperation clear in the lines of his shoulders. "How do you figure that?"

She looked at him silently for a moment. He needed a haircut. His hair curled the way vines did when they got too long, in looping tendrils, the color of white gold in the moonlight. The scars on his face and throat looked like they had been etched there with metallic ink. He was beautiful, she thought miserably, beautiful and there was nothing there in him, not an expression, not a slant of cheekbone or shape of jaw or curve of lips that bespoke any family resemblance to herself or her mother at all. He didn't even really look like Valentine.

"What?" he said. "Why are you looking at me like that?"

She wanted to throw herself into his arms and sob at the exact same time that she wanted to pound on him with her fists. Instead, she said, "If it weren't for what happened in the faerie court, Simon would still be alive."

He reached down and savagely yanked a hunk of grass out of the ground. Dirt still clung to the roots. He tossed it aside. "We were forced to do what we did. It's not as if we did it for fun, or to hurt him. Besides," he said, with the ghost of a smile, "you're my sister."

"Don't say it like that—"

"What, 'sister'?" He shook his head. "When I was a little kid, I realized that if you say any word over and over fast enough, it loses all its meaning. I'd lie awake saying the words over and over to myself—'sugar,' 'mirror,' 'whisper,' 'dark.' 'Sister,'" he said, softly. "You're my sister."

"It doesn't matter how many times you say it. It'll still be true."

"And it doesn't matter what you won't let me say, that'll still be true too."

*"Jace!"* Another voice, calling his name. It was Alec, slightly out of breath from running. He was holding a black plastic bag in one hand. Behind him stalked Magnus, impossibly tall and thin and glowering in a long leather coat that flapped in the wind like a bat's wing. Alec came to a stop in front of Jace and held out the bag. "I brought blood," he said. "Like you asked."

Jace opened the top of the bag, peered in, and wrinkled his nose. "Do I want to ask you where you got this?"

"From a butcher shop in Greenpoint," said Magnus, joining them. "They bleed their meat to make it halal. It's animal blood."

"Blood is blood," said Jace, and stood up. He looked down at Clary and hesitated. "When Raphael said this wouldn't be pleasant, he wasn't lying. You can stay here. I'll send Isabelle down to wait with you."

She tipped her head back to look up at him. The moonlight cast the shadow of branches across his face. "Have you ever seen a vampire rise?"

"No, but I—"

"Then you don't really know, do you?" She stood up, and Isabelle's blue coat fell around her in rustling folds. "I want to be there. I *have* to be there."

She could see only part of his face in the shadows, but she thought he looked almost—impressed. "I know better than to tell you there's anything you can't do," he said. "Let's go."

Raphael was tamping down a large rectangle of dirt when they came back into the clearing, Jace and Clary a little ahead of Magnus and Alec, who seemed to be arguing about something. Simon's body was gone. Isabelle was sitting on the ground, her whip coiled at her ankles in a golden circle. She was shivering. "Jesus, it's cold," Clary said, pulling Isabelle's heavy coat close around her. The velvet was warm, at least. She tried to ignore the fact that the hem of it was stained with Simon's blood. "It's as if it turned to winter overnight."

"Be glad it isn't winter," said Raphael, setting the spade against the trunk of a nearby tree. "The ground freezes like iron in winter. Sometimes it is impossible to dig and the fledgling must wait months, starving underground, before it can be born."

"Is that what you call them? Fledglings?" said Clary. The word seemed wrong, too friendly somehow. It reminded her of ducklings.

"Yes," said Raphael. "It means the not-yet or newly born." He caught sight of Magnus then, and for a split second looked surprised before he wiped the expression carefully from his features. "High Warlock," he said. "I hadn't expected to see you here."

"I was curious," said Magnus, his cat eyes glittering. "I've never seen one of the Night Children rise."

Raphael glanced at Jace, who was lounging against a tree trunk. "You keep surprisingly illustrious company, Shadowhunter."

"Are you talking about yourself again?" asked Jace. He smoothed the churned dirt with the tip of a boot. "That seems boastful."

"Maybe he meant me," said Alec. Everyone looked at him in surprise. Alec so rarely made jokes. He smiled nervously. "Sorry," he said. "Nerves."

"There's no need for that," said Magnus, reaching to touch Alec's shoulder. Alec moved quickly out of range, and Magnus's outstretched hand fell to his side.

"So what do we do now?" Clary demanded, hugging herself for warmth. Cold seemed to have seeped into every pore of her body. Surely it was too cold for late summer.

Raphael, noticing her gesture, smiled minutely. "It is always cold at a rising," he said. "The fledgling draws strength from the living things that surround it, taking from them the energy to rise."

Clary glared at him resentfully. "You don't seem cold."

"I'm not living." He stepped back a little from the edge of the grave—Clary forced herself to think of it as a grave, since that's exactly what it was—and gestured to the others to do the same. "Make room," he said. "Simon can hardly rise if you are all standing on top of him."

They moved hastily backward. Clary found Isabelle clutching her elbow and turned to see that the other girl was white to the lips. "What's wrong?"

"Everything," Isabelle said. "Clary, maybe we should have just let him go—"

"Let him die, you mean." Clary jerked her arm out of Isabelle's grip. "Of course that's what you think. You think everyone who isn't just like you is better off dead anyway."

Isabelle's face was the picture of misery. "That isn't—"

A sound tore through the clearing, a sound unlike any Clary had ever heard before—a sort of pounding rhythm coming from deep underground, as if suddenly the heartbeat of the world had become audible.

*What's happening?* Clary thought, and then the ground buckled and heaved under her. She fell to her knees. The grave was roiling like the surface of an unsteady ocean. Ripples appeared in its surface. Suddenly it burst apart, clods of dirt flying. A small mountain of dirt, like an anthill, heaved itself upward. At the center of the mountain was a hand, fingers splayed, clawing at the dirt.

"*Simon!*" Clary tried to rush forward, but Raphael yanked her back.

"Let me go!" She tried to pull herself free, but Raphael's grip was like steel. "Can't you see he needs our help?"

"He should do this himself," Raphael said, without

loosening his hold on her. "It is better that way."

"It's your way! It's not mine!" She jerked herself out of his grip and ran toward the grave, just as it heaved upward, hurling her back to the ground. A hunched shape was forcing itself out of the hastily dug grave, fingers like filthy claws sunk deep into the earth. Its bare arms were streaked black with dirt and blood. It tore itself free of the sucking earth, crawled a few feet, and collapsed onto the ground.

"Simon," she whispered. Because of course it was Simon, *Simon*, not an *it*. She scrambled to her feet and ran toward him, her sneakers sinking deep into the churned earth.

"Clary!" Jace shouted. "What are you doing?"

She stumbled, her ankle twisting as her leg sank into the dirt. She fell onto her knees next to Simon, who lay as still as if he really were dead. His hair was filthy and matted with clots of dirt, his glasses gone, his T-shirt torn down the side, blood on the skin that showed under it. "Simon," she said, and reached to touch his shoulder. "Simon, are you—"

His body tensed under her fingers, every muscle tightening, his skin hard as iron.

"—all right?" she finished.

He turned his head, and she saw his eyes. They were blank, lifeless. With a sharp cry he rolled over and sprang at her, swift as a striking snake. He struck her squarely, knocking her back into the dirt. "Simon!" she shouted, but he didn't seem to hear. His face was twisted, unrecognizable as he loomed up over her, his lips curling back, and she saw his sharp canines, the fang-teeth, gleam in the moonlight like white bone needles. Suddenly terrified, she kicked out at him, but he grabbed her shoulders and forced her back down into the dirt. His hands were bloody, the nails broken, but he was incredibly strong, stronger even than her own Shadowhunter muscles. The bones in her shoulders ground together painfully as he bent down over her—

And was plucked away and sent flying as if he weighed no more than a pebble. Clary shot to her feet, gasping, and met Raphael's grim gaze. "I told you to stay away from him," he said, and turned to kneel down by Simon, who had landed a short distance away and was curled, twitching, on the ground.

Clary sucked in a breath. It sounded like a sob. "He doesn't know me."

"He knows you. He doesn't care." Raphael looked over his shoulder at Jace. "He is starving. He needs blood."

Jace, who had been standing white-faced and frozen at the grave's edge, stepped forward and held out the plastic bag mutely, like an offering. Raphael snatched it and tore it open. A number of plastic packets of red fluid fell out. He seized one, muttering, and tore it open with sharp nails, spattering blood down the front of his dirt-stained white shirt.

Simon, as if scenting the blood, curled up and let out a piteous wail. He was still twitching; his broken-nailed hands gouged at the dirt and his eyes were rolled back to the whites. Raphael held out the blood packet, letting some of the red fluid drip onto Simon's face, streaking the white skin with scarlet. "There you go," he said, almost in a croon. "Drink, little fledgling. Drink."

And Simon, who had been a vegetarian since he was ten years old, who wouldn't drink milk that wasn't organic, who fainted at the sight of needles—Simon snatched the packet of blood out of Raphael's thin brown hand and tore into it with his teeth. He swallowed the blood in a few gulps and tossed the packet aside with another wail; Raphael was ready with a second one, and pressed it into his hand. "Do not drink too fast," he cautioned. "You will make yourself sick." Simon, of course, ignored him; he had managed to get the second packet open without help and was gulping greedily at the contents. Blood ran from the corners of his mouth, down his throat, and spattered his hands with fat red drops. His eyes were closed.

Raphael turned to look at Clary. She could feel Jace staring at her too, and the others, all with identical expressions of horror and disgust. "Next time he feeds," Raphael said calmly, "it will not be quite so messy."

*Messy*. Clary turned away and stumbled out of the clearing, hearing Jace call out for her but ignoring him, starting to run when she reached the trees. She was halfway down the hill when the pain hit. She went to her knees, gagging, as everything in her stomach came up in a wrenching flood. When it was over, she crawled a short distance away and collapsed against the ground. She knew she was probably lying on someone's grave, but she didn't care. She rested her hot face against the cool dirt and thought, for the first time, that maybe the dead weren't so unlucky after all.

# 11

## Smoke and Steel

**The critical care unit of Beth Israel hospital always** reminded Clary of photos she'd seen of Antarctica: It was cold and remote-feeling, and everything was either gray, white, or pale blue. The walls of her mother's room were white, the tubes that snaked around her head and the endless beeping banks of instruments around the bed were gray, and the blanket pulled up around her chest was pale blue. Her face was white. The only color in the room was her red hair, flaring across the snowy expanse of pillow like a bright, incongruous flag planted at the south pole.

Clary wondered how Luke was managing to pay for this private room, where the money had come from and how he'd gotten it. She supposed she could ask him when he got back from buying vending machine coffee in the ugly little café on the third floor. The coffee from the machine down there looked like tar and tasted like it too, but Luke seemed addicted to the stuff.

The metal legs of the bedside chair squeaked across the floor as Clary pulled it out and sat down slowly, smoothing her skirt down over her legs. Whenever she came to see her mother in the hospital she felt nervous and dry-mouthed, as if she were about to get in trouble for something. Maybe because the only times she'd ever seen her mother's face like this, flat and without animation, was when her mother was about to explode with rage.

"Mom," she said. She reached out and took her mother's left hand; there was a puncture mark on the wrist still, where Valentine had shoved one end of a tube. The skin of her mother's hand—always rough and chapped, spattered with paint and turpentine—felt like the dry bark of a tree. Clary folded her fingers around Jocelyn's, feeling a hard lump come into her throat. "Mom, I . . ." She cleared her throat. "Luke says you can hear me. I don't know if that's true or not. Anyway, I came because I needed to talk to you. It's okay if you can't say anything back. See, the thing is, it's . . ." She swallowed again and looked toward the window, the strip of blue sky visible at the edge of the brick wall that faced the hospital. "It's Simon. Something's happened to him. Something that was my fault."

Now that she wasn't looking at her mother's face, the story poured out of her, all of it: how she'd met Jace and the other Shadowhunters, the search for the Mortal Cup, Hodge's betrayal and the battle at Renwick's, the realization that Valentine was her father as well as Jace's. More recent events too: the nighttime visit to the Bone City, the Soul-Sword, the Inquisitor's hatred of Jace, and the woman with the silver hair. And then she told her mother about the Seelie Court, about the price the Queen had demanded, and what had happened to Simon afterward. She could feel tears burn her throat while she talked, but it was a relief to tell it, to unburden herself to someone, even someone who—probably—couldn't hear her.

"So, basically," she said, "I've screwed everything up royally. I remember you saying that growing up happens when you start having things you look back on and wish you could change. I guess that means I've grown up now. It's just that—that I—" *I thought you'd be there when I did.* She choked on tears just as someone behind her cleared his throat.

Clary wheeled around and saw Luke standing in the doorway, a Styrofoam cup in his hand. Under the hospital's fluorescent lights, she could see how tired he looked. There was gray in his hair, and his blue flannel shirt was rumpled.

"How long have you been standing there?"

"Not long," he said. "I brought you some coffee." He held out the cup but she waved it away.

"I hate that stuff. It tastes like feet."

At that he smiled. "How would you know what feet taste like?"

"I just know." She leaned forward and kissed Jocelyn's cold cheek before standing up. "Bye, Mom."

Luke's blue pickup was parked in the concrete lot under the hospital. They had pulled out onto the FDR highway before he spoke.

"I heard what you said back at the hospital."

"I *thought* you were eavesdropping." She spoke without anger. There was nothing in what she'd said to her mother that Luke couldn't know.

"What happened to Simon wasn't your fault."

She heard the words, but they seemed to bounce off her as if there were an invisible wall surrounding her. Like the wall Hodge had built around her when he'd betrayed her to Valentine, but this time she couldn't hear anything through it, couldn't feel anything through it either. She was as numb as if she'd been encased in ice.

"Did you hear me, Clary?"

"It's a nice thing to say, but of course it was my fault. Everything that happened to Simon was my fault."

"Because he was angry at you when he went back to the hotel? He didn't go back to the hotel *because* he was angry at you, Clary. I've heard of situations like this before. They call them 'darklings,' those who are half-turned. He would have felt drawn back to the hotel by a compulsion he couldn't control."

"Because he had Raphael's blood in him. But that would never have happened either if it weren't for me. If I hadn't brought him to that party—"

"You thought it would be safe there. You weren't putting him in any danger you hadn't put yourself in. You can't torture yourself like this," said Luke, turning onto the Brooklyn Bridge. The water slid by under them in sheets of silvery gray. "There's no point to it."

She slumped lower in her seat, curling her fingers into the sleeves of her knitted green hoodie. Its edges were frayed and the yarn tickled her cheek.

"Look," Luke went on. "In all the years I've known him,

there's always been exactly one place Simon wanted to be, and he's always fought like hell to make sure he got there and stayed there."

"Where's that?"

"Wherever you were," said Luke. "Remember when you fell out of that tree on the farm when you were ten, and broke your arm? Remember how he made them let him ride with you in the ambulance on the way to the hospital? He kicked and yelled till they gave in."

"You laughed," said Clary, remembering, "and my mom hit you in the shoulder."

"It was hard not to laugh. Determination like that in a ten-year-old is something to see. He was like a pit bull."

"If pit bulls wore glasses and were allergic to ragweed."

"You can't put a price on that kind of loyalty," said Luke, more seriously.

"I know. Don't make me feel worse."

"Clary, I'm telling you he made his own decisions. What you're blaming yourself for is *being what you are*. And that's no one's fault and nothing you can change. You told him the truth and he made up his own mind what he wanted to do about that. Everyone has choices to make; no one has the right to take those choices away from us. Not even out of love."

"But that's just it," Clary said. "When you love someone, you don't have a choice." She thought of the way her heart had contracted when Isabelle had called to tell her Jace was missing. She'd left the house without a moment's thought or hesitation. "Love takes your choices away."

"It's a lot better than the alternative." Luke guided the truck onto Flatbush. Clary didn't reply; just gazed dully out the window. The area just off the bridge was not one of the prettier parts of Brooklyn; either side of the avenue was lined with ugly office buildings and auto body shops. Normally she hated it but right now the surroundings suited her mood. "So, have you heard from—?" Luke began, apparently deciding it was time to change the subject.

"Simon? Yes, you know I have."

"Actually, I was going to say Jace."

"Oh." Jace had called her cell phone several times and left messages. She hadn't picked up or called him back. Not talking to him was her penance for what had happened to Simon. It was the worst way she could think to punish herself. "No, I haven't."

Luke's voice was carefully neutral. "You might want to. Just to see if he's all right. He's probably having a pretty bad time of it, considering—"

Clary shifted in her seat. "I thought you checked in with Magnus. I heard you talking to him about Valentine and the whole reversing the Soul-Sword thing. I'm sure he'd tell you if Jace wasn't okay."

"Magnus can reassure me about Jace's physical health. His mental health, on the other hand—"

"Forget it. I'm not calling Jace." Clary heard the coldness in her own voice and was almost shocked at herself. "I have to be there for Simon right now. It's not like his mental health is so great either."

Luke sighed. "If he's having trouble coming to terms with his condition, maybe he should—"

"Of course he's having trouble!" She shot Luke an accusing look, though he was concentrating on traffic and didn't notice.

"You of all people ought to understand what it's like to—"

"Wake up a monster one day?" Luke didn't sound bitter, just weary. "You're right, I do understand. And if he ever wants to talk to me, I'd be happy to tell him all about it. He will get through this, even if he thinks he won't."

Clary frowned. The sun was setting just behind them, making the rearview mirror shine like gold. Her eyes stung from the brightness. "It's not the same," she said. "At least you grew up knowing werewolves were real. Before he can tell anyone he's a vampire, he'll have to convince them that vampires *exist* in the first place."

Luke looked as if he were about to say something, then changed his mind. "I'm sure you're right." They were in Williamsburg now, driving down half-empty Kent Avenue, warehouses rising above them on either side. "Still. I got him something. It's in the glove compartment. Just in case . . ."

Clary snapped the compartment open and frowned. She took out a shiny folded pamphlet, the kind they kept stacked in clear plastic stands in hospital waiting rooms. "*How to Come Out to Your Parents*," she read out loud. "LUKE. Don't be ridiculous. Simon's not gay, he's a vampire."

"I recognize that, but the pamphlet's all about telling your parents difficult truths about yourself they may not want to face. Maybe he could adapt one of the speeches, or just listen to the advice in general—"

"Luke!" She spoke so sharply that he pulled the truck to a stop with a loud screech of brakes. They were just in front of his house, the water of the East River glittering darkly on their left, the sky streaked with soot and shadows. Another, darker shadow crouched on Luke's front porch.

Luke narrowed his eyes. In wolf form, he'd told her, his eyesight was perfect; in human form, he remained nearsighted. "Is that . . . ?"

"Simon. Yes." She knew him even as an outline. "I'd better go talk to him."

"Sure. I'll, ah, run some errands. I have things to pick up."

"What kind of things?"

He waved her away. "Food things. I'll be back in a half hour. Don't stay outside, though. Go in the house and lock up."

"You know I will."

She watched as the pickup sped away, then turned toward the house. Her heart was pounding. She'd talked to Simon on the phone a few times but she hadn't seen him since they'd brought him, groggy and blood-splattered, to Luke's house in the dark early hours of that horrible morning to clean up before driving him home. She'd thought he ought to go to the Institute, but of course that was impossible. Simon would never see the inside of a church or synagogue again.

She'd watched him walking up the path to his front door, shoulders hunched forward as if he were walking against a heavy wind. When the porch light came on automatically, he flinched away from it, and she knew it was because he had thought it was the light of the sun; and she started to cry, silently, in the backseat of the pickup, the tears splashing down onto the strange black Mark on her forearm.

"Clary," Jace had whispered, and he'd reached for her hand, but she'd recoiled from him just as Simon had recoiled from the light. She wouldn't touch him. She'd never touch him again. That was her penance, her payment for what she'd done to Simon.

Now, as she mounted the steps to Luke's porch, her mouth went dry and her throat swelled with the pressure of tears. She told herself not to cry. Crying would only make him feel worse.

He was sitting in the shadows at the corner of the porch, watching her. She could see the gleam of his eyes in the darkness. She wondered if they'd held that sort of light in them before; she couldn't remember. "Simon?"

He stood up in one single smooth graceful movement that sent a chill up her spine. There was one thing Simon had never been, and that was graceful. There was something else about him, something different—

"Sorry if I startled you." He spoke carefully, almost formally, as if they were strangers.

"It's all right, it's just—How long have you been here?"

"Not long. I can only travel after the sun starts going down, remember? I accidentally put my hand about an inch out the window yesterday and nearly charred off my fingers. Luckily I heal fast."

She fumbled for her key, unlocked the door, swung it open. Pale light spilled out onto the porch. "Luke said we should stay inside."

"Because the nasty things," Simon said, pushing past her, "they come out in the dark."

The living room was full of warm yellow light. Clary shut the door behind them and flipped the dead bolts closed. Isabelle's blue coat was still hanging on a hook by the door. She'd meant to take it to a dry cleaner to see if they could get the bloodstains out, but she hadn't had a chance. She stared at it for a moment, steeling herself, before turning to look at Simon.

He was standing in the middle of the room, hands awkwardly in the pockets of his jacket. He was wearing jeans and a frayed I ♥ NEW YORK T-shirt that had belonged to his dad. Everything about him was familiar to Clary, and yet he seemed like a stranger. "Your glasses," she said, belatedly realizing what had seemed strange to her out on the porch. "You're not wearing them."

"Have *you* ever seen a vampire wearing glasses?"

"Well, no, but—"

"I don't need them anymore. Perfect vision seems to come with the territory." He sat down on the couch and Clary joined him, sitting beside him but not too near. Up close she could see how pale his skin looked, blue traceries of veins apparent just beneath the surface. His eyes without the glasses looked huge and dark, the lashes like black ink strokes. "Of course I still have to wear them around the house or my mother would freak out. I'm going to have to tell her I'm getting contacts."

"You're going to have to tell her, period," Clary said, more firmly than she felt. "You can't hide your—your condition forever."

"I can try." He raked a hand through his dark hair, his mouth twisting. "Clary, what am I going to *do*? My mom keeps bringing me food and I have to throw it out the window—I haven't been outside in two days, but I don't know how much longer I can go on pretending I have the flu. Eventually she's going to bring me to the doctor, and then what? I don't have a *heartbeat*. He'll tell her that I'm *dead*."

"Or write you up as a medical miracle," said Clary.

"It's not funny."

"I know, I was just trying to—"

"I keep thinking about blood," Simon said. "I dream about it. Wake up thinking about it. Pretty soon I'll be writing morbid emo poetry about it."

"Don't you have those bottles of blood Magnus gave you? You're not running out, are you?"

"I have them. They're in my mini-fridge. But I've only got three left." His voice sounded thin with tension. "What about when I run out?"

"You won't. We'll get you some more," Clary said, with more confidence than she felt. She supposed she could always hit up Magnus's friendly local supplier of lamb's blood, but the whole business made her queasy. "Look, Simon, Luke thinks you should tell your mom. You can't hide it from her forever."

"I can damn well try."

"Think about Luke," she said desperately. "You can still live a normal life."

"And what about us? Do you want a vampire boyfriend?" He laughed bitterly. "Because I foresee many romantic picnics in our future. You, drinking a virgin piña colada. Me, drinking the blood of a virgin."

"Think of it as a handicap," Clary urged. "You just have to learn how to work your life around it. Lots of people do it."

"I'm not sure I'm people. Not anymore."

"You are to me," she said. "Anyway, being human is overrated."

"At least Jace can't call me *mundane* anymore. What's that you're holding?" he asked, noticing the pamphlet, still rolled up in her left hand.

"Oh, this?" She held it up. "*How to Come Out to Your Parents.*"

He widened his eyes. "Something you want to tell me?"

"It's not for me. It's for you." She handed it to him.

"I don't have to come out to my mother," said Simon. "She already thinks I'm gay because I'm not interested in sports and I haven't had a serious girlfriend yet. Not that she knows about, anyway."

"But you have to come out as a vampire," Clary pointed out. "Luke thought maybe you could, you know, use one of the suggested speeches in the pamphlet, except use the word 'undead' instead of—"

"I get it, I get it." Simon spread the pamphlet open. "Here, I'll practice on you." He cleared his throat. "Mom. I have something to tell you. I'm undead. Now, I know you may have some preconceived notions about the undead. I know you may not be comfortable with the idea of me being undead. But I'm here to tell you that the undead are just like you and me." Simon paused. "Well, okay. Possibly more like me than you."

"SIMON."

"All right, all right." He went on. "The first thing you need to understand is that I'm the same person I always was. Being undead isn't the most important thing about me. It's just part of who I am. The second thing you should know is that it isn't a choice. I was born this way." Simon squinted at her over the pamphlet. "Sorry, *reborn* this way."

Clary sighed. "You're not *trying*."

"At least I can tell her you buried me in a Jewish cemetery," Simon said, abandoning the pamphlet. "Maybe I should start small. Tell my sister first."

"I'll go with you if you want. Maybe I can help make them understand."

He looked up at her, surprised, and she saw the cracks in his armor of bitter humor, and the fear that was underneath. "You'd do that?"

"I—," Clary began, and was cut off by a sudden deafening screech of tires and the sound of shattering glass. She leaped to her feet and raced to the window, Simon beside her. She yanked the curtain aside and stared out.

Luke's pickup truck was pulled up onto the lawn, its motor grinding, dark strips of burned rubber laid across the sidewalk. One of the truck's headlights was blazing; the other had been smashed and there was a dark stain across the front grille of the truck—and something humped, white and motionless lying underneath the front wheels. Bile rose in Clary's throat. Had Luke run someone over? But no—impatiently she scraped the glamour from her vision as if she were scraping dirt from a window. The thing under Luke's wheels wasn't human. It was smooth, white, almost larval, and it twitched like a worm pinned to a board.

The driver's side door of the truck burst open and Luke leaped out. Ignoring the creature pinned under his wheels, he dashed across the lawn toward the porch. Following him with her gaze, Clary saw that there was a dark shape sprawled in the shadows there. This shape *was* human—small, with light, braided hair—

"That's that werewolf girl. Maia." Simon sounded astonished. "What *happened?*"

"I don't know." Clary grabbed her stele off the top of a bookcase. They clattered down the steps, and dashed for the shadows where Luke crouched, his hands on Maia's shoulders, lifting her and propping her gently against the side of the porch. Up close, Clary could see that the front of her shirt was torn and there was a gash in her shoulder, leaking a slow pulse of blood.

Simon stopped dead. Clary, nearly crashing into him, gave a gasp of surprise and shot him an angry look before she realized. *The blood.* He was afraid of it, afraid of looking at it.

"She's all right," said Luke, as Maia's head rolled and she groaned. He slapped her cheek lightly and her eyes fluttered open. "Maia. Maia, can you hear me?"

She blinked and nodded, looking dazed. "Luke?" she whispered. "What happened?" She winced. "My shoulder—"

"Come on. I'd better get you inside." Luke hoisted her in his arms, and Clary remembered that she'd always thought he was surprisingly strong for someone who worked in a bookstore. She'd put it down to all that hauling around of heavy boxes. Now she knew better. "Clary. Simon. Come on."

They headed back inside, where Luke laid Maia down on the tattered gray velour couch. He sent Simon running for a blanket and Clary to the kitchen for a wet towel. When Clary returned, she found Maia propped up against one of the cushions, looking flushed and feverish. She was chattering rapidly and nervously to Luke, "I was coming across the lawn when—I smelled something. Something rotten, like garbage. I turned around and it hit me—"

"What hit you?" said Clary, handing Luke the towel.

Maia frowned. "I didn't see it. It knocked me over and then—I tried to kick it off, but it was too fast—"

"I saw it," said Luke, his voice flat. "I was driving up to the house and I saw you crossing the lawn—and then I saw it following you, in the shadows at your heels. I tried to yell out the window to you, but you didn't hear me. Then it knocked you down."

"*What* was following her?" asked Clary.

"It was a Drevak demon," said Luke, his voice grim. "They're blind. They track by smell. I drove the car up onto the lawn and crushed it."

Clary glanced out the window at the truck. The thing that had been twitching under the wheels was gone, unsurprisingly—demons always returned to their home dimensions when they died. "Why would it attack Maia?" She dropped her voice as a thought occurred to her: "Do you think it was Valentine? Looking for werewolf blood for his spell? He got interrupted the last time—"

"I don't think so," Luke said, to her surprise. "Drevak demons aren't bloodsuckers and they definitely couldn't cause the kind of mayhem you saw in the Silent City. Mostly they're spies and messengers. I think Maia just got in its way." He bent to look at Maia, who was moaning softly, her eyes closed. "Can you pull your sleeve up so I can see your shoulder?"

The werewolf girl bit her lip and nodded, then reached over to roll up the sleeve of her sweater. There was a long gash just below her shoulder. Blood had dried to a crust on her arm. Clary sucked her breath in as she saw that the jagged red cut was lined with what looked like thin black needles poking grotesquely out of the skin.

Maia stared down at her arm in obvious horror. "What *are* those?"

"Drevak demons don't have teeth; they have poisonous spines in their mouths," Luke said. "Some of the spines have broken off in your skin."

Maia's teeth had begun to chatter. "Poison? Am I going to die?"

"Not if we work fast," Luke reassured her. "I'm going to have to pull them out, though, and it's going to hurt. Do you think you can handle it?"

Maia's face was contorted into a grimace of pain. She managed to nod. "Just . . . get them out of me."

"Get what out?" asked Simon, coming into the room with a rolled-up blanket. He dropped the blanket when he saw Maia's arm, and took an involuntary step back. "What are *those*?"

"Squeamish about blood, mundane?" Maia said, with a small, twisted smile. Then she gasped. "Oh. It hurts—"

"I know," Luke said, gently wrapping the towel around the lower part of her arm. From his belt he drew a thin-bladed knife. Maia took a look at the knife and squeezed her eyes shut.

"Do what you have to," she said in a small voice. "But—I don't want the others watching."

"I understand." Luke turned to Simon and Clary. "Go in the kitchen, both of you," he said. "Call the Institute. Tell them what's happened and have them send someone. They can't send one of the Brothers, so preferably someone with medical training, or a warlock." Simon and Clary stared at him, paralyzed by the sight of the knife and Maia's slowly purpling arm. "Go!" he said, more sharply, and this time they went.

# 12

## The Hostility of Dreams

**Simon watched Clary as she leaned against the refrigerator,** biting her lip like she always did when she was upset. Often he forgot how small she was, how light-boned and fragile, but at times like this—times when he wanted to put his arms around her—he was restrained by the thought that holding her too hard might hurt her, especially now when he no longer knew his own strength.

Jace, he knew, didn't feel that way. Simon had watched with a sick feeling in his stomach, unable to look away, as Jace had taken Clary in his arms and kissed her with such force Simon had thought one or the both of them might shatter. He'd held her as if he wanted to crush her into himself, as if he could fold the two of them into one person.

Of course Clary was strong, stronger than Simon gave her credit for. She was a Shadowhunter, with all that entailed. But that didn't matter; what they had between them was still as fragile as a flickering candle flame, as delicate as eggshell—and he knew that if it shattered, if he somehow let it break and be destroyed, something inside him would shatter too, something that could never be fixed.

"Simon." Her voice brought him back down to earth. "Simon, are you listening to me?"

"What? Yes, I am. Of course." He leaned against the sink, trying to look as if he'd been paying attention. The tap was dripping, which momentarily distracted him again—each silvery drop of water seemed to shimmer, tear-shaped and perfect, just before it fell. Vampire sight was a strange thing, he thought. His attention kept getting caught by the most ordinary things—the glitter of water, the flowering cracks in a bit of pavement, the sheen of oil on a road—as if he'd never seen them before.

"Simon!" Clary said again, exasperated. He realized she was holding something pink and metallic out to him. Her new cell phone. "I said I want you to call Jace."

That snapped him back to attention. "*Me* call him? He hates me."

"No, he doesn't," she said, though he could tell from the look in her eyes that she only half-believed that. "Anyway, I don't want to talk to him. Please?"

"Fine." He took the phone from her and scrolled through to Jace's number. "What do you want me to say?"

"Just tell him what happened. He'll know what to do."

Jace picked up the phone on the third ring, sounding out of

breath. "Clary," he said, startling Simon until he realized that of course Clary's name would have popped up on Jace's phone. "Clary, are you all right?"

Simon hesitated. There was a tone in Jace's voice he'd never heard before, an anxious concern devoid of sarcasm or defense. Was that how he spoke to Clary when they were alone? Simon glanced at her; she was watching him with wide green eyes, biting unself-consciously on her right index fingernail.

"Clary." Jace again. "I thought you were avoiding me—"

A flash of irritation shot through Simon. *You're her brother,* he wanted to shout down the phone line, *that's all. You don't own her. You've got no right to sound so—so—*

*Brokenhearted.* That was the word. Though he'd never thought of Jace as having a heart to break.

"You were right," he said finally, his voice cold. "She still is. This is Simon."

There was such a long silence that Simon wondered if Jace had dropped the phone.

"Hello?"

"I'm here." Jace's voice was crisp and cool as autumn leaves, all vulnerability gone. "If you're calling me up just to chat, mundane, you must be lonelier than I thought."

"Believe me, I wouldn't be calling you if I had a choice. I'm doing this because of Clary."

"Is she all right?" Jace's voice was still crisp and cool but with an edge to it now, autumn leaves frosted with a sheen of hard ice. "If something's happened to her—"

"Nothing's happened to her." Simon fought to keep the anger out of his voice. As briefly as he could, he gave Jace a rundown of the night's events and Maia's resultant condition. Jace waited until he was done, then rapped out a set of short instructions. Simon listened in a daze and found himself nodding before realizing that of course Jace couldn't see him. He began to speak and realized he was listening to silence; the other boy had hung up. Wordlessly, Simon flipped the phone shut and handed it to Clary. "He's coming here."

She sagged against the sink. "Now?"

"Now. Magnus and Alec will be with him."

"Magnus?" she said dazedly, and then, "Oh, of course. Jace would have been at Magnus's. I was thinking he was at the Institute, but of course he wouldn't have been there. I—"

A harsh cry from the living room cut her off. Her eyes widened. Simon felt the hair on his neck stand up like wires. "It's all right," he said, as soothingly as he could. "Luke wouldn't hurt Maia."

"He *is* hurting her. He has no choice," Clary said. She was shaking her head. "That's how it always is these days. There's never any choice." Maia cried out again and Clary gripped the edge of the counter as if she were in pain herself. "I *hate* this!" she burst out. "I hate all of it! Always being scared, always being hunted, always wondering who's going to get hurt next. I wish I could go back to the way things used to be!"

"But you can't. None of us can," Simon said. "At least you can still go out in daylight."

She turned to him, lips parted, her eyes wide and dark. "Simon, I didn't mean—"

"I know you didn't." He backed away, feeling as if there were something caught in his throat. "I'm going to go see how they're doing." For a moment he thought she might follow him, but she let the kitchen door fall shut between them without protest.

All the lights were on in the living room. Maia lay gray-faced on the couch, the blanket he had brought pulled up to her chest. She was holding a wad of cloth against her right arm; the cloth was partly soaked through with blood. Her eyes were shut.

"Where's Luke?" Simon said, then winced, wondering if his tone was too harsh, too demanding. She looked awful, her eyes sunken into gray hollows, her mouth tight with pain. Her eyes fluttered open and fixed on him.

"Simon," she breathed. "Luke went outside to move the car off the lawn. He was worried about the neighbors."

Simon glanced toward the window. He could see the sweep of the headlights grazing the house as Luke swung the car into the driveway. "How about you?" he asked. "Did he get those things out of your arm?"

She nodded dully. "I'm just so tired," she whispered through cracked lips. "And—thirsty."

"I'll get you some water." There was a pitcher of water and a stack of glasses on the sideboard next to the dining room table. Simon poured a glass full of the tepid liquid and brought it to Maia. His hands were shaking slightly and some of the water spilled as she took the glass from him. She was lifting her head, about to say something—*Thank you*, probably—when their fingers touched and she jerked back so hard that the glass went flying. It hit the edge of the coffee table and shattered, splashing water across the polished wood floor.

"Maia? Are you all right?"

She shrank away from him, her shoulders pressed against the back of the sofa, her lips pulled away from bared teeth. Her eyes had gone a luminous yellow. A low growl came from her throat, the sound of a cornered dog at bay.

"Maia?" Simon said again, appalled.

"*Vampire*," she snarled.

He felt his head rock back as if she had slapped him. "Maia—"

"I thought you were *human*. But you're a monster. A blood-sucking leech."

"I am human—I mean, I *was* human. I got turned. A few days ago." His mind was swimming; he felt dizzy and sick. "Just like you were—"

"Don't ever compare yourself to me!" She had struggled up into a sitting position, those ghastly yellow eyes still on him, scouring him with their disgust. "I'm still human, still alive—you're a dead thing that feeds on blood."

"*Animal* blood—"

"Just because you can't get human, or the Shadowhunters will burn you alive—"

"Maia," he said, and her name in his mouth was half fury and half a plea; he took a step toward her and her hand whipped out, nails shooting out like talons, suddenly impossibly long. They raked his cheek, sending him staggering back, his hand clapped to his face. Blood coursed down his cheek, into his mouth. He tasted the salt of it and his stomach rumbled.

Maia was crouched on the sofa's arm now, her knees drawn up, clawed fingers leaving deep gouges in the gray velveteen. A low growl poured from her throat and her ears were long and flat against her head. When she bared her teeth, they were sharply jagged—not needle-thin like his own, but strong, whitely pointed canines. She had dropped the bloody cloth that had wrapped her arm and he could see the punctures where the spines had gone in, the glimmer of blood, welling, spilling—

A sharp pain in his lower lip told him that his fangs had slid from their sheaths. Some part of him wanted to fight her, to wrestle her down and puncture her skin with his teeth, to gulp her hot blood. The rest of him felt as if it were screaming. He took a step back and then another, his hands out as if he could hold her back.

She tensed to spring, just as the door to the kitchen flew open and Clary burst into the room. She leaped onto the coffee table, landing lightly as a cat. She held something in her hand, something that flashed a bright white-silver when she raised her arm. Simon saw that it was a dagger as elegantly curved as a bird's wing; a dagger that whipped past Maia's hair, millimeters from her face, and sank to the hilt in gray velveteen. Maia tried to pull away and gasped; the blade had gone through her sleeve and pinned it to the sofa.

Clary yanked the blade back. It was one of Luke's. The moment she'd cracked the kitchen door and gotten a look at what was going on in the living room, she'd made a beeline for the personal weapons stash he kept in his office. Maia might be weakened and sick, but she'd looked mad enough to kill, and Clary didn't doubt her abilities.

"What the hell is it with you?" As if from a distance, Clary heard herself speaking, and the steel in her own voice astonished her. "Werewolves, vampires—you're both Downworlders."

"Werewolves don't hurt people, or each other. Vampires are murderers. One killed a boy down at the Hunter's Moon just the other day—"

"That wasn't a vampire." Clary saw Maia blanch at the certainty in her voice. "And if you could stop blaming each other all the time for every bad thing that happens Downworld, maybe the Nephilim would start taking you seriously and actually *do* something about it." She turned to Simon. The vicious cuts across his cheek were already healing to silvery red lines. "Are you all right?"

"Yes." His voice was barely audible. She could see the hurt in his eyes, and for a moment she wrestled the urge to call Maia a number of unprintable names. "I'm fine."

Clary turned back to the werewolf girl. "You're lucky he's not as much of a bigot as you are, or I'd complain to the Clave and make the whole pack pay for your behavior."

Maia bristled. "You don't get it. Vampires are what they are because they're infected with demon energies—"

"So are lycanthropes!" Clary said. "I may not know much, but I do know that."

"But that's the problem. The demon energies change us, make us different—you can call it a sickness or whatever you want, but the demons who created vampires and the demons who created werewolves came from species who were at war with each other. They hated each other, so it's in our blood to hate each other too. We can't help it. A werewolf and a vampire can never be friends because of it." She looked at Simon. Her eyes were bright with anger and something else. "You'll start hating me soon enough," she said. "You'll hate Luke, too. You won't be able to help it."

"Hate *Luke*?" Simon was ashen, but before Clary could reassure him, the front door banged open. She looked around, expecting Luke, but it wasn't Luke. It was Jace. He was all in black, two seraph blades stuck through the belt that circled his narrow hips. Alec and Magnus were just behind him, Magnus in a long, swirling cape that looked as if it were decorated with bits of crushed glass.

Jace's golden eyes, with the precision of a laser, fixed immediately on Clary. If she'd thought he might look apologetic, concerned, or even ashamed after all that had happened, she was wrong. All he looked was angry. "What," he said, with a sharp and deliberate annoyance, "do you think you're doing?"

Clary glanced down at herself. She was still perched on the coffee table, knife in hand. She fought the urge to hide it behind her back. "We had an incident. I took care of it."

"Really." Jace's voice dripped sarcasm. "Do you even know how to use that knife, Clarissa? *Without* poking a hole in yourself or any innocent bystanders?"

"I didn't hurt anyone," Clary said between her teeth.

"She stabbed the couch," said Maia in a dull voice, her eyes falling shut. Her cheeks were still flushed red with fever and rage, but the rest of her face was alarmingly pale.

Simon looked at her worriedly. "I think she's getting worse."

Magnus cleared his throat. When Simon didn't move, he said, "Get out of the *way*, mundane," in a tone of immense annoyance. He flung his cloak back as he stalked across the room to where Maia lay on the couch. "I take it you're my patient?" he inquired, gazing down at her through glitter-crusted lashes.

Maia stared up at him with unfocused eyes.

"I'm Magnus Bane," he went on in a soothing tone, stretching out his ringed hands. Blue sparks had begun to dance between them like bioluminescence dancing in water. "I'm the warlock who's here to cure you. Didn't they tell you I was coming?"

"I know who you are, but . . ." Maia looked dazed. "You look so . . . so . . . *shiny*."

Alec made a noise that sounded very much like a laugh stifled by a cough as Magnus's thin hands wove a shimmering blue curtain of magic around the werewolf girl.

Jace wasn't laughing. "Where," he asked, "is Luke?"

"He's outside," Simon said. "He was moving the truck off the lawn."

Jace and Alec exchanged a quick look.

"Funny," Jace said. He didn't sound amused. "I didn't see him when we were coming up the stairs."

A thin tendril of panic unfurled like a leaf inside Clary's chest. "Did you see his pickup?"

"I saw it," Alec said. "It was in the driveway. The lights were off."

At that even Magnus, intent on Maia, looked up. Through the net of enchantment he had woven around himself and the werewolf girl, his features seemed blurred and indistinct, as if he were looking at them through water. "I don't like it," he said, his voice sounding hollow and far away. "Not after a Drevak attack. They roam in packs."

Jace's hand was already reaching for one of his seraph blades. "I'll go check on him. Alec, you stay here, keep the house secure."

Clary jumped down from the table. "I'm coming with you."

"No, you're not." He headed for the door, not glancing behind him to see if she was following.

She put on a burst of speed and threw herself between him and the front door. "*Stop*."

For a moment she thought he was going to keep right on

going even if he had to walk *through* her, but he paused, just inches from her, so close she could feel his breath stir her hair when he spoke. "I *will* knock you down if I have to, Clarissa."

"Stop calling me that."

"Clary," he said in a low voice, and the sound of her name in his mouth was so intimate that a shudder ran up her spine. The gold in his eyes had turned hard, metallic. She wondered for a moment if he might actually spring at her, what it would be like if he struck her, knocked her down, grabbed her wrists even. Fighting to him was like sex to other people. The thought of him touching her like that brought the blood to her cheeks in a hot flood.

She spoke around the breathless catch in her voice. "He's my uncle, not yours—"

A savage humor flashed across his face. "Any uncle of yours is an uncle of mine, darling sister," he said, "and he's no blood relation to either of us."

"Jace—"

"Besides, I haven't got time to Mark you," he said, lazy gold eyes raking her, "and all you've got is that knife. It won't be much use if it's demons we're dealing with."

She jammed the knife into the wall beside the door, point-first, and was rewarded by the look of surprise on his face. "So what? You've got two seraph blades; give me one."

"Oh, for the love of—" It was Simon, hands jammed into his pockets, eyes burning like black coals in his white face. "*I'll* go."

Clary said, "Simon, don't—"

"At least I'm not wasting my time standing here flirting while we don't know what's happened to Luke." He gestured for her to move aside from the door.

Jace's lips thinned. "We'll *all* go." To Clary's surprise he jerked a seraph blade out of his belt and handed it to her. "Take it."

"What's its name?" she asked, moving away from the door.

"Nakir."

Clary had left her jacket in the kitchen, and the cold air sheeting off the East River cut through her thin shirt the moment she stepped out onto the dark porch. "Luke?" she called. "*Luke!*"

The truck was pulled up in the driveway, one of the doors hanging open. The roof light was on, shedding a faint glow. Jace frowned. "The keys are in the ignition. The car's idling."

Simon shut the front door behind them. "How do you know that?"

"I can hear it." Jace looked at Simon speculatively. "And so could you if you tried, bloodsucker." He loped down the stairs, a faint chuckle drifting behind him on the wind.

"I think I liked 'mundane' better than 'bloodsucker,'" Simon muttered.

"With Jace, you don't really get to choose your insulting nickname." Clary felt in her jeans pocket until her fingers encountered cool, smooth stone. She raised the witchlight in her hand, its glow raying out between her fingers like the light of a tiny sun. "Come on."

Jace had been right; the truck *was* idling. Clary smelled the exhaust as they approached, her heart sinking. Luke would never have left the car door open and the keys in the ignition like that unless something had happened.

Jace was circling the truck, frowning. "Bring that witch-light closer." He knelt down in the grass, running his fingers lightly over it. From an inner pocket he drew an object Clary recognized: a smooth piece of metal, engraved all over with delicate runes. A Sensor. Jace ran it over the grass and it obliged with a series of loud clicking noises, like a Geiger counter gone berserk. "Definite demonic action. I'm picking up heavy traces."

"Could that be left over from the demon who attacked Maia?" Simon asked.

"The levels are too high. There's been more than one demon here tonight." Jace rose to his feet, all business. "Maybe you two should go back inside. Send Alec out here. He's dealt with this sort of thing before."

"Jace—" Clary was furious all over again. She broke off as something caught her eye. It was a flicker of movement, across the street, down by the cement rock-strewn bank of the East River. There was something about the movement—an angle as a gesture caught the light, something too quick, too *elongated* to be human. . . .

Clary flung an arm out, pointing. "Look! By the water!"

Jace's gaze followed hers and he sucked in his breath. Then he was running, and they were running after him, over the asphalt of Kent Street and onto the scrubby grass that bordered the waterfront. The witchlight swung in Clary's hand as she ran, lighting bits of the riverbank with haphazard illumination: a patch of weeds there, a jut of broken concrete that nearly tripped her up, a heap of trash and broken glass—and then, as they came in clear sight of the lapping water, the crumpled figure of a man.

It was Luke—Clary saw that instantly, though the two dark, humped shapes crouching over him blocked his face from her view. He was on his back, so close to the water that she wondered for a panicked moment if the hunched creatures were holding him under, trying to drown him. Then they drew back, hissing through perfectly circular lipless mouths, and she saw that his head was resting on the gravelly riverbank. His face was slack and gray.

"Raum demons," Jace whispered.

Simon's eyes were wide. "Are those the same things that attacked Maia—?"

"No. These are much worse." Jace gestured at Simon and Clary to get behind him. "You two, stay back." He raised his seraph blade. "*Israfiel!*" he cried, and there was a sudden hot burst of light as it blazed up. Jace leaped forward, sweeping his weapon at the nearest of the demons. In the light of the seraph blade, the demon's appearance was unpleasantly visible: dead-white, scaled skin, a black hole for a mouth, bulging, toadlike eyes, and arms that ended in tentacles where hands should have been. It lashed out now with those tentacles, whipping them toward Jace with incredible speed.

But Jace was faster. There was a nasty *snick* sort of noise as Israfiel sheared through the demon's wrist and its tentacled appendage flew through the air. The tentacle tip came to rest at Clary's feet, still twitching. It was gray-white, tipped with blood-red suckers. Inside each sucker was a cluster of tiny, needle-sharp teeth.

Simon made a gagging noise. Clary was inclined to agree. She kicked at the spasming clot of tentacles, sending it rolling across the dirty grass. When she looked up, she saw that Jace had knocked the injured demon down and they were tumbling together across the rocks at the river's edge. The glow of Jace's seraph blade sent elegant arcs of light shattering across the water as he writhed and twisted to avoid the creature's remaining tentacles—not to mention the black blood spraying from its severed wrist. Clary hesitated—should she go to Luke or run to help Jace?—and in that moment of hesitation she heard Simon shout, "Clary, watch *out*!" and turned to see the second demon lunging straight at her.

There was no time to reach for the seraph blade at her belt, no time to remember and shout out its name. She threw her hands out and the demon struck her, knocking her backward. She went down with a cry, hitting her shoulder painfully against the uneven ground. Slick tentacles rasped against her skin. One braceleted her arm, squeezing painfully; the other whipped forward, wrapping her throat.

She grabbed frantically at her neck, trying to pull the lashing, flexible limb away from her windpipe. Already her lungs were aching. She kicked and twisted—

And suddenly the pressure was gone; the thing was off her. She sucked in a whistling breath and rolled to her knees. The demon was in a half crouch, staring at her with black, pupilless eyes. Getting ready to lunge again? She grabbed for her blade, spat: "*Nakir*," and a spear of light shot from her fingers. She'd never held an angel knife before. The hilt of it trembled and vibrated in her hand; it felt alive. "*NAKIR!*" she cried, staggering to her feet, the blade outstretched and pointed at the Raum demon.

To her surprise, the demon skittered backward, tentacles waving, almost as if it were—but this wasn't possible—*afraid* of her. She saw Simon, running toward her, a length of what looked like steel pipe in his hand; behind him, Jace was getting to his knees. She couldn't see the demon he'd been fighting; perhaps he'd killed it. As for the second Raum demon, its mouth was open and it was making a distressed, hooting noise, like a monstrous owl. Abruptly, it turned and, with tentacles waving, dashed toward the bank and leaped into the river. A gush of blackish water splashed upward, and then the demon was gone, vanishing beneath the river's surface without even a telltale spray of bubbles to mark its place.

Jace reached her side just as it vanished. He was bent over, panting, smeared with black demon blood. "What—happened?" he demanded between gasps for breath.

"I don't know," Clary admitted. "It came at me—I tried to fight it off but it was too fast—and then it just *left*. Like it saw something that scared it."

"Are you all right?" It was Simon, skidding to a stop in front of her, not panting—he didn't breathe anymore, she reminded herself—but anxious, clutching a thick length of pipe in his hand.

"Where did you get that?" Jace demanded.

"I wrenched it off the side of a telephone pole." Simon looked as if the recollection surprised him. "I guess you can do anything when your adrenaline is up."

"Or when you have the unholy strength of the damned," Jace said.

"Oh, shut up, both of you," snapped Clary, earning herself a martyred look from Simon and a leer from Jace. She pushed past the two of them, heading for the riverbank. "Or have you forgotten about Luke?"

Luke was still unconscious, but breathing. He was as pale as

Maia had been, and his sleeve was torn across the shoulder. When Clary drew the blood-stiffened fabric away from the skin, working as gingerly as she could, she saw that across his shoulder was a cluster of circular red wounds where a tentacle had gripped him. Each was oozing a mixture of blood and blackish fluid. She sucked in her breath. "We have to get him inside."

Magnus was waiting for them on the front porch when Simon and Jace carried Luke, slumped between them, up the stairs. Having finished with Maia, Magnus had put her to bed in Luke's room, so they set Luke down on the sofa where she'd been lying and let Magnus go to work on him.

"Will he be all right?" Clary demanded, hovering around the couch as Magnus summoned blue fire that shimmered between his hands.

"He'll be fine. Raum poison is a little more complex than a Drevak sting, but nothing I can't handle." Magnus motioned her away. "At least not if you get back and let me work."

Reluctantly, she sank down into an armchair. Jace and Alec were over by the window, heads close together. Jace was gesturing with his hands. She guessed he was explaining to Alec what had happened with the demons. Simon, looking uncomfortable, was leaning against the wall beside the kitchen door. He seemed lost in thought. Not wanting to look at Luke's slack gray face and sunken eyes, Clary let her gaze rest on Simon, gauging the ways in which he looked both familiar and very alien. Without the glasses, his eyes seemed twice their size, and very dark, more black than brown. His skin was pale and smooth as white marble, traced with darker veins at the temples and the sharply angled cheekbones. Even his hair seemed darker, in stark contrast to the white of his skin. She remembered looking at the crowd in Raphael's hotel, wondering why there didn't seem to be any ugly or unattractive vampires. Maybe there was some rule about not making vampires out of the physically unappealing, she'd thought then, but now she wondered if the vampirism itself wasn't transformative, smoothing out blotched skin, adding color and luster to eyes and hair. Perhaps it was an evolutionary advantage to the species. Good looks could only help vampires lure their prey.

She realized then that Simon was staring back at her, his dark eyes wide. Snapping out of her reverie, she turned back to see Magnus getting to his feet. The blue light was gone. Luke's eyes were still closed but the ugly grayish tint had gone from his skin, and his breathing was deep and regular.

"He's all right!" Clary exclaimed, and Alec, Jace, and Simon came hurrying over to have a look. Simon slid his hand into Clary's, and she wrapped her fingers around his, glad for the reassurance.

"So he'll live?" Simon said, as Magnus sank down onto the armrest of the nearest chair. He looked exhausted, drawn and bluish. "You're sure?"

"Yes, I'm sure," Magnus said. "I'm the High Warlock of Brooklyn; I know what I'm doing." His eyes moved to Jace, who had just said something to Alec in a voice too low for any of the rest of them to hear. "Which reminds me," Magnus went on, sounding stiff—and Clary had never heard him sound stiff before—"that I'm not exactly sure what it is you think you're doing, calling on me every time one of you has so much as an ingrown toenail that needs clipping. As High Warlock, my time is valuable. There are plenty of lesser warlocks who'd be happy to do a job for you at a greatly reduced rate."

Clary blinked at him in surprise. "You're *charging* us? But Luke is a friend!"

Magnus took a thin blue cigarette out of his shirt pocket. "Not a friend of mine," he said. "I met him only on the few occasions when your mother brought him along when your memory spells were being refreshed." He passed his hand across the cigarette's tip and it lit with a multicolored flame. "Did you think I was helping you out of the goodness of my heart? Or am I just the only warlock you happen to know?"

Jace had listened to this short speech with a smolder of fury sparking his amber eyes to gold. "No," he said now, "but you *are* the only warlock we know who happens to be dating a friend of ours."

For a moment everyone stared at him—Alec in sheer horror, Magnus in astonished anger, and Clary and Simon in surprise. It was Alec who spoke first, his voice shaking. "Why would you say something like that?"

Jace looked baffled. "Something like what?"

"That I'm dating—that we're—it's not *true*," Alec said, his voice rising and dropping several octaves as he fought to control it.

Jace looked at him steadily. "I didn't say he was dating *you*," he said, "but funny that you knew just what I meant, isn't it?"

"We're not dating," Alec said again.

"Oh?" Magnus said. "So you're just that friendly with everybody, is that it?"

"*Magnus.*" Alec stared imploringly at the warlock. Magnus,

however, it seemed, had had enough. He crossed his arms over his chest and leaned back in silence, regarding the scene before him with slitted eyes.

Alec turned to Jace. "You don't—," he began. "I mean, you couldn't possibly think—"

Jace was shaking his head in puzzlement. "What I don't get is you going to all these lengths to hide your relationship with Magnus from me when it's not as if I would mind if you *did* tell me about it."

If he meant his words to be reassuring, it was clear that they weren't. Alec went a pale gray color, and said nothing. Jace turned to Magnus. "Help me convince him," he said, "that I really don't care."

"Oh," Magnus said quietly, "I think he believes you about that."

"Then I don't . . ." Bewilderment was plain on Jace's face, and for a moment Clary saw Magnus's expression and knew he was strongly tempted to answer. Moved by a hasty pity for Alec, she pulled her hand out of Simon's and said,

"Jace, that's enough. Let it alone."

"Let what alone?" Luke inquired. Clary whirled around to find him sitting up on the couch, wincing a little with pain but looking otherwise healthy enough.

"Luke!" She darted to the side of the sofa, considered hugging him, saw the way he was holding his shoulder, and decided against it. "Do you remember what happened?"

"Not really." Luke passed a hand across his face. "The last thing I remember was going out to the truck. Something hit my shoulder and jerked me sideways. I remember the most incredible pain—Anyway, I must have passed out after that.

The next thing I knew I was listening to five people shouting. What was all that about, anyway?"

"Nothing," chorused Clary, Simon, Alec, Magnus, and Jace, in surprising and probably never-to-be-repeated unison.

Despite his obvious exhaustion, Luke's eyebrows shot up. But "I see," was all he said.

Since Maia was still asleep in Luke's bedroom, he announced that he'd be just fine on the couch. Clary tried to give him the bed in her room, but he refused to take it. Giving up, she headed into the narrow hallway to retrieve sheets and blankets from the linen closet. She was dragging a comforter down from a high shelf when she sensed someone behind her. Clary whirled, dropping the blanket she'd been holding into a soft pile at her feet.

It was Jace. "Sorry to startle you."

"It's fine." She bent to retrieve the blanket.

"Actually, I'm not sorry," he said. "That's the most emotion I've seen from you in days."

"I haven't seen you in days."

"And whose fault is that? I've called you. You don't pick up the phone. And it's not as if I could simply come see you. I've been in prison, in case you've forgotten."

"Not exactly prison." She tried to sound light as she straightened up. "You've got Magnus to keep you company. And *Gilligan's Island.*"

Jace suggested that the cast of *Gilligan's Island* could do something anatomically unlikely with themselves.

Clary sighed. "Aren't you supposed to be leaving with Magnus?"

His mouth twisted and she saw something fracture behind his eyes, a starburst of pain. "Can't wait to get rid of me?"

"No." She hugged the blanket against herself and stared down at his hands, unable to meet his eyes. His slender fingers were scarred and beautiful, with the faint white band of paler skin still visible where he had worn the Morgenstern ring on his right index finger. The yearning to touch him was so bad she wanted to let go of the blankets and scream. "I mean, no, it's not that. I don't hate you, Jace."

"I don't hate you, either."

She looked up at him, relieved. "I'm glad to hear that—"

"I wish I could hate you," he said. His voice was light, his mouth curved in an unconcerned half smile, his eyes sick with misery. "I want to hate you. I try to hate you. It would be so much easier if I did hate you. Sometimes I think I do hate you and then I see you and I—"

Her hands had grown numb with their grip on the blanket. "And you what?"

"What do you *think*?" Jace shook his head. "Why should I tell you everything about how I feel when you never tell me anything? It's like banging my head on a wall, except at least if I were banging my head on a wall, I'd be able to make myself stop."

Clary's lips were trembling so violently that she found it hard to speak. "Do you think it's easy for me?" she demanded. "Do you think—"

"Clary?" It was Simon, coming into the hallway with that new soundless grace of his, startling her so badly that she dropped the blanket again. She turned aside, but not fast enough to hide her expression from him, or the telltale shine in her eyes. "I see," he said, after a long pause. "Sorry to interrupt." He vanished back into the living room, leaving Clary staring after him through a wavering lens of tears.

"*Damn* it." She turned on Jace. "What is it about you?" she said, with more savagery than she'd intended. "Why do you have to ruin *everything*?" She shoved the blanket at him hastily and darted out of the room after Simon.

He was already out the front door. She caught up to him on the porch, letting the front door bang shut behind her. "Simon! Where are you going?"

He turned around almost reluctantly. "Home. It's late—I don't want to get caught here with the sun coming up."

Since the sun wasn't coming up for hours, this struck Clary as a feeble excuse. "You know you're welcome to stay and sleep here during the day if you want to avoid your mom. You can sleep in my room—"

"I don't think that's a good idea."

"Why not? I don't understand why you're going."

He smiled at her. It was a sad smile with something else underneath. "You know what the worst thing I can imagine is?"

She blinked at him. "No."

"Not trusting someone I love."

She put her hand on his sleeve. He didn't move away, but he didn't respond to her touch, either. "Do you mean—"

"Yes," he said, knowing what she was about to ask. "I mean you."

"But you *can* trust me."

"I used to think I could," he said. "But I get the feeling you'd rather pine over someone you can never possibly be with than try being with someone you can."

There was no point pretending. "Just give me time," she said. "I just need some time to get over—to get over it all."

"You're not going to tell me I'm wrong, are you?" he said. His eyes looked very wide and dark in the dim porch light. "Not this time."

"Not this time. I'm sorry."

"Don't be." He turned away from her and her outstretched hand, heading for the porch steps. "At least it's the truth."

*For whatever that's worth.* She shoved her hands into her pockets, watching him as he walked away from her until he was swallowed up by the darkness.

It turned out that Magnus and Jace weren't leaving after all; Magnus wanted to spend a few more hours at the house to make sure that Maia and Luke were recovering as expected. After a few minutes of awkward conversation with a bored Magnus while Jace, sitting on Luke's piano bench and industriously studying some sheet music, ignored her, Clary decided to go to bed early.

But sleep didn't come. She could hear Jace's soft piano playing through the walls, but that wasn't what was keeping her awake. She was thinking of Simon, leaving for a house that no longer felt like home to him, of the despair in Jace's voice as he said *I want to hate you*, and of Magnus, not telling Jace the truth: that Alec did not want Jace to know about his relationship because he was still in love with him. She thought of the satisfaction it would have brought Magnus to say the words out loud, to acknowledge what the truth was, and the fact that he hadn't said them—

had let Alec go on lying and pretending—because that was what Alec wanted, and Magnus cared about Alec enough to give him that. Maybe it was true what the Seelie Queen had said, after all: Love made you a liar.

# 13

## A Host of Rebel Angels

**There are three distinct sections to Ravel's *Gaspard de la*** *Nuit*; Jace had played his way through the first when he got up from the piano, went into the kitchen, picked up Luke's phone, and made a single call. Then he went back to the piano and the *Gaspard*.

He was halfway through the third section when he saw a light sweep across Luke's front lawn. It cut off a moment later, plunging the view from the front window into darkness, but Jace was already on his feet and reaching for his jacket.

He closed Luke's front door behind him soundlessly and loped down the front steps two at a time. On the lawn by the footpath was a motorcycle, the engine still rumbling. It had a weirdly organic look to it: Pipes like ropy veins wound up and over the chassis, and the single headlight, now dim, resembled a gleaming eye. In a way, it looked as alive as the boy who was leaning against the cycle, looking at Jace curiously. He was wearing a brown leather jacket and his dark hair curled down to the collar of it and fell over his narrowed eyes. He was grinning, exposing pointed white teeth. Of course, Jace thought, neither the boy nor the motorcycle was *really* alive; they both ran on demon energies, fed by the night.

"Raphael," Jace said, by way of greeting.

"You see," Raphael said, "I have brought it, as you asked me to."

"I see that."

"Though, I might add, I have been very curious as to why you should want such a thing as a demonic motorcycle. They are not exactly Covenant, for one thing, and for another, it is rumored you already have one."

"I do have one," Jace admitted, circling the cycle so as to examine it from all angles. "But it's on the roof of the Institute, and I can't get to it right now."

Raphael chuckled softly. "It seems we're both unwelcome at the Institute."

"You bloodsuckers still on the Most Wanted list?"

Raphael leaned to the side and spit, delicately, onto the ground. "They accuse us of murders," he said angrily. "The death of the were-creature, the faerie, even the warlock, though I have told them we do not drink warlock blood. It is bitter and can work strange changes in those who consume it."

"You told Maryse this?"

"Maryse." Raphael's eyes glittered. "I could not speak with her if I wanted to. All decisions are made through the

Inquisitor now, all inquiries and requests routed through her. It is a bad situation, friend, a bad situation."

"You're telling me," said Jace. "And we're not friends. I agreed not to tell the Clave what happened with Simon because I needed your help. Not because I like you."

Raphael grinned, his teeth flashing white in the dark. "You like me." He tilted his head to the side. "It is odd," he reflected. "I would have thought you would seem different now that you are in disgrace with the Clave. No longer their favored son. I thought some of that arrogance might have been beaten out of you. But you are just the same."

"I believe in consistency," Jace said. "Are you going to let me have the bike, or not? I've only got a few hours until sunrise."

"I take it that means you're not going to give me a ride home?" Raphael moved gracefully away from the motorcycle; as he moved, Jace caught the bright glint of the gold chain around his throat.

"Nope." Jace climbed onto the bike. "But you can sleep in the cellar under the house if you're worried about sunrise."

"Mmm." Raphael seemed thoughtful; he was a few inches shorter than Jace, and though he looked younger physically, his eyes were much older. "So are we even for Simon now, Shadowhunter?"

Jace gunned the bike, turning it toward the river. "We'll never be even, bloodsucker, but at least this is a start."

Jace hadn't ridden a cycle since the weather had changed, and he was caught short by the icy wind that arced off the river, piercing his thin jacket and the denim of his jeans with dozens of ice-tipped needles of cold. Jace shivered, glad that at least he had worn leather gloves to protect his hands.

Though the sun had just gone down, the world already seemed leached of color. The river was the color of steel, the sky gray as a dove, the horizon a thick black painted line in the distance. Lights winked and glittered along the spans of the Williamsburg and Manhattan Bridges. The air tasted of snow, though winter was months away.

The last time he'd flown over the river, Clary had been with him, her arms around him and her small hands bunched in the material of his jacket. He hadn't been cold then. He banked the cycle viciously and felt it lurch sideways; he thought he saw his own shadow flung against the water, tilted crazily to the side. As he righted himself, he saw it: a ship with black metal sides, unmarked and almost lightless, its prow a narrow blade scything the water ahead. It reminded him of a shark, lean and quick and deadly.

He braked and drifted carefully downward, soundless, a leaf caught in a tide. He didn't feel as if he were falling, more as if the ship were lifting itself to meet him, buoyed on a rising current. The wheels of the cycle touched down onto the deck and he glided slowly to a stop. There was no need to cut the engine; he swung his legs off the cycle and its rumble subsided to a growl, then a purr, then silence. When he glanced back at it, it looked a little as if it were glowering at him, like an unhappy dog after being told to stay.

He grinned at it. "I'll be back for you," he said. "I've got to check out this boat first."

There was a lot to check out. He was standing on a wide deck, the water to his left. Everything was painted black: the deck, the metal guardrail that encircled it; even the windows in the long, narrow cabin were blacked out. The boat was bigger than he'd expected it to be: probably the length of a football field, maybe more. It wasn't like any ship he'd ever seen before: too big to be a yacht, too small to be a naval vessel, and he'd never seen a ship where everything was painted black. Jace wondered where his father had gotten it.

Leaving the bike, he started a slow circuit around the deck. The clouds had cleared and the stars shone down, impossibly bright. He could see the city illuminated on both sides of him as if he stood in an empty narrow-walled passage made of light. His boots echoed hollowly against the deck. He wondered suddenly if Valentine was even here. Jace had rarely been anywhere that seemed so thoroughly deserted.

He paused for a moment at the bow of the boat, looking out over the river that sliced between Manhattan and Long Island like a scar. The water was churned to gray peaks, lashed with silver along their tops, and a strong and steady wind was blowing, the kind of wind that blew only across water. He stretched his arms out and let the wind take his jacket and blow it back like wings, whip his hair across his face, sting his eyes to tears.

There had been a lake by the manor house in Idris. His father had taught him to sail on it, taught him the language of wind and water, of buoyancy and air. *All men should know how to sail*, he had said. It was one of the few times he'd ever spoken like that, saying *all men* and not *all Shadowhunters*. It was a brief reminder that whatever else Jace might be, he was still part of the human race.

Turning away from the bow with his eyes stinging, Jace saw a door set into the wall of the cabin between two blacked-out windows. Crossing the deck quickly, he tried the handle; it was locked. With his stele, he carved a quick set of Opening runes into the metal and the door swung open, the hinges shrieking in protest and shedding red flakes of rust. Jace ducked under the low doorway and found himself in a dimly lit metal stairwell. The air smelled of rust and disuse. He took another step forward and the door shut behind him with an echoing metallic slam, plunging him into darkness.

He swore, feeling for the witchlight rune-stone in his pocket. His gloves felt suddenly clunky, his fingers stiff with cold. He was colder inside than he had been out on the deck. The air was like ice. He drew his hand out of his pocket, shivering, and not just from the temperature. The hair along the back of his neck was prickling, his every nerve screaming. Something was wrong.

He raised the rune-stone and it flared into light, making his eyes water even more. Through the blur he saw the slender figure of a girl standing in front of him, her hands clasped across her chest, her hair a splash of red color against the black metal all around them.

His hand shook, scattering leaping darts of witchlight as if a host of fireflies had risen out of the darkness below. "*Clary?*"

She stared at him, white-faced, her lips trembling. Questions died in his throat—what was she doing here? How had she gotten to the ship? A spasm of terror gripped him, worse than any fear he'd ever felt for himself. Something was wrong with her, with Clary. He took a step forward, just as she moved her hands away from her chest and held them out to him. They were sticky with blood. Blood covered the front of her white dress like a scarlet bib.

He caught her with one arm as she sagged forward. He nearly dropped the witchlight as her weight fell against him. He could feel the beat of her heart, the brush of her soft hair against his chin, so familiar. The scent of her was different, though. That scent he associated with Clary, a mix of floral soap and clean cotton, was gone; he smelled only blood and metal. Her head tilted back, her eyes rolling up to the whites. The wild beating of her heart was slowing—stopping—

"No!" He shook her, hard enough that her head rolled against his arm. "Clary! Wake up!" He shook her again, and this time her lashes fluttered; he felt his relief like a sudden cold sweat, and then her eyes were open, but they were no longer green; they were an opaque and glowing white, white and blinding as headlights on a dark road, white as the clamoring noise inside his own mind. *I've seen those eyes before*, he thought, and then darkness surged up over him like a wave, bringing silence with it.

There were holes punched into the darkness, glimmering dots of light against shadow. Jace closed his eyes, trying to calm his own breathing. There was a coppery taste in his mouth, like blood, and he could tell that he was lying on a cold metal surface and that the chill was seeping through his clothes and into his skin. He counted backward from one hundred inside his head until his breathing slowed. Then he opened his eyes again.

The darkness was still there, but it had resolved itself into familiar night sky punctuated by stars. He was on the deck of the ship, flat on his back in the shadow of the Brooklyn Bridge, which loomed at the ship's bow like a gray mountain of metal and stone. He groaned and lifted himself onto his elbows—then froze as he became aware of another shadow, this one recognizably human, leaning over him. "That was a nasty knock to the head you got," said the voice that haunted his nightmares. "How do you feel?"

Jace sat up and immediately regretted it as his stomach lurched. If he'd eaten anything in the past ten hours, he was fairly sure he would have thrown it up. As it was, the sour taste of bile flooded his mouth. "I feel like hell."

Valentine smiled. He was sitting on a stack of empty, flattened boxes, wearing a neat gray suit and tie, as if he were seated behind the elegant mahogany desk at the Wayland manor house in Idris. "I have another obvious question for you. How did you find me?"

"I tortured it out of your Raum demon," said Jace. "You're the one who taught me where they keep their hearts. I threatened it and it told me—well, they're not very bright, but it managed to tell me it had come from a ship on the river. I looked up and saw the shadow of your boat on the water. It told me you'd summoned it too, but I already knew that."

"I see." Valentine seemed to be hiding a smile. "Next time you should at least tell me you're coming before you drop by. It would save you a nasty run-in with my guards."

"Guards?" Jace propped himself against the cold metal railing and took in deep breaths of clean, cold air. "You mean demons, don't you? You used the Sword to summon them."

"I don't deny that," Valentine said. "Lucian's beasts shattered my army of Forsaken, and I had neither time nor inclination to create more. Now that I have the Mortal Sword, I no longer need them. I have others."

Jace thought of Clary, bloody and dying in his arms. He put

a hand to his forehead. It was cool where the metal railing had touched it. "That thing in the stairwell," he said. "It wasn't Clary, was it?"

"Clary?" Valentine sounded mildly surprised. "Is that what you saw?"

"Why wouldn't it be what I saw?" Jace struggled to keep his voice flat, nonchalant. He wasn't unfamiliar or uncomfortable with secrets—either his own or other people's—but his feelings for Clary were something he had told himself he could bear only if he did not look at them too closely.

But this was Valentine. He looked at everything closely, studying it, analyzing in what way it could be turned to his advantage. In that way he reminded Jace of the Queen of the Seelie Court: cool, menacing, calculating.

"What you encountered in the stairwell," Valentine said, "was Agramon—the Demon of Fear. Agramon takes the form of whatever most terrifies you. When it is done feeding on your terror, it kills you, presuming you are still alive at that point. Most men—and women—die of fear before that. You are to be congratulated for holding out as long as you did."

"Agramon?" Jace was astonished. "That's a Greater Demon. Where did you get hold of *that*?"

"I paid a young and hubristic warlock to summon it for me. He thought that if the demon remained inside his pentagram, he could control it. Unfortunately for him, his greatest fear was that a demon he summoned would break the wards of the pentagram and attack him, and that's exactly what happened when Agramon came through."

"So that's how he died," Jace said.

"How who died?"

"The warlock," Jace said. "His name was Elias. He was sixteen. But you knew that, didn't you? The Ritual of Infernal Conversion—"

Valentine laughed. "You *have* been busy, haven't you? So you know why I sent those demons to Lucian's house, don't you?"

"You wanted Maia," said Jace. "Because she's a werewolf child. You need her blood."

"I sent the Drevak demons to spy out what there was to see at Lucian's and report back to me," Valentine said. "Lucian killed one of them, but when the other reported the presence of a young lycanthrope—"

"You sent the Raum demons to take her." Jace felt suddenly very tired. "Because Luke is fond of her and you wanted to hurt him if you could." He paused, and then said, in a measured tone: "Which is pretty low, even for you."

For a moment a spark of anger lit Valentine's eyes; then he threw his head back and roared with mirth. "I admire your stubbornness. It's so much like mine." He got to his feet then and held a hand out for Jace to take. "Come. Walk around the deck with me. There's something I want to show you."

Jace wanted to spurn the offered hand, but wasn't sure, considering the pain in his head, that he could make it to his feet unaided. Besides, it was probably better not to anger his father so soon; whatever Valentine might say about prizing Jace's rebelliousness, he had never had much patience with disobedient behavior.

Valentine's hand was cool and dry, his grip oddly reassuring. When Jace was on his feet, Valentine released his hold and drew a stele out of his pocket. "Let me take those injuries away," he said, reaching out for his son.

Jace drew away—after a second's hesitation that Valentine would surely have noticed. "I don't want your help."

Valentine put the stele away. "As you like." He began to walk, and Jace, after a moment, followed him, jogging to catch up. He knew his father well enough to know he would never turn around to see if Jace had pursued him, but would just expect that he had and begin talking accordingly.

He was right. By the time Jace reached his father's side, Valentine had already started speaking. He had his hands loosely clasped behind his back and moved with an easy, careless grace, unusual in a big, broad-shouldered man. He leaned forward as he walked, almost as if he were striding into a heavy wind.

". . . if I recall correctly," Valentine was saying, "you are in fact familiar with Milton's *Paradise Lost*?"

"You only made me read it ten or fifteen times," said Jace. "It's better to reign in hell than serve in heaven, etcetera, and so on."

"*Non serviam*," said Valentine. "'I will not serve.' It's what Lucifer had inscribed upon his banner when he rode with his host of rebel angels against a corrupt authority."

"What's your point? That you're on the devil's side?"

"Some say Milton was on the devil's side himself. His Satan is certainly a more interesting figure than his God." They had nearly reached the front of the ship. He stopped and leaned against the guardrail.

Jace joined him there. They had passed the bridges of the East River and were heading out into the open water between Staten Island and Manhattan. The lights of the downtown financial district shimmered like witchlight on the water. The sky was powdered with diamond dust and the river hid its secrets under a slick black sheet, broken here and there with a silvery flash that could have been a fish's tail—or a mermaid's. *My city*, Jace thought, experimentally, but the words still brought to mind Alicante and its crystal towers, not the skyscrapers of Manhattan.

After a moment Valentine said, "Why are you here, Jonathan? I wondered after I saw you in the Bone City if your hatred for me was implacable. I had nearly given up on you."

His tone was level, as it almost always was, but there was something in it—not vulnerability but at least a sort of genuine curiosity, as if he had realized that Jace was capable of surprising him.

Jace looked out at the water. "The Queen of the Seelie Court wanted me to ask you a question," he said. "She told me to ask you what blood runs in my veins."

Surprise passed over Valentine's face like a hand smoothing away all expression. "You spoke with the Queen?"

Jace said nothing.

"It is the way of the Folk. Everything they say has more than one meaning. Tell her, if she asks again, that the blood of the Angel runs in your veins."

"And in every Shadowhunter's veins," said Jace, disappointed. He'd hoped for a better answer. "You wouldn't lie to the Queen of the Seelie Court, would you?"

Valentine's tone was short. "No. And you wouldn't come here just to ask me that ridiculous question. Why are you really here, Jonathan?"

"I had to talk to someone." He wasn't as good at controlling his voice as his father was; he could hear the pain in it, like a bleeding wound just under the surface. "The Lightwoods—I'm nothing but trouble for them. Luke must hate me by now. The Inquisitor wants me dead. I did something to hurt Alec and I'm not even sure what."

"And your sister?" Valentine said. "What about Clarissa?"

*Why do you have to ruin everything?* "She's not too pleased with me either." He hesitated. "I remembered what you said at the Bone City. That you never got a chance to tell me the truth. I don't trust you," he added. "I want you to know that. But I thought I'd give you the chance to tell me *why*."

"You have to ask me more than why, Jonathan." There was a note in his father's voice that startled Jace—a fierce humility that seemed to temper Valentine's pride, as steel might be tempered by fire. "There are so many *whys*."

"Why did you kill the Silent Brothers? Why did you take the Mortal Sword? What are you planning? Why wasn't the Mortal Cup enough for you?" Jace caught himself before he could ask any more questions. *Why did you leave me a second time? Why did you tell me I wasn't your son anymore, then come back for me anyway?*

"You know what I want. The Clave is hopelessly corrupt and must be destroyed and built again. Idris must be freed from the influence of the degenerate races, and Earth made proof against the demonic threat."

"Yeah, about that demonic threat." Jace glanced around, as if he half-expected to see the black shadow of Agramon hulking toward him. "I thought you hated demons. Now you use them like servants. The Ravener, the Drevak demons, Agramon—they're your *employees*. Guards, butler—personal chef, for all I know."

Valentine tapped his fingers on the railing. "I'm no friend to demons," he said. "I am Nephilim, no matter how much I might think the Covenant is useless and the Law fraudulent. A man doesn't have to agree with his government to be a patriot, does he? It takes a true patriot to dissent, to say he loves his country more than he cares for his own place in the social order. I've been vilified for my choice, forced into hiding, banished from Idris. But I am—I will always be—Nephilim. I can't change the blood in my veins if I wished to—and I don't."

*I do.* Jace thought of Clary. He glanced down at the dark water again, knowing it wasn't true. To give up the hunt, the kill, the knowledge of one's own soaring speed and sure abilities: It was impossible. He *was* a warrior. He could be nothing else.

"Do you?" Valentine asked. Jace looked away quickly, wondering if his father could read his face. It had been just the two of them alone for so many years. He'd known his father's face better than his own, once. Valentine was the one person from whom he felt he could never hide what he was feeling. Or the first person, at least. Sometimes he felt as if Clary could look right through him as if he were glass.

"No," he said. "I don't."

"You're a Shadowhunter forever?"

"I am," Jace said, "in the end, what you made me."

"Good," said Valentine. "That's what I wanted to hear." He leaned back against the railing, looking up at the night sky. There was gray in his silvery white hair; Jace had never noticed it before. "This is a war," Valentine said. "The only question is, what side will you fight on?"

"I thought we were all on the same side. I thought it was us against the demon worlds."

"If only it could be. Don't you understand that if I felt that the Clave had the best interests of this world at heart, if I thought they were doing the best job they possibly could—by the Angel, why would I fight them? What reason would I have?"

*Power*, Jace thought, but he said nothing. He was no longer sure what to say, much less what to believe.

"If the Clave goes on as they are," Valentine said, "the demons will see their weakness and attack, and the Clave, distracted by their endless courting of the degenerate races, will be in no condition to fight them off. The demons will attack and they will destroy and there will be nothing left."

*The degenerate races*. The words carried an uncomfortable familiarity; they recalled Jace's childhood to him, in a way that was not entirely unpleasant. When he thought of his father and of Idris, it was always the same blurred memory of hot sunshine burning down on the green lawns in front of their country house, and of a big, dark, broad-shouldered figure leaning down to lift him off the grass and carry him inside. He must have been very young then, and he had never forgotten it, not the way the grass had smelled—green and bright and newly cut—or the way the sun had turned his father's hair to a white halo, nor the feeling of being carried. Of being safe.

"Luke," Jace said, with some difficulty. "Luke isn't a degenerate—"

"Lucian is different. He was a Shadowhunter once." Valentine's tone was flat and final. "This isn't about specific Downworlders, Jonathan. This is about the survival of every living creature in this world. The Angel chose the Nephilim for a reason. We are the best of this world, and we are meant to save it. We are the closest thing that exists in this world to gods—

and we must use that power to save this world from destruction, whatever the cost to us."

Jace leaned his elbows on the railing. It was cold here: The icy wind cut through his clothes, and the tips of his fingers were numb. But in his mind, he saw green hills and blue water and the honey-colored stones of the Wayland manor house.

"In the old tale," he said, "Satan said to Adam and Eve 'You shall be as gods' when he tempted them into sin. And they were cast out of the garden because of it."

There was a pause before Valentine laughed. He said, "See, that's what I need you for, Jonathan. You keep me from the sin of pride."

"There are all sorts of sins." Jace straightened up and turned to face his father. "You didn't answer my question about the demons, Father. How can you justify summoning them, *associating* with them? Do you plan to send them against the Clave?"

"Of course I do," said Valentine, without hesitation, without a moment's pause to consider whether it might be wise to reveal his plans to someone who might share them with his enemies. Nothing could have shaken Jace more than to realize how sure his father was of success. "The Clave won't yield to reason, only to force. I tried to build an army of Forsaken; with the Cup, I could create an army of new Shadowhunters, but that will take years. I don't have years. *We*, the human race, don't have years. With the Sword I can call to me an obedient army of demons. They will serve me as tools, do whatever I demand. They will have no choice. And when I am done with them, I will command them to destroy themselves, and they will do it." His voice was emotionless.

Jace was gripping the railing so hard that his fingers had

begun to ache. "You can't slaughter every Shadowhunter who opposes you. That's murder."

"I won't have to. When the Clave sees the power arrayed against them, they'll surrender. They're not suicidal. And there are those among them who support me." There was no arrogance in Valentine's voice, only a calm certainty. "They will step forward when the time comes."

"I think you're underestimating the Clave." Jace tried to make his voice steady. "I don't think you understand how much they hate you."

"Hate is nothing when weighed against survival." Valentine's hand went to his belt, where the hilt of the Sword gleamed dully. "But don't take my word for it. I told you there was something I wanted to show you. Here it is."

He drew the Sword from its sheath and held it out to Jace. Jace had seen Maellartach before in the Bone City, hanging on the wall in the pavilion of the Speaking Stars. And he had seen the hilt of it protruding from Valentine's shoulder sheath, but he'd never really examined it up close. *The Angel's Sword.* It was a dark, heavy silver, glimmering with a dull sheen. Light seemed to move over and through it, as if it were made of water. In its hilt bloomed a fiery rose of light.

Jace spoke through his dry mouth. "Very nice."

"I want you to hold it." Valentine presented the Sword to his son, the way he'd always taught him, hilt first. The Sword seemed to shimmer blackly in the starlight.

Jace hesitated. "I don't . . ."

"Take it." Valentine pressed it into his hand.

The moment Jace's fingers closed around the grip, a spear of light shot up the hilt of the Sword and down the core of it into the blade. He looked quickly to his father, but Valentine was expressionless.

A dark pain spread up Jace's arm and through his chest. It wasn't that the Sword was heavy; it wasn't. It was that it seemed to want to pull him downward, to drag him through the ship, through the green ocean water, through the fragile crust of the earth itself. Jace felt as if the breath were being torn out of his lungs. He flung his head up and looked around—

And saw that the night had changed. A glimmering net of thin gold wires had been flung across the sky, and the stars shone down through it, bright as nail heads hammered into the darkness. Jace saw the curve of the world as it slipped away from him, and for a moment was struck by the beauty of it all. Then the night sky seemed to crack open like a glass and pouring through the shards came a horde of dark shapes, humped and twisted, gnarled and faceless, howling out a soundless scream that seared the inside of his mind. Icy wind burned him as six-legged horses hurtled past, their hooves striking bloody sparks from the deck of the ship. The things that rode them were indescribable. Overhead eyeless, leathery-winged creatures circled, screeching and dripping a venomous green slime.

Jace bent over the railing, retching uncontrollably, the Sword still gripped in his hand. Below him the water churned with demons like a poisonous stew. He saw spiny creatures with bloody saucerlike eyes struggling as they were dragged under by boiling masses of slippery black tentacles. A mermaid caught in the grip of a ten-legged water spider screamed hopelessly as it sank its fangs into her thrashing tail, its red eyes glittering like beads of blood.

The Sword fell from Jace's hand and clattered to the deck. Abruptly the sound and spectacle were gone and the night was silent. He hung tightly to the railing, staring down at the sea below in disbelief. It was empty, its surface ruffled only by wind.

"What *was* that?" Jace whispered. His throat felt rough, as if it had been scraped with sandpaper. He looked wildly at his father, who had bent to retrieve the Soul-Sword from the deck where Jace had dropped it. "Are those the demons you've already called?"

"No." Valentine slid Maellartach into its sheath. "Those are the demons that have been drawn to the edges of this world by the Sword. I brought my ship to this place because the wards are thin here. What you saw is my army, waiting on the other side of the wards—waiting for me to call them to my side." His eyes were grave. "Do you still think the Clave won't capitulate?"

Jace closed his eyes and said, "Not all of them—not the Lightwoods—"

"You could convince them. If you stand with me, I swear no harm will come to them."

The darkness behind Jace's eyes began to turn red. He had been imagining the ashes of Valentine's old house, the blackened bones of the grandparents he'd never met. Now he saw other faces. Alec's. Isabelle's. Max's. Clary's.

"I've done so much to hurt them already," he whispered. "Nothing else must happen to any of them. Nothing."

"Of course. I understand." And Jace realized, to his astonishment, that Valentine *did* understand, that somehow he saw what no one else seemed to be able to understand. "You think it is your fault, all the harm that has befallen your friends, your family."

"It *is* my fault."

"You're right. It is." At that, Jace looked up in absolute astonishment. Surprise at being agreed with battled with horror and relief in equal measures.

"Is it?"

"The harm is not deliberate, of course. But you are like me. We poison and destroy everything we love. There *is* a reason for that."

"What reason?"

Valentine glanced up at the sky. "We are meant for a higher purpose, you and I. The distractions of the world are just that, distractions. If we allow ourselves to be turned aside from our course by them, we are duly punished."

"And our punishment is visited on everyone we care about? That seems a little hard on *them*."

"Fate is never fair. You are caught in a current much stronger than you are, Jonathan; struggle against it and you'll drown not just yourself but those who try to save you. Swim with it, and you'll survive."

"Clary—"

"No harm will come to your sister if you join with me. I will go to the ends of the earth to protect her. I will bring her to Idris, where nothing can happen to her. I promise you that."

"Alec. Isabelle. Max—"

"The Lightwood children, also, will have my protection."

Jace said softly, "Luke—"

Valentine hesitated, then said, "All your friends will be protected. Why can't you believe me, Jonathan? This is the only way that you can save them. I swear it."

Jace couldn't speak. He shut his eyes again. Inside him the cold of fall battled with the memory of summer.

"Have you made your decision?" Valentine said; Jace couldn't see him, but he could hear the finality in the question. He even sounded eager.

Jace opened his eyes. The starlight was a white burst against his irises; for a moment he could see nothing else. He said, "Yes, Father. I've made my decision."

# Part Three
# Day of Wrath

*Day of wrath, that day of burning,*
*Seer and Sibyl speak concerning,*
*All the world to ashes turning.*
—Abraham Coles

# 14

## FEARLESS

**When Clary awoke, light was streaming in through the** windows and there was a sharp pain in her left cheek. Rolling over, she saw that she'd fallen asleep on her sketchpad and the corner of it had been digging into her face. She'd also dropped her pen onto the duvet, and there was a black stain spreading across the cloth. With a groan she sat up, rubbed her cheek ruefully, and went in search of a shower.

The bathroom showed telltale signs of the activities of the night before; there were bloody cloths shoved into the trash and a smear of dried blood across the sink. With a shudder Clary ducked into the shower with a bottle of grapefruit body wash, determined to scrub away her lingering feelings of unease.

Afterward, wrapped in one of Luke's robes and with a towel around her damp hair, she pushed the bathroom door open to discover Magnus lurking on the other side, clutching a towel in one hand and his glittery hair in the other. He must have slept on it, she thought, because one side of the glittered spikes looked dented in. "Why does it take girls so long to shower?" he demanded. "Mortal girls, Shadowhunters, female warlocks, you're all the same. I'm not getting any younger waiting out here."

Clary stepped aside to let him pass. "How old *are* you, anyway?" she asked curiously.

Magnus winked at her. "I was alive when the Dead Sea was just a lake that was feeling a little poorly."

Clary rolled her eyes.

Magnus made a shooing motion. "Now move your petite behind. I need to get in there; my hair is a *wreck*."

"Don't use up all my body wash, it's expensive," Clary told him, and headed into the kitchen, where she rooted around for some filters and plugged in the Mr. Coffee machine. The familiar burble of the percolator and the smell of coffee damped down her feeling of unease. As long as there was coffee in the world, how bad could things be?

She headed back to the bedroom to get dressed. Ten minutes later, in jeans and a blue-and-green striped sweater, she was in the living room shaking Luke awake. He sat up with a groan, his hair rumpled and his face creased with sleep.

"How are you feeling?" Clary asked, handing him a chipped mug full of steaming coffee.

"Better now." Luke glanced down at the torn fabric of his shirt; the edges of the tear were stained with blood. "Where's Maia?"

"She's asleep in your room, remember? You said she could have it." Clary perched on the arm of the sofa.

Luke rubbed at his shadowed eyes. "I don't remember last night all that well," he admitted. "I remember going out to the truck and not much after that."

"There were more demons hiding outside. They attacked you. Jace and I took care of them."

"More Drevak demons?"

"No." Clary spoke with reluctance. "Jace called them Raum demons."

"Raum demons?" Luke sat up straight. "That's serious stuff. Drevak demons are dangerous pests, but the Raum—"

"It's all right," Clary told him. "We got rid of them."

"You got rid of them? Or Jace did? Clary, I don't want you—"

"It wasn't like that." She shook her head. "It was like . . ."

"Wasn't Magnus around? Why didn't he go with you?" Luke interrupted, clearly upset.

"I was healing *Maia*, that's why," Magnus said, coming into the living room smelling strongly of grapefruit. His hair was wrapped in a towel and he was dressed in a blue satin tracksuit with silver stripes down the side. "Where is the gratitude?"

"I *am* grateful." Luke looked as if he were both angry and trying not to laugh at the same time. "It's just that if anything had happened to Clary—"

"Maia would have died if I'd gone out there with them," Magnus said, flopping down into a chair. "Clary and Jace handled the demons just fine on their own, didn't you?" He turned to Clary.

She squirmed. "You see, that's just it—"

"What's just it?" It was Maia, still in the clothes she'd worn the night before, with one of Luke's big flannel shirts thrown over her T-shirt. She moved stiffly across the room and sat down gingerly in a chair. "Is that coffee I smell?" she asked hopefully, wrinkling her nose.

Honestly, Clary thought, it was hardly fair for a werewolf to be curvy and pretty; she ought to be big and hirsute, possibly with hair coming out of her ears. *And this,* Clary added silently, *is exactly why I don't have any female friends and spend all my time with Simon. I've got to get a grip.* She rose to her feet. "You want me to get you some?"

"Sure." Maia nodded. "Milk and sugar!" she called as Clary left the room, but by the time she was back from the kitchen, steaming mug in hand, the werewolf girl was frowning. "I don't really remember what happened last night," she said, "but there's something about Simon, something that's bothering me . . ."

"Well, you did try to kill him," Clary said, settling back onto the arm of the sofa. "Maybe that's it."

Maia paled, staring down into her coffee. "I'd forgotten. He's a vampire now." She looked up at Clary. "I didn't mean to hurt him. I was just . . ."

"Yes?" Clary raised her eyebrows. "Just what?"

Maia's face went a slow, dark red. She set her coffee down on the table beside her.

"You might want to lie down," Magnus advised. "I find that helps when the crushing sense of horrible realization sets in."

Maia's eyes filled suddenly with tears. Clary looked toward Magnus in horror—he looked equally shocked, she noticed—and then to Luke. "*Do something,*" she hissed at him under her breath. Magnus might be a warlock who could heal fatal injuries with a flash of blue fire, but Luke was hands down the top choice between the two for dealing with crying teenage girls.

Luke began to kick back his blanket in preparation for rising, but before he could get to his feet, the front door banged open and Jace came in, followed by Alec, who was carrying a white box. Magnus hastily pulled the towel off his head and dropped it behind the armchair. Without the gel and glitter, his hair was dark and straight, halfway to his shoulders.

Clary's eyes went immediately to Jace, as they always did; she couldn't help it, but at least no one else seemed to notice. Jace looked strung up, wired and tense, but also exhausted, his eyes ringed with gray. His eyes slid over her without expression and landed on Maia, who was still weeping soundlessly and didn't seem to have heard them come in. "Everyone in a good mood, I see," he observed. "Keeping up morale?"

Maia rubbed at her eyes. "Crap," she muttered. "I hate crying in front of Shadowhunters."

"So go cry in another room," Jace said, his voice devoid of warmth. "We certainly don't need you sniveling in here while we're talking, do we?"

"Jace," Luke began warningly, but Maia had already gotten to her feet and stalked out of the room through the kitchen door.

Clary turned on Jace. "Talking? We weren't talking."

"But we will be," Jace said, flopping down onto the piano bench and stretching out his long legs. "Magnus wants to shout at me, don't you, Magnus?"

"Yes," Magnus said, tearing his eyes away from Alec long enough to scowl. "Where the hell were you? I thought I was clear with you that you were to stay in the house."

"*I* thought he didn't have a choice," Clary said. "I thought he *had* to stay where you are. You know, because of magic."

"Normally, yes," Magnus said crossly, "but last night, after everything I did, my magic was—depleted."

"Depleted?"

"Yes." Magnus looked angrier than ever. "Even the High Warlock of Brooklyn doesn't have inexhaustible resources. I'm only human. Well," he amended, "half-human, anyway."

"But you must have known your resources were depleted," Luke said, not unkindly, "didn't you?"

"Yes, and I made the little bastard swear to stay in the house." Magnus glared at Jace. "Now I know what your much-vaunted Shadowhunter vows are worth."

"You need to know how to make me swear properly," Jace said, unfazed. "Only an oath on the Angel has any meaning."

"It's true," Alec said. It was the first thing he'd said since they'd come into the house.

"Of course it's true." Jace picked up Maia's untouched mug of coffee and took a sip. He made a face. "Sugar."

"Where were you all night, anyway?" Magnus asked, his voice sour. "With Alec?"

"I couldn't sleep, so I went for a walk," Jace said. "When I got back, I bumped into this sad bastard mooning around the porch." He pointed at Alec.

Magnus brightened. "Were you there all night?" he asked Alec.

"No," Alec said. "I went home and then came back. I'm wearing different clothes, aren't I? Look."

Everyone looked. Alec was wearing a dark sweater and jeans, which was exactly what he'd been wearing the day before. Clary decided to give him the benefit of the doubt. "What's in the box?" she asked.

"Oh. Ah." Alec looked at the box as if he'd forgotten it. "Doughnuts, actually." He opened the box and set it down on the coffee table. "Does anyone want one?"

Everyone, as it turned out, wanted a doughnut. Jace wanted two. After downing the Boston cream that Clary brought him, Luke seemed moderately revitalized; he kicked the blanket the rest of the way off and sat up against the back of the couch. "There's one thing I don't get," he said.

"Just one thing? You're way ahead of the rest of us," said Jace.

"The two of you went out after me when I didn't come back to the house," Luke said, looking from Clary to Jace.

"Three of us," Clary said. "Simon came with."

Luke looked pained. "Fine. The three of you. There were two demons, but Clary says you killed neither of them. So what happened?"

"I would have killed mine, but it ran off," Jace said. "Otherwise—"

"But why would it do that?" Alec inquired. "Two of them, three of you—maybe it felt outnumbered?"

"No offense to anyone involved, but the only one among you who seems formidable is Jace," Magnus said. "An untrained Shadowhunter and a scared vampire . . ."

"I think it might have been me," Clary said. "I think maybe I scared it off."

Magnus blinked. "Didn't I just say—"

"I don't mean I scared it off because I'm so terrifying," Clary said. "I think it was this." She raised her hand, turning it so that they could see the Mark on her inner arm.

There was a sudden quiet. Jace looked at her steadily, then away; Alec blinked, and Luke looked astounded. "I've never seen that Mark before," he said finally. "Has anyone else?"

"No," Magnus said. "But I don't like it."

"I'm not sure what it is, or what it means," Clary said, lowering her arm. "But it doesn't come from the Gray Book."

"All runes come from the Gray Book." Jace's voice was firm.

"Not this one," Clary said. "I saw it in a dream."

"In a *dream*?" Jace looked as furious as if she were personally insulting him. "What are you playing at, Clary?"

"I'm not playing at anything. Don't you remember when we were in the Seelie Court—"

Jace looked as if she had hit him. Clary went on, quickly, before he could say anything:

"—and the Seelie Queen told us we were experiments? That Valentine had done—had done *things* to us, to make us different, special? She told me that mine was the gift of words that cannot be spoken, and yours was the Angel's own gift?"

"That was faerie nonsense."

"Faeries don't lie, Jace. Words that cannot be spoken—she meant runes. Each has a different meaning, but they're meant to be drawn, not said aloud." She went on, ignoring his doubtful look. "Remember when you asked me how I'd gotten into your cell in the Silent City? I told you I just used a regular Opening rune—"

"Was that all you did?" Alec looked surprised. "I got there just after you did and it looked like someone had ripped that door off its hinges."

"And my rune didn't just unlock the door," Clary said. "It unlocked everything inside the cell, too. It broke Jace's manacles open." She took a breath. "I think the Queen meant I can draw runes that are more powerful than ordinary runes. And maybe even create new ones."

Jace shook his head. "No one can create new runes—"

"Maybe she can, Jace." Alec sounded thoughtful. "It's true, none of us have ever seen that Mark on her arm before."

"Alec's right," Luke said. "Clary, why don't you go and get your sketchbook?"

She looked at him in some surprise. His gray-blue eyes were tired, a little sunken, but held the same steadiness they'd held when she was six years old and he'd promised her that if she climbed the jungle gym in the Prospect Park playground, he'd always be standing underneath it to catch her if she fell. And he always had been.

"Okay," she said. "I'll be right back."

To get to the spare bedroom, Clary had to cross through the kitchen, where she found Maia seated on a stool pulled up to the counter, looking miserable. "Clary," she said, jumping down from the stool. "Can I talk to you for a second?"

"I'm just going to my room to get something—"

"Look, I'm sorry about what happened with Simon. I was delirious."

"Oh, yeah? What happened to all that werewolves are destined to hate vampires business?"

Maia blew out an exasperated breath. "We are, but—I guess I don't have to hurry the process along."

"Don't explain it to me; explain it to Simon."

Maia flushed again, her cheeks turning dark red. "I doubt he'll want to talk to me."

"He might. He's pretty forgiving."

Maia looked at her more closely. "Not that I want to pry, but are you two going out?"

Clary felt *herself* start to flush and thanked her freckles for providing at least some cover-up. "Why do you want to know?"

Maia shrugged. "The first time I met him he referred to you as his best friend, but the second time he called you his girlfriend. I wondered if it was an on-off thing."

"Sort of. We were friends first. It's a long story."

"I see." Maia's blush had vanished and her tough-girl smirk was back on her face. "Well, you're lucky, that's all. Even if he is a vampire now. You must be pretty used to all sorts of weird stuff, being a Shadowhunter, so I bet it doesn't faze you."

"It fazes me," Clary said, more sharply than she'd intended. "I'm not Jace."

The smirk widened. "No one is. And I get the feeling he knows it."

"What's that supposed to mean?"

"Oh, you know. Jace reminds me of an old boyfriend. Some guys look at you like they want sex. Jace looks at you like you've already *had* sex, it was great, and now you're just friends—even though you want more. Drives girls crazy. You know what I mean?"

*Yes*, Clary thought. "No," she said.

"I guess you wouldn't, being his sister. You'll have to take my word on it."

"I have to go." Clary was almost out the kitchen door when something occurred to her and she turned around. "What happened to him?"

Maia blinked. "What happened to who?"

"The old boyfriend. The one Jace reminds you of."

"Oh," Maia said. "He's the one who turned me into a werewolf."

"All right, I got it," Clary said, coming back into the living room with her sketchpad in one hand and a box of Prismacolor pencils in the other. She pulled a chair out from the little-used dining room table—Luke always ate in the kitchen or in his office, and the table was covered in paper and old bills—and sat down, sketchpad in front of her. She felt as if she were taking a test at art school. *Draw this apple.* "What do you want me to do?"

"What do you think?" Jace was still sitting on the piano bench, his shoulders slumped forward; he looked as if he hadn't slept all night. Alec was leaning against the piano behind him, probably because it was as far away from Magnus as he could get.

"Jace, that's enough." Luke was sitting up straight but looked as if it were something of an effort. "You said you could draw new runes, Clary?"

"I said I thought so."

"Well, I'd like you to try."

"Now?"

Luke smiled faintly. "Unless you've got something else in mind?"

Clary flipped the sketchpad to a blank page and stared down at it. Never had a sheet of paper looked quite so empty to her before. She could sense the stillness in the room, everyone watching her: Magnus with his ancient, tempered curiosity; Alec too preoccupied with his own problems to care much for hers; Luke hopefully; and Jace with a cold, frightening blankness. She remembered him saying that he wished he could hate her and wondered if someday he might succeed.

She threw her pencil down. "I can't just do it on command like that. Not without an idea."

"What kind of idea?" said Luke.

"I mean, I don't even know what runes already exist. I need to know a meaning, a word, before I can draw a rune for it."

"It's hard enough for us to remember every rune—," Alec began, but Jace, to Clary's surprise, cut him off.

"How about," he said quietly, "Fearless?"

"Fearless?" she echoed.

"There are runes for bravery," said Jace. "But never anything to take away fear. But if you, as you say, can create new runes . . ." He glanced around, and saw Alec's and Luke's surprised expressions. "Look, I just remembered that there isn't one, that's all. And it seems harmless enough."

Clary looked over at Luke, who shrugged. "Fine," he said.

Clary took a dark gray pencil from the box and set the tip of it to the paper. She thought of shapes, lines, curlicues; she thought of the signs in the Gray Book, ancient and perfect, embodiments of a language too faultless for speech. A soft voice spoke inside her head: *Who are you, to think you can speak the language of heaven?*

The pencil moved. She was almost sure she hadn't moved it, but it slid across the paper, describing a single line. She felt her heart skip. She thought of her mother, sitting dreamily before her canvas, creating her own vision of the world in ink and oil paint. She thought, *Who am I? I am Jocelyn Fray's daughter.* The pencil moved again, and this time her breath caught; she found she was whispering the word, under her breath: "Fearless. Fearless." The pencil looped back up, and now she was guiding it rather than being guided by it. When she was done, she set the pencil down and gazed for a moment, wonderingly, at the result.

The completed Fearless rune was a matrix of strongly swirling lines: a rune as bold and aerodynamic as an eagle. She tore the page free and held it up so the others could see it. "There," she said, and was rewarded by the startled look on Luke's face—so he *hadn't* believed her—and the fractional widening of Jace's eyes.

"Cool," Alec said.

Jace got to his feet and crossed the room, taking the sheet of paper out of her hand. "But does it work?"

Clary wondered if he meant the question or if he was just being nasty. "What do you mean?"

"I mean, how do we know it works? Right now it's just a drawing—you can't take fear away from a piece of paper, it doesn't have any to begin with. We have to try it out on one of us before we can be sure it's a real rune."

"I'm not sure that's such a great idea," Luke said.

"It's a fabulous idea." Jace dropped the paper back onto the table, and began to slide off his jacket. "I've got a stele we can use. Who wants to do me?"

"A regrettable choice of words," muttered Magnus.

Luke stood up. "No," he said. "Jace, you already behave as if you've never heard the word 'fear.' I fail to see how we're going to be able to tell the difference if it *does* work on you."

Alec stifled what sounded like a laugh. Jace simply smiled a tight, unfriendly smile. "I've heard the word 'fear,'" he said.

"I simply choose to believe it doesn't apply to me."

"Exactly the problem," said Luke.

"Well, why don't I try it on you, then?" Clary said, but Luke shook his head.

"You can't Mark Downworlders, Clary, not with any real effect. The demon disease that causes lycanthropy prevents the Marks from taking effect."

"Then . . ."

"Try it on me," Alec said unexpectedly. "I could do with some fearlessness." He slid his jacket off, tossed it over the piano stool, and crossed the room to stand in front of Jace. "Here. Mark my arm."

Jace glanced over at Clary. "Unless you think you should do it?"

She shook her head. "No. You're probably better at actually applying Marks than I am."

Jace shrugged. "Roll up your sleeve, Alec."

Obediently, Alec rolled his sleeve up. There was already a permanent Mark on his upper arm, an elegant scroll of lines meant to give him perfect balance. They all leaned forward, even Magnus, as Jace carefully traced the outlines of the Fearless rune on Alec's arm, just below the existing Mark. Alec winced as the stele traced its burning path across his skin. When Jace was done, he slid his stele back into his pocket and stood a moment admiring his handiwork. "Well, it *looks* nice at least," he announced. "Whether it works or not . . ."

Alec touched the new Mark with his fingertips, then glanced up to find everyone else in the room staring at him.

"So?" Clary said.

"So what?" Alec rolled his sleeve down, covering the Mark.

"So, how do you *feel*? Any different?"

Alec looked considering. "Not really."

Jace threw his hands up. "So it doesn't work."

"Not necessarily," Luke said. "There might simply be nothing going on that might activate it. Perhaps there isn't anything here that Alec is afraid of."

Magnus glanced at Alec and raised his eyebrows. "Boo," he said.

Jace was grinning. "Come on, surely you've got a phobia or two. What scares you?"

Alec thought for a moment. "Spiders," he said.

Clary turned to Luke. "Have you got a spider anywhere?"

Luke looked exasperated. "Why would I have a *spider*? Do I look like someone who would collect them?"

"No offense," Jace said, "but you kind of do."

"You know"—Alec's tone was sour—"maybe this was a stupid experiment."

"What about the dark?" Clary suggested. "We could lock you in the basement."

"I'm a demon hunter," Alec said, with exaggerated patience. "Clearly, I am *not afraid of the dark*."

"Well, you might be."

"But I'm not."

Clary was spared replying by the buzz of the doorbell. She looked over at Luke, raising her eyebrows. "Simon?"

"Couldn't be. It's daylight."

"Oh, right." She'd forgotten again. "Do you want me to get it?"

"No." He stood up with only a short grunt of pain. "I'm fine. It's probably someone wondering why the bookstore's shut."

He crossed the room and threw the door open. His shoulders went stiff with surprise; Clary heard the bark of a familiar, stridently angry female voice, and a moment later Isabelle and Maryse Lightwood pushed past Luke and strode into the room, followed by the gray, menacing figure of the Inquisitor. Behind them was a tall and burly man, dark-haired and olive-skinned, with a thick black beard. Though it had been taken many years ago, Clary recognized him from the old photo Hodge had showed her: This was Robert Lightwood, Alec and Isabelle's father.

Magnus's head went up with a snap. Jace paled markedly, but showed no other emotion. And Alec—Alec stared from his sister, to his mother, to his father, and then looked at Magnus, his clear, light blue eyes darkened with a hard resolution. He took a step forward, placing himself between his parents and everyone else in the room.

Maryse, on seeing her eldest son in the middle of Luke's living room, did a double take. "Alec, what on *earth* are you doing here? I thought I made it clear that—"

"Mother." Alec's voice as he interrupted his mother was firm, implacable, and not unkind. "Father. There's something I have to tell you." He smiled at them. "I'm seeing someone."

Robert Lightwood looked at his son with some exasperation. "Alec," he said. "This is hardly the time."

"Yes, it is. This is important. You see, I'm not just seeing anyone." Words seemed to be pouring out of Alec in a torrent, while his parents looked on in confusion. Isabelle and Magnus were staring at him with expressions of nearly identical astonishment. "I'm seeing a Downworlder. In fact, I'm seeing a war—"

Magnus's fingers moved, quick as a flash of light, in Alec's direction. There was a faint shimmer in the air around Alec—his eyes rolled up—and he dropped to the floor, felled like a tree.

"Alec!" Maryse clapped her hand to her mouth. Isabelle, who had been standing closest to her brother, dropped down beside him. But Alec had already begun to stir, his eyelids fluttering open. "Wha—what—why am I on the floor?"

"That's a good question." Isabelle glowered down at her brother. "What *was* that?"

"What was what?" Alec sat up, holding his head. A look of alarm crossed his face. "Wait—did I say anything? Before I passed out, I mean."

Jace snorted. "You know how we were wondering if that thing Clary did would work or not?" he asked. "It works all right."

Alec looked supremely horrified. "What did I say?"

"You said you were seeing someone," his father told him. "Though you weren't clear as to why that was important."

"It's not," Alec said. "I mean, I'm not seeing anyone. And it's not important. Or it wouldn't be if I was seeing someone, which I'm not."

Magnus looked at him as if he were an idiot. "Alec's been delirious," he said. "Side effect of some demon toxins. Most unfortunate, but he'll be fine soon."

"Demon toxins?" Maryse's voice had become shrill. "No one reported a demon attack to the Institute. *What* is going on here, Lucian? This is your house, isn't it? You know perfectly well if there's been a demon attack you're supposed to report it—"

"Luke was attacked too," Clary said. "He's been unconscious."

"How convenient. Everyone's either unconscious or apparently delirious," said the Inquisitor. Her knifelike voice cut through the room, silencing everyone. "Downworlder, you know perfectly well that Jonathan Morgenstern should not be in your house. He should have been locked up in the warlock's care."

"I have a name, you know," Magnus said. "Not," he added, seeming to think twice about interrupting the Inquisitor, "that that matters, really. In fact, forget all about it."

"I know your name, Magnus Bane," said the Inquisitor. "You've failed in your duty once; you won't get another chance."

"Failed in my duty?" Magnus frowned. "Just by bringing the boy here? There was nothing in the contract I signed that said I couldn't bring him with me at my own discretion."

"That wasn't your failure," the Inquisitor said. "Letting him see his father last night, *that* was your failure."

There was a stunned silence. Alec scrambled up off the floor, his eyes seeking out Jace's—but Jace wouldn't look at him. His face was a mask.

"That's ridiculous," Luke said. Clary had rarely seen him look so angry. "Jace doesn't even know where Valentine is. Stop hounding him."

"Hounding is what I do, Downworlder," said the Inquisitor. "It's my job." She turned to Jace. "Tell the truth, now, boy," she said, "and it will all be much easier."

Jace raised his chin. "I don't have to tell you anything."

"If you're innocent, why not exonerate yourself? Tell us where you really were last night. Tell us about Valentine's little pleasure boat."

Clary stared at him. *I went for a walk*, he'd said. But that didn't mean anything. Maybe he really had gone for a walk. But her heart, her stomach, felt sick. *You know what the worst thing I can imagine is?* Simon had said. *Not trusting someone I love.*

When Jace didn't speak, Robert Lightwood said, in his deep bass voice: "Imogen? You're saying Valentine is—was—"

"On a boat in the middle of the East River," said the Inquisitor. "That's correct."

"That's why I couldn't find him," Magnus said, half to himself. "All that water—it disrupted my spell."

"What's Valentine doing in the middle of the river?" Luke said, bewildered.

"Ask Jonathan," said the Inquisitor. "He borrowed a motorcycle from the head of the city's vampire clan and he flew it to the boat. Isn't that right, Jonathan?"

Jace said nothing. His face was unreadable. The Inquisitor, though, looked hungry, as if she were feeding off the suspense in the room.

"Reach into the pocket of your jacket," she said. "Take out the object you've been carrying with you since you last left the Institute."

Slowly, Jace did as she asked. As he drew his hand out of his pocket, Clary recognized the shimmering blue-gray object he held. The piece of the Portal mirror.

"Give it to me." The Inquisitor snatched it out of his hand. He winced; the edge of the glass had cut him, and blood welled up along his palm. Maryse made a soft noise, but didn't move. "I knew you'd return to the Institute for this," said the Inquisitor, positively gloating now. "I knew your sentimentality wouldn't allow you to leave it behind."

"What is it?" Robert Lightwood sounded bewildered.

"A bit of a Portal in mirror form," said the Inquisitor. "When the Portal was destroyed, the image of its last destination was preserved." She turned the bit of glass over in her long, spidery fingers. "In this case, the Wayland country house."

Jace's eyes followed the movement of the mirror. In the bit of it Clary could see, there seemed to be a trapped piece of blue sky. She wondered if it ever rained in Idris.

With a sudden, violent motion at odds with her calm tone, the Inquisitor dashed the piece of mirror to the ground. It shattered instantly into powdery shards. Clary heard Jace suck his breath in, but he didn't move.

The Inquisitor drew on a pair of gray gloves and knelt among the bits of mirror, sifting them through her fingers until she found what she was looking for—a single sheet of thin paper. She stood, holding it up for everyone in the room to see the thick rune written on it in black ink. "I marked this paper with a tracking rune and slipped it between the bit of mirror and its backing. Then I replaced it in the boy's room. Don't feel bad for not noticing it," she said to Jace. "Older heads and wiser than yours have been fooled by the Clave."

"You've been spying on me," Jace said, and now his voice was colored with anger. "Is that what the Clave does, invade the privacy of its fellow Shadowhunters to—"

"Be careful what you say to me. You are not the only one who's broken the Law." The Inquisitor's chilly gaze slid around the room. "In releasing you from the Silent City, in freeing you from the warlock's control, your friends have done the same."

"Jace isn't our friend," said Isabelle. "He's our brother."

"I'd be careful what you say, Isabelle Lightwood," said the Inquisitor. "You could be considered complicit."

"Complicit?" To everyone's surprise, it was Robert Lightwood who had spoken. "The girl was just trying to keep you from shattering our family. For God's sake, Imogen, these are all just children—"

"Children?" The Inquisitor turned her icicle gaze on Robert. "Just as you were children when the Circle plotted the destruction of the Clave? Just as my son was a child when he—" She caught herself with a sort of gasp, as if gaining control of herself by main force.

"So this is about Stephen after all," said Luke, with a sort of pity in his voice. "Imogen—"

The Inquisitor's face contorted. "This is not about Stephen! This is about the *Law*!"

Maryse's thin fingers twisted as her hands worked at each other. "And Jace," she said. "What's going to happen to him?"

"He will return to Idris with me tomorrow," said the Inquisitor. "You've forfeited your right to know any more than that."

"How can you take him back to that place?" Clary demanded. "When will he come *back*?"

"Clary, *don't*," Jace said. The words were a plea, but she battled on.

"Jace isn't the problem here! Valentine is the problem!"

"Leave it alone, Clary!" Jace yelled. "For your own good, leave it alone!"

Clary couldn't help herself, she flinched away from him—he'd never shouted at her like that, not even when she'd dragged him to their mother's hospital room. She saw the look on his face as he registered her flinch and wished she could take it back somehow.

Before she could say anything else, Luke's hand descended onto her shoulder. He spoke, sounding as grave as he had the night he'd told her the story of his life. "If the boy went to his father," he said, "knowing the kind of father Valentine was, it is because we failed him, not because he has failed us."

"Save your sophistry, Lucian," said the Inquisitor. "You've gone as soft as a mundane."

"She's right." Alec was sitting on the edge of the sofa, his arms crossed and his jaw set. "Jace lied to us. There's no excuse for that."

Jace's jaw dropped. He'd been sure of Alec's loyalty, at least, and Clary didn't blame him. Even Isabelle was staring at her brother in horror. "Alec, how can you *say* that?"

"The Law is the Law, Izzy," said Alec, not looking at his sister. "There's no way around that."

At that, Isabelle gave a little gasping cry of rage and astonishment and bolted out the front door, letting it swing open behind her. Maryse made a move as if to follow her, but Robert drew his wife back, saying something in a low voice.

Magnus got to his feet. "I do believe that's my cue to leave as well," he said. Clary noticed he was avoiding looking at Alec. "I'd say it's been nice meeting you all, but, in fact, it hasn't. It's been quite awkward, and frankly, the next time I see a single one of you will be far too soon."

Alec stared at the ground as Magnus stalked out of the living room and through the front door. This time it shut behind him with a bang.

"Two down," said Jace, with ghastly amusement. "Who's next?"

"That's enough from you," said the Inquisitor. "Give me your hands."

Jace held his hands out as the Inquisitor produced a stele from some hidden pocket and proceeded to trace a Mark around the circumference of his wrists. When she took her hands away, Jace's wrists were crossed, one over the other, bound together with what looked like a circlet of burning flames.

Clary cried out. "What are you doing? You'll hurt him—"

"I'm fine, little sister." Jace spoke calmly enough, but she noticed that he couldn't seem to look at her. "The flames won't burn me unless I try to get my hands free."

"And as for you," the Inquisitor added, and turned on Clary, much to Clary's surprise. Up until now the Inquisitor had barely seemed to notice she was alive. "You were lucky enough to be raised by Jocelyn and escape your father's taint. Nevertheless, I'll be keeping an eye on you."

Luke's grip tightened on Clary's shoulder. "Is that a threat?"

"The Clave does not make threats, Lucian Graymark. The Clave makes promises and keeps them." The Inquisitor sounded almost cheerful. She was the only one in the room who could be described that way; everyone else looked shell-shocked, except for Jace. His teeth were bared in a snarl Clary doubted he was even aware of. He looked like a lion in a trap.

"Come, Jonathan," the Inquisitor said. "Walk in front of me. If you make a single move to flee, I'll put a blade between your shoulders."

Jace had to struggle to turn the front doorknob with his bound hands. Clary set her teeth to keep from screaming, and then the door was open and Jace was gone and so was the Inquisitor. The Lightwoods followed in a line, Alec still staring at the ground. The door shut behind them and Clary and Luke were alone in the living room, silent in shared disbelief.

# 15

## The Serpent's Tooth

**"Luke," Clary began, the moment the door had shut behind** the Lightwoods. "What are we going to *do*—"

Luke had his hands pressed to either side of his head as if he were keeping it from splitting in half. "Coffee," he declared. "I need coffee."

"I brought you coffee."

He dropped his hands and sighed. "I need more."

Clary followed him into the kitchen, where he helped himself to yet more coffee before sitting down at the kitchen table and running his hands distractedly through his hair. "This is bad," he said. "Very bad."

"You think?" Clary couldn't imagine drinking coffee right now. Her nerves already felt like they were stretched out as thin as wires. "What happens if they take him to Idris?"

"Trial before the Clave. They'll probably find him guilty. Then punishment. He's young, so they might just strip his Marks, not curse him."

"What does that mean?"

Luke didn't meet her eyes. "It means they'll take his Marks away, unmake him as a Shadowhunter, and throw him out of the Clave. He'll be a mundane."

"But that would kill him. It really would. He'd rather die."

"Don't you think I know that?" Luke had finished his coffee and stared morosely at the mug before setting it back down. "But that won't make any difference to the Clave. They can't get their hands on Valentine, so they'll punish his son instead."

"What about me? I'm his daughter."

"But you're not of their world. Jace is. Not that I don't suggest you lie low for a while yourself. I wish we could head up to the farmhouse—"

"We can't just leave Jace with them!" Clary was appalled. "I'm not going anywhere."

"Of course you aren't." Luke waved away her protest. "I said I wish we could, not that I thought we should. There's the question of what Imogen will do now that she knows where Valentine is, of course. We could find ourselves in the middle of a war."

"I don't care if she wants to kill Valentine. She's welcome to Valentine. I just want to get Jace back."

"That may not be so easy," said Luke, "considering that in this case, he actually did what he's accused of doing."

Clary was outraged. "What, you think he killed the Silent Brothers? You think—"

"No. I don't think he killed the Silent Brothers. I think he did exactly what Imogen saw him do: He went to see his father."

Remembering something, Clary asked: "What did you mean when you said we'd failed him, not the other way around? You mean you don't blame him?"

"I do and I don't." Luke looked weary. "It was a stupid thing to do. Valentine isn't to be trusted. But when the Lightwoods turned their backs on him, what did they expect him to do? He's still just a child, he still needs parents. If they won't have him, he'll go looking for someone who will."

"I thought maybe," said Clary, "maybe he was looking to *you* for that."

Luke looked unutterably sad. "I thought so too, Clary. I thought so too."

Very faintly, Maia could hear the sound of voices coming from the kitchen. They were done with all their shouting in the living room. Time to get out. She folded up the note she'd scribbled hastily, left it on Luke's bed, and crossed the room to the window she'd spent the past twenty minutes forcing open. Cool air spilled through it—it was one of those early fall days when the sky seemed impossibly blue and distant and the air was faintly tinged with the smell of smoke.

She scooted onto the windowsill and looked down. It would have been a worrying jump for her before she'd been Changed; now she spared only a moment's thought for her injured shoulder before leaping. She landed in a crouch on the cracked concrete of Luke's backyard. Straightening up, she glanced back at the house, but no one threw a door open or called out to her to come back.

She fought down an errant stab of disappointment. It wasn't as if they'd paid that much attention to her when she *was* in the house, she thought, scrambling up the high chain-link fence that separated Luke's backyard from the alley, so why would they notice that she'd left it? She was clearly an afterthought, just as she'd always been. The only one of them who'd treated her as if she were of any importance was Simon.

The thought of Simon made her wince as she dropped down onto the other side of the fence and jogged up the alley to Kent Avenue. She'd said to Clary that she didn't remember the previous night, but it wasn't true. She remembered the look on his face when she'd recoiled from him—as if it were imprinted on the backs of her eyelids. The strangest thing was that in that moment he had still looked human to her, more human than almost anyone she'd ever known.

She crossed the street to avoid passing right in front of Luke's house. The street was nearly deserted, Brooklyners sleeping their late Sunday-morning sleep. She headed toward the Bedford Avenue subway, her mind still on Simon. There was a hollow place in the pit of her stomach that ached when she thought of him. He was the first person she'd wanted to trust in years, and he'd made trusting him impossible.

*Of course, if trusting him is impossible, then why are you on your way to see him right now?* came the whisper in the back of her mind that always spoke to her in Daniel's voice. *Shut up*, she told it firmly. *Even if we can't be friends, I owe him an apology at least.*

Someone laughed. The sound echoed off the high factory walls on her left. Her heart contracting with sudden fear, Maia whirled around, but the street behind her was empty. There was an old woman walking her dogs along the riverside, but Maia doubted she was within shouting distance.

She sped up her pace anyway. She could outwalk most humans, she reminded herself, not to mention outrun them. Even in her present state, with her arm aching like someone had slammed a sledgehammer into her shoulder, it wasn't as if she had anything to fear from a mugger or rapist. Two teenage boys armed with knives had tried to grab her while she was walking through Central Park one night after she'd first come to the city, and only Bat had kept her from killing them both.

*So why was she so panicked?*

She glanced behind her. The old woman was gone; Kent was empty. The old abandoned Domino sugar factory rose up in front of her. Seized by a sudden urge to get off the street, she ducked down the alley beside it.

She found herself in a narrow space between two buildings, full of garbage, discarded bottles, the skittering of rats. The roofs above her touched, blocking out the sun and making her feel as if she had ducked into a tunnel. The walls were brick, set with small, dirty windows, many of which had been smashed in by vandals. Through them she could see the abandoned factory floor and row after row of metal boilers, furnaces, and vats. The air smelled of burned sugar. She leaned against one of the walls, trying to still the pounding of her heart. She had almost succeeded in calming herself down when an impossibly familiar voice spoke to her out of the shadows:

"Maia?"

She whirled around. He was standing at the entrance to the alley, his hair lit from behind, shining like a halo around his beautiful face. Dark eyes fringed with long lashes regarded her curiously. He was wearing jeans and, despite the chill in the air, a short-sleeved T-shirt. He still looked fifteen.

*"Daniel,"* she whispered.

He moved toward her, his steps making no sound. "It's been a long time, little sister."

She wanted to run, but her legs felt like bags of water. She pressed herself back against the wall as if she could disappear into it. "But—you're *dead*."

"And you didn't cry at my funeral, did you, Maia? No tears for your big brother?"

"You were a monster," she whispered. "You tried to kill me—"

"Not hard enough." There was something long and sharp in his hand now, something that gleamed like silver fire in the dimness. Maia wasn't sure what it was; her vision was blurred by terror. She slid to the ground as he moved toward her, her legs no longer able to hold her up.

Daniel knelt down beside her. She could see what it was in his hand now: a snapped-off jagged edge of glass from one of the broken windows. Terror rose and broke over her like a wave, but it wasn't fear of the weapon in her brother's hand that was crushing her, it was the emptiness in his eyes. She could look into them and through them and see only darkness. "Do you remember," he said, "when I told you I'd cut out your tongue before I'd let you tattle on me to Mom and Dad?"

Paralyzed with fear, she could only stare at him. Already she could feel the glass cutting into her skin, the choking taste of blood filling her mouth, and she wished she were dead, already dead, anything was better than this horror and this dread—

"Enough, Agramon." A man's voice cut through the fog in

her head. Not Daniel's voice—it was soft, cultured, undeniably human. It reminded her of someone—but who?

*"As you wish, Lord Valentine."* Daniel breathed outward, a soft sigh of disappointment—and then his face began to fade and crumble. In a moment he was gone, and with him the sense of paralyzing, bone-crushing terror that had threatened to choke the life out of her. She sucked in a desperate breath.

"Good. She's breathing." The man's voice again, irritable now. "Really, Agramon. A few more seconds and she'd have been dead."

Maia looked up. The man—Valentine—was standing over her, very tall, dressed all in black, even the gloves on his hands and the thick-soled boots on his feet. He used the tip of a boot now to force her chin up. His voice when he spoke was cool, perfunctory. "How old are you?"

The face gazing down at hers was narrow, sharp-boned, leached of all color, his eyes black and his hair so white he looked like a photograph in negative. On the left side of his throat, just above the collar of his coat, was a spiraling Mark.

"You're Valentine?" she whispered. "But I thought that you—"

The boot came down on her hand, sending a stab of pain shooting up her arm. She screamed.

"I asked you a question," he said. "How old are you?"

"How *old* am I?" The pain in her hand, mixed with the acrid stench of garbage all around made her stomach turn. "Screw you."

A bar of light seemed to leap between his fingers; he slashed it down and across her face so quickly that she didn't have time to jerk back. A hot line of pain burned its way across her cheek; she slapped a hand to her face and felt blood slick her fingers.

"Now," Valentine said, in the same precise and cultured voice. "How old are you?"

"Fifteen. I'm fifteen."

She sensed, rather than saw, him smile. *"Perfect."*

Once back at the Institute, the Inquisitor herded Jace away from the Lightwoods and up the stairs to the training room. Catching sight of himself in the long mirrors that ran along the walls, he stiffened in shock. He hadn't really looked at himself in days, and last night had been a bad one. His eyes were surrounded by black shadows, his shirt smeared with dried blood and filthy mud from the East River. His face looked hollow and drawn.

"Admiring yourself?" The Inquisitor's voice cut through his reverie. "You won't look so pretty when the Clave gets through with you."

"You do seem obsessed with my looks." Jace turned away from the mirror with some relief. "Could it be that all this is because you're attracted to me?"

"Don't be revolting." The Inquisitor had taken four long strips of metal from the gray pouch that hung at her waist. Angel blades. "You could be my son."

"Stephen." Jace remembered what Luke had said back at the house. "That's what he's called, right?"

The Inquisitor whirled on him. The blades she gripped were vibrating with her rage. *"Don't you ever say his name."*

For a moment Jace wondered if she might really try to kill him. He said nothing as she got herself under control. Without looking at him, she pointed with one of the blades. "Stand there in the center of the room, please."

Jace obeyed. Though he tried not to look at the mirrors, he could see his reflection—and the Inquisitor's—out of the corner of his eye, the mirrors reflecting back at each other until an infinite number of Inquisitors stood there, threatening an infinite number of Jaces.

He glanced down at his bound hands. His wrists and shoulders had gone from aching to a hard, stabbing pain, but he didn't wince as the Inquisitor regarded one of the blades, named it Jophiel, and plunged it into the polished wooden floorboards at her feet. He waited, but nothing happened.

"Boom?" he said eventually. "Was something supposed to happen there?"

"Shut up." The Inquisitor's tone was final. "And stay where you are."

Jace stayed, watching with growing curiosity as she moved to his other side, named a second blade Harahel, and proceeded to drive that one into the floorboards as well.

With the third blade—Sandalphon—he realized what she was doing. The first blade had been driven into the floor just south of him, the next to the east, and the next to the north. She was marking out the points of a compass. He struggled to remember what this might mean, came up with nothing. This was clearly Clave ritual, beyond anything he'd been taught. By the time she reached the last blade, Taharial, his palms were sweating, chafing where they rubbed against each other.

The Inquisitor straightened, looking pleased with herself. "There."

"There what?" Jace demanded, but she held a hand up.

"Not quite yet, Jonathan. There's one more thing." She moved to the southernmost blade and knelt in front of it. With a quick movement she produced a stele and marked a single dark rune into the floor just below the knife. As she rose to her feet, a high sharp sweet chime sounded through the room, the sound of a delicate bell being struck. Light poured from the four angel blades, so blinding that Jace turned his face away, half-closing his eyes. When he turned back, a moment later, he saw that he was standing inside a cage whose walls looked as if they had been woven out of filaments of light. They were not static, but moving, like sheets of illuminated rain.

The Inquisitor was now a blurred figure behind a glowing wall. When Jace called out to her, even his voice sounded wavering and hollow, as if he were calling to her through water. "What is this? What have you done?"

She laughed.

Jace took an angry step forward, and then another; his shoulder brushed a glowing wall. As if he'd touched an electrified fence, the shock that pulsed through him was like a blow, knocking him off his feet. He tumbled awkwardly to the floor, unable to use his hands to break his fall.

The Inquisitor laughed again. "If you try to walk *through* the wall, you'll get more than a shock. The Clave calls this particular punishment the Malachi Configuration. These walls can't be broken as long as the seraph blades remain where they are. I wouldn't," she added, as Jace, kneeling, made a move toward the blade closest to him. "Touch the blades and you'll die."

"But *you* can touch them," he said, unable to keep the loathing out of his voice.

"I can, but I won't."

"But what about food? Water?"

"All in good time, Jonathan."

He got to his feet. Through the blurred wall, he saw her turn as if to go.

"But my hands—" He looked down at his bound wrists. The burning metal was eating into his skin like acid. Blood welled around the fiery manacles.

"You should have thought of that before you went to see Valentine."

"You're not exactly making me fear the revenge of the Council. They can't be worse than you."

"Oh, you're not going to the Council," the Inquisitor said. There was a quiet calm in her tone that Jace did not like.

"What do you mean, I'm not going to the Council? I thought you said you were taking me to Idris tomorrow?"

"No. I'm planning to return you to your father."

The shock of her words almost knocked him back off his feet. "*My father?*"

"Your father. I'm planning to trade you to him for the Mortal Instruments."

Jace stared at her. "You must be joking."

"Not at all. It's simpler than a trial. Of course, you'll be banned from the Clave," she added, as a sort of afterthought, "but I assume you expected that."

Jace was shaking his head. "You have the wrong guy. I hope you realize that."

A look of annoyance flashed across her face. "I thought we'd dispensed with your pretense of innocence, Jonathan."

"I didn't mean me. I meant my father."

For the first time since he'd met her, she looked confused. "I don't understand what you mean."

"My father won't trade the Mortal Instruments for me." The

words were bitter, but Jace's tone wasn't. It was matter-of-fact. "He'd let you kill me in front of him before he'd hand you either the Sword or the Cup."

The Inquisitor shook her head. "You don't understand," she said, and there was a puzzling trace of resentment in her voice. "Children never do. The love a parent has for a child, there *is* nothing else like it. No other love so consuming. No father—not even Valentine—would sacrifice his son for a hunk of metal, no matter how powerful."

"You don't know my father. He'll laugh in your face and offer you some money to mail my body back to Idris."

"Don't be absurd—"

"You're right," Jace said. "Come to think of it, he'll probably make you pay the shipping charges yourself."

"I see that you're still your father's son. You don't want him to lose the Mortal Instruments—it would be a loss of power to you as well. You don't want to live out your life as the disgraced son of a criminal, so you'll say anything to sway my decision. But you don't fool me."

"Listen." Jace's heart was pounding, but he tried to speak calmly. She *had* to believe him. "I know you hate me. I know you think I'm a liar like my father. But I'm telling you the truth now. My father absolutely believes in what he's doing. You think he's evil. But he thinks he's *right*. He thinks he's doing God's work. He won't give that up for me. You were tracking me when I went out there, you must have heard what he said—"

"I *saw* you speak to him," said the Inquisitor. "I *heard* nothing."

Jace cursed under his breath. "Look, I'll swear any oath you want to prove I'm not lying. He's using the Sword and the Cup to summon demons and control them. The more you waste your time with me, the more he can build up his army. By the time you realize he won't make the trade, you'll have no chance against him—"

The Inquisitor turned away with a noise of disgust. "I'm tired of your lies."

Jace caught his breath in disbelief as she turned her back on him and stalked toward the door.

*"Please!"* he cried.

She stopped at the door and turned to look at him. Jace could only see the angular shadows of her face, the pointed chin, and dark hollows at her temples. Her gray clothes vanished into the shadows so that she looked like a bodiless floating skull. "Don't think," she said, "that returning you to your father is what I *want* to do. It's better than Valentine Morgenstern deserves."

"What does he deserve?"

"To hold the dead body of his child in his arms. To see his dead son and know that there is nothing he can do, no spell, no incantation, no bargain with hell that will bring him back—" She broke off. "He should *know*," she said, in a whisper, and pushed at the door, her hands scrabbling against the wood. It shut behind her with a click, leaving Jace, his wrists burning, staring after her in confusion.

Clary hung up the phone with a frown. "No answer."

"Who is it you were trying to call?" Luke was on his fifth cup of coffee and Clary was starting to worry about him. Surely there was such a thing as caffeine poisoning? He didn't seem on the verge of a fit or anything, but she surreptitiously unplugged the percolator on her way back to the table, just in case. "Simon?"

"No. I feel weird waking him up during the daytime, though he said it doesn't bother him as long as he doesn't have to see day*light*."

"So . . ."

"I was calling Isabelle. I want to know what's going on with Jace."

"She didn't answer?"

"No." Clary's stomach rumbled. She went to the refrigerator, removed a peach yogurt, and ate it mechanically, tasting nothing. She was halfway through the container when she remembered something. "Maia," she said. "We should check and see if she's okay." She set the yogurt down. "I'll go."

"No, I'm her pack leader. She trusts me. I can calm her down if she's upset," Luke said. "I'll be right back."

"Don't say that," Clary begged. "I hate it when people say that."

He smiled at her crookedly and ducked out into the hallway. Within a few minutes he was back, looking stunned. "She's gone."

"Gone? Gone how?"

"I mean she snuck out of the house. She left this." He tossed a folded piece of paper onto the table. Clary picked it up and read the scrawled sentences with a frown:

*Sorry about everything. Gone to make amends. Thanks for all you've done. Maia.*

"Gone to make amends? What does that mean?"

Luke sighed. "I was hoping you would know."

"Are you worried?"

"Raum demons are retrievers," Luke said. "They find people and bring them back to whoever summoned them. That demon could still be looking for her."

"Oh," Clary said in a small voice. "Well, my guess would be that she means she went to see Simon."

Luke looked surprised. "Does she know where he lives?"

"I don't know," Clary admitted. "They seem kind of close in a way. She might." She fished into her pocket for her phone. "I'll call him."

"I thought calling him made you feel weird."

"Not as weird as everything else that's going on." She scrolled through her address book for Simon's number. It rang three times before he picked up, sounding groggy.

"Hello?"

"It's me." She turned away from Luke as she spoke, more out of habit than from any desire to hide the conversation from him.

"You do know I'm nocturnal now," he said with groan. She could hear him rolling over in bed. "That means I sleep all day."

"Are you at home?"

"Yeah, where else would I be?" His voice sharpened, sleep falling away. "What is it, Clary, what's wrong?"

"Maia ran off. She left a note saying she might be going to your house."

Simon sounded puzzled. "Well, she didn't. Or if she did, she hasn't shown up yet."

"Is anyone else home but you?"

"No, my mom's at work and Rebecca has classes. Why, you really think Maia's going to show up here?"

"Just give us a call if she does—"

Simon cut her off. "Clary." His tone was urgent. "Hang on a second. I think someone's trying to break into my house."

Time passed inside the prison, and Jace watched the shocking silver rain falling all around him with a detached sort of interest. His fingers had started to go numb, which he suspected was a bad sign, but he couldn't bring himself to care. He wondered if the Lightwoods knew he was up here, or if someone entering the training room would get a nasty surprise when they found him locked up in it. But no, the Inquisitor wasn't that sloppy. She would have told them the room was off-limits until she disposed of the prisoner in whatever manner she saw fit. He supposed he ought to be angry, even afraid, but he couldn't bring himself to care about that either. Nothing seemed real anymore: not the Clave, not the Covenant, not the Law, not even his father.

A soft footfall alerted him to the presence of someone else in the room. He'd been lying on his back, staring at the ceiling; now he sat up, his gaze flicking around the room. He could see a dark shape just beyond the shimmering rain-curtain. *It must be the Inquisitor*, back to sneer at him some more. He braced himself—then saw, with a jolt, the dark hair and familiar face.

Maybe there were still some things he cared about, after all. "Alec?"

"It's me." Alec knelt down on the other side of the glimmering wall. It was like looking at someone through clear water rippled with current; Jace could see Alec clearly now, but occasionally his features would seem to waver and dissolve as the fiery rain shimmered and undulated.

It was enough to make you seasick, Jace thought.

"What in the Angel's name is this stuff?" Alec reached out to touch the wall.

"Don't." Jace reached out, then drew back quickly before he made contact with the wall. "It'll shock you, maybe kill you if you try to pass through it."

Alec drew his hand back with a low whistle. "The Inquisitor meant business."

"Of course she did. I'm a dangerous criminal. Or hadn't you heard?" Jace heard the acid in his own tone, saw Alec flinch, and was meanly, momentarily, glad.

"She didn't call you a criminal, exactly . . ."

"No, I'm just a very naughty boy. I do all sorts of bad things. I kick kittens. I make rude gestures at nuns."

"Don't joke. This is serious stuff." Alec's eyes were somber. "What the hell were you thinking, going to see Valentine? I mean, seriously, what was going through your head?"

A number of smart remarks occurred to Jace, but he found he didn't want to make any of them. He was too tired. "I was thinking that he's my father."

Alec looked as if he were mentally counting to ten to maintain his patience. "Jace—"

"What if it was your father? What would you do?"

"*My* father? My father would never do the things that Valentine—"

Jace's head jerked up. "Your father *did do those things*! He was in the Circle along with my father! Your mother, too! Our parents were all the same. The only difference is that yours got caught and punished, and mine didn't!"

Alec's face tightened. But "The *only* difference?" was all he said.

Jace looked down at his hands. The burning cuffs weren't meant to be left on so long. The skin underneath them was dotted with beads of blood.

"I just meant," Alec said, "that I don't see how you could want to see him, not after what's he's done in general, but after what he did to *you*."

Jace said nothing.

"All those years," Alec said. "He let you think he was dead. Maybe you don't remember what it was like when you were ten years old, but I do. Nobody who loved you could do—could do anything like that."

Thin lines of blood were making their way down Jace's hands, like red string unraveling. "Valentine told me," he said quietly, "that if I supported him against the Clave, if I did that, he'd make sure no one I cared about was hurt. Not you or Isabelle or Max. Not Clary. Not your parents. He said—"

"No one would be hurt?" Alec echoed derisively. "You mean he wouldn't hurt them himself. Nice."

"I saw what he can do, Alec. The kind of demonic force he can summon. If he brings his demon army against the Clave, there *will* be a war. And people get hurt in wars. They die in wars." He hesitated. "If you had the chance to save everyone you loved—"

"But what kind of chance is it? What's Valentine's word even worth?"

"If he swears on the Angel that he'll do something, he'll do it. I know him."

"*If* you support him against the Clave."

Jace nodded.

"He must have been pretty pissed when you said no," Alec observed.

Jace looked up from his bleeding wrists and stared. "What?"

"I said—"

"I know what you said. What makes you think I said no?"

"Well, you did. Didn't you?"

Very slowly, Jace nodded.

"I know you," Alec said, with supreme confidence, and stood up. "You told the Inquisitor about Valentine and his plans, didn't you? And she didn't care?"

"I wouldn't say she didn't care. More like she didn't really believe me. She's got a plan she thinks will take care of Valentine. The only problem is, her plan sucks."

Alec nodded. "You can fill me in on that later. First things first: We have to figure out how to get you out of here."

"*What?*" Disbelief made Jace feel slightly dizzy. "I thought you came down right on the side of go directly to jail, do not pass Go, do not collect two hundred dollars. 'The Law is the Law, Isabelle.' What was all that you were spouting?"

Alec looked astonished. "You can't have thought I *meant* that. I just wanted the Inquisitor to trust me so she wouldn't be watching me all the time like she's watching Izzy and Max. She knows they're on your side."

"And you? Are you on my side?" Jace could hear the roughness in his own question and was almost overwhelmed by how much the answer meant to him.

"I'm with you," Alec said, "always. Why do you even have to ask? I may respect the Law, but what the Inquisitor has been doing to you has nothing to do with the Law. I don't know exactly what's going on, but the hatred she has for you is personal. It has nothing to do with the Clave."

"I bait her," said Jace. "I can't help it. Vicious bureaucrats get under my skin."

Alec shook his head. "It's not that either. It's an old hate. I can feel it."

Jace was about to answer when the cathedral bells began to ring. This close to the roof, the sound was echoingly loud. He glanced up—he still half-expected to see Hugo flying among the wooden rafters in his slow, thoughtful circles. The raven had always liked it up there between the rafters and the arched stone ceiling. At the time Jace had thought the bird liked to dig his claws into the soft wood; now he realized the rafters had lent him an excellent vantage point for spying.

An idea began to take shape in the back of Jace's mind, dark and formless. Out loud he said only, "Luke said something about the Inquisitor having a son named Stephen. He said she was trying to get even for him. I asked her about him and she freaked out. I think it might have something to do with why she hates me so much."

The bells had stopped ringing. Alec said, "Maybe. I could ask my parents, but I doubt they'd tell me."

"No, don't ask them. Ask Luke."

"Go all the way back to Brooklyn, you mean? Look, sneaking out of here is going to be all but impossible—"

"Use Isabelle's phone. Text Clary. Tell her to ask Luke."

"Okay." Alec paused. "Do you want me to say anything else to her for you? To Clary, I mean, not Isabelle."

"No," Jace said. "I don't have anything to say to her."

* * *

"Simon!" Clutching the phone, Clary whirled toward Luke. "He says someone's trying to break into his house."

"Tell him to get out of there."

"I can't get out of here," Simon said tightly. "Not unless I want to catch on fire."

"Daylight," she said to Luke, but she saw he'd already realized the problem and was searching for something in his pockets. Car keys. He held them up.

"Tell Simon we're coming. Tell him to lock himself in a room until we get there."

"Did you hear that? Lock yourself in a room."

"I heard." Simon's voice sounded tense; Clary could hear a soft scraping sound, then a heavy thump.

"Simon!"

"I'm fine. I'm just piling things against the door."

"What kind of things?" She was out on the porch now, shivering in her thin sweater. Luke, behind her, was locking up the house.

"A desk," Simon said with some satisfaction. "And my bed."

"Your *bed*?" Clary climbed up into the truck beside Luke, struggling one-handed with her seat belt as Luke peeled out of the driveway and rocketed down Kent. He reached over and buckled it for her. "How did you lift your bed?"

"You forget. Super vampire strength."

"Ask him what he's hearing," Luke said. They were speeding down the street, which would have been fine if the Brooklyn waterfront had been better maintained. Clary gasped every time they hit a pothole.

"What are you hearing?" she asked, catching her breath.

"I heard the front door crash in. I think someone must

have kicked it open. Then Yossarian came streaking into my room and hid under the bed. That's how I knew there was definitely someone in the house."

"And now?"

"Now I don't hear anything."

"That's good, right?" Clary turned to Luke. "He says he doesn't hear anything now. Maybe they went away."

"Maybe." Luke sounded doubtful. They were on the expressway now, speeding toward Simon's neighborhood. "Keep him on the phone anyway."

"What are you doing now, Simon?"

"Nothing. I've shoved everything in the room against the door. Now I'm trying to get Yossarian out from behind the heating vent."

"Leave him where he is."

"This is all going to be very hard to explain to my mom," Simon said, and the phone went dead. There was a click and then nothing. CALL DISCONNECTED flashed on the digital display.

"No. *No!*" Clary hit the redial button, her fingers trembling.

Simon picked up immediately. "Sorry. Yossarian scratched me and I dropped the phone."

Her throat burned with relief. "That's fine, just as long as you're still okay and—"

A noise like a tidal wave crashed through the phone, obliterating Simon's voice. She yanked the phone away from her ear. The display still read CALL CONNECTED.

"*Simon!*" she screamed into the phone. "Simon, can you hear me?"

The crashing noise stopped. There was the sound of

something shattering, and a high, unearthly yowl—Yossarian? Then the sound of something heavy striking the ground.

"Simon?" she whispered.

There was a click and then a drawling, amused voice spoke in her ear. "Clarissa," it said. "I should have known you'd be on the other end of this phone line."

She squeezed her eyes shut, her stomach falling out from under her as if she were on a roller coaster that had just made its first drop. "Valentine."

"You mean 'Father,'" he said, sounding genuinely annoyed. "I deplore this modern habit of calling one's parents by their first names."

"What I actually want to call you is a hell of a lot more unprintable than your name," she snapped. "Where's Simon?"

"You mean the vampire boy? Questionable company for a Shadowhunter girl of good family, don't you think? From now on I'll be expecting to have a say in your choice of friends."

*"What did you do to Simon?"*

"Nothing," said Valentine, amused. "Yet."

And he hung up.

By the time Alec came back into the training room, Jace was lying on the floor, envisioning lines of dancing girls in an effort to ignore the pain in his wrists. It wasn't working.

"What are you doing?" Alec asked, kneeling down as close to the shimmering wall of the prison as he could get. Jace tried to remind himself that when Alec asked this sort of question, he really meant it, and that it was something he had once found endearing rather than annoying. He failed.

"I thought I'd lie on the floor and writhe in pain for a while," he grunted. "It relaxes me."

"It does? Oh—you're being sarcastic. That's a good sign, probably," Alec said. "If you can sit up, you might want to. I'm going to try to slide something through the wall."

Jace sat up so quickly that his head spun. "Alec, don't—"

But Alec had already moved to push something toward him with both hands, as if he were rolling a ball to a child. A red sphere broke through the shimmering curtain and rolled to Jace, bumping gently against his knee.

"An apple." He picked it up with some difficulty. "How appropriate."

"I thought you might be hungry."

"I am." Jace took a bite of the apple; juice ran down his hands and sizzled in the blue flames that cuffed his wrists. "Did you text Clary?"

"No. Isabelle won't let me into her room. She just throws things against the door and screams. She said if I came in she'd jump out the window. She'd do it too."

"Probably."

"I get the feeling," Alec said, and smiled, "she hasn't forgiven me for betraying you, as she sees it."

"Good girl," said Jace with appreciation.

"I *didn't* betray you, idiot."

"It's the thought that counts."

"Good, because I brought you something else, too. I don't know if it'll work, but it's worth a try." He slid something small and metallic through the wall. It was a silvery disk about the size of a quarter. Jace set the apple aside and picked the disk up curiously. "What's this?"

"I got it off the desk in the library. I've seen my parents use it before to take off restraints. I think it's an Unlocking rune. It's worth trying—"

He broke off as Jace touched the disk to his wrists, holding it awkwardly between two fingers. The moment it touched the line of blue flame, the cuff flickered and vanished.

"Thanks." Jace rubbed his wrists, each one braceleted with a line of chafed, bleeding skin. He was starting to be able to feel his fingertips again. "It's not a file hidden in a birthday cake, but it'll keep my hands from falling off."

Alec looked at him. The wavering lines of the rain-curtain made his face look elongated, worried—or maybe he *was* worried. "You know, something occurred to me when I was talking to Isabelle earlier. I told her she couldn't jump out the window—and not to try or she'd get herself killed."

Jace nodded. "Sound big-brotherly advice."

"But then I started wondering if that was true in your case—I mean, I've seen you do things that were practically flying. I've seen you fall three stories and land like a cat, jump from the ground to a roof—"

"Hearing my achievements recited is certainly gratifying, but I'm not sure what your point is, Alec."

"My point is that there are four walls to this prison, not five."

Jace stared at him. "So Hodge wasn't lying when he said we'd actually use geometry in our daily lives. You're right, Alec. There are four walls to this cage. Now if the Inquisitor had gone with two, I might—"

"JACE," Alec said, losing patience. "I mean, there's no *top* to the cage. Nothing between you and the ceiling."

Jace craned his head back. The rafters seemed to sway dizzily high above him, lost in shadow. "You're crazy."

"Maybe," Alec said. "Maybe I just know what you can do." He shrugged. "You could try, at least."

Jace looked at Alec—at his open, honest face and steady blue eyes. *He* is *crazy*, Jace thought. It was true, in the heat of fighting, he'd done some amazing things, but so had they all. Shadowhunter blood, years of training . . . but he couldn't jump thirty feet straight up into the air.

*How do you know you can't,* said a soft voice in his head, *if you've never tried it?*

Clary's voice. He thought of her and her runes, of the Silent City and the handcuff popping off his wrist as if it had cracked under some enormous pressure. He and Clary shared the same blood. If Clary could do things that shouldn't be possible . . .

He got to his feet, almost reluctantly, and looked around, taking slow stock of the room. He could still see the floor-length mirrors and the multitude of weapons hanging on the walls, their blades glinting dully, through the curtain of silver fire that surrounded him. He bent and retrieved the half-eaten apple off the floor, looked at it for a thoughtful moment—then cocked his arm back and threw it as hard as he could. The apple sailed through the air, hit a shimmering silver wall, and burst into a corona of molten blue flame.

Jace heard Alec gasp. So the Inquisitor *hadn't* been exaggerating. If he hit one of the prison walls too hard, he'd die.

Alec was on his feet, suddenly wavering. "Jace, I don't know—"

"Shut up, Alec. And don't watch me. It's not helping."

Whatever Alec said in response, Jace didn't hear it. He was doing a slow pivot in place, his eyes focused on the rafters. The runes that gave him excellent long sight kicked in, the rafters coming into better focus: He could see their chipped edges, their whorls and knots, the black stains of age. But they were solid. They'd held up the Institute roof for hundreds of years. They could hold a teenage boy. He flexed his fingers, taking deep, slow, controlled breaths, just as his father had taught him. In his mind's eye he saw himself leaping, soaring, catching hold of a rafter with ease and swinging himself up onto it. He was light, he told himself, light as an arrow, winging its way easily through the air, swift and unstoppable. It would be easy, he told himself. Easy.

"I am Valentine's arrow," Jace whispered. "Whether he knows it or not."

And he jumped.

# 16

## A Stone of the Heart

**Clary hit the button to call Simon back, but the phone went** straight to voice mail. Hot tears splashed down her cheeks and she threw her own phone at the dashboard. "Damn it, damn it—"

"We're almost there," Luke said. They'd gotten off the expressway and she hadn't even noticed. They pulled up in front of Simon's house, a wooden one-family whose front was painted a cheerful red. Clary was out of the car and running up the front walk before Luke had even yanked on the security brake. She could hear him yelling her name as she dashed up the steps and pounded frantically on the front door.

"Simon!" she shouted. "*Simon!*"

"Clary, enough." Luke caught up to her on the front porch. "The neighbors—"

"Screw the neighbors." She fumbled for the key ring on her belt, found the right key, and slid it into the lock. She swung the door open and stepped warily into the hallway, Luke just behind her. They peered through the first door on the left into the kitchen. Everything looked exactly as it always had, from the meticulously clean counter to the fridge magnets. There was the sink where she'd kissed Simon just a few days ago. Sunshine streamed in through the windows, filling the room with pale yellow light. Light that was capable of charring Simon away to ashes.

Simon's room was the last one at the end of the hall. The door stood slightly open, though Clary could see nothing but darkness through the crack.

She slid her stele out of her pocket and gripped it tightly. She knew it wasn't really a weapon, but the feel of it in her hand was calming. Inside, the room was dark, black curtains drawn across the windows, the only light coming from the digital clock on the bedside table. Luke was reaching across her to flip on the light when something—something that hissed and spit and snarled like a demon—launched itself at him out of the darkness.

Clary screamed as Luke seized her shoulders and pushed her roughly aside. She stumbled and nearly fell; when she righted herself, she turned to see an astonished-looking Luke holding a yowling, struggling white cat, its fur sticking out all over. It looked like a ball of cotton with claws.

"Yossarian!" Clary exclaimed.

Luke dropped the cat. Yossarian immediately shot between his legs and disappeared down the hall.

"Stupid cat," Clary said.

"It's not his fault. Cats don't like me." Luke reached for the light switch and flipped it on. Clary gasped. The room was completely in order, nothing at all out of place, not even the rug askew. Even the coverlet was folded neatly on the bed.

"Is it a glamour?"

"Probably not. Probably just magic." Luke moved into the center of the room, looking around him thoughtfully. As he moved to pull one of the curtains aside, Clary saw something gleam in the carpet at his feet.

"Luke, wait." She went to where he was standing and knelt to retrieve the object. It was Simon's silver cell phone, badly bent out of shape, the antenna snapped off. Heart pounding, she flipped the phone open. Despite the crack that ran the length of the display screen, a single text message was still visible: *Now I have them all.*

Clary sank down on the bed in a daze. Distantly, she felt Luke pluck the phone out of her hand. She heard him suck in his breath as he read the message.

"What does that mean? 'Now I have them all'?" asked Clary.

Luke set Simon's phone down on the desk and passed a hand over his face. "I'm afraid it means that now he has Simon and, we might as well face it, Maia, too. It means he has everything he needs for the Ritual of Conversion."

Clary stared at him. "You mean this isn't just about getting at me—and you?"

"I'm sure Valentine regards that as a pleasant side effect. But it's not his main goal. His main goal is to reverse the characteristics of the Soul-Sword. And for that he needs—"

"The blood of Downworlder children. But Maia and Simon aren't children. They're teenagers."

"When that spell was created, the spell to turn the Soul-Sword to darkness, the word 'teenager' hadn't even been invented. In Shadowhunter society, you're an adult when you're eighteen. Before that, you're a child. For Valentine's purposes, Maia and Simon are children. He has the blood of a faerie child already, and the blood of a warlock child. All he needed was a werewolf and a vampire."

Clary felt as if the air had been punched out of her. "Then why didn't we do something? Why didn't we think of protecting them somehow?"

"So far Valentine has done what's convenient. None of his victims were chosen for any other reason than that they were there and available. The warlock was easy to find; all Valentine had to do was hire him under the pretense of wanting a demon raised. It's simple enough to spot faeries in the park if you know where to look. And the Hunter's Moon is exactly where you'd go if you wanted to find a werewolf. Putting himself to this extra danger and trouble just to strike out at us when nothing's changed—"

"Jace," said Clary.

"What do you mean, Jace? What about him?"

"I think it's Jace he's trying to get back at. Jace must have done something last night on the boat, something that really pissed Valentine off. Pissed him off enough to abandon whatever plan he had before and make a new one."

Luke looked baffled. "What makes you think that Valentine's change of plans had anything to do with your brother?"

"Because," Clary said with grim certainty, "only Jace can piss someone off *that* much."

* * *

"Isabelle!" Alec pounded on his sister's door. "Isabelle, open the door. I know you're in there."

The door opened a crack. Alec tried to peer through it, but no one appeared to be on the other side. "She doesn't want to talk to you," said a well-known voice.

Alec glanced down and saw gray eyes glaring at him from behind a bent pair of spectacles. "Max," he said. "Come on, little brother, let me in."

"I don't want to talk to you either." Max started to push the door shut, but Alec, quick as a flick of Isabelle's whip, wedged his foot into the gap.

"Don't make me knock you over, Max."

"You wouldn't." Max pushed back with all his might.

"No, but I might go get our parents, and I have a feeling Isabelle doesn't want that. Do you, Izzy?" he demanded, pitching his voice loud enough for his sister, inside the room, to hear.

"Oh, for God's sake." Isabelle sounded furious. "All right, Max. Let him in."

Max stepped away and Alec pushed his way in, letting the door swing half-shut behind him. Isabelle was kneeling in the embrasure of the window beside her bed, her gold whip coiled around her left arm. She was wearing her hunting gear, the tough black trousers and skintight shirt with their silvery, near-invisible design of runes. Her boots were buckled up to her knees and her black hair whipped in the breeze from the open window. She glared at him, reminding him for a moment of nothing more than Hugo, Hodge's black raven.

"What the hell are you doing? Trying to get yourself killed?" he demanded, striding furiously across the room toward his sister.

Her whip snaked out, coiling around his ankles. Alec stopped dead, knowing that with a single flick of her wrist Isabelle could jerk him off his feet and land him in a trussed bundle on the hardwood floor. "Don't come any closer to me, Alexander Lightwood," she said in her angriest voice. "I'm not feeling very charitable toward you at the moment."

"Isabelle—"

"How could you just turn on Jace like that? After all he's been through? And you swore that oath to watch out for each other too—"

"Not," he reminded her, "if it meant breaking the Law."

"The *Law*!" Isabelle snapped in disgust. "There's a higher law than the Clave, Alec. The law of family. Jace is your family."

"The law of family? I've never heard of that before," Alec said, nettled. He knew he ought to be defending himself, but it was hard not to be distracted by the lifelong habit of correcting one's younger siblings when they were wrong. "Could that be because you just made it up?"

Isabelle flicked her wrist. Alec felt his feet go out from under him and twisted to absorb the impact of falling with his hands and wrists. He landed, rolled onto his back, and looked up to see Isabelle looming over him. Max was beside her. "What should we do with him, Maxwell?" Isabelle asked. "Leave him tied up here for the parents to find?"

Alec had had enough. He whipped a blade from the sheath at his wrist, twisted, and slashed it through the whip around his ankles. The electrum wire parted with a snap and he sprang to his feet as Isabelle drew her arm back, the wire hissing around her.

A low chuckle broke the tension. "All right, all right, you've tortured him enough. I'm here."

Isabelle's eyes flew wide. "Jace!"

"The same." Jace ducked into Isabelle's room, shutting the door behind him. "No need for the two of you to fight—" He winced as Max careened into him, yelping his name. "Careful there," he said, gently disentangling the boy. "I'm not in the best shape right now."

"I can see that," Isabelle said, her eyes raking him anxiously. His wrists were bloody, his fair hair was plastered sweatily to his neck and forehead, and his face and hands were stained with dirt and ichor. "Did the Inquisitor hurt you?"

"Not too badly." Jace's eyes met Alec's across the room. "She just locked me up in the weapons gallery. Alec helped me get out."

The whip drooped in Isabelle's hand like a flower. "Alec, is that true?"

"Yes." Alec brushed dust from the floor off his clothes with deliberate ostentation. He couldn't resist adding: "So there."

"Well, you should have *said*."

"And you should have had some faith in me—"

"Enough. There's no time for bickering," Jace said. "Isabelle, what kind of weapons do you have in here? And bandages, any bandages?"

"Bandages?" Isabelle set her whip down and took her stele out of a drawer. "I can fix you up with an *iratze*—"

Jace raised his wrists. "An *iratze* would be good for my bruises, but it won't help these. These are rune burns." They looked even worse in the bright light of Isabelle's room—the circular scars were black and cracked in places, oozing blood and clear fluid. He lowered his hands as Isabelle paled. "And I'll need some weapons, too, before I—"

"Bandages first. Weapons later." She set her stele down on top of the dresser and herded Jace into the bathroom with a basketful of ointments, gauze pads, and bandage strips. Alec watched them through the half-open door, Jace leaning against the sink as his adoptive sister sponged his wrists and wrapped them in white gauze. "Okay, now take your shirt off."

"I knew there was something in this for you." Jace slid off his jacket and drew his T-shirt over his head, wincing. His skin was pale gold, layered over hard muscle. Black ink Marks twined his slim arms. A mundane might have thought the white scars that snowflaked Jace's skin, remnants of old runes, made him less than perfect, but Alec didn't. They all had those scars; they were badges of honor, not flaws.

Jace, seeing Alec watching him through the half-open door, said, "Alec, can you get the phone?"

"It's on the dresser." Isabelle didn't look up. She and Jace were conversing in low tones; Alec couldn't hear them, but suspected this was because they were trying not to scare Max.

Alec looked. "It's *not* on the dresser."

Isabelle, tracing an *iratze* on Jace's back, swore in annoyance. "Oh, hell. I left my phone in the kitchen. Crap. I don't want to go looking for it in case the Inquisitor's around."

"I'll get it," Max offered. "She doesn't care about me, I'm too young."

"I suppose." Isabelle sounded reluctant. "What do you need the phone for, Alec?"

"We just need it," Alec said impatiently. "Izzy—"

"If you're texting Magnus to say 'I think u r kewl,' I'm going to kill you."

"Who's Magnus?" Max inquired.

"He's a warlock," said Alec.

"A sexy, sexy warlock," Isabelle told Max, ignoring Alec's look of total fury.

"But warlocks are bad," protested Max, looking baffled.

"Exactly," said Isabelle.

"I don't understand," said Max. "But I'm going to get the phone. I'll be right back."

He slipped out the door as Jace pulled his shirt and jacket back on and came back into the bedroom, where he commenced looking for weapons in the piles of Isabelle's belongings that were strewn around the floor. Isabelle followed him, shaking her head. "What's the plan now? Are we all leaving? The Inquisitor's going to freak when she finds out you're not there anymore."

"Not as much as she'll freak when Valentine turns her down." Tersely, Jace outlined the Inquisitor's plan. "The only problem is, he'll never go for it."

"The—the *only* problem?" Isabelle was so furious she was almost stuttering, something she hadn't done since she was six. "She can't do that! She can't just trade you away to a psychopath! You're a member of the Clave! You're our *brother*!"

"The Inquisitor doesn't think so."

"I don't care what she thinks. She's a hideous bitch and she has *got* to be stopped."

"Once she finds out her plan is seriously flawed, she might be able to be talked down," Jace observed. "But I'm not sticking around to find out. I'm getting out of here."

"It's not going to be easy," Alec said. "The Inquisitor's got this place locked up tighter than a pentagram. You know there are guards downstairs? She's called in half the Conclave."

"She must think highly of me," said Jace, tossing aside a pile of magazines.

"Maybe she's not wrong." Isabelle looked at him thoughtfully. "Did you seriously jump thirty feet out of a Malachi Configuration? Did he, Alec?"

"He did," Alec confirmed. "I've never seen anything like it."

"I've never seen anything like *this*." Jace lifted a ten-inch dagger from the floor. One of Isabelle's pink brassieres was speared on the wickedly sharp tip. Isabelle snatched it off, scowling.

"That's not the point. How did you *do* it? Do you know?"

"I jumped." Jace pulled two razor-edged spinning disks out from under the bed. They were covered in gray cat hair. He blew on them, scattering fur. "*Chakhrams*. Cool. Especially if I meet any demons with serious dander allergies."

Isabelle thwacked him with the bra. "You're not answering me!"

"Because I don't know, Izzy." Jace scrambled to his feet. "Maybe the Seelie Queen was right. Maybe I have powers I don't even know about because I've never tested them. Clary certainly does."

Isabelle wrinkled her forehead. "She does?"

Alec's eyes widened suddenly. "Jace—is that vampire cycle of yours still up on the roof?"

"Possibly. But it's daylight, so it's not much use."

"Besides," Isabelle pointed out, "we can't all fit on it."

Jace slid the *chakhrams* onto his belt, along with the ten-inch dagger. Several angel blades went into his jacket pockets. "That doesn't matter," he said. "You're not coming with me."

Isabelle spluttered. "What do you mean, we're not—" She

broke off as Max returned, out of breath and clutching her battered pink phone. "Max, you're a hero." She snatched the phone from him, shooting a glare at Jace. "I'll get back to you in a minute. Meanwhile, who are we calling? Clary?"

"I'll call her—," Alec began.

"No." Isabelle batted his hand away. "She likes me better." She was already dialing; she stuck her tongue out as she held the phone up to her ear. "Clary? It's Isabelle. I—*What?*" The color in her face vanished as if it had been wiped away, leaving her gray and staring. "How is that possible? But why—"

"How is what possible?" Jace was at her side in two strides. "Isabelle, what's happened? Is Clary—"

Isabelle drew the phone away from her ear, her knuckles white. "It's Valentine. He's taken Simon and Maia. He's going to use them to perform the Ritual."

In one smooth motion, Jace reached over and plucked the phone out of Isabelle's hand. He put it to his ear. "Drive to the Institute," he said. "Don't come in. Wait for me. I'll meet you outside." He snapped the phone shut and handed it to Alec. "Call Magnus," he said. "Tell him to meet us down by the waterfront in Brooklyn. He can pick the place, but it should be somewhere deserted. We're going to need his help getting to Valentine's ship."

"We?" Isabelle perked up visibly.

"Magnus, Luke, and myself," Jace clarified. "You two are staying here and dealing with the Inquisitor for me. When Valentine doesn't come through with his part of her deal, you're the ones who are going to have to convince her to send all the backup the Conclave has got after Valentine."

"I don't get it," Alec said. "How do you plan to get out of here in the first place?"

Jace grinned. "Watch," he said, and jumped up onto Isabelle's windowsill. Isabelle cried out, but Jace was already ducking through the window opening. He balanced for a moment on the sill outside—and then he was gone.

Alec raced to the window and stared out in horror, but there was nothing to see: just the garden of the Institute far below, brown and empty, and the narrow path that led up to the front door. There were no screaming pedestrians on Ninety-sixth Street, no cars pulled over at the sight of a falling body. It was as if Jace had vanished into thin air.

The sound of water woke him. It was a heavy repetitive sound—water sloshing against something solid, over and over, as if he were lying in the bottom of a pool that was rapidly draining and refilling itself. There was the taste of metal in his mouth and the smell of metal all around. He was conscious of a nagging, persistent pain in his left hand. With a groan, Simon opened his eyes.

He was lying on a hard, bumpy metal floor painted an ugly gray-green. The walls were the same green metal. There was a single high round window in one wall, letting in only a little sunlight, but it was enough. He'd been lying with his hand in a patch of it and his fingers were red and blistered. With another groan, he rolled away from the light and sat up.

And realized he wasn't alone in the room. Though the shadows were thick, he could see in the dark just fine. Across from him, her hands bound together and chained to a large steam pipe, was Maia. Her clothes were torn and there was a massive bruise across her left cheek. He could see where her braids had been torn away from her scalp on one side, her hair matted with blood. The moment he sat up, she stared at him and burst immediately into tears. "I thought," she hiccupped between sobs, "that you—were dead."

"I *am* dead," Simon said. He was staring at his hand. As he watched, the blisters faded, the pain lessening, the skin resuming its normal pallor.

"I know, but I meant—really dead." She swiped at her face with her bound hands. Simon tried to move toward her, but something brought him up short. A metal cuff around his ankle was attached to a thick metal chain sunk into the floor. Valentine was taking no chances.

"Don't cry," he said, and immediately regretted it. It wasn't as if the situation didn't warrant tears. "I'm fine."

"For now," said Maia, rubbing her wet face against her sleeve. "That man—the one with the white hair—his name is Valentine?"

"You saw him?" Simon said. "I didn't see anything. Just my front door blowing in and then a massive shape that came at me like a freight train."

"He's *the* Valentine, right? The one everyone talks about. The one who started the Uprising."

"He's Jace and Clary's father," Simon said. "That's what I know about him."

"I thought his voice sounded familiar. He sounds just like Jace." She looked momentarily rueful. "No wonder Jace is such an ass."

Simon could only agree.

"So you didn't . . ." Maia's voice trailed off. She tried again. "Look, I know this sounds weird, but when Valentine came for you, did you see someone you recognized with him, someone who's dead? Like a ghost?"

Simon shook his head, bewildered. "No. Why?"

Maia hesitated. "I saw my brother. The ghost of my brother. I think Valentine was making me hallucinate."

"Well, he didn't try anything like that on me. I was on the phone with Clary. I remember dropping it when the shape came at me—" He shrugged. "That's it."

"With Clary?" Maia looked almost hopeful. "Then maybe they'll figure out where we are. Maybe they'll come after us."

"Maybe," Simon said. "Where are we, anyway?"

"On a boat. I was still conscious when he brought me onto it. It's a big black hulking metal thing. There are no lights and there are—*things* everywhere. One of them jumped out at me and I started screaming. That was when he grabbed my head and banged it into the wall. I passed out for a while after that."

"Things? What do you mean things?"

"Demons," she said, and shuddered. "He has all sorts of demons here. Big ones and little ones and flying ones. They do whatever he tells them."

"But Valentine's a Shadowhunter. And from all I've heard, he *hates* demons."

"Well, they don't appear to know that," said Maia. "What I don't get is what he wants with us. I know he hates Downworlders, but this seems like a lot of effort just to kill two of them." She had started to shiver, her jaws clicking together like the chattery-teeth toys you could buy in novelty stores. "He must want something from the Shadowhunters. Or Luke."

*I know what he wants,* Simon thought, but there was no point in telling Maia; she was upset enough already. He shrugged his jacket off. "Here," he said, and tossed it across the room to her.

Twisting around her manacles, she managed to drape it awkwardly around her shoulders. She offered him a wan but grateful smile. "Thanks. But aren't you cold?"

Simon shook his head. The burn on his hand was entirely gone now. "I don't feel the cold. Not anymore."

She opened her mouth, then closed it again. A struggle was taking place behind her eyes. "I'm sorry. About the way I reacted to you yesterday." She paused, almost holding her breath. "Vampires scare me to death," she whispered at last. "When I first came to the city, I had a pack I used to hang out with—Bat, and two other boys, Steve and Gregg. We were in the park once and we ran into some vamps sucking on blood bags under a bridge—there was a fight and I mostly remember one of the vamps just picking Gregg up, just picking him up, and *ripping* him in half—" Her voice rose, and she clamped a hand over her mouth. She was shaking. "In half," she whispered. "All his insides fell out. And then they started eating."

Simon felt a dull pang of nausea roll over him. He was almost glad that the story made him sick to his stomach, rather than something else. Like hungry. "I wouldn't do that," he said. "I like werewolves. I like Luke—"

"I know you do." Her mouth worked. "It's just that when I met you, you seemed so *human*. You reminded me what I used to be like, before."

"Maia," Simon said. "You're still human."

"No, I'm not."

"In the ways that count, you are. Just like me."

She tried to smile. He could tell she didn't believe him, and he hardly blamed her. He wasn't sure he believed himself.

* * *

The sky had turned to gunmetal, weighted with heavy clouds. In the gray light the Institute loomed up, huge as the slabbed side of a mountain. The angled slate roof shone like unpolished silver. Clary thought she had caught the movement of hooded figures in the shadows by the front door, but she wasn't sure. It was hard to tell anything clearly when they were parked over a block away, peering through the smeared windows of Luke's truck.

"How long has it been?" she asked, for either the fourth or fifth time, she wasn't sure.

"Five minutes longer than the last time you asked me," Luke said. He was leaning back in his seat, his head back, looking utterly exhausted. The stubble coating his jaw and cheek was silvery gray and there were black lines of shadow under his eyes. All those nights at the hospital, the demon attack, and now this, Clary thought, suddenly worried. She could see why he and her mother had hidden from this life for so long. She wished she could hide from it herself. "Do you want to go in?"

"No. Jace said to wait outside." She peered out the window again. Now she was sure there were figures in the doorway. As one of them turned, she thought she caught a flash of silvery hair—

"Look." Luke was sitting bolt upright, rolling his window down hastily.

Clary looked. Nothing appeared to have changed. "You mean the people in the doorway?"

"No. The guards were there before. Look on the roof." He pointed.

Clary pressed her face to the truck window. The slate roof of the cathedral was a riot of Gothic turrets and spires, carved angels, and arched embrasures. She was about to say irritably that she didn't notice anything other than some crumbling gargoyles, when a flash of movement caught her eyes. Someone was up on the roof. A slim, dark figure, moving swiftly among the turrets, darting from one overhang to another, now dropping flat, to edge down the impossibly steep roof—someone with pale hair that glinted in the gunmetal light like brass—

*Jace.*

Clary was out of the truck before she knew what she was doing, pounding down the street toward the church, Luke shouting after her. The huge edifice seemed to sway overhead, hundreds of feet high, a sheer cliff of stone. Jace was at the edge of the roof now, looking down, and Clary thought, *It can't be, he wouldn't, he wouldn't do this, not Jace*, and then he stepped off the roof into empty air, as calmly as if he were stepping off a porch. Clary screamed out loud as he fell like a stone—

And landed lightly on his feet just in front of her. Clary stared with her mouth open as he rose up out of a shallow crouch and grinned at her. "If I made a joke about just dropping in," he said, "would you write me off as a cliché?"

"How—how did you—how did you *do that*?" she whispered, feeling as if she were about to throw up. She could see Luke out of the truck, standing with his hands clasped behind his head and staring past her. She whirled around to see the two guards from the front door running toward them. One was Malik; the other was the woman with the silver hair.

"Crap." Jace grabbed her hand and yanked her after him. They raced toward the truck and piled in beside Luke, who gunned the engine and took off while the passenger side door was still hanging open. Jace reached across Clary and jerked it shut. The truck veered around the two Shadowhunters—Malik, Clary saw, had what looked like a flinging knife in his hand. He was aiming at one of the tires. She heard Jace swear as he fumbled in his jacket for a weapon—Malik drew his arm back, the blade shining—and the silvery-haired woman threw herself onto his back, seizing at his arm. He tried to shake her off—Clary twisted around in her seat, gasping—and then the truck hurtled around the corner and lost itself in the traffic on York Avenue, the Institute receding into the distance behind them.

Maia had fallen into a fitful doze against the steam pipe, Simon's jacket draped around her shoulders. Simon watched the light from the porthole move across the room and tried in vain to calculate the hours. Usually he used his cell phone to tell him what time it was, but that was gone—he'd searched his pockets in vain. He must have dropped it when Valentine charged into his room.

He had bigger concerns, though. His mouth was dry and papery, his throat aching. He was thirsty in a way that was like every thirst and hunger he'd ever known blended together to form a sort of exquisite torture. And it was only going to get worse.

Blood was what he needed. He thought of the blood in the refrigerator beside his bed at home, and his veins burned like hot silver wires running just under his skin.

"Simon?" It was Maia, lifting her head groggily. Her cheek was printed with white dents where it had lain against the bumpy pipe. As he watched, the white faded into pink as the blood returned to her face.

*Blood.* He ran his dry tongue around his lips. "Yeah?"

"How long was I asleep?"

"Three hours. Maybe four. It's probably afternoon by now."

"Oh. Thanks for keeping watch."

He hadn't been. He felt vaguely ashamed as he said, "Of course. No problem."

"Simon . . ."

"Yes?"

"I hope you know what I mean when I say I'm sorry you're here, but I'm glad you're with me."

He felt his face crack into a smile. His dry lower lip split and he tasted blood in his mouth. His stomach groaned. "Thanks."

She leaned toward him, the jacket slipping from her shoulders. Her eyes were a light amber-gray that changed as she moved. "Can you reach me?" she asked, holding out her hand.

Simon reached for her. The chain that secured his ankle rattled as he stretched his hand as far as it would go. Maia smiled as their fingertips brushed—

"How touching." Simon jerked his hand back, staring. The voice that had spoken out of the shadows was cool, cultured, vaguely foreign in a way he couldn't quite place. Maia dropped her hand and twisted around, the color draining from her face as she stared up at the man in the doorway. The man had come in so quietly neither one of them had heard him. "The children of Moon and Night, getting along at last."

"Valentine," Maia whispered.

Simon said nothing. He couldn't stop staring. So this was Clary and Jace's father. With his cap of white-silver hair and burning black eyes, he didn't look much like either one of them, though there was something of Clary in his sharp bone structure and the shape of his eyes, and something of Jace in the lounging insolence with which he moved. He was a big man, broad-shouldered with a thick frame that didn't resemble either of his children's. He padded into the green metal room like a cat, despite being weighted down with what looked like enough weaponry to outfit a platoon. Thick black leather straps with silver buckles crisscrossed his chest, holding a wide-hilted silver sword across his back. Another thick strap circled his waist, and through it was thrust a butcher's array of knives, daggers, and narrow shimmering blades like enormous needles.

"Get up," he said to Simon. "Keep your back against the wall."

Simon tilted his chin up. He could see Maia watching him, white-faced and scared, and felt a rush of fierce protectiveness. He would keep Valentine from hurting her if it was the last thing he did. "So you're Clary's father," he said. "No offense, but I can kind of see why she hates you."

Valentine's face was impassive, almost motionless. His lips barely moved as he said, "And why is that?"

"Because," Simon said, "you're obviously psychotic."

Now Valentine smiled. It was a smile that moved no part of his face other than his lips, and those twisted only slightly. Then he brought his fist up. It was clenched; Simon thought for a moment that Valentine was going to swing at him, and he flinched reflexively. But Valentine didn't throw the punch. Instead, he opened his fingers, revealing a shimmering pile of what looked like glitter in the center of his broad palm. Turning toward Maia, he bent his head and blew the powder at her in a grotesque parody of a blown kiss. The powder settled on her like a swarm of shimmering bees.

Maia screamed. Gasping and jerking wildly, she thrashed

from side to side as if she could twist *away* from the powder, her voice rising in a sobbing scream.

"What did you do to her?" Simon shouted, leaping to his feet. He ran at Valentine, but the leg chain jerked him back. "*What did you do?*"

Valentine's thin smile widened. "Silver powder," he said. "It burns lycanthropes."

Maia had stopped twitching and was curled into a fetal position on the floor, weeping quietly. Blood ran from vicious red scores along her hands and arms. Simon's stomach lurched again and he fell back against the wall, sickened by himself, by all of it. "You bastard," he said as Valentine idly brushed the last of the powder from his fingers. "She's just a girl, she wasn't going to hurt you, she's *chained up*, for—"

He choked, his throat burning.

Valentine laughed. "For God's sake?" he said. "Is that what you were going to say?"

Simon said nothing. Valentine reached over his shoulder and drew the heavy silver Sword from its sheath. Light played along its blade like water slipping down a sheer silver wall, like sunlight itself refracted. Simon's eyes stung and he turned his face away.

"The Angel blade burns you, just as God's name chokes you," said Valentine, his cool voice sharp as crystal. "They say that those who die upon its point will achieve the gates of heaven. In which case, revenant, I am doing you a favor." He lowered the blade so that the tip touched Simon's throat. Valentine's eyes were the color of black water and there was nothing in them: no anger, no compassion, not even any hate. They were empty as a hollowed-out grave. "Any last words?"

Simon knew what he was supposed to say. *Sh'ma Yisrael, adonai elohanu, adonai echod.* Hear, oh Israel, the Lord our God, the Lord is One. He tried to speak the words, but a searing pain burned his throat. "*Clary,*" he whispered instead.

A look of annoyance passed across Valentine's face, as if the sound of his daughter's name in a vampire's mouth displeased him. With a sharp flick of his wrist, he brought the Sword level and slashed it with a single smooth gesture across Simon's throat.

# 17

## East of Eden

**"How did you do that?" Clary demanded as the truck sped** uptown, Luke hunched over the wheel.

"You mean how did I get onto the roof?" Jace was leaning back against the seat, his eyes half-closed. There were white bandages tied around his wrists and flecks of dried blood at his hairline. "First I climbed out Isabelle's window and up the wall. There are a number of ornamental gargoyles that make good handholds. Also, I'd like to note for the record that my motorcycle is no longer where I left it. I bet the Inquisitor took it on a joyride around Hoboken."

"I *meant*," Clary said, "how did you jump off the cathedral roof and not die?"

"I don't know." His arm brushed hers as he raised his

hands to rub at his eyes. "How did you create that rune?"

"I don't know either," she whispered. "The Seelie Queen was right, wasn't she? Valentine, he—he *did* things to us." She glanced over at Luke, who was pretending to be absorbed in turning left. "Didn't he?"

"This isn't the time to talk about that," Luke said. "Jace, did you have a particular destination in mind or did you just want to get away from the Institute?"

"Valentine's taken Maia and Simon to the boat to perform the Ritual. He'll want to do it as soon as possible." Jace tugged at one of the bandages on his wrist. "I've got to get there and stop him."

"No," Luke said sharply.

"Okay, *we* have to get there and stop him."

"Jace, I'm not having you go back to that ship. It's too dangerous."

"You saw what I just did," Jace said, incredulity rising in his voice, "and you're worried about me?"

"I'm worried about you."

"There's no time for that. After my father kills your friends, he'll call on an army of demons you can't even imagine. After *that*, he'll be unstoppable."

"Then the Clave—"

"The Inquisitor won't do anything," Jace said. "She's blocked the Lightwoods' access to the Clave. She wouldn't call for reinforcements, even when I told her what Valentine has planned. She's obsessed with this insane plan she has."

"What plan?" Clary said.

Jace's voice was bitter. "She wanted to trade me to my father for the Mortal Instruments. I told her Valentine would never go for it, but she didn't believe me." He laughed, a sharp staccato laugh. "Isabelle and Alec are going to tell her what happened with Simon and Maia. I'm not too optimistic, though. She doesn't believe me about Valentine and she's not going to upset her precious plan just to save a couple of Downworlders."

"We can't just wait to hear from them, anyway," Clary said. "We have to get to the boat now. If you can take us to it—"

"I hate to break it to you, but we need a boat to get to another boat," said Luke. "I'm not sure even Jace can walk on water."

At that moment Clary's phone buzzed. It was a text message from Isabelle. Clary frowned. "It's an address. Down by the waterfront."

Jace looked over her shoulder. "That's where we have to go to meet Magnus." He read the address off to Luke, who executed an irritable U-turn and headed south. "Magnus will get us across the water," Jace explained. "The ship is surrounded by protection wards. I got onto it before because my father wanted me to get onto it. This time he won't. We'll need Magnus to deal with the wardings."

"I don't like this." Luke tapped his fingers on the steering wheel. "I think I should go and you two should stay with Magnus."

Jace's eyes flashed. "No. It has to be me who goes."

"Why?" Clary asked.

"Because Valentine's using a fear demon," Jace explained. "That's how he was able to kill the Silent Brothers. It's what slaughtered that warlock, the werewolf in the alley outside the Hunter's Moon, and probably what killed that fey child in the park. And it's why the Brothers had those looks on their faces. Those terrified looks. They were literally scared to death."

"But the blood—"

"He drained the blood later. And in the alley he was interrupted by one of the lycanthropes. That's why he didn't have enough time to get the blood he needed. And that's why he still needs Maia." Jace raked a hand through his hair. "No one can stand up against the fear demon. It gets in your head and destroys your mind."

"Agramon," said Luke. He'd been silent, staring through the windshield. His face looked gray and pinched.

"Yeah, that's what Valentine called it."

"He's not a fear demon. He's *the* fear demon. The Demon of Fear. How did Valentine get Agramon to do his bidding? Even a warlock would have trouble binding a Greater Demon, and *outside* the pentagram—" Luke sucked his breath in. "That's how the warlock child died, isn't it? Summoning Agramon?"

Jace nodded assent, and explained quickly the trick that Valentine had played on Elias. "The Mortal Cup," he finished, "lets him control Agramon. Apparently it gives you some power over demons. Not like the Sword does, though."

"Now I'm even less inclined to let you go," Luke said. "It's a Greater Demon, Jace. It would take this city's worth of Shadowhunters to deal with it."

"I know it's a Greater Demon. But its weapon is fear. If Clary can put the Fearless rune on me, I can take it down. Or at least try."

"No!" Clary protested. "I don't want your safety dependent on my stupid rune. What if it doesn't work?"

"It worked before," Jace said as they turned off the bridge and headed back into Brooklyn. They were rolling down narrow Van Brunt Street, between high brick factories whose boarded-up windows and padlocked doors betrayed no hint of what lay inside. In the distance, the waterfront glimmered between buildings.

"What if I mess it up this time?"

Jace turned his head toward her, and for a moment their eyes met. His were the gold of distant sunlight. "You won't," he said.

"Are you sure this is the address?" asked Luke, bringing the truck to a slow stop. "Magnus isn't here."

Clary glanced around. They had drawn up in front of a large factory, which looked as if it had been destroyed by a terrible fire. The hollow brick and plaster walls still stood, but metal struts poked through them, bent and pitted with burns. In the distance Clary could see the financial district of lower Manhattan and the black hump of Governors Island, farther out to sea. "He'll come," she said. "If he told Alec he was coming, he'll do it."

They got out of the truck. Though the factory stood on a street lined with similar buildings, it was quiet, even for a Sunday. There was no one else around and none of the sounds of commerce—trucks backing up, men shouting—that Clary associated with warehouse districts. Instead there was silence, a cool breeze off the river, and the cries of seabirds. Clary drew her hood up, zipped her jacket, and shivered.

Luke slammed the truck door shut and zipped his flannel jacket closed. Silently, he offered Clary a pair of his thick woolly gloves. She slid them on and wiggled her fingers. They were so big for her that it was like wearing paws. She glanced around. "Wait—where's Jace?"

Luke pointed. Jace was kneeling down by the waterline, a dark figure whose bright hair was the only spot of color against the blue-gray sky and brown river.

"You think he wants privacy?" she asked.

"In this situation, privacy is a luxury none of us can afford. Come on." Luke strode off down the driveway, and Clary followed him. The factory itself backed up right onto the waterline, but there was a wide gravelly beach next to it. Shallow waves lapped at the weed-choked rocks. Logs had been placed in a rough square around a black pit where a fire had once burned. There were rusty cans and bottles strewn everywhere. Jace was standing by the edge of the water, his jacket off. As Clary watched, he threw something small and white toward the water; it hit with a splash and vanished.

"What are you doing?" she said.

Jace turned to face them, the wind whipping his fair hair across his face. "Sending a message."

Over his shoulder Clary thought she saw a shimmering tendril—like a living piece of seaweed—emerge from the gray river water, a bit of white caught in its grip. A moment later it vanished and she was left blinking.

"A message to who?"

Jace scowled. "No one." He turned away from the water and stalked across the pebbled beach to where he'd spread his jacket out. There were three long blades laid out on it. As he turned, Clary saw the sharpened metal disks threaded through his belt.

Jace stroked his fingers along the blades—they were flat and gray-white, waiting to be named. "I didn't have a chance to get to the armory, so these are the weapons we have. I thought we might as well get as ready as we can before Magnus gets here." He lifted the first blade. *"Abrariel."* The seraph knife shimmered and changed color as he named it. He held it out to Luke.

"I'm all right," Luke said, and drew his jacket aside to show the *kindjal* thrust through his belt.

Jace handed Abrariel to Clary, who took the weapon silently. It was warm in her hand, as if a secret life vibrated inside it.

*"Camael,"* Jace said to the next blade, making it shudder and glow. *"Telantes,"* he said to the third.

"Do you ever use Raziel's name?" Clary asked as Jace slid the blades into his belt and shrugged his jacket back on, getting to his feet.

"Never," Luke said. "That's not done." His gaze scanned the road behind Clary, looking for Magnus. She could sense his anxiety, but before she could say anything else, her phone buzzed. She flipped it open and handed it wordlessly to Jace. He read the text message, his eyebrows lifting.

"It looks like the Inquisitor gave Valentine until sunset to decide whether he wants me or the Mortal Instruments more," he said. "She and Maryse have been fighting for hours, so she hasn't noticed I'm gone yet."

He handed Clary back her phone. Their fingers brushed and Clary jerked her hand back, despite the thick woolly glove that covered her skin. She saw a shadow pass over his features, but he said nothing to her. Instead, he turned to Luke and demanded, with surprising abruptness, "Did the Inquisitor's son die? Is that why she's like this?"

Luke sighed and thrust his hands into the pockets of his coat. "How did you figure that out?"

"The way she reacts when someone says his name. It's the only time I've ever seen her show any human feelings."

Luke expelled a breath. He had pushed his glasses up and his eyes were squinted against the harsh wind off the river. "The Inquisitor is the way she is for many reasons. Stephen is only one of them."

"It's weird," Jace said. "She doesn't seem like someone who even *likes* kids."

"Not other people's," said Luke. "It was different with her own. Stephen was her golden boy. In fact, he was everyone's . . . everyone who knew him. He was one of those people who was good at everything, unfailingly nice without being boring, handsome without everyone hating him. Well, maybe we hated him a little."

"He went to school with you?" Clary said. "And my mother—and Valentine? Is that how you knew him?"

"The Herondales were in charge of running the London Institute, and Stephen went to school there. I saw him more after we all graduated, when he moved back to Alicante. And there was a time when I saw him very often indeed." Luke's eyes had gone distant, the same blue-gray as the river. "After he was married."

"So he was in the Circle?" Clary asked.

"Not then," Luke said. "He joined the Circle after I—well, after what happened to me. Valentine needed a new second in command and he wanted Stephen. Imogen, who was utterly loyal to the Clave, was hysterical—she begged Stephen to reconsider—but he cut her off. Wouldn't speak to her, or his father. He was absolutely in thrall to Valentine. Went everywhere trailing after him like a shadow." Luke paused. "The thing is, Valentine didn't think Stephen's wife was suitable for him. Not for someone who was going to be second in command of the Circle. She had—undesirable family connections." The pain in Luke's voice surprised Clary. Had he cared that much about these people? "Valentine forced Stephen to divorce Amatis and remarry—his second wife was a very young girl, only eighteen years old, named Céline. She, too, was utterly under Valentine's influence, did everything he told her to, no matter how bizarre. Then Stephen was killed in a Circle raid on a vampire nest. Céline killed herself when she found out. She was eight months pregnant at the time. And Stephen's father died, too, of heartbreak. So that was Imogen's whole family, all gone. They couldn't even bury her daughter-in-law and grandchild's ashes in the Bone City, because Céline was a suicide. She was buried at a crossroads outside Alicante. Imogen survived, but—she turned to ice. When the Inquisitor was killed in the Uprising, Imogen was offered his job. She returned from London to Idris—but never, as far as I heard, spoke about Stephen again. But it does explain why she hates Valentine as much as she does."

"Because my father poisons everything he touches?" Jace said bitterly.

"Because your father, for all his sins, still has a son, and she doesn't. And because she blames him for Stephen's death."

"And she's right," said Jace. "It was his fault."

"Not entirely," said Luke. "He offered Stephen a choice, and Stephen chose. Whatever else his faults were, Valentine never blackmailed or threatened anyone into joining the Circle. He wanted only willing followers. The responsibility for Stephen's choices rests with him."

"Free will," said Clary.

"There's nothing free about it," said Jace. "Valentine—"

"Offered you a choice, didn't he?" Luke said. "When you went to see him. He wanted you to stay, didn't he? Stay and join up with him?"

"Yes." Jace looked out across the water toward Governors Island. "He did." Clary could see the river reflected in his eyes; they looked steely, as if the gray water had drowned all their gold.

"And you said no," said Luke.

Jace glared. "I wish people would stop guessing that. It's making me feel predictable."

Luke turned away as if to hide a smile, and paused. "Someone's coming."

Someone was indeed coming, someone very tall with black hair that blew in the wind. "Magnus," Clary said. "But he looks . . . different."

As he drew closer, she saw that his hair, normally spiked up and glittered like a disco ball, hung cleanly past his ears like a sheet of black silk. The rainbow leather pants had been replaced by a neat, old-fashioned dark suit and a black frock coat with glimmering silver buttons. His cat's eyes glowed amber and green. "You look surprised to see me," he said.

Jace glanced at his watch. "We did wonder if you were coming."

"I said I would come, so I came. I just needed time to prepare. This isn't some hat trick, Shadowhunter. This is going to take some serious magic." He turned to Luke. "How's the arm?"

"Fine. Thank you." Luke was always polite.

"That's your truck parked up by the factory, isn't it?"

Magnus pointed. "It's awfully butch for a bookseller."

"Oh, I don't know," said Luke. "All that lugging around heavy book boxes, climbing stacks, hard-core alphabetizing . . ."

Magnus laughed. "Can you unlock the truck for me? I mean, I could do it myself"—he wiggled his fingers—"but that seems rude."

"Sure." Luke shrugged and they headed back toward the factory. When Clary made as if to follow them, though, Jace caught her arm. "Wait. I want to talk to you for a second."

Clary watched as Magnus and Luke headed for the truck. They made an odd pair, the tall warlock in a long black coat and the shorter, stockier man in jeans and flannel, but they were both Downworlders, both trapped in the same space between the mundane and the supernatural worlds.

"Clary," Jace said. "Earth to Clary. Where are you?"

She looked back at him. The sun was setting off the water now, behind him, leaving his face in shadow and turning his hair to a halo of gold. "Sorry."

"It's all right." He touched her face, gently, with the back of his hand. "You disappear so completely into your head sometimes," he said. "I wish I could follow you."

*You do,* she wanted to say. *You live in my head all the time.* Instead, she said, "What did you want to tell me?"

He dropped his hand. "I want you to put the Fearless rune on me. Before Luke gets back."

"Why before he gets back?"

"Because he's going to say it's a bad idea. But it's the only chance of defeating Agramon. Luke hasn't—encountered it, he doesn't know what it's like. But I do."

She searched his face. "What was it like?"

His eyes were unreadable. "You see what you fear the most in the world."

"I don't even know what that is."

"Trust me. You don't want to." He glanced down. "Do you have your stele?"

"Yeah, I have it." She pulled the woolly glove off her right hand and fished for the stele. Her hand was shaking a little as she drew it out. "Where do you want the Mark?"

"The closer it is to the heart, the more effective." He turned his back on her hand and drew off his jacket, dropping it on the ground. He shrugged his T-shirt up, baring his back. "On the shoulder blade would be good."

Clary placed a hand on his shoulder to steady herself. His skin there was a paler gold than the skin of his hands and face, and smooth where it was not scarred. She traced the tip of the stele along the blade of his shoulder and felt him wince, his muscles tightening. "Don't press so hard—"

"Sorry." She eased up, letting the rune flow from her mind, down through her arm, into the stele. The black line it left behind looked like charring, a line of ash. "There. You're finished."

He turned around, shrugging his shirt back on. "Thanks." The sun was burning down beyond the horizon now, flooding the sky with blood and roses, turning the edge of the river to liquid gold, softening the ugliness of the urban waste all around them. "What about you?"

"What about me what?"

He took a step closer. "Push your sleeves up. I'll Mark you."

"Oh. Right." She did as he asked, pushing up her sleeves, holding her bare arms out to him.

The sting of the stele on her skin was like the light touch of a needle's tip, scraping without puncturing. She watched the black lines appear with a sort of fascination. The Mark she'd gotten in her dream was still visible, faded only a little around the edges.

"'*And the Lord said unto him, Therefore whosoever slayeth Cain, vengeance shall be taken on him sevenfold. And the Lord set a Mark upon Cain, lest any finding him should kill him.*'"

Clary turned around, pulling her sleeves down. Magnus stood watching them, his black coat seeming to float around him in the wind off the river. A small smile played around his mouth.

"You can quote the Bible?" asked Jace, bending to retrieve his jacket.

"I was born in a deeply religious century, my boy," said Magnus. "I always thought Cain's might have been the first recorded Mark. It certainly protected him."

"But he was hardly one of the angels," said Clary. "Didn't he kill his brother?"

"Aren't we planning to kill our father?" said Jace.

"That's different," said Clary, but didn't get a chance to elaborate on *how* it was different, because at that moment, Luke's truck pulled up onto the beach, spraying gravel from its tires. Luke leaned out the window.

"Okay," he said to Magnus. "Here we go. Get in."

"Are we going to drive to the boat?" Clary said, bewildered. "I thought . . ."

"What boat?" Magnus cackled, as he swung himself up into the cab next to Luke. He jerked a thumb behind him. "You two, get into the back."

Jace climbed up into the back of the truck and leaned down to help Clary up after him. As she settled herself against the spare tire, she saw that a black pentagram inside a circle had been painted onto the metal floor of the truck bed. The arms of the pentagram were decorated with wildly curlicuing symbols. They weren't quite the runes she was familiar with—there was something about looking at them that was like trying to understand a person speaking a language that was close to, but not quite, English.

Luke leaned out the window and looked back at them. "You know I don't like this," he said, the wind muffling his voice. "Clary, you're going to stay in the truck with Magnus. Jace and I will go up onto the ship. You understand?"

Clary nodded and huddled into a corner of the truck bed. Jace sat beside her, bracing his feet. "This is going to be interesting."

"What—," Clary began, but the truck started up again, tires roaring against gravel, drowning her words. It lurched forward into the shallow water at the edge of the river. Clary was flung against the cab's back window as the truck moved forward into the river—was Luke planning to drown them all? She twisted around and saw that the cab was full of dizzying blue columns of light, snaking and twisting. The truck seemed to bump over something bulky, as if it had driven over a log. Then they were moving smoothly forward, almost gliding.

Clary hauled herself to her knees and looked over the side of the truck, already fairly sure what she would see.

They were moving—no, *driving*—atop the dark water, the bottom of the truck's tires just brushing the river's surface, spreading tiny ripples outward along with the occasional shower of Magnus-created blue sparks. Everything was suddenly very quiet, except for the faint roar of the motor and the call of the seabirds overhead. Clary stared across the truck bed at Jace, who was grinning. "Now this is *really* going to impress Valentine."

"I don't know," Clary said. "Other crack teams get bat boomerangs and wall-crawling powers; we get the Aquatruck."

"If you don't like it, Nephilim," came Magnus's voice, faintly, from the truck cab, "you're welcome to see if you can walk on the water."

"I think we should go in," said Isabelle, her ear pressed to the library door. She beckoned for Alec to come closer. "Can you hear anything?"

Alec leaned in beside his sister, careful not to drop the phone he was holding. Magnus said he'd call if he had news or if anything happened. So far, he hadn't. "No."

"Exactly. They've stopped yelling at each other." Isabelle's dark eyes gleamed. "They're waiting for Valentine now."

Alec moved away from the door and strode partway down the hall to the nearest window. The sky outside was the color of charcoal half-sunk into ruby ashes. "It's sunset."

Isabelle reached for the door handle. "Let's go."

"Isabelle, wait—"

"I don't want her to be able to lie to us about what Valentine says," Isabelle said. "Or what happens. Besides, I want to see him. Jace's father. Don't you?"

Alec moved back to the library door. "Yes, but this isn't a good idea because—"

Isabelle pushed down on the handle of the library door. It

swung wide open. With a half-amused glance over her shoulder at him, she ducked inside; swearing under his breath, Alec followed her.

His mother and the Inquisitor stood at opposite ends of the huge desk, like boxers facing each other across a ring. Maryse's cheeks were bright red, her hair straggling around her face. Isabelle shot Alec a look, as if to say, *Maybe we shouldn't have come in here. Mom looks mad.*

On the other hand, if Maryse looked angry, the Inquisitor looked positively demented. She whirled around as the library door opened, her mouth twisted into an ugly shape. "What are you two doing here?" she shouted.

"Imogen," said Maryse.

"Maryse!" The Inquisitor's voice rose. "I've had about enough of you and your delinquent children—"

*"Imogen,"* Maryse said again. There was something in her voice—an urgency—that made even the Inquisitor turn and look.

The air just by the freestanding brass globe was shimmering like water. A shape began to coalesce out of it, like black paint being stroked over white canvas, evolving into the figure of a man with broad, planklike shoulders. The image was wavering, too much for Alec to see more than that the man was tall, with a shock of close-cropped salt-white hair.

"Valentine." The Inquisitor looked caught off guard, Alec thought, though surely she must have been expecting him.

The air by the globe was shimmering more violently now. Isabelle gasped as a man stepped out of the wavering air, as if he were coming up through layers of water. Jace's father was a formidable man, over six feet tall with a wide chest and hard, thick arms corded with ropy muscles. His face was almost triangular, sharpening to a hard, pointed chin. He might have been considered handsome, Alec thought, but he was startlingly unlike Jace, lacking anything of his son's pale-gold looks. The hilt of a sword was visible just over his left shoulder—the Mortal Sword. It wasn't as if he needed to be armed, since he wasn't corporeally present, so he must have worn it to annoy the Inquisitor. Not that she needed to be more annoyed than she was.

"Imogen," Valentine said, his dark eyes grazing the Inquisitor with a look of satisfied amusement. *That's Jace all over, that look,* Alec thought. "And Maryse, my Maryse—it *has* been a long time."

Maryse, swallowing hard, said with some difficulty, "I'm not your Maryse, Valentine."

"And these must be your children," Valentine went on as if she hadn't spoken. His eyes came to rest on Isabelle and Alec. A faint shiver went through Alec, as if something had plucked at his nerves. Jace's father's words were perfectly ordinary, even polite, but there was something in his blank and predatory gaze that made Alec want to step in front of his sister and block her from Valentine's view. "They look just like you."

"Leave my children out of this, Valentine," Maryse said, clearly struggling to keep her voice steady.

"Well, that hardly seems fair," Valentine said, "considering you haven't left *my* child out of this." He turned to the Inquisitor. "I got your message. Surely that's not the best you can do?"

She hadn't moved; now she blinked slowly, like a lizard. "I hope the terms of my offer were perfectly clear."

"My son in return for the Mortal Instruments. That was it, correct? Otherwise you'll kill him."

"*Kill* him?" Isabelle echoed. "MOM!"

"Isabelle," Maryse said tightly. "Shut up."

The Inquisitor shot Isabelle and Alec a venomous glare between her slitted eyelids. "You have the terms correct, Morgenstern."

"Then my answer is no."

"*No?*" The Inquisitor looked as if she'd taken a step forward on solid ground and it had collapsed under her feet. "You can't bluff me, Valentine. I will do exactly as I threatened."

"Oh, I have no doubt in you, Imogen. You have always been a woman of single-minded and ruthless focus. I recognize these qualities in you because I possess them myself."

"I am nothing like you. I follow the Law—"

"Even when it instructs you to kill a boy still in his teens just to punish his father? This is not about the Law, Imogen, it is that you hate and blame me for the death of your son and this is your manner of recompensing me. It will make no difference. I will not give up the Mortal Instruments, not even for Jonathan."

The Inquisitor simply stared at him. "But he's your son," she said. "Your *child*."

"Children make their own choices," said Valentine. "That's something you never understood. I offered Jonathan safety if he stayed with me; he spurned it and returned to you, and you'll exact your revenge on him as I told him you would. You are nothing, Imogen," he finished, "if not predictable."

The Inquisitor didn't seem to notice the insult. "The Clave

will insist on his death, should you not give me the Mortal Instruments," she said, like someone caught in a bad dream. "I won't be able to stop them."

"I'm aware of that," said Valentine. "But there is nothing I can do. I offered him a chance. He didn't take it."

"Bastard!" Isabelle shouted suddenly, and made as if to run forward; Alec grabbed her arm and dragged her backward, holding her there. "He's a dickhead," she hissed, then raised her voice, shouting at Valentine: "You're a—"

"*Isabelle!*" Alec covered his sister's mouth with his hand as Valentine spared them both a single, amused glance.

"You . . . offered him . . ." The Inquisitor was starting to remind Alec of a robot whose circuits were shorting out. "And he turned you *down*?" She shook her head. "But he's your spy—your weapon—"

"Is that what you thought?" he said, with apparently genuine surprise. "I am hardly interested in spying out the secrets of the Clave. I'm only interested in its destruction, and to achieve that end I have far more powerful weapons in my arsenal than a boy."

"But—"

"Believe what you like," Valentine said with a shrug. "You are nothing, Imogen Herondale. The figurehead of a regime whose power is soon to be shattered, its rule ended. There is nothing you have to offer me that I could possibly want."

"*Valentine!*" The Inquisitor threw herself forward, as if she could stop him, catch at him, but her hands only went through him as if through water. With a look of supreme disgust, he stepped back and vanished.

* * *

The sky was licked with the last tongues of a fading fire, the water had turned to iron. Clary drew her jacket closer around her body and shivered.

"Are you cold?" Jace had been standing at the back of the truck bed, looking down at the wake the car left behind it: two white lines of foam cutting the water. Now he came and slid down beside her, his back against the rear window of the cab. The window itself was almost entirely fogged up with bluish smoke.

"Aren't you?"

"No." He shook his head and slid his jacket off, handing it across to her. She put it on, reveling in the softness of the leather. It was too big in that comforting way. "You're going to stay in the truck like Luke told you to, right?"

"Do I have a choice?"

"Not in the literal sense, no."

She slid her glove off and reached out her hand to him. He took it, gripping it tightly. She looked down at their interlaced fingers, hers so small, squared-off at the tips, his long and thin. "You'll find Simon for me," she said. "I know you will."

"Clary." She could see the water all around them mirrored in his eyes. "He may be—I mean, it may be—"

"No." Her tone left no room for doubt. "He'll be all right. He has to be."

Jace exhaled. His irises rippled with dark blue water—like tears, Clary thought, but they weren't tears, only reflections. "There's something I want to ask you," he said. "I was afraid to ask before. But now I'm not afraid of anything." His hand moved to cup her cheek, his palm warm against her cold skin, and she found that her own fear was gone, as if he could pass the power of the Fearless rune to her through his touch. Her chin went up, her lips parting in expectation—his mouth brushed hers lightly, so lightly it felt like the brush of a feather, the memory of a kiss—and then he pulled back, his eyes widening; she saw the black wall in them, rising up to blot out the incredulous gold: the shadow of the ship.

Jace let go of her with an exclamation and scrambled to his feet. Clary got up awkwardly, Jace's heavy jacket throwing her off balance. Blue sparks were flying from the windows of the cab, and in their light she could see that the side of the ship was corrugated black metal, that there was a thin ladder crawling down one side, and that an iron railing ran around the top. What looked like big, awkwardly shaped birds were perched on the railing. Waves of cold seemed to roll off the boat like freezing air off an iceberg. When Jace called out to her, his breath came out in white puffs, his words lost in the sudden engine roar of the big ship.

She frowned at him. "What? What did you say?"

He grabbed for her, sliding a hand up under her jacket, his fingertips grazing her bare skin. She yelped in surprise. He yanked the seraph blade he'd give her earlier from her belt and pressed it into her hand. "I said"—and he let her go—"to get Abrariel out, because they're coming."

"Who are coming?"

"The demons." He pointed up. At first Clary saw nothing. Then she noticed the huge, awkward birds she'd seen before. They were dropping off the railing one by one, falling like stones down the side of the boat—then leveling out and heading straight for the truck where it floated on top of the waves. As they got closer, she saw that they weren't birds at all, but ugly flying things like pterodactyls, with wide, leathery wings and bony triangular heads. Their mouths were full of serrated shark teeth, row on row of them, and their claws glinted like straight razors.

Jace scrambled up onto the roof of the cab, Telantes blazing in his hand. As the first of the flying things reached them, he flung the blade. It struck the demon, slicing off the top of its skull the way you might slice the top off an egg. With a high windy screech, the thing toppled sideways, wings spasming. When it struck the ocean, the water boiled.

The second demon hit the hood of the truck, its claws raking long furrows in the metal. It flung itself against the windshield, spiderwebbing the glass. Clary shouted for Luke, but another one of them dive-bombed her, hurtling down from the steel sky like an arrow. She yanked the sleeve of Jace's jacket up, flinging her arm out to show the defensive rune. The demon *skreeked* as the other one had, wings flapping backward—but it had already come too close, within her reach. She saw that it had no eyes, only indentations on each side of its skull, as she smashed Abrariel into its chest. It burst apart, leaving a wisp of black smoke behind.

"Well done," said Jace. He had jumped down from the truck cab to dispatch another one of the screeching flying things. He had a dagger out now, its hilt slicked with black blood.

"What *are* these things?' Clary panted, swinging Abrariel in a wide arc that slashed across the chest of a flying demon. It cawed and swiped at her with a wing. This close, she could see that the wings ended in blade-sharp ridges of bone. This one caught the sleeve of Jace's jacket and tore it across.

"My *jacket*," said Jace in a rage, and stabbed down at the

thing as it rose, piercing its back. It shrieked and disappeared. "I *loved* that jacket."

Clary stared at him, then spun around as the rending screech of metal assailed her ears. Two of the flying demons had their claws in the top of the truck cab, ripping it off the frame. The air was filled with the screech of tearing metal. Luke was down on the hood of the truck, slashing at the creatures with his *kindjal*. One toppled off the side of the truck, vanishing before it hit the water. The other burst into the air, the cab roof clutched in its claws, *skreeking* triumphantly, and winged back toward the boat.

For the moment the sky was clear. Clary raced up and peered down into the cab. Magnus was slumped down in his seat, his face gray. It was too dark for her to see if he was wounded. "Magnus!" she shouted. "Are you hurt?"

"No." He struggled to sit upright, then fell back against the seat. "I'm just—drained. The protection spells on the ship are strong. Stripping them, keeping them off, is—difficult." His voice faded. "But if I don't do it, anyone who sets foot on that ship, other than Valentine, will die."

"Maybe you should come with us," said Luke.

"I can't work on the wards if I'm on the ship itself. I have to do it from here. That's the way it works." Magnus's grin looked painful. "Besides, I'm no good in a fight. My talents lie elsewhere."

Clary, still hanging down into the cab, began, "But what if we need—"

*"Clary!"* Luke shouted, but it was too late. None of them had seen the flying creature clinging motionless to the side of the truck. It launched itself upward now, winging sideways, claws sinking deep into the back of Clary's jacket, a blur of

shadowy wings and reeking, jagged teeth. With a howling screech of triumph, it took off into the air, Clary dangling helplessly from its claws.

*"Clary!"* Luke shouted again, and raced to the edge of the truck's hood and stopped there, staring hopelessly upward at the dwindling winged shape with its slackly hanging burden.

"It won't kill her," said Jace, joining him on the hood. "It's retrieving her for Valentine."

There was something about his tone that sent a chill through Luke's blood. He turned to stare at the boy next to him. "But—"

He didn't finish. Jace had already dived from the truck, in a single smooth movement. He splashed down in the filthy river water and struck out toward the boat, his strong kicks churning the water to froth.

Luke turned back to Magnus, whose pale face was just visible through the cracked windshield, a white smudge against the darkness. Luke held a hand up, thought he saw Magnus nod in response.

Sheathing his *kindjal* at his side, he dived into the river after Jace.

Alec released his hold on Isabelle, half-expecting her to start screaming the moment he took his hand off her mouth. She didn't. She stood beside him and stared as the Inquisitor stood, swaying slightly, her face a chalky gray-white.

"Imogen," Maryse said. There was no feeling in her voice, not even any anger.

The Inquisitor didn't seem to hear her. Her expression didn't change as she sank bonelessly into Hodge's old chair.

"My God," she said, staring down at the desk. "What have I done?"

Maryse glanced over at Isabelle. "Get your father."

Isabelle, looking as frightened as Alec had ever seen her, nodded and slipped out of the room.

Maryse crossed the room to the Inquisitor and looked down at her. "What have you done, Imogen?" she said. "You've handed victory to Valentine. That's what you've done."

"No," the Inquisitor breathed.

"You knew exactly what Valentine was planning when you locked Jace up. You refused to allow the Clave to become involved because it would have interfered with your plan. You wanted to make Valentine suffer as he had made you suffer; to show him you had the power to kill his son the way he killed yours. You wanted to humble him."

"Yes. . . ."

"But Valentine will not be humbled," said Maryse. "I could have told you that. You never had a hold over him. He only pretended to consider your offer to make absolutely certain that we would have no time to call for reinforcements from Idris. And now it's too late."

The Inquisitor looked up wildly. Her hair had come loose from its knot and hung in lank strips around her face. It was the most human Alec had seen her look, but he got no pleasure out of it. His mother's words chilled him: *too late*. "No, Maryse," she said. "We can still—"

"Still *what*?" Maryse's voice cracked. "Call on the Clave? We don't have the days, the hours, it would take them to get here. If we're going to face Valentine—and God knows we have no choice—"

"We're going to have to do it now," interrupted a deep voice. Behind Alec, glowering darkly, was Robert Lightwood.

Alec stared at his father. It had been years since he'd seen him in hunting gear; his time had been taken up with administrative tasks, with running the Conclave and dealing with Downworlder issues. Something about seeing his father in his heavy, dark armored clothes, his broadsword strapped across his back, reminded Alec of being a child again, when his father had been the biggest, strongest and most terrifying man he could imagine. And he was still terrifying. He hadn't seen his father since he'd embarrassed himself at Luke's. He tried to catch his eye now, but Robert was looking at Maryse. "The Conclave stands ready," Robert said. "The boats are waiting at the dock."

The Inquisitor's hands fluttered around her face. "It's no good," she said. "There aren't enough of us—we can't possibly—"

Robert ignored her. Instead, he looked at Maryse. "We should go very soon," he said, and in his tone there was the respect that had been lacking when he had addressed the Inquisitor.

"But the Clave," the Inquisitor began. "They should be informed."

Maryse shoved the phone on the desk toward the Inquisitor, hard. "*You* tell them. Tell them what you've done. It's your job, after all."

The Inquisitor said nothing, just stared at the phone, one hand over her mouth.

Before Alec could start to feel sorry for her, the door opened again and Isabelle came in, in her Shadowhunter gear, with her long silver-gold whip in one hand and a wooden-bladed *naginata* in the other. She frowned at her brother. "Go get ready," she said. "We're sailing for Valentine's ship right away."

Alec couldn't help it; the corner of his mouth twitched upward. Isabelle was always so *determined*. "Is that for me?" he asked, indicating the *naginata*.

Isabelle jerked it away from him. "Get your own!"

*Some things never change*. Alec headed toward the door, but was stopped by a hand on his shoulder. He looked up in surprise.

It was his father. He was looking down at Alec, and though he wasn't smiling, there was a look of pride on his lined and tired face. "If you're in need of a blade, Alexander, my *guisarme* is in the entryway. If you'd like to use it."

Alec swallowed and nodded, but before he could thank his father, Isabelle spoke from behind him:

"Here you go, Mom," she said. Alec turned and saw his sister in the process of handing the *naginata* to his mother, who took it and spun it expertly in her grasp.

"Thank you, Isabelle," Maryse said, and with a movement as swift as any of her daughter's, she lowered the blade so that it pointed directly at the Inquisitor's heart.

Imogen Herondale looked up at Maryse with the blank, shattered eyes of a ruined statue. "Are you going to kill me, Maryse?"

Maryse hissed through her teeth. "Not even close," she said. "We need every Shadowhunter in the city, and right now, that includes you. Get up, Imogen, and get yourself ready for battle. From now on, the orders around here are going to come from *me*." She smiled grimly. "And the first thing you're going to do is free my son from that accursed Malachi Configuration."

She looked magnificent as she spoke, Alec thought with pride, a true Shadowhunter warrior, every line of her blazing with righteous fury.

He hated to spoil the moment—but they were going to find out Jace was gone on their own soon enough. Better that someone cushioned the shock.

He cleared his throat. "Actually," he said, "there's something you should probably know . . ."

# 18

# Darkness Visible

**Clary had always hated roller coasters, hated that feeling** of her stomach dropping out through her feet when the coaster hurtled downward. Being snatched from the truck and dragged through the air like a mouse in the claws of an eagle was ten times worse. She screamed out loud as her feet left the truck bed and her body soared upward, unbelievably fast. She screamed and twisted—until she looked down and saw how high she already was above the water and realized what would happen if the flying demon released her.

She went still. The pickup truck looked like a toy below, drifting impossibly on the waves. The city swung around her, blurred walls of glittering light. It might have been beautiful if she weren't so terrified. The demon banked and dived, and suddenly instead of rising she was falling. She thought of the thing dropping her hundreds of feet through the air until she crashed into the icy black water, and shut her eyes—but falling through blind darkness was worse. She opened them again and saw the black deck of the ship rising up from below her like a hand about to swat them both out of the sky. She screamed a second time as they dropped toward the deck—and through a dark square cut into its surface. Now they were inside the ship.

The flying creature slowed its pace. They were dropping through the center of the boat, surrounded by railed metal decks. Clary caught glimpses of dark machinery; none of it looked in working order, and there were gears and tools abandoned in various places. If there had been electrical lights before, they were no longer working, though a faint glow permeated everything. Whatever had powered the ship before, Valentine was now powering it with something else.

Something that had sucked the warmth right out of the atmosphere. Icy air lashed at her face as the demon reached the bottom of the ship and ducked down a long, poorly lit corridor. It wasn't being particularly careful with her. Her knee slammed against a pipe as the creature turned a corner, sending a shock wave of pain up her leg. She cried out and heard its hissing laughter above her. Then it released her and she was falling. Twisting in the air, Clary tried to get her hands and knees under her before she hit the ground. It almost worked. She struck the floor with a jarring impact and rolled to the side, stunned.

She was lying on a hard metal surface, in semidarkness. This had probably been a storage space at one point, because the walls were smooth and doorless. There was a square opening high above her through which the only light filtered. Her whole body felt like one big bruise.

"Clary?" A whispered voice. She rolled onto her side, wincing. A shadow knelt beside her. As her eyes adjusted to the darkness, she saw the small, curvy figure, braided hair, dark brown eyes. *Maia.* "Clary, is that you?"

Clary sat up, ignoring the screaming pain in her back. "Maia. Maia, oh my God." She stared at the other girl, then wildly around the room. It was empty but for the two of them. "Maia, where is he? Where's Simon?"

Maia bit her lip. Her wrists were bloody, Clary saw, her face streaked with dried tears. "Clary, I'm so sorry," she said, in her soft and husky voice. "Simon's dead."

Soaked through and half-frozen, Jace collapsed onto the deck of the ship, water streaming from his hair and clothes. He stared up at the cloudy night sky, gasping in breaths. It had been no easy task to climb the rickety iron ladder badly bolted to the ship's metal side, especially with slippery hands and drenched clothes dragging him down.

If it hadn't been for the Fearless rune, he reflected, he probably would have been worried that one of the flying demons would pick him off the ladder like a bird picking a bug off a vine. Fortunately, they seemed to have returned to the ship once they'd seized Clary. Jace couldn't imagine why, but he'd long ago given up trying to fathom why his father did anything.

Above him a head appeared, silhouetted against the sky. It was Luke, having reached the top of the ladder. He clambered laboriously onto the railing and dropped down onto the other side of it. He looked down at Jace. "You all right?"

"Fine." Jace got to his feet. He was shivering. It was cold on the boat, colder than it had been down by the water—and his jacket was gone. He'd given it to Clary.

Jace looked around. "Somewhere there's a door that leads into the ship. I found it last time. We just have to walk around the deck until we find it again."

Luke started forward.

"And let me go first," Jace added, stepping in front of him. Luke shot him an extremely puzzled look, seemed as if he were about to say something, and finally fell into step just beside Jace as they approached the curved front of the ship, where Jace had stood with Valentine the night before. He could hear the oily slap of water against the bow, far below.

"Your father," Luke said, "what did he say to you when you saw him? What did he promise you?"

"Oh, you know. The usual. A lifetime's supply of Knicks tickets." Jace spoke lightly but the memory bit into him deeper than the cold. "He said he'd make sure no harm came to me or anyone I cared about if I'd leave the Clave and return to Idris with him."

"Do you think—" Luke hesitated. "Do you think he'd hurt Clary to get back at you?"

They rounded the bow and Jace caught a brief glimpse of the Statue of Liberty off in the distance, a pillar of glowing light. "No. I think he took her to make us come onto the boat like this, to give him a bargaining chip. That's all."

"I'm not sure he needs a bargaining chip." Luke spoke in a low voice as he unsheathed his *kindjal*. Jace turned to follow Luke's gaze, and for a moment could only stare.

There was a black hole in the deck on the west side of the ship, a hole like a square that had been cut into the metal, and out of its depths poured a dark cloud of monsters. Jace flashed back to the last time he had stood here, with the Mortal Sword in his hand, staring around him in horror as the sky above him and the sea below him turned to roiling masses of nightmares. Only now they stood in front of him, a cacophony of demons: the bone-white Raum that had attacked them at Luke's; Oni demons with their green bodies, wide mouths, and horns; the slinking black Kuri demons, spider demons with their eight pincer-tipped arms and the poison-dripping fangs that protruded from their eye sockets—

Jace couldn't count them all. He felt for Camael and took it from his belt, its white glare lighting the deck. The demons hissed at the sight of it, but none of them backed away. The Fearless rune on Jace's shoulder blade began to burn. He wondered how many demons he could kill before it burned itself away.

"Stop! *Stop!*" Luke's hand, knotted in the back of Jace's shirt, jerked him backward. "There's too many, Jace. If we can get back to the ladder—"

"We can't." Jace yanked himself out of Luke's grip and pointed. "They've cut us off on both sides."

It was true. A phalanx of Moloch demons, flames jetting from their empty eyes, blocked their retreat. Luke swore, fluently and viciously. "Jump over the side, then. I'll hold them off."

"*You* jump," Jace said. "I'm fine here."

Luke threw his head back. His ears had gone pointed, and when he snarled at Jace, his lips drew back over canines that were suddenly sharp. "You—" He broke off as a Moloch demon leaped at him, claws outstretched. Jace stabbed it casually in the spine as it went by, and it staggered into Luke, yowling. Luke seized it in clawed hands and hurled it over the railing. "You used that Fearless rune, didn't you?" Luke said, turning back to Jace with eyes that glowed amber.

There was a distant splash.

"You're not wrong," Jace admitted.

"Christ," said Luke. "Did you put it on yourself?"

"No. Clary put it on me." Jace's seraph blade cut the air with white fire; two Drevak demons fell. There were dozens more where it had come from, lurching toward them, their needle-tipped hands outstretched. "She's good at that, you know."

"*Teenagers,*" said Luke, as if it were the filthiest word he knew, and threw himself into the oncoming horde.

"Dead?" Clary stared at Maia as if she'd spoken in Bulgarian. "He can't be dead."

Maia said nothing, just watched her with sad, dark eyes.

"I would know." Clary pressed her hand, clenched into a fist, against her chest. "I would know it *here*."

"I thought that myself," Maia said. "Once. But you don't know. You never know."

Clary scrambled to her feet. Jace's jacket hung off her shoulders, the back of it nearly shredded through. She shrugged it off impatiently and dropped it onto the floor. It was ruined, the back scored through with a dozen razored claw marks. *Jace will be upset that I wrecked his jacket*, she thought. *I should buy him a new one. I should—*

She drew a long, ragged breath. She could hear her own heart pounding, but that sounded distant too. "What—happened to him?"

Maia was still kneeling on the floor. "Valentine got us both," she said. "He chained us up in a room together. Then he came in with a weapon—a sword, really long and bright, as if it was glowing. He threw silver powder at me so I couldn't fight him, and he—he stabbed Simon in the throat." Her voice faded to a whisper. "He cut his wrists open and he poured the blood into bowls. Some of those demon creatures of his came in and helped him take it. Then he just left Simon lying there, like some toy he'd ripped all the insides out of so he had no use for it anymore. I screamed—but I knew he was dead. Then one of the demons picked me up and brought me down here."

Clary pressed the back of her hand against her mouth, pressed and pressed until she tasted salty blood. The sharp taste of the blood seemed to cut through the fog in her brain. "We have to get out of here."

"No offense, but that's pretty obvious." Maia got to her feet, wincing. "There's no way out of here. Not even for a Shadowhunter. Maybe if you were . . ."

"If I were what?" Clary demanded, pacing the square of their cell. "Jace? Well, I'm not." She kicked at the wall. It echoed hollowly. She dug into her pocket and pulled out her stele. "But I have my own talents."

She shoved the tip of the stele against the wall and began to draw. The lines seemed to flow out of her, black and charred-looking, hot as her furious anger. She slammed the stele against the wall again and again and the black lines flowed up out of its tip like flames. When she drew back, breathing hard, she saw Maia staring at her in astonishment.

"Girl," she said, "what did you *do*?"

Clary wasn't sure. It looked as if she had thrown a bucket of acid against the wall. The metal all around the rune was sagging and dripping like ice cream on a hot day. She stepped back, eyeing it warily as a hole the size of a large dog opened in the wall. Clary could see steel struts behind it, more of the ship's metal innards. The edges of the hole still sizzled, though it had stopped spreading outward. Maia took a step forward, pushing Clary's arm away.

"Wait." Clary was suddenly nervous. "The melted metal—it could be, like, toxic sludge or something."

Maia snorted. "I'm from New Jersey. I was *born* in toxic sludge." She marched up to the hole and peered through it. "There's a metal catwalk on the other side," she announced. "Here—I'm going to pull myself through." She turned around and stuck her feet through the hole, then her legs, moving backward slowly. She grimaced as she wriggled her body through, then froze. "Ouch! My shoulders are stuck. Push me?" She held her hands out.

Clary took her hands and pushed. Maia's face turned white, then red—and she suddenly pulled free, like a champagne cork popped from the bottle. With a shriek, she tumbled backward. There was a crash and Clary stuck her head anxiously through the hole. "Are you all right?"

Maia was lying on a narrow metal catwalk several feet below. She rolled over slowly and pushed herself into a sitting position, wincing. "My ankle—but I'll be fine," she added, seeing Clary's face. "We heal fast too, you know."

"I know. Okay, my turn." Clary's stele poked uncomfortably into her stomach as she bent, prepared to slide through the hole after Maia. The drop to the catwalk was intimidating, but not as intimidating as the idea of waiting in the storage space for whatever came to claim them. She turned over onto her stomach, sliding her feet into the hole—

And something seized her by the back of her shirt, hauling her upward. Her stele fell out of her belt and rattled to the floor. She gasped in sudden shock and pain; the neck band of her sweater cut into her throat, and she choked. A moment later she was released. She crashed to the floor, her knees hitting the metal with a hollow clang. Gagging, she rolled onto her back and looked up, knowing what she would see.

Valentine stood over her. In one hand he held a seraph blade, glittering with a harsh white light. His other hand, which had gripped the back of her shirt, was clenched into a fist. His carved white face was set into a sneer of disdain. "Always your mother's daughter, Clarissa," he said. "What have you done now?"

Clary pulled herself painfully up to her knees. Her mouth was filled with the salty blood from where her lip had torn open. As she looked at Valentine, her simmering rage bloomed like a poisonous flower inside her chest. This man, her father, had killed Simon and left him dead on the floor like so much discarded trash. She had thought she had hated people before in her life; she'd been wrong. *This* was hatred.

"The werewolf girl," Valentine went on, frowning, "where is she?"

Clary leaned forward and spat her mouthful of blood onto his shoes. With a sharp exclamation of disgust and surprise, he stepped backward, raising the blade in his hand, and for a moment Clary saw the unguarded fury in his eyes and thought he was really going to do it, was really going to kill her right there where she crouched at his feet, for spitting on his shoes.

Slowly, he lowered the blade. Without a word, he walked past Clary, and stared through the hole she had made in the wall. Slowly, she turned, her eyes raking the floor until she saw it. Her mother's stele. She reached for it, her breath catching—

Valentine, turning, saw what she was doing. With a single stride, he was across the room. He kicked the stele out of her reach; it spun across the metal floor and fell through the hole in the wall. She half-closed her eyes, feeling the loss of the stele like the loss of her mother all over again.

"The demons will find your Downworlder friend," said Valentine, in his cold, still voice, sliding his seraph blade into a sheath at his waist. "There is nowhere for her to flee to. Nowhere for any of you to go. Now get up, Clarissa."

Slowly, Clary got to her feet. Her whole body ached from the pummeling it had taken. A moment later she gasped in surprise as Valentine seized her by the shoulders, turning her so that her back was to him. He whistled; a high, sharp, and unpleasant sound. The air stirred overhead and she heard the ugly flap of leathery wings. With a little cry, she tried to break away, but Valentine was too strong. The wings settled around them both and then they were rising into the air together, Valentine holding her in his arms, as if he really were her father.

Jace had thought he and Luke would be dead by now. He wasn't sure why they weren't. The deck of the ship was slippery with blood. He was covered in filth. Even his hair was lank and sticky with ichor, and his eyes stung with blood and sweat. There was a deep cut along the top of his right arm, and no time to carve a Healing rune into the skin. Every time he lifted the arm, a searing pain shot through his side.

They had managed to wedge themselves into a recess in the metal wall of the ship, and they fought from this shelter as the demons lurched at them. Jace had used both his chakhrams and was down to his last seraph blade and the dagger he'd taken from Isabelle. It wasn't much—he wouldn't have gone out to face only a few demons this poorly armed, and now he was facing a horde. He ought to be frightened, he knew, but he felt almost nothing at all—only a disgust for the demons, who did not belong in this world, and rage at Valentine, who had summoned them here. Distantly, he knew his lack of fear wasn't entirely a good thing. He wasn't even afraid of how much blood he was losing from his arm.

A spider demon scuttled toward Jace, chittering and jetting yellow poison. He ducked away, not quite fast enough to keep a few drops of the poison from splattering his shirt. It hissed as it ate through the material; he felt the sting as it burned his skin like a dozen tiny superheated needles.

The spider demon clicked in satisfaction, and sprayed another jet of poison. Jace ducked and the venom hit an Oni demon coming toward him from the side; the Oni screamed in agony and thrashed its way to the spider demon, claws extended. The two grappled together, rolling across the deck.

The surrounding demons surged away from the spilled poison, which made a barrier between them and the Shadowhunter. Jace took advantage of the momentary breather to turn to Luke beside him. Luke was almost unrecognizable. His ears rose to sharp, wolfish points; his lips were pulled back from his snarling muzzle in a permanent rictus, his clawed hands black with demon ichor.

"We should go for the railings." Luke's voice was half a growl. "Get off the ship. We can't kill them all. Maybe Magnus—"

"I don't think we're doing so badly." Jace twirled his seraph blade—which was a bad idea; his hand was wet with blood and the blade almost slipped out of his grasp. "All things considered."

Luke made a noise that might have been a snarl or a laugh, or a combination of both. Then something huge and shapeless fell out of the sky, knocking them both to the ground.

Jace hit the ground hard, his seraph blade flying out of his hand. It struck the deck, skittered across the metal surface, and slid over the edge of the boat, out of sight. Jace swore and staggered to his feet.

The thing that had landed on them was an Oni demon. It was unusually big for its kind—not to mention unusually smart to have thought of climbing up onto the roof and dropping down on them from above. It was sitting on top of Luke now, slashing at him with the sharp tusks that sprouted from its forehead. Luke was defending himself as best he could with his own claws, but he was already drenched in blood; his *kindjal* lay a foot away from him on the deck. Luke grabbed for it and the Oni seized one of his legs in a spadelike hand, bringing the leg down like a tree branch over its knee. Jace heard the bone break with a snap as Luke cried out.

Jace dived for the *kindjal*, grabbed it, and rolled to his feet, flinging the dagger hard at the back of the Oni demon's neck. It sliced through with enough force to decapitate the creature, which sagged forward, black blood gushing from its neck stump. A moment later it was gone. The *kindjal* thumped to the deck beside Luke.

Jace ran to him and knelt down. "Your leg—"

"It's broken." Luke struggled into a sitting position. His face twisted in pain.

"But you heal fast."

Luke looked around, his face grim. The Oni might have been dead, but the other demons had learned from its example. They were swarming up onto the roof. Jace couldn't tell, in the dim moonlight, how many of them there were—dozens? Hundreds? After a certain number it didn't matter anymore.

Luke closed his hand around the hilt of the *kindjal*. "Not fast enough."

Jace drew Isabelle's dagger from his belt. It was the last of his weapons and it seemed suddenly and pitifully small. A sharp emotion pierced him—not fear, he was still beyond that, but sorrow. He saw Alec and Isabelle as if they were standing in front of him, smiling at him, and then he saw Clary with her arms out as if she were welcoming him home.

He rose to his feet just as they fell from the roof in a wave, a shadow tide blotting out the moon. Jace moved to try to block Luke, but it was no use; the demons were all around. One reared up in front of him. It was a six-foot skeleton, grinning with broken teeth. Scraps of brightly colored Tibetan prayer flags hung from its rotting bones. It gripped a *katana* sword in a bony hand, which was unusual—most demons didn't arm themselves. The blade, inscribed with demonic runes, was longer than Jace's arm, curling and sharp and deadly.

Jace flung the dagger. It struck the demon's bony rib cage and stuck there. The demon barely seemed to notice; it only kept moving, inexorable as death. The air around it stank of death and graveyards. It raised the *katana* in a clawed hand—

A gray shadow cut the darkness in front of Jace, a shadow that moved with a whirling, precise, and deadly motion. The downward swing of the *katana* met with the grinding screech of metal on metal; the shadowy figure thrust the *katana* back at the demon, stabbing upward with the other hand with a swiftness that Jace's eye could barely follow. The demon fell back, its skull shattering as it crumpled into nothingness. All around him he could hear the shrieks of demons howling in pain and surprise. Whirling, he saw that dozens of shapes—*human* shapes—were crawling up over the railings, dropping to the ground, and racing to close with the mass of demons that crawled, slithered, hissed, and flew upon the deck. They carried blades of light and wore the dark, tough clothing of—

"*Shadowhunters?*" Jace said, so startled that he spoke out loud.

"Who else?" A grin flashed in the darkness.

"Malik? Is that you?"

Malik inclined his head. "Sorry about earlier today," he said. "I was under orders."

Jace was about to tell Malik that his having just saved his life more than made up for his earlier attempt to prevent Jace from leaving the Institute, when a group of Raum demons surged toward them, tentacles lashing the air. Malik whirled and charged to meet them with a shout, his seraph blade blazing like a star. Jace was about to follow him when a hand seized him by the arm and pulled him sideways.

It was a Shadowhunter, all in black, a hood shading the face beneath. "Come with me."

The hand tugged insistently at his sleeve.

"I need to get to Luke. He's been hurt." He jerked his arm back. "Let *go* of me."

"Oh, for the Angel's sake—" The figure released him and reached up to push back the hood of its long cloak, revealing a narrow white face and gray eyes that blazed like chips of diamond. "*Now* will you do what you're told, Jonathan?"

It was the Inquisitor.

Despite the whirling speed with which they flew through the air, Clary would have kicked out at Valentine if she could. But he held her as if his arms were iron bands. Her feet swung free, but struggle as she might, she didn't seem to be able to connect with anything.

When the demon banked and swerved suddenly, she let out a scream. Valentine laughed. Then they were spinning through a narrow metal tunnel and into a much larger, wider room. Instead of dropping them unceremoniously, the flying demon set them down gently on the floor.

Much to Clary's surprise, Valentine let her go. She jerked away from him and stumbled into the middle of the room, looking around wildly. It was a big space, probably once some kind of machine room. Machinery still lined the walls, shoved out of the way to create a wide square space in the center. The floor was thick black metal, splotched here and there with darker stains. In the middle of the empty space were four basins, big enough to wash a dog in. The interiors of the first two were stained a dark rust brown. The third was full of dark red liquid. The fourth was empty.

A metal footlocker stood behind the bowls. A dark cloth had

been thrown over it. As she drew closer, she saw that on top of the cloth rested a silver sword that glowed with a blackish light, almost an absence of illumination: a radiant, visible darkness.

Clary whirled around and stared at Valentine, who was quietly watching her. "How could you do it?" she demanded. "How could you kill Simon? He was just a—he was just a boy, just an ordinary human—"

"He wasn't human," said Valentine, in his silky voice. "He had become a monster. You just couldn't see it, Clarissa, because it wore the face of a friend."

"He wasn't a monster." She moved a little closer to the Sword. It looked huge, heavy. She wondered if she could lift it—and even if she could, could she swing it? "He was still Simon."

"Don't think I'm not sympathetic to your situation," said Valentine. He stood unmoving in the single shaft of light that came down from the trapdoor in the ceiling. "It was the same for me when Lucian was bitten."

"He told me," she spat at him. "You gave him a dagger and told him to kill himself."

"That was a mistake," said Valentine.

"At least you admit it—"

"I should have killed him myself. It would have showed that I cared."

Clary shook her head. "But you didn't. You've never cared about anyone. Not even my mother. Not even Jace. They were just things that belonged to you."

"But isn't that what love is, Clarissa? Ownership? 'I am my beloved's and my beloved is mine,' as the Song of Songs goes."

"No. And don't quote the Bible at me. I don't think you get it."

She was standing very near to the locker now, the hilt of the Sword within reaching distance. Her fingers were wet with sweat and she dried them surreptitiously on her jeans. "It's not just that someone belongs to you, it's that you give yourself to them. I doubt *you've* ever given anything to anyone. Except maybe nightmares."

"To give yourself to someone?" The thin smile didn't waver. "As you've given yourself to Jonathan?"

Her hand, which had been lifting toward the Sword, spasmed into a fist. She pulled it back against her chest, staring at him unbelievingly. "*What?*"

"You think I haven't seen the way you two look at each other? The way he says your name? You may not think I can feel, but that doesn't mean I can't see feelings in others." Valentine's tone was cool, every word a sliver of ice stabbing into her ears. "I suppose we have only ourselves to blame, your mother and I; having kept you two apart so long, you never developed the revulsion toward each other that would be more natural between siblings."

"I don't know what you mean." Clary's teeth were chattering.

"I think I make myself plain enough." He had moved out of the light. His face was a study in shadow. "I saw Jonathan after he faced the fear demon, you know. It showed itself to him as you. That told me all I needed to know. The greatest fear in Jonathan's life is the love he feels for his sister."

"I don't do what I'm told," said Jace. "But I might do what you want if you ask me nicely."

The Inquisitor looked as if she wanted to roll her eyes but had forgotten how. "I need to talk to you."

Jace stared at the Inquisitor. "*Now?*"

She put a hand on his arm. "Now."

"You're insane." Jace looked down the length of the ship. It looked like a Bosch painting of hell. The darkness was full of demons: lumbering, howling, squawking, and slashing out with claws and teeth. Nephilim darted back and forth, their weapons bright in the shadows. Jace could see already that there weren't enough Shadowhunters. Not nearly enough. "There's no way—we're in the middle of a battle—"

The Inquisitor's bony grip was surprisingly strong. "*Now.*" She pushed him, and he took a step back, too surprised to do anything else, and then another, until they were standing in the recess of a wall. She let go of Jace and felt in the folds of her dark cloak, drawing forth two seraph blades. She whispered their names, and then several words Jace didn't know, and flung them at the deck, one on either side of him. They stuck, points down, and a single blue-white sheet of light sprang up from them, walling Jace and the Inquisitor off from the rest of the ship.

"Are you locking me up *again?*" Jace demanded, staring at the Inquisitor in disbelief.

"This isn't a Malachi Configuration. You can get out of it if you want." Her thin hands clasped each other tightly. "Jonathan—"

"You mean Jace." He could no longer see the battle past the wall of white light, but he could still hear the sounds of it, the screams and the howling of the demons. If he turned his head, he could just catch a glimpse of a small section of ocean, sparkling with light like diamonds scattered over the surface of a mirror. There were about a dozen boats down there, the sleek, multi-hulled trimarans used on the lakes in Idris. Shadowhunter boats. "What are you doing here, Inquisitor? Why did you come?"

"You were right," she said. "About Valentine. He wouldn't make the trade."

"He told you to let me die." Jace felt suddenly light-headed.

"The moment he refused, of course, I called the Conclave together and brought them here. I—I owe you and your family an apology."

"Noted," said Jace. He hated apologies. "Alec and Isabelle? Are they here? They won't be punished for helping me?"

"They're here, and no, they won't be punished." She was still staring at him, eyes searching. "I can't understand Valentine," she said. "For a father to throw away the life of his child, his only son—"

"Yeah," said Jace. His head ached and he wished she would shut up, or that a demon would attack them. "It's a conundrum, all right."

"Unless . . ."

Now he looked at her in surprise. "Unless what?"

She jabbed a finger at his shoulder. "When did you get that?"

Jace looked down and saw that the spider demon's poison had eaten a hole in his shirt, leaving a good deal of his left shoulder bare. "The shirt? At Macy's. Winter sale."

"The *scar*. This scar, here on your shoulder."

"Oh, that." Jace wondered at the intensity of her gaze. "I'm not sure. Something that happened when I was very young, my father said. An accident of some kind. Why?"

Breath hissed through the Inquisitor's teeth. "It can't be," she murmured. "*You* can't be—"

"I can't be what?"

There was a note of uncertainty in the Inquisitor's voice.

"All those years," she said, "when you were growing up—you *truly* thought you were Michael Wayland's son—?"

Sharp fury went through Jace, made all the more painful by the tiny stab of disappointment that accompanied it. "By the *Angel*," he spat, "you dragged me off here in the middle of battle just to ask me the same goddamned questions again? You didn't believe me the first time and you still don't believe me. You'll never believe me, despite everything that's happened, even though *everything I told you was the truth*." He jabbed a finger toward whatever was happening on the other side of the wall of light. "I should be out there fighting. Why are you keeping me here? So after this is all over, if any of us are still even alive, you can go to the Clave and tell them I wouldn't fight on your side against my father? *Nice* try."

She had gone even paler than he'd thought possible. "Jonathan, that's not what I—"

*"My name is Jace!"* he shouted. The Inquisitor flinched, her mouth half-open, as if she were still about to say something. Jace didn't want to hear it. He stalked past her, nearly knocking her to the side, and kicked at one of the seraph blades in the deck. It toppled over and the wall of light vanished.

Beyond it was chaos. Dark shapes hurtled to and fro on deck, demons clambered over crumpled bodies, and the air was full of smoke and screaming. He strained to see anyone he knew in the melee. Where was Alec? Isabelle?

"Jace!" The Inquisitor hurried after him, her face pulled tight with fear. "Jace, you don't have a weapon, at least take—"

She broke off as a demon loomed up out of the darkness in front of Jace like an iceberg off the bow of a ship. It wasn't one he'd seen before tonight; this one had the wrinkled face and agile hands of a huge monkey, but the long, barbed tail of a scorpion. Its eyes were rolling and yellow. It hissed at him through broken needle teeth. Before Jace could duck, its tail shot forward with the speed of a striking cobra. He saw the needle tip whipping toward his face—

And for the second time that night, a shadow passed between him and death. Drawing a long-bladed knife, the Inquisitor threw herself in front of him, just in time for the scorpion's sting to bury itself in her chest.

She screamed, but stayed on her feet. The demon's tail whipped back, ready for another strike—but the Inquisitor's knife had already left her hand, flying straight and true. The runes carved on its blade gleamed as it sliced through the demon's throat. With a hiss, as of air escaping from a punctured balloon, it folded inward, its tail spasming as it vanished.

The Inquisitor crumpled to the deck. Jace knelt down beside her and laid a hand on her shoulder, rolling her onto her back. Blood was spreading across the gray front of her blouse. Her face was slack and yellow, and for a moment Jace thought she was already dead.

"Inquisitor?" He couldn't say her first name, not even now.

Her eyes fluttered open. Their whites were already dulling. With a great effort she beckoned him toward her. He bent closer, close enough to hear her whisper in his ear, whisper on a last exhale of breath—

"What?" Jace said, bewildered. "What does that mean?"

There was no answer. The Inquisitor had slumped back against the deck, her eyes wide open and staring, her mouth curved into what almost looked like a smile.

Jace sat back on his heels, numb and staring. She was dead. Dead because of him.

Something seized hold of the back of his shirt and hauled him to his feet. Jace clapped a hand to his belt—realized he was weaponless—and twisted around to see a familiar pair of blue eyes staring into his with utter incredulity.

"You're alive," Alec said—two short words, but there was a wealth of feeling behind them. The relief on his face was plain, as was his exhaustion. Despite the chill in the air, his black hair was plastered to his cheeks and forehead with sweat. His clothes and skin were streaked with blood and there was a long rip in the sleeve of his armored jacket, as if something jagged and sharp had torn it open. He clutched a bloody *guisarme* in his right hand and Jace's collar in the other.

"I seem to be," Jace admitted. "I won't be for long if you don't give me a weapon, though."

With a quick glance around, Alec let go of Jace, took a seraph blade from his belt, and handed it over. "Here," he said. "It's called Samandiriel."

Jace barely had the blade in his hand when a medium-size Drevak demon scuttled toward them, chittering imperiously. Jace raised Samandiriel, but Alec had already dispatched the creature with a jabbing blow from his *guisarme*.

"Nice weapon," Jace said, but Alec was looking past him, at the crumpled gray figure on the deck.

"Is that the Inquisitor? Is she . . . ?"

"She's dead," Jace said.

Alec's jaw set. "Good riddance. How'd she get it?"

Jace was about to reply when he was interrupted by a loud cry of "Alec! *Jace*!" It was Isabelle, hurrying toward them through the stench and smoke. She wore a close-fitting dark jacket, smeared with yellowish blood. Gold chains hung with rune charms circled her wrists and ankles, and her whip curled around her like a net of electrum wire.

She held her arms out. "Jace, we thought—"

"No." Something made Jace step back, shying away from her touch. "I'm all covered in blood, Isabelle. Don't."

A hurt expression crossed her face. "But we've all been looking for you—Mom and Dad, they—"

*"Isabelle!"* Jace shouted, but it was too late: A massive spider demon reared up behind her, jetting yellow poison from its fangs. Isabelle screamed as the poison struck her, but her whip shot out with blinding speed, slicing the demon in half. It thudded to the deck in two pieces, then vanished.

Jace darted toward Isabelle just as she slumped forward. Her whip slipped from her hand as he caught her, cradling her awkwardly against him. He could see how much of the poison had gotten on her: It had splashed mostly onto her jacket, but some of it spattered her throat, and where it touched, the skin burned and sizzled. Barely audibly, she whimpered—Isabelle, who never showed pain.

"Give her to me." It was Alec, dropping his weapon as he hurried to help his sister. He took Isabelle from Jace's arms and lowered her gently to the deck. Kneeling beside her, stele in hand, he looked up at Jace. "Hold off whatever comes while I heal her."

Jace couldn't drag his eyes away from Isabelle. Blood streamed from her neck down onto her jacket, soaking her hair. "We have to get her off this boat," he said roughly. "If she stays here—"

"She'll die?" Alec was tracing the tip of his stele as gently as he could over his sister's throat. "We're all going to die. There are too many of them. We're being slaughtered. The Inquisitor deserved to die for this—this is all her fault."

"A Scorpios demon tried to kill me," Jace said, wondering why he was saying it, why he was defending someone he hated. "The Inquisitor got in its way. Saved my life."

"She *did*?" Astonishment was clear in Alec's tone. "Why?"

"I guess she decided I was worth saving."

"But she always—" Alec broke off, his expression changing to one of alarm. "Jace, behind you—two of them—"

Jace whirled. Two demons were approaching: a Ravener, with its alligator-like body and serrated teeth, its scorpion tail curling forward over its back, and a Drevak, its pale white maggot-flesh gleaming in the moonlight. Jace heard Alec, behind him, suck in an alarmed breath; then Samandiriel left his hand, cutting a silvery path through the air. It sliced through the Ravener's tail, just below the pendulous poison sac at the end of its long stinger.

The Ravener howled. The Drevak turned, confused—and got the poison sac full in the face. The sac broke open, drenching the Drevak in venom. It emitted a single garbled scream and crumpled, its head eaten away to the bone. Blood and poison splattered the deck as the Drevak vanished. The Ravener, blood gushing from its tail stump, dragged itself a few more paces forward before it, too, disappeared.

Jace bent and picked up Samandiriel gingerly. The metal deck was still sizzling where the Ravener's poison had spilled on it, pocking it with tiny spreading holes like cheesecloth.

"Jace." Alec was on his feet, holding a pale but upright

Isabelle by the arm. "We need to get Isabelle out of here."

"Fine," Jace said. "You get her out of here. I'm going to deal with *that*."

"With what?" Alec said, bewildered.

"With that," Jace said again, and pointed. Something was coming toward them through the smoke and flames, something huge, humped, and massive. Easily five times the size of any other demon on the ship, it had an armored body, many-limbed, each appendage ending in a spiked chitinous talon. Its feet were elephant feet, huge and splayed. It had the head of a giant mosquito, Jace saw as it came closer, complete with insectile eyes and a dangling blood-red feeding tube.

Alec sucked in his breath. "What the hell is it?"

Jace thought for a moment. "Big," he said finally. "Very."

"Jace—"

Jace turned and looked at Alec, and then at Isabelle. Something inside him told him that this might very well be the last time he ever saw them, and yet he still wasn't afraid, not for himself. He wanted to say something to them, maybe that he loved them, that either one of them was worth more to him than a thousand Mortal Instruments and the power they could bring. But the words wouldn't come.

"Alec," he heard himself say. "Get Isabelle to the ladder, now, or we'll all die."

Alec met his gaze and held it for a moment. Then he nodded and pushed Isabelle, still protesting, toward the railing. He helped her up onto it and then over, and with immense relief Jace saw her dark head disappearing as she began to descend the ladder. *And now you, Alec,* he thought. *Go.*

But Alec wasn't going. Isabelle, now out of view, cried out

sharply as her brother jumped back down from the railing, onto the deck of the ship. His *guisarme* lay on the deck where he'd dropped it; he seized it now and moved to stand next to Jace and face the demon as it came.

He never got that far. The demon, bearing down on Jace, made a sudden swerve and rushed toward Alec, its bloody feeding tube whipping back and forth hungrily. Jace spun to block Alec, but the metal deck he was standing on, rotted with poison, crumbled underneath him. His foot plunged through and he fell hard against the deck.

Alec had time to shout Jace's name, and then the demon was on him. He stabbed at it with his *guisarme*, plunging the sharp end of it deep into the demon's flesh. The creature reared back, screaming a weirdly human scream, black blood spraying from the wound. Alec retreated, reaching for another weapon, just as the demon's talon whipped around, knocking him to the deck. Then its feeding tube wrapped around him.

Somewhere, Isabelle was screaming. Jace struggled desperately to pull his leg from the deck; sharp edges of metal stabbed into him as he jerked himself free and staggered to his feet.

He raised Samandiriel. Light blazed forth from the seraph blade, bright as a falling star. The demon flinched back, making a low hissing sound. It relaxed its grip on Alec and for a moment Jace thought it might be going to let him go. Then it whipped its head back with a sudden, startling speed and flung Alec with immense force. Alec hit the blood-slippery deck hard, skidded across it—and fell, with a single hoarse cry, over the side of the ship.

Isabelle was screaming Alec's name; her screams were like

spikes being driven into Jace's ears. Samandiriel was still blazing in his hand. Its light illuminated the demon stalking toward him, its insectile gaze bright and predatory, but all he could see was Alec; Alec falling over the side of the ship, Alec drowning in the black water far below. He thought he tasted seawater in his own mouth, or it might have been blood. The demon was almost on him; he raised Samandiriel in his hand and flung it—the demon squealed, a high, agonized sound—and then the deck gave way beneath Jace with a screech of crumbling metal and he fell into darkness.

# 19

## Dies Irae

**"You're wrong," Clary said, but her voice held no conviction.** "You don't know anything about me or Jace. You're just trying to—"

"To what? I'm trying to reach you, Clarissa. To make you understand." There was no feeling in Valentine's voice that Clary could detect beyond a faint amusement.

"You're laughing at us. You think you can use me to hurt Jace, so you're laughing at us. You're not even angry anymore," she added. "A real father would be angry."

"I am a real father. The same blood that runs in my veins runs in yours."

"You're not my father. Luke is," said Clary, almost wearily. "We've been over this."

"You only look to Luke as your father because of his relationship with your mother—"

"Their *relationship?*" Clary laughed out loud. "Luke and my mother are friends."

For a moment she was sure she saw a look of surprise pass over his face. But "Is that so," was all he said. And then, "You really think he endured all this—Lucian, I mean—this life of silence and hiding and running, this devotion to the protection of a secret even he didn't fully understand, just for *friendship?* You know very little about people, Clary, at your age, and less about men."

"You can make all the innuendoes about Luke you want. It won't make any difference. You're wrong about him, just like you're wrong about Jace. You have to give everyone ugly motives for everything they do, because ugly motives are all you understand."

"Is that what it would be if he loved your mother? Ugly?" said Valentine. "What's so ugly about love, Clarissa? Or is it that you sense, deep down, that your precious Lucian is neither truly human nor truly capable of feelings as we would understand them—"

"Luke's as human as I am," Clary flung at him. "You're just a bigot."

"Oh, no," Valentine said. "I'm anything but that." He moved a little closer to her, and she stepped in front of the Sword, blocking it from his view. "You think of me that way because you look at me and at what I do through the lens of your mundane understanding of the world. Mundane humans create distinctions between themselves, distinctions that seem ridiculous to any Shadowhunter. Their distinctions are based on race, religion, national identity, any of a dozen minor and irrelevant markers. To mundanes these seem logical, for though mundanes cannot see, understand, or acknowledge the demon worlds, still somewhere buried in their ancient memories, they know that there are those that walk this earth that are *other*. That do not belong, that mean only harm and destruction. Since the demon threat is invisible to mundanes, they must assign the threat to others of their own kind. They place the face of their enemy onto the face of their neighbor, and thus are generations of misery assured." He took another step toward her, and Clary instinctively moved backward; she was pressed up against the footlocker now. "I'm not like that," he went on. "I can see the truth of it. Mundanes see as through a glass, darkly, but Shadowhunters—we see face-to-face. We know the truth of evil, and know that while it walks among us, it is not *of* us. What does not belong to our world must not be allowed to take root here, to grow like a poisonous flower and extinguish all life."

Clary had meant to go for the Sword and then for Valentine, but his words shook her. His voice was so soft, so persuasive, and it wasn't as if she thought demons *should* be allowed to stay on earth, to drain it away to ashes as they'd drained away so many other worlds. . . . It almost made sense, what he said, but—

"Luke isn't a demon," she said.

"It seems to me, Clarissa," said Valentine, "that you've had very little experience of what a demon is and what it is not. You have met a few Downworlders who seemed to you to be kind enough, and it is through the lens of their kindness that you view the world. Demons, to you, are hideous creatures that leap out from the shadows to rend and attack. And there are such creatures. But there are also demons of deep subtlety and secrecy, demons who walk among humans unrecognized and unhindered. Yet I have seen them do such dreadful things that their more bestial colleagues seem gentle in comparison. There was a demon in London that I once knew, who posed as a very powerful financier. He was never alone, so it was difficult for me to get close enough to kill him, though I knew what he was. He would have his servants bring him animals and young children—anything that was small and helpless—"

"Stop." Clary put her hands up to her ears. "I don't want to hear this."

But Valentine's voice droned on, inexorable, muffled but not inaudible. "He would eat them slowly, over the course of many days. He had his tricks, his ways of keeping them alive through the worst imaginable tortures. If you can imagine a child trying to crawl to you with half its body torn away—"

"*Stop!*" Clary tore her hands away from her ears. "That's enough, *enough!*"

"Demons feed on death and pain and madness," Valentine said. "When I kill, it is because I must. You grew up in a falsely beautiful paradise surrounded by fragile glass walls, my daughter. Your mother created the world she wanted to live in and she brought you up in it, but she never told you it was an illusion. And all the time the demons waited with their weapons of blood and terror to smash the glass and pull you free of the lie."

"You smashed the walls," Clary whispered. "*You* dragged me into all this. No one but you."

"And the glass that cut you, the pain you felt, the blood? Do you blame me for that as well? I was not the one who put you into the prison."

"Stop it. Just stop talking." Clary's head was ringing. She wanted to scream at him, *You kidnapped my mother, you did this, it's your fault!* But she had begun to see what Luke had meant when he'd said you couldn't argue with Valentine. Somehow he'd made it impossible for her to disagree with him without feeling as if she were standing up for demons who bit children in half. She wondered how Jace had stood it all those years, living in the shadow of that demanding, overwhelming personality. She began to see where Jace's arrogance came from, his arrogance and his carefully controlled emotions.

The edge of the locker behind her was biting into the back of her legs. She could feel the cold coming off the Sword, making the hair on the back of her neck prickle. "What is it you want from me?" she asked Valentine.

"What makes you think I want anything from you?"

"You wouldn't be talking to me otherwise. You'd have whacked me on the head and be waiting around for—for whatever the next step is after this."

"The next step," said Valentine, "is for your Shadowhunter friends to track you down and for me to tell them that if they want to retrieve you alive, they'll trade the werewolf girl for you. I still need her blood."

"They'll never trade Maia for me!"

"That's where you're wrong," said Valentine. "They know the value of a Downworlder as compared to that of a Shadowhunter child. They'll make the trade. The Clave requires it."

"The Clave? You mean—that's part of the Law?"

"Codified into its very being," said Valentine. "Now do you see? We are not so very different, the Clave and I, or Jonathan and I, or even you and I, Clarissa. We merely have a small disagreement as to method." He smiled, and stepped forward to close the space between them.

Moving more quickly that she would have thought she could, Clary reached behind her and snatched up the Soul-Sword. It was as heavy as she'd thought it would be, so heavy she nearly overbalanced. Putting out a hand to steady herself, she lifted it, pointing the blade directly at Valentine.

Jace's fall ended abruptly when he struck a hard metal surface with enough force to rattle his teeth. He coughed, tasting blood in his mouth, and staggered painfully to his feet.

He was standing on a bare metal catwalk painted a dull green. The inside of the ship was hollow, a great echoing chamber of metal with dark outward-curving walls. Looking up, Jace could see a tiny patch of starry sky through the smoking hole in the hull far above.

The belly of the ship was a maze of catwalks and ladders that seemed to lead nowhere, twisting in on each other like the guts of a giant snake. It was freezing cold. Jace could see his breath puffing out in white clouds when he exhaled. There was very little light. He squinted into the shadows, then reached into his pocket to retrieve his witchlight rune-stone.

Its white glow lit the dimness. The catwalk was long, with a ladder at the far end leading down to a lower level. As Jace moved toward it, something glinted at his feet.

He bent down. It was a stele. He couldn't help but stare around him, as if half-expecting someone to materialize out of the shadows; how the *hell* had a Shadowhunter stele gotten down here? He picked it up carefully. All steles had a sort of aura to them, a ghostly imprint of their owner's personality. This one sent a shot of painful recognition through him. *Clary*.

A sudden, soft laugh broke the silence. Jace spun around, shoving the stele through his belt. In the glare of the witchlight, Jace could see a dark figure standing at the end of the catwalk. The face was hidden in shadow.

"Who's there?" he called.

There was no answer, only a sense that someone was laughing at him. Jace's hand went automatically to his belt, but he had dropped the seraph blade when he fell. He was out of weapons.

But what had his father always taught him? Used correctly, almost anything could be a weapon. He moved slowly toward the figure, his eyes taking in the various details around him—a strut he could catch hold of and swing from, kicking out with his feet; an exposed bit of broken metal he could throw an opponent against, puncturing their spine. All these thoughts went through his head in a split second, the single split second before the figure at the end of the catwalk turned, his white hair shining in the witchlight, and Jace recognized him.

Jace stopped dead in his tracks. "Father? Is that you?"

The first thing Alec was aware of was freezing cold. The second was that he couldn't breathe. He tried to suck in air and his body spasmed. He sat upright, expelling dirty river water from his lungs in a bitter flood that made him gag and choke.

Finally he could breathe, though his lungs felt like they were on fire. Gasping, he looked around. He was sitting on a corrugated metal platform—no, it was the back of a truck. A pickup truck, floating in the middle of the river. His hair and clothes were streaming cold water. And Magnus Bane was sitting opposite him, regarding him with amber cat's eyes that glowed in the dark.

His teeth began to chatter. "What—what *happened?*"

"You tried to drink the East River," Magnus said, and Alec saw, as if for the first time, that Magnus's clothes were soaking wet too, sticking to his body like a dark second skin. "I pulled you out."

Alec's head was pounding. He felt at his belt for his stele, but it was gone. He tried to think back—the ship, overrun with demons; Isabelle falling and Jace catching her; blood, everywhere underfoot, the demon attacking—

"Isabelle! She was climbing down when I fell—"

"She's fine. She made it to a boat. I saw her." Magnus reached out to touch Alec's head. "You, on the other hand, might have a concussion."

"I need to get back to the battle." Alec pushed his hand away. "You're a warlock. Can't you, I don't know, *fly* me back to the boat or something? And fix my concussion while you're at it?"

Magnus, his hand still outstretched, sank back against the side of the truck bed. In the starlight his eyes were chips of green and gold, hard and flat as jewels.

"Sorry," Alec said, realizing how he had sounded, though he still felt that Magnus ought to see that getting to the ship was the most important thing. "I know you don't have to help us out—it's a favor—"

"Stop. I don't do you favors, Alec. I do things for you because—well, why do you think I do them?"

Something rose up in Alec's throat, cutting off his response. It was always like this when he was with Magnus. It was as if there were a bubble of pain or regret that lived inside his heart, and when he wanted to say something, anything, that seemed meaningful or true, it rose up and choked off his words. "I need to get back to the ship," he said, finally.

Magnus sounded too tired to even be angry. "I would help you," he said. "But I can't. Stripping the protection wards off the ship was bad enough—it's a strong, strong enchantment, demon-based—but when you fell, I had to put a fast spell on the truck so it wouldn't sink when I lost consciousness. And I will lose consciousness, Alec. It's just a matter of time." He passed a hand across his eyes. "I didn't want you to drown," he said. "The enchantment should hold enough for you to get the truck back to land."

"I—didn't realize." Alec looked at Magnus, who was three hundred years old but had always looked timeless, as if he had stopped getting older around the age of nineteen. Now there were sharp lines cut into the skin around his eyes and mouth. His hair hung lankly over his forehead, and the slump in his shoulders was not his usual careless posture but true exhaustion.

Alec put his hands out. They were pale in the moonlight, wrinkled from water and dotted with dozens of silver scars. Magnus looked down at them, and then back at Alec, confusion darkening his gaze.

"Take my hands," Alec said. "And take my strength too. Whatever of it you can use to—to keep yourself going."

Magnus didn't move. "I thought you had to get back to the ship."

"I have to fight," said Alec. "But that's what you're doing, isn't it? You're part of the fight just as much as the Shadowhunters on the ship—and I know you can take some of my strength, I've heard of warlocks doing that—so I'm offering. Take it. It's yours."

Valentine smiled. He was wearing his black armor, and gauntlet gloves that shone like the carapaces of black insects. "My son."

"Don't call me that," Jace said, and then, feeling a tremor begin in his hands, "Where's Clary?"

Valentine was still smiling. "She defied me," he said. "I had to teach her a lesson."

*"What have you done to her?"*

"Nothing." Valentine came closer to Jace, close enough to touch him if he had chosen to extend his hand. He didn't. "Nothing she won't recover from."

Jace closed his hand into a fist so his father wouldn't see it shaking. "I want to see her."

"Really? With all this going on?" Valentine glanced up, as if he could see through the hull of the ship to the carnage on deck. "I would have thought you'd want to be fighting with the rest of your Shadowhunter friends. Pity their efforts are for nothing."

"You don't know that."

"I do know it. For every one of them, I can summon a thousand demons. Even the best Nephilim can't hold out against those odds. As in the case," Valentine added, "of poor Imogen."

"How do you—"

"I see everything that happens on my ship." Valentine's eyes narrowed. "You do know it's your fault she died, don't you?"

Jace sucked in a breath. He could feel his heart pounding as if it wanted to tear its way out of his chest.

"If it weren't for you, none of them would have come to the ship. They thought they were rescuing you, you know. If it had just been about the two Downworlders, they wouldn't have bothered."

Jace had almost forgotten. "Simon and Maia—"

"Oh, they're dead. Both of them." Valentine's tone was casual, even soft. "How many have to die, Jace, before you see the truth?"

Jace's head felt as if it were full of swirling smoke. His shoulder burned with pain. "We've had this conversation. You're wrong, Father. You might be right about demons, you might even be right about the Clave, but this is not the way—"

"I meant," said Valentine, "when will you see that you're *just like me?*"

Despite the cold, Jace had begun to sweat. "What?"

"You and I, we're alike," said Valentine. "As you said to me before, you are what I made you to be, and I made you as a copy of myself. You have my arrogance. You have my courage. And you have that quality that causes others to give their lives for you without question."

Something hammered at the back of Jace's mind. Something he ought to know, or had forgotten—his shoulder *burned*—"I don't *want* people giving their lives for me," he cried.

"No. You do. You like knowing that Alec and Isabelle would die for you. That your sister would. The Inquisitor *did* die for you, didn't she, Jonathan? And you stood by and let her—"

"No!"

"You're just like me—it isn't surprising, is it? We're father and son, why shouldn't we be alike?"

*"No!"* Jace's hand shot out and seized the twisted metal strut. It came off in his hand with an explosive snap, its broken edge jagged and wickedly sharp. *"I am not like you!"* he cried, and drove the strut directly into his father's chest.

Valentine's mouth opened. He staggered back, the end of the strut protruding from his chest. For a moment Jace could only stare, thinking, *I was wrong—it's really him*—and then Valentine seemed to collapse in on himself, his body crumbling away like sand. The air was full of the smell of burning as Valentine's body turned to ash that blew away on the cold air.

Jace put a hand to his shoulder. The skin where the Fearless rune had burned itself away felt hot to the touch. A great sense of weakness overwhelmed him. *"Agramon,"* he whispered, and fell to his knees on the catwalk.

It was only a few moments that he knelt on the ground as his hammering pulse slowed, but to Jace it felt like forever. When he finally stood up, his legs were stiff with cold. His fingertips were blue. The air still stank of something burned, though there was no sign of Agramon.

Still gripping the piece of metal strut, Jace made for the ladder at the end of the catwalk. The effort of clambering down one-handed cleared his head. He dropped from the last rung to find himself on a second narrow catwalk that ran along the side of a vast metal chamber. There were dozens of other catwalks laddering the walls and a variety of pipes and machinery. Banging sounds came from inside the pipes, and every once in a while one of the pipes would give off a blast of what looked like steam, though the air remained bitterly cold.

*Quite a place you've got for yourself here, Father,* Jace thought. The bare industrial interior of the ship didn't fit with the Valentine he knew, who was particular about the type of cut crystal his decanters were made out of. Jace glanced around. It was a labyrinth down here; there was no way to know which direction he should go. He turned to climb down the next ladder and noticed a dark red smear on the metal floor.

Blood. He scraped the toe of his boot through it. It was still damp, slightly tacky. Fresh blood. His pulse quickened. Partway down the catwalk, he saw another spot of red, and then another a farther distance away, like a trail of bread crumbs in a fairy tale.

Jace followed the blood, his boots echoing loudly on the metal catwalk. The pattern of the blood splatters was peculiar, not as if there had been a fight, but more as if someone had been carried, bleeding, along the catwalk—

He reached a door. It was made of black metal, silvered here and there with dents and chips. There was a bloody handprint around the knob. Gripping the jagged strut more tightly, Jace pushed the door open.

A wave of even colder air hit him and he sucked in a breath. The room was empty except for a metal pipe that ran along one wall, and what looked like a heap of sacking in the corner. A little light came in through a porthole high up in the wall. As Jace stepped gingerly forward, the light from the porthole fell on the heap in the corner and he realized that it wasn't a pile of trash after all, but a body.

Jace's heart started to bang like an unlocked door in a windstorm.

The metal floor was sticky with blood. His boots pulled away from it with an ugly suctioning sound as he crossed the room and bent down beside the crumpled figure in the corner. A boy, dark-haired and dressed in jeans and a blood-soaked blue T-shirt.

Jace took the body by the shoulder and heaved. It flipped over, limp and boneless, brown eyes staring sightlessly upward. Jace's breath caught in his throat. It *was* Simon. He was white as paper. There was an ugly gash at the base of his throat, and both wrists had been slashed, leaving gaping, ragged-edged wounds.

Jace sank to his knees, still holding Simon's shoulder. He thought hopelessly of Clary, of her pain when she found out, of the way she'd crushed his hands in hers, so much strength in those small fingers. *Find Simon. I know you will.*

And he had. But it was too late.

When Jace was ten, his father had explained to him all the ways to kill vampires. Stake them. Cut their heads off and set them to burning like eerie jack-o'-lanterns. Let the sun scorch them to ashes. Or drain their blood. They needed blood to live, they ran on it, like cars ran on gasoline. Looking at the ragged wound in Simon's throat, it wasn't hard to see what Valentine had done.

Jace reached out to close Simon's staring eyes. If Clary had to see him dead, better she not see him like this. He moved his hand down to the collar of Simon's shirt, meaning to tug it up, to cover the gash.

Simon moved. His eyelids twitched and opened, his eyes rolled back to the whites. He gurgled then, a faint sound, lips curling back, showing the points of vampire fangs. The breath rattled in his slashed throat.

Nausea rose in the back of Jace's throat, his hand tightening on Simon's collar. *He wasn't dead.* But God, the pain, it must be incredible. He couldn't heal, couldn't regenerate, not without—

Not without blood. Jace let go of Simon's shirt and dragged his right sleeve up with his teeth. Using the jagged tip of the broken strut, he slashed a deep cut lengthwise down his wrist. Blood gushed to the surface of the skin. He dropped the strut; it hit the metal floor with a clang. He could smell his own blood in the air, sharp and coppery.

He looked down at Simon, who hadn't moved. The blood was running down Jace's hand now, his wrist stinging. He held it out over Simon's face, letting the blood drip down his fingers, spill onto Simon's mouth. There was no reaction. Simon wasn't moving. Jace moved closer; he was kneeling over Simon now, his breath making white puffs in the icy air. He leaned down, pressed his bleeding wrist against Simon's mouth. "Drink my blood, idiot," he whispered. "*Drink it.*"

For a moment nothing happened. Then Simon's eyes fluttered shut. Jace felt a sharp sting in his wrist, a sort of pull, a hard pressure—and Simon's right hand flew up and clamped onto Jace's arm, just above the elbow. Simon's back arched off the floor, the pressure on Jace's wrist increasing as Simon's fangs sank deeper. Pain shot up Jace's arm. "Okay," Jace said. "Okay, enough."

Simon's eyes opened. The whites were gone, the dark brown irises focused on Jace. There was color in his cheeks, a hectic flush like a fever. His lips were slightly parted, the white fangs stained with blood.

"Simon?" Jace said.

Simon rose up. He moved with incredible speed, knocking Jace sideways and rolling on top of him. Jace's head hit the metal floor, his ears ringing as Simon's teeth sank into his neck. He tried to twist away, but the other boy's arms were like iron bars, pinning him to the ground, fingers digging into his shoulders.

But Simon wasn't hurting him—not really—the pain that had started out sharp faded to a sort of dull burn, pleasant the way the burn of the stele was sometimes pleasant. A drowsy sense of peace stole through Jace's veins and he felt his muscles relax; the hands that had been trying to push Simon away a moment ago now pressed him closer. He could feel the beat of his own heart, feel it slowing, its hammering fading to a softer echo. A shimmering darkness crept in at the corners of his vision, beautiful and strange. Jace closed his eyes—

Pain lanced through his neck. He gasped and his eyes flew open; Simon was sitting up on him, staring down with wide eyes, his hand across his own mouth. Simon's wounds were gone, though fresh blood stained the front of his shirt.

Jace could feel the pain of his bruised shoulders again, the slash across his wrist, his punctured throat. He could no longer hear his heart beating, but knew it was slamming away inside his chest.

Simon took his hand away from his mouth. The fangs were gone. "I could have killed you," he said. There was a sort of pleading in his voice.

"I would have let you," said Jace.

Simon stared down at him, then made a noise in the back of his throat. He rolled off Jace and hit the floor on his knees, hugging his elbows. Jace could see the dark tracery of Simon's veins through the pale skin of his throat, branching blue and purple lines. Veins full of blood.

*My blood.* Jace sat up. He fumbled for his stele. Dragging it across his arm felt like hauling a lead pipe across a football field. His head throbbed. When he finished the *iratze*, he leaned his head back against the wall behind him, breathing hard, the pain leaving him as the healing rune took effect. *My blood in his veins.*

"I'm sorry," Simon said. "I'm so sorry."

The healing rune was having its effect. Jace's head started to clear and the banging in his chest slowed. He got to his feet, carefully, expecting a wave of dizziness, but he felt only a little weak and tired. Simon was still on his knees, staring down at his hands. Jace reached down and grabbed the back of his shirt, hauling him to his feet. "Don't apologize," he said, letting Simon go. "Just get moving. Valentine has Clary and we haven't got much time."

The second her fingers closed around the hilt of Maellartach, a searing blast of cold shot up Clary's arm. Valentine watched with an expression of mild interest as she gasped with pain, her fingers going numb. She clutched desperately at the Sword, but it slipped from her grasp and clattered to the ground at her feet.

She barely saw Valentine move. A moment later he was standing in front of her with the Sword in his grasp. Clary's hand was stinging. She glanced down and saw that a red, burning weal was rising along her palm.

"Did you really think," Valentine said, a tinge of disgust coloring his voice, "that I'd let you near a weapon I thought you could *use*?" He shook his head. "You didn't understand a word I said, did you? It appears that of my two children, only one seems capable of understanding the truth."

Clary closed her injured hand into a fist, almost welcoming the pain. "If you mean Jace, he hates you too."

Valentine swung the Sword up, bringing the tip of it level with Clary's collarbone. "That is enough," he said, "out of you."

The tip of the Sword was sharp; when she breathed, it pricked her throat, and a trickle of blood threaded its way down her chest. The Sword's touch seemed to spill cold through her veins, sending sizzling ice particles through her arms and legs, numbing her hands.

"Ruined by your upbringing," Valentine said. "Your mother was always a stubborn woman. It was one of the things I loved about her in the beginning. I thought she would stand by her ideals."

It was strange, Clary thought with a detached sort of horror, that when she had seen her father before at Renwick's, his considerable personal charisma had been on display for Jace's benefit. Now he wasn't bothering, and without the surface patina of charm, he seemed—empty. Like a hollow statue, eyes cut out to show only darkness inside.

"Tell me, Clarissa—did your mother ever talk about me?"

"She told me my father was dead." *Don't say anything else,* she warned herself, but she was sure he could read the rest of the words in her eyes. *And I wish she had been telling the truth.*

"And she never told you you were different? Special?"

Clary swallowed, and the tip of the blade cut a little deeper. More blood trickled down her chest. "She never told me I was a Shadowhunter."

"Do you know why," Valentine said, looking down the

length of the Sword at her, "your mother left me?"

Tears burned the back of Clary's throat. She made a choking noise. "You mean there was only *one* reason?"

"She told me," he went on, as if Clary hadn't spoken, "that I had turned her first child into a monster. She left me before I could do the same to her second. You. *But she was too late.*"

The cold at her throat, in her limbs, was so intense that she was beyond shivering. It was as if the Sword was turning her to ice. "She'd never say that," Clary whispered. "Jace isn't a monster. Neither am I."

"I wasn't talking about—"

The trapdoor over their heads slammed open and two shadowy figures dropped from the hole, landing just behind Valentine. The first, Clary saw with a bright shock of relief, was Jace, falling through the air like an arrow shot from a bow, sure of its target. He hit the floor with an assured lightness. He was clutching a bloodstained steel strut in one hand, its end broken off to a wicked point.

The second figure landed beside Jace with the same lightness if not the same grace. Clary saw the outline of a slender boy with dark hair and thought, *Alec.* It was only when he straightened and she recognized the familiar face that she realized who it was.

She forgot the Sword, the cold, the pain in her throat, forgot everything. *"Simon!"*

Simon looked across the room at her. Their eyes met for just a moment and Clary hoped he could read in her face her full and overwhelming relief. The tears that had been threatening came, and spilled down her face. She didn't move to wipe them away.

Valentine turned his head to look behind him, and his mouth sagged in the first expression of honest surprise Clary had ever seen on his face. He whirled to face Jace and Simon.

The moment the point of the Sword left Clary's throat, the ice drained from her, taking all her strength with it. She sank to her knees, shivering uncontrollably. When she raised her hands to wipe the tears away from her face, she saw that the tips of her fingers were white with the beginnings of frostbite.

Jace stared at her in horror, then at his father. "What did you do to her?"

"Nothing," Valentine said, regaining control of himself. "Yet."

To Clary's surprise, Jace paled, as if his father's words had shocked him.

"I'm the one who should be asking you what you've done, Jonathan," Valentine said, and though he spoke to Jace, his eyes were on Simon. "Why is it still alive? Revenants can regenerate, but not with such little blood in them."

"You mean me?" Simon demanded. Clary stared. Simon sounded *different*. He didn't sound like a kid smarting off to an adult; he sounded like someone who felt like he could face Valentine Morgenstern on equal footing. Like someone who *deserved* to face him on equal footing. "Oh, that's right, you left me for dead. Well, dead-*er*."

"Shut *up*." Jace shot a glare at Simon; his eyes were very dark. "Let me answer this." He turned to his father. "I let Simon drink my blood," he said. "So he wouldn't die."

Valentine's already severe face settled into harder lines, as if the bones were pushing out through the skin. "You *willingly* let a vampire drink your blood?"

Jace seemed to hesitate for a moment—he glanced over at Simon, who was staring fixedly at Valentine with a look of intense hatred. Then he said, carefully, "Yes."

"You have no idea what you've done, Jonathan," said Valentine in a terrible voice. "No idea."

"I saved a life," said Jace. "One you tried to take. I know that much."

"Not a human life," said Valentine. "You resurrected a monster that will only kill to feed again. His kind are always hungry—"

"I'm hungry right now," Simon said, and smiled to reveal that his fang teeth had slid from their sheaths. They glittered white and pointed against his lower lip. "I wouldn't mind a little more blood. Of course your blood would probably choke me, you poisonous piece of—"

Valentine laughed. "I'd like to see you try it, revenant," he said. "When the Soul-Sword cuts you, you will burn as you die."

Clary saw Jace's eyes go to the Sword, and then to her. There was an unspoken question in them. Quickly, she said, "The Sword isn't turned. Not quite. He didn't get Maia's blood, so he didn't finish the ceremony—"

Valentine turned toward her, Sword in hand, and she saw him smile. The Sword seemed to flick in his grasp, and then something hit her—it was like being knocked over by a wave, thrown down and then lifted against your will and tossed through the air. She rolled across the floor, helpless to stop herself, until she struck the bulkhead with bruising force. She crumpled at the base of it, gasping with breathlessness and pain.

Simon started toward her at a run. Valentine swung the

Soul-Sword and a sheet of sheer, blazing fire rose up, sending him stumbling backward with its surging heat.

Clary struggled to raise herself onto her elbows. Her mouth was full of blood. The world swayed around her and she wondered how hard she'd hit her head and if she was going to pass out. She willed herself to stay conscious.

The fire had receded, but Simon was still crouched on the floor, looking dazed. Valentine glanced briefly at him, and then at Jace. "If you kill the revenant now," he said, "you can still undo what you've done."

"No," Jace whispered.

"Just take the weapon you hold in your hand and drive it through his heart." Valentine's voice was soft. "One simple motion. Nothing you haven't done before."

Jace met his father's stare with a level gaze. "I saw Agramon," he said. "It had your face."

"You *saw* Agramon?" The Soul-Sword glittered as Valentine moved toward his son. "And you lived?"

"I killed it."

"You killed the Demon of Fear, but you won't kill a single vampire, not even at my order?"

Jace stood watching Valentine without expression. "He's a vampire, that's true," he said. "But his name is Simon."

Valentine stopped in front of Jace, the Soul-Sword in his hand, burning with a harsh black light. Clary wondered for a terrified moment if Valentine meant to stab Jace where he stood, and if Jace meant to let him. "I take it, then," Valentine said, "that you haven't changed your mind? What you told me when you came to me before, that was your final word, or do you regret having disobeyed me?"

Jace shook his head slowly. One hand still clutched the broken strut, but his other hand—his right—was at his waist, drawing something from his belt. His eyes, though, never left Valentine's, and Clary wasn't sure Valentine saw what he was doing. She hoped not.

"Yes," Jace said, "I regret having disobeyed you."

*No!* Clary thought, but her heart sank. Was he giving up, did he think it was the only way to save her and Simon?

Valentine's face softened. "Jonathan—"

"Especially," Jace said, "since I plan to do it again. Right now." His hand moved, quick as a flash of light, and something hurtled through the air toward Clary. It fell a few inches from her, hitting the metal with a clang and rolling. Her eyes widened.

It was her mother's stele.

Valentine began to laugh. "A *stele?* Jace, is this some sort of joke? Or have you finally—"

Clary didn't hear the rest of what he said; she heaved herself up, gasping as pain lanced through her head. Her eyes watered, her vision blurred; she reached out a shaking hand for the stele—and as her fingers touched it, she heard a voice, as clear inside her head as if her mother stood beside her. *Take the stele, Clary. Use it. You know what to do.*

Her fingers closed spasmodically around it. She sat up, ignoring the wave of pain that went through her head and down her spine. She was a Shadowhunter, and pain was something you lived with. Dimly, she could hear Valentine call her name, hear his footsteps, coming nearer—and she flung herself at the bulkhead, thrusting the stele forward with such force that when its tip touched the metal, she thought she heard the sizzle of something burning.

She began to draw. As always happened when she drew, the world fell away and there was only herself and the stele and the metal she drew on. She remembered standing outside Jace's cell whispering to herself, *Open, open, open,* and knew that she had drawn on all her strength to create the rune that had broken Jace's bonds. And she knew that the strength she had put into that rune was not a tenth, not a hundredth, of the strength she was putting into *this*. Her hands burned and she cried out as she dragged the stele down the metal wall, leaving a thick black line like char behind it. *Open.*

All her frustration, all her disappointment, all her rage went through her fingers and into the stele and into the rune. *Open.* All her love, all her relief at seeing Simon alive, all her hope that they still might survive. *Open!*

Her hand, still holding the stele, dropped to her lap. For a moment there was utter silence as all of them—Jace, Valentine, even Simon—stared along with her at the rune that burned on the ship's bulkhead.

It was Simon who spoke, turning to Jace. "What does it say?"

But it was Valentine who answered, not taking his eyes from the wall. There was a look on his face—not at all the look Clary had expected, a look that mixed triumph and horror, despair and delight. "It says," he said, "'*Mene mene tekel upharsin.*'"

Clary staggered to her feet. "That's not what it says," she whispered. "It says *open.*"

Valentine met her eyes with his own. "Clary—"

The scream of metal drowned out his words. The wall Clary had drawn on, a wall made of sheets of solid steel, warped and shuddered. Rivets tore free of their housings and jets of water sprayed into the room.

She could hear Valentine calling, but his voice was drowned out by the deafening sounds of metal being wrenched from metal as every nail, every screw, and every rivet that held together the enormous ship began tearing free from its moorings.

She tried to run toward Jace and Simon, but fell to her knees as another surge of water came through the widening hole in the wall. This time the wave knocked her down, icy water drawing her under. Somewhere Jace was calling her name, his voice loud and desperate over the screaming of the ship. She shouted his name only once before she was sucked out the jagged hole in the bulkhead and into the river.

She spun and kicked in the black water. Terror gripped her, terror of the blind darkness and of the depths of the river, the millions of tons of water all around her, pressing in on her, choking out the air in her lungs. She couldn't tell which way was up or which direction to swim. She could no longer hold her breath. She sucked in a lungful of filthy water, her chest bursting with the pain, stars exploding behind her eyes. In her ears the sound of rushing water was replaced by a high, sweet, impossible singing. *I'm dying*, she thought in wonder. A pair of pale hands reached out of the black water and drew her close. Long hair drifted around her. *Mom*, Clary thought, but before she could clearly see her mother's face, the darkness closed her eyes.

Clary came back to consciousness with voices all around her and lights shining in her eyes. She was flat on her back on the corrugated steel of Luke's truck bed. The gray-black sky swam overhead. She could smell river water all around her, mixed with the smell of smoke and blood. White faces hovered over her like balloons on strings. They swam into focus as she blinked her eyes.

Luke. And Simon. They were both looking down at her with expressions of anxious concern. For a moment she thought Luke's hair had gone white; then, blinking, she realized it was full of ashes. In fact, so was the air—it tasted of ashes—and their clothes and skin were streaked with blackish grime.

She coughed, tasting ash in her mouth. "Where's Jace?"

"He's . . ." Simon's eyes went to Luke, and Clary felt her heart contract.

"He's all right, isn't he?" she demanded. She struggled to sit up and a hard pain shot through her head. "Where is he? Where *is he?*"

"I'm here." Jace appeared at the edge of her vision, his face in shadow. He knelt down next to her. "I'm sorry. I should have been here when you woke up. It's just . . ."

His voice cracked.

"It's just what?" She stared at him; backlit by starlight, his hair was more silver than gold, his eyes bleached of color. His skin was streaked with black and gray.

"He thought you were dead too," Luke said, and stood up abruptly. He was staring out at the river, at something Clary couldn't see. The sky was full of swirls of black and scarlet smoke, as if it were on fire.

"Dead too? Who else—?" She broke off as a nauseating pain gripped her. Jace saw her expression and reached into his pocket, bringing out his stele.

"Hold still, Clary." There was a burning pain in her forearm, and then her head began to clear. She sat up and saw that she was sitting on a wet plank shoved up against the back of the truck cab. The bed was full of several inches of sloshing water, mixed with swirls of the ash that was sifting down from the sky in a fine black rain.

She glanced at the place where Jace had drawn a healing Mark on the inside of her arm. Her weakness was already receding, as if he'd shot a jolt of strength into her veins.

He traced the line of the *iratze* he'd drawn on her arm with his fingers before he drew back. His hand felt as cold and wet as her skin did. The rest of him was wet too; his hair damp and his soaked clothes sticking to his body.

There was an acrid taste in her mouth, as if she'd licked the bottom of an ashtray. "What happened? Was there a fire?"

Jace glanced toward Luke, who was staring out at the heaving black-gray river. The water was dotted here and there with small boats, but there was no sign of Valentine's ship. "Yes," he said. "Valentine's ship burned down to the waterline. There's nothing left."

"Where is everyone?" Clary moved her gaze to Simon, who was the only one of them who was dry. There was a faint greenish cast to his already pale skin, as if he were sick or feverish. "Where are Isabelle and Alec?"

"They're on one of the other Shadowhunter boats. They're fine."

"And Magnus?" She twisted around to look into the truck cab, but it was empty.

"He was needed to tend to some of the more badly wounded Shadowhunters," said Luke.

"But everyone's all right? Alec, Isabelle, Maia—they are all right, aren't they?" Clary's voice sounded small and thin in her own ears.

"Isabelle was injured," said Luke. "So was Robert Lightwood. He'll be needing a good amount of time to heal. Many of the other Shadowhunters, including Malik and Imogen, are dead. This was a very hard battle, Clary, and it didn't go well for us. Valentine is gone. So is the Sword. The Conclave is in tatters. I don't know—"

He broke off. Clary stared at him. There was something in his voice that frightened her. "I'm sorry," she said. "This was my fault. If I hadn't—"

"If you hadn't done what you did, Valentine would have killed everyone on the ship," said Jace fiercely. "You're the only thing that kept this from being a massacre."

Clary stared at him. "You mean what I did with the rune?"

"You tore that ship to fragments," Luke said. "Every bolt, every rivet, anything that might have held it together, just snapped apart. The whole thing shuddered into pieces. The oil tanks came apart too. Most of us barely had time to jump into the water before it all started to burn. What you did—no one's ever seen anything like it."

"Oh," Clary said in a small voice. "Was anyone—did I hurt anyone?"

"Quite a few of the demons drowned when the ship sank," said Jace. "But none of the Shadowhunters were hurt, no."

"Because they can swim?"

"Because they were rescued. Nixies pulled us all out of the water."

Clary thought of the hands in the water, the impossible

sweet singing that had surrounded her. So it hadn't been her mother after all. "You mean water faeries?"

"The Queen of the Seelie Court came through, in her way," said Jace. "She did promise us what aid was in her power."

"But how did she . . ." *How did she know?* Clary was going to say, but she thought of the Queen's wise and cunning eyes, and of Jace throwing that bit of white paper into the water by the beach in Red Hook, and decided not to ask.

"The Shadowhunter boats are starting to move," said Simon, looking out at the river. "I guess they've picked up everyone they could."

"Right." Luke squared his shoulders. "Time to get going." He moved slowly toward the truck cab—he was limping, though he seemed otherwise mostly uninjured.

Luke swung himself into the driver's seat, and in a moment the truck's engine was roiling again. They took off, skimming the water, the drops splashed up by the wheels catching the gray-silver of the lightening sky.

"This is so weird," said Simon. "I keep expecting the truck to start sinking."

"I can't believe you just went through what we went through and you think *this* is weird," said Jace, but there was no malice in his tone and no annoyance. He sounded only very, very tired.

"What will happen to the Lightwoods?" Clary asked. "After everything that's happened—the Clave—"

Jace shrugged. "The Clave works in mysterious ways. I don't know what they'll do. They'll be very interested in *you*, though. And in what you can do."

Simon made a noise. Clary thought at first that it was a

noise of protest, but when she looked closely at him, she saw he was greener than ever. "What's wrong, Simon?"

"It's the river," he said. "Running water isn't good for vampires. It's pure, and—we're not."

"The East River's hardly pure," said Clary, but she reached out and touched his arm gently anyway. He smiled at her. "Didn't you fall into the water when the ship came apart?"

"No. There was a piece of metal floating in the water and Jace tossed me onto it. I stayed out of the river."

Clary looked over her shoulder at Jace. She could see him a little more clearly now; the darkness was fading. "Thank you," she said. "Do you think . . ."

He raised his eyebrows. "Do I think what?"

"That Valentine might have drowned?"

"Never believe the bad guy is dead until you see a body," said Simon. "That just leads to unhappiness and surprise ambushes."

"You're not wrong," said Jace. "My guess is he isn't dead. Otherwise we would have found the Mortal Instruments."

"Can the Clave go on without them? Whether Valentine's alive or not?" Clary wondered.

"The Clave always goes on," said Jace. "That's all it knows how to do." He turned his face toward the eastern horizon. "The sun's coming up."

Simon went rigid. Clary stared at him in surprise for a moment, and then in shocked horror. She whirled to follow Jace's gaze. He was right—the eastern horizon was a blood-red stain spreading out from a golden disc. Clary could see the first edge of the sun staining the water around them unearthly hues of green and scarlet and gold.

*"No!"* she whispered.

Jace looked at her in surprise, and then at Simon, who sat motionless, staring at the rising sun like a trapped mouse staring at a cat. Jace got quickly to his feet and walked over to the truck cab. He spoke in a low voice. Clary saw Luke turn to look at her and Simon, and then back at Jace. He shook his head.

The truck lurched forward. Luke must have pressed his foot to the gas. Clary grabbed for the side of the truck bed to steady herself. Up front, Jace was shouting at Luke that there had to be some way to make the damn thing go faster, but Clary knew they'd never outrun the dawn.

"There must be something," she said to Simon. She couldn't believe that in less than five minutes she'd gone from incredulous relief to incredulous horror. "We could cover you, maybe, with our clothes—"

Simon was still staring at the sun, white-faced. "A pile of rags won't work," he said. "Raphael explained—it takes walls to protect us from sunlight. It'll burn through cloth."

"But there must be something—"

"Clary." She could see him clearly now, in the gray predawn light, his eyes huge and dark in his white face. He held out his hands to her. "Come here."

She fell against him, trying to cover as much of his body as she could with her own. She knew it was useless. When the sun touched him, he'd fall away to ashes.

They sat for a moment in perfect stillness, arms wrapped around each other. Clary could feel the rise and fall of his chest—habit, she reminded herself, not necessity. He might not breathe, but he could still die.

"I won't let you die," she said.

"I don't think you get a choice." She felt him smile. "I didn't think I'd get to see the sun again," he said. "I guess I was wrong."

"Simon—"

Jace shouted something. Clary looked up. The sky was flooded with rose-colored light, like dye poured into clear water. Simon tensed under her. "I love you," he said. "I have never loved anyone else but you."

Gold threads shot through the rosy sky like the gold veining in expensive marble. The water around them blazed with light and Simon went rigid, his head falling back, his open eyes filling with gold as if molten liquid were rising inside of him. Black lines appeared on his skin like cracks in a shattered statue.

*"Simon!"* Clary screamed. She reached for him but felt herself hauled suddenly backward; it was Jace, his hands gripping her shoulders. She tried to pull away but he held her tightly; he was saying something in her ear, over and over, and only after a few moments did she even begin to understand him:

"Clary, look. *Look.*"

"No!" Her hands flew to her face. She could taste the brackish water from the bottom of the truck bed on her palms. It was salty, like tears. "I don't want to look. I don't want to—"

"Clary." Jace's hands were at her wrists, pulling her hands away from her face. The dawn light stung her eyes. *"Look."*

She looked. And heard her own breath whistle harshly in her lungs as she gasped. Simon was sitting up at the back of the truck, in a patch of sunlight, openmouthed and staring down at himself. The sun danced on the water behind him and the edges of his hair glinted like gold. He had not burned away to ash, but sat unscorched in the sunlight, and the pale skin of his face and arms and hands was entirely unmarked.

Outside the Institute, night was falling. The faint red of sunset glowed in through the windows of Jace's bedroom as he stared at the pile of his belongings on the bed. The pile was much smaller than he thought it would be. Seven whole years of life in this place, and this was all he had to show for it: half a duffel bag's worth of clothes, a small stack of books, and a few weapons.

He had debated whether he should bring the few things he'd saved from the manor house in Idris with him when he left tonight. Magnus had given him back his father's silver ring, which he no longer felt comfortable wearing. He had hung it on a loop of chain around his throat. In the end, he had decided to take everything: There was no point leaving anything of himself behind in this place.

He was packing the duffel with clothes when a knock sounded at the door. He went to it, expecting Alec or Isabelle.

It was Maryse. She wore a severe black dress and her hair was pulled back sharply from her face. She looked older than he remembered her. Two deep lines ran from the corners of her mouth to her jaw. Only her eyes had any color. "Jace," she said. "Can I come in?"

"You can do what you like," he said, returning to the bed. "It's your house." He grabbed up a handful of shirts and stuffed them into the duffel bag with possibly unnecessary force.

"Actually, it's the Clave's house," said Maryse. "We're only its guardians."

Jace shoved books into the bag. "Whatever."

"What are you doing?" If Jace hadn't known better, he would have thought her voice wavered slightly.

"I'm packing," he said. "It's what people generally do when they're moving out."

She blanched. "Don't leave," she said. "If you want to stay—"

"I don't want to stay. I don't belong here."

"Where will you go?"

"Luke's," he said, and saw her flinch. "For a while. After that, I don't know. Maybe to Idris."

"Is that where you think you belong?" There was an aching sadness in her voice.

Jace stopped packing for a moment and stared down at his bag. "I don't know where I belong."

"With your family." Maryse took a tentative step forward. "With us."

"*You* threw me out." Jace heard the harshness in his own voice, and tried to soften it. "I'm sorry," he said, turning to look at her. "About everything that's happened. But you didn't want me before, and I can't imagine you want me now. Robert's going to be sick awhile; you'll be needing to take care of him. I'll just be in the way."

"In the way?" She sounded incredulous. "Robert wants to *see* you, Jace—"

"I doubt that."

"What about Alec? Isabelle, Max—they need you. If you don't believe me that I want you here—and I couldn't blame you if you didn't—you must know that they do. We've been through a bad time, Jace. Don't hurt them more than they're already hurt."

"That's not fair."

"I don't blame you if you hate me." Her voice *was* wavering. Jace swung around to stare at her in surprise. "But what I did—even throwing you out—treating you as I did, it was to protect you. And because I was afraid."

"Afraid of me?"

She nodded.

"Well, that makes me feel *much* better."

Maryse took a deep breath. "I thought you would break my heart like Valentine did," she said. "You were the first thing I loved, you see, after him, that wasn't my own blood. The first living creature. And you were just a child—"

"You thought I was someone else."

"No. I've always known just who you are. Ever since the first time I saw you getting off the ship from Idris, when you were ten years old—you walked into my heart, just as my own children did when they were born." She shook her head. "You can't understand. You've never been a parent. You never love anything like you love your children. And nothing can make you angrier."

"I did notice the angry part," Jace said, after a pause.

"I don't expect you to forgive me," Maryse said. "But if you'd stay for Isabelle and Alec and Max, I'd be so grateful—"

It was the wrong thing to say. "I don't want your gratitude," Jace said, and turned back to the duffel bag. There was nothing left to put in it. He tugged at the zipper.

*"A la claire fontaine,"* Maryse said, *"m'en allant promener."*

He turned to look at her. "What?"

*"Il y a longtemps que je t'aime. Jamais je ne t'oublierai*—it's the old French ballad I used to sing to Alec and Isabelle. The one you asked me about."

There was very little light in the room now, and in the dimness Maryse looked to him almost as she had when he was ten years old, as if she had not changed at all in the past seven years. She looked severe and worried, anxious—and hopeful. She looked like the only mother he'd ever known.

"You were wrong that I never sang it to you," she said. "It's just that you never heard me."

Jace said nothing, but he reached out and yanked the zipper open on the duffel bag, letting his belongings spill out onto the bed.

# Epilogue

**"*Clary!*" Simon's mother beamed all over her face at the** sight of the girl standing on her doorstep. "I haven't seen you for ages. I was starting to worry you and Simon had had a fight."

"Oh, no," Clary said. "I just wasn't feeling well, that's all." *Even when you've got magic healing runes, apparently you're not invulnerable.* She hadn't been surprised to wake up the morning after the battle to find she had a pounding headache and a fever; she'd thought she had a cold—who wouldn't, after freezing in wet clothes on the open water for hours at night?—but Magnus said she had most likely exhausted herself creating the rune that had destroyed Valentine's ship.

Simon's mother clucked sympathetically. "The same bug

Simon had the week before last, I bet. He could barely get out of bed."

"He's better now, though, right?" Clary said. She knew it was true, but she didn't mind hearing it again.

"He's fine. He's out in the back garden, I think. Just go on through the gate." She smiled. "He'll be happy to see you."

The redbrick row houses on Simon's street were divided by pretty white wrought iron fences, each of which had a gate that led to a tiny patch of garden in the back of the house. The sky was bright blue and the air cool, despite the sunny skies. Clary could taste the tang of future snow on the air.

She fastened the gate shut behind her and went looking for Simon. He was in the back garden, as promised, lying on a plastic lounging chair with a comic open in his lap. He pushed it aside when he saw Clary, sat up, and grinned. "Hey, baby."

"*Baby?*" She perched beside him on the chair. "You're kidding me, right?"

"I was trying it out. No?"

"No," she said firmly, and leaned over to kiss him on the mouth. When she drew back, his fingers lingered in her hair, but his eyes were thoughtful.

"I'm glad you came over," he said.

"Me too. I would have come sooner, but—"

"You were sick. I know." She'd spent the week texting him from Luke's couch, where she'd lain wrapped up in a blanket watching *CSI* reruns. It was comforting to spend time in a world where every puzzle had a detectable, scientific answer.

"I'm better now." She glanced around and shivered, pulling her white cardigan closer around her body. "What are you doing lying around outside in this weather, anyway? Aren't you freezing?"

Simon shook his head. "I don't really feel cold or heat anymore. Besides"—his mouth curled into a smile—"I want to spend as much time in the sunlight as I can. I still get sleepy during the day, but I'm fighting it."

She touched the back of her hand to his cheek. His face was warm from the sun, but underneath, the skin was cool. "But everything else is still . . . still the same?"

"You mean am I still a vampire? Yeah. It looks like it. Still want to drink blood, still no heartbeat. I'll have to avoid the doctor, but since vampires don't get sick . . ." He shrugged.

"And you talked to Raphael? He still has no idea why you can go out into the sun?"

"None. He seems pretty pissed about it too." Simon blinked at her sleepily, as if it were two in the morning instead of the afternoon. "I think it upsets his ideas about the way things should be. Plus he's going to have a harder job getting me to roam the night when I'm determined to roam the day instead."

"You'd think he'd be thrilled."

"Vampires don't like change. They're very traditional." He smiled at her, and she thought, *He'll always look like this. When I'm fifty or sixty, he'll still look sixteen.* It wasn't a happy thought. "Anyway, this'll be good for my music career. If that Anne Rice stuff is anything to go by, vampires make great rock stars."

"I'm not sure that information is reliable."

He leaned back against the chair. "What is? Besides you, of course."

"*Reliable?* Is that how you think of me?" she demanded in mock indignation. "That's not very romantic."

A shadow passed across his face. "Clary . . ."

"What? What is it?" She reached for his hand and held it. "You're using your bad news voice."

He looked away from her. "I don't know if it's bad news or not."

"Everything's one or the other," Clary said. "Just tell me you're all right."

"I'm all right," he said. "But—I don't think we should see each other anymore."

Clary almost fell off the lounge chair. "*You don't want to be friends anymore?*"

"Clary—"

"Is it because of the demons? Because I got you turned into a vampire?" Her voice was rising higher and higher. "I know everything's been crazy, but I can keep you away from all that. I can—"

Simon winced. "You're starting to sound like a dolphin, do you know that? Stop."

Clary stopped.

"I still want to be friends," he said. "It's the *other* stuff I'm not so sure about."

"Other stuff?"

He started to blush. She hadn't known vampires *could* blush. It looked startling against his pale skin. "The girlfriend-boyfriend stuff."

She was silent for a long moment, searching for words. Finally, she said: "At least you didn't say 'the kissing stuff.' I was afraid you were going to call it that."

He looked down at their hands, where they lay intertwined on the plastic of the lounge chair. Her fingers looked small against his, but for the first time, her skin was a shade darker. He stroked his thumb absently over her knuckles and said, "I wouldn't have called it that."

"I thought this was what you wanted," she said. "I thought you said that—"

He looked up at her through his dark lashes. "That I loved you? I do love you. But that's not the whole story."

"Is this because of Maia?" Her teeth had started to chatter, only partly from the cold. "Because you like her?"

Simon hesitated. "No. I mean, yes, I like her, but not the way you mean. It's just that when I'm around her—I know what it's like to have someone like *me* that way. And it's not like it is with you."

"But you don't love her—"

"Maybe I could someday."

"Maybe I could love *you* someday."

"If you ever do," he said, "come and let me know. You know where to find me."

Her teeth were chattering harder. "I can't lose you, Simon. I *can't*."

"You never will. I'm not leaving you. But I'd rather have what we have, which is real and true and important, than have you pretend anything else. When I'm with you, I want to know I'm with the real you, the real Clary."

She leaned her head against his, closing her eyes. He still felt like Simon, despite everything; still smelled like him, like his laundry soap. "Maybe I don't know who that is."

"But I do."

* * *

Luke's brand-new pickup was idling by the curb when Clary left Simon's house, fastening the gate shut behind her.

"You dropped me off. You didn't have to pick me up too," she said, swinging herself up into the cab beside him. Trust Luke to replace his old, destroyed truck with a new one that was exactly like it.

"Forgive me my paternal panic," said Luke, handing her a waxed paper cup of coffee. She took a sip—no milk and lots of sugar, the way she liked it. "I tend to get a little nervous when you're not in my immediate line of sight these days."

"Oh, yeah?" Clary held the coffee tightly to keep it from spilling as they bumped down the potholed road. "How long do you think that's going to go on for?"

Luke looked considering. "Not long. Five, maybe six years."

"Luke!"

"I plan to let you start dating when you're thirty, if that helps."

"Actually, that doesn't sound so bad. I may not be ready until I'm thirty."

Luke looked at her sideways. "You and Simon . . . ?"

She waved the hand that wasn't holding the coffee cup. "Don't ask."

"I see." He probably did. "Did you want me to drop you at home?"

"You're going to the hospital, right?" She could tell from the nervous tension underlying his jokes. "I'll go with you."

They were on the bridge now, and Clary looked out over the river, nursing her coffee thoughtfully. She never got tired of this view, the narrow river of water between the canyon walls of

Manhattan and Brooklyn. It glittered in the sun like aluminum foil. She wondered why she'd never tried to draw it. She remembered asking her mother once why she'd never used her as a model, never drawn her own daughter. "To draw something is to try to capture it forever," Jocelyn had said, sitting on the floor with a paintbrush dripping cadmium blue onto her jeans. "If you really love something, you never try to keep it the way it is forever. You have to let it be free to change."

*But I hate change.* She took a deep breath. "Luke," she said. "Valentine said something to me when I was on the ship, something about—"

"Nothing good ever starts with the words 'Valentine said,'" muttered Luke.

"Maybe not. But it was about you and my mom. He said you were in love with her."

Silence. They were stopped in traffic on the bridge. She could hear the sound of the Q train rumbling past. "Do *you* think that's true?" Luke said at last.

"Well." Clary could sense the tension in the air and tried to choose her words carefully. "I don't know. I mean, he said it before and I just dismissed it as paranoia and hatred. But this time I started thinking, and well—it is sort of weird that you've always been around, you've been like a dad to me, we practically lived on the farm in the summer, and yet neither you nor my mom ever dated anyone else. So I thought maybe . . ."

"You thought maybe what?"

"That maybe you've been together all this time and you just didn't want to tell me. Maybe you thought I was too young to get it. Maybe you were afraid it would start me asking questions about my dad. But I'm not too young to get it anymore.

You can tell me. I guess that's what I'm saying. You can tell me anything."

"Maybe not anything." There was another silence as the truck inched forward in the crawling traffic. Luke squinted into the sun, his fingers tapping on the wheel. Finally, he said, "You're right. I am in love with your mother."

"That's great," Clary said, trying to sound supportive despite how gross the idea happened to be of people her mom's and Luke's age being in love.

"But," he said, finishing, "she doesn't know it."

"She doesn't know it?" Clary made a wide sweeping gesture with her arm. Fortunately, her coffee cup was empty. "How could she not know? Haven't you told her?"

"As a matter of fact," said Luke, slamming his foot down on the gas so that the truck lurched forward, "no."

"Why not?"

Luke sighed and rubbed his stubbled chin tiredly. "Because," he said. "It never seemed like the right time."

"That is a lame excuse, and you know it."

Luke managed to make a noise halfway between a chuckle and a grunt of annoyance. "Maybe, but it's the truth. When I first realized how I felt about Jocelyn, I was the same age you are. Sixteen. And we'd all just met Valentine. I wasn't any competition for him. I was even a little glad that if it wasn't going to be me she wanted, it was going to be someone who really deserved her." His voice hardened. "When I realized how wrong I was about that, it was too late. When we ran away together from Idris, and she was pregnant with you, I offered to marry her, to take care of her. I said it didn't matter who the father of her baby was, I'd raise it like my own. She thought I was being charitable. I couldn't convince her I was being as selfish as I knew how to be. She told me she didn't want to be a burden on me, that it was too much to ask of anyone. After she left me in Paris, I went back to Idris but I was always restless, never happy. There was always that part of me missing, the part that was Jocelyn. I would dream that she was somewhere needing my help, that she was calling out to me and I couldn't hear her. Finally I went looking for her."

"I remember she was happy," Clary said in a small voice. "When you found her."

"She was and she wasn't. She was glad to see me, but at the same time I symbolized for her that whole world she'd run from, and she wanted no part of it. She agreed to let me stay when I promised I'd give up all ties to the pack, to the Clave, to Idris, to all of it. I would have offered to move in with both of you, but Jocelyn thought my transformations would be too hard to hide from you, and I had to agree. I bought the bookstore, took a new name, and pretended Lucian Graymark was dead. And for all intents and purposes, he has been."

"You really did a lot for my mom. You gave up a whole life."

"I would have done more," Luke said matter-of-factly. "But she was so adamant about wanting nothing to do with the Clave or Downworld, and whatever I might pretend, I'm still a lycanthrope. I'm a living reminder of all of that. And she was so sure she wanted *you* never to know any of it. You know, I never agreed with the trips to Magnus, to altering your memories or your Sight, but it was what she wanted and I let her do it because if I'd tried to stop her, she would have sent me away. And there's no way—no way—she would have let me marry her, be your father and *not* tell you the truth about myself. And that would have brought down everything, all those fragile walls she'd tried so hard to build between herself and the Invisible World. I couldn't do that to her. So I stayed silent."

"You mean you never told her how you felt?'

"Your mother isn't stupid, Clary," said Luke. He sounded calm, but there was a certain tightness in his voice. "She must have known. I offered to *marry* her. However kind her denials might have been, I do know one thing: She knows how I feel and she doesn't feel the same way."

Clary was silent.

"It's all right," Luke said, trying for lightness. "I accepted it a long time ago."

Clary's nerves were singing with a sudden tension that she didn't think was from the caffeine. She pushed back thoughts about her own life. "You offered to marry her, but did you say it was because you loved her? It doesn't sound like it."

Luke was silent.

"I think you should have told her the truth. I think you're wrong about how she feels."

"I'm not, Clary." Luke's voice was firm: *That's enough now.*

"I remember once I asked her why she didn't date," Clary said, ignoring his admonishing tone. "She said it was because she'd already given her heart. I thought she meant to my dad, but now—now I'm not so sure."

Luke looked actually astonished. "She *said* that?" He caught himself, and added, "Probably she did mean Valentine, you know."

"I don't think so." She shot him a look out of the corner of her eye. "Besides, don't you hate it? Not ever saying how you really feel?"

This time the silence lasted until they were off the bridge and rumbling down Orchard Street, lined with shops and restaurants whose signs were in beautiful Chinese characters of curling gold and red. "Yes, I hated it," Luke said. "At the time, I thought what I had with you and your mother was better than nothing. But if you can't tell the truth to the people you care about the most, eventually you stop being able to tell the truth to yourself."

There was a sound like rushing water in Clary's ears. Looking down, she saw that she'd crushed the empty waxed-paper cup she was holding into an unrecognizable ball.

"Take me to the Institute," she said. "Please."

Luke looked over at her in surprise. "I thought you wanted to come to the hospital?"

"I'll meet you there when I'm finished," she said. "There's something I have to do first."

The lower level of the Institute was full of sunlight and pale dust motes. Clary ran down the narrow aisle between the pews, threw herself at the elevator, and stabbed at the button. "Come on, come *on*," she muttered. "Come—"

The golden doors creaked open. Jace was standing inside the elevator. His eyes widened when he saw her.

"—on," Clary finished, and dropped her arm. "Oh. Hi."

He stared at her. "Clary?"

"You cut your hair," she said without thinking. It was true—the long metallic strands were no longer falling in his face, but were neatly and evenly cut. It made him look more civilized, even a little older. He was dressed neatly too, in a dark blue sweater and jeans. Something silver glinted at his throat, just under the collar of the sweater.

He raised a hand. "Oh. Right. Maryse cut it." The door of the elevator began to slide closed; he held it back. "Did you need to come up to the Institute?"

She shook her head. "I just wanted to talk to you."

"Oh." He looked a little surprised at that, but stepped out of the elevator, letting the door clang shut behind him. "I was just running over to Taki's to pick up some food. No one really feels like cooking. . . ."

"I understand," Clary said, then wished she hadn't. It wasn't as if the Lightwoods' desire to cook or not cook had anything to do with her.

"We can talk there," Jace said. He started toward the door, then paused and looked back at her. Standing between two of the burning candelabras, their light casting a pale gold overlay onto his hair and skin, he looked like a painting of an angel. Her heart constricted. "Are you coming, or not?" he snapped, not sounding angelic in the least.

"Oh. Right. I'm coming." She hurried to catch up with him.

As they walked to Taki's, Clary tried to keep the conversation away from topics related to her, Jace, or her and Jace. Instead, she asked him how Isabelle, Max, and Alec were doing.

Jace hesitated. They were crossing First and a cool breeze was blowing up the avenue. The sky was a cloudless blue, a perfect New York autumn day.

"I'm sorry." Clary winced at her own stupidity. "They must be pretty miserable. All these people they knew are dead."

"It's different for Shadowhunters," Jace said. "We're warriors. We expect death in a way you—"

Clary couldn't help a sigh. "'You *mundanes* don't.' That's what you were going to say, isn't it?"

"I was," he admitted. "Sometimes it's hard even for me to know what you really are."

They had stopped in front of Taki's, with its sagging roof and windowless facade. The ifrit who guarded the front door gazed down at them with suspicious red eyes.

"I'm Clary," she said.

Jace looked down at her. The wind was blowing her hair across her face. He reached out and pushed it back, almost absently. "I know."

Inside, they found a corner booth and slid into it. The diner was nearly empty: Kaelie, the pixie waitress, lounged against the counter, lazily fluttering her blue-white wings. She and Jace had dated once. A pair of werewolves occupied another booth. They were eating raw shanks of lamb and arguing about who would win in a fight: Dumbledore from the Harry Potter books or Magnus Bane.

"Dumbledore would totally win," said the first one. "He has the badass Killing Curse."

The second lycanthrope made a trenchant point. "But Dumbledore isn't real."

"I don't think Magnus Bane is real either," scoffed the first. "Have you ever *met* him?"

"This is so weird," said Clary, slinking down in her seat. "Are you listening to them?"

"No. It's rude to eavesdrop." Jace was studying the menu, which gave Clary the opportunity to covertly study *him. I never look at you*, she'd told him. It was true too, or at least she never looked at him the way she wanted to, with an artist's eye. She would always get lost, distracted by a detail: the curve of his cheekbone, the angle of his eyelashes, the shape of his mouth.

"You're staring at me," he said, without looking up from the menu. "Why are you staring at me? Is something wrong?"

Kaelie's arrival at their table saved Clary from having to answer. Her pen, Clary noticed, was a silvery birch twig. She regarded Clary curiously out of all-blue eyes. "Do you know what you want?"

Unprepared, Clary ordered a few random items off the menu. Jace asked for a plate of sweet potato fries and a number of dishes to be boxed up and brought home to the Lightwoods. Kaelie departed, leaving behind the faint smell of flowers.

"Tell Alec and Isabelle I'm sorry about everything that happened," Clary said when Kaelie was out of earshot. "And tell Max that I'll take him to Forbidden Planet anytime."

"Only mundanes say they're sorry when what they mean is 'I share your grief,'" Jace observed. "None of it was your fault, Clary." His eyes were suddenly bright with hate. "It was Valentine's."

"I take it there's been no . . ."

"No sign of him? No. I'd guess he's holed up somewhere until he can finish what he started with the Sword. After that . . ." Jace shrugged.

"After that, what?"

"I don't know. He's a lunatic. It's hard to guess what a lunatic will do next." But he avoided her eyes, and Clary knew what he was thinking: *War.* That was what Valentine wanted. War with the Shadowhunters. And he would get it too. It was only a matter of where he would strike first. "Anyway, I doubt that's what you came to talk to me about, is it?"

"No." Now that the moment had come, Clary was having a hard time finding words. She caught a glimpse of her reflection in the silvery side of the napkin holder. White cardigan, white face, hectic flush in her cheeks. She looked like she had a fever. She felt a little like it too. "I've been wanting to talk to you for the past few days—"

"You could have fooled me." His voice was unnaturally sharp. "Every time I called you, Luke said you were sick. I figured you were avoiding me. Again."

"I wasn't." It seemed to her that there were vast amounts of empty space between them, though the booth wasn't that big and they weren't sitting that far apart. "I did want to talk to you. I've been thinking about you all the time."

He made a noise of surprise and held his hand out across the table. She took it, a wave of relief breaking over her. "I've been thinking about you, too."

His grip was warm on hers, comforting, and she remembered how she'd taken the bloody shard of the Portal out of his hand at Renwick's—the only thing that was left of his old life—and how he had pulled her into his arms. "I really was sick," she said. "I swear. I almost died back there on the ship, you know."

He let her hand go, but he was staring at her, almost as if he meant to memorize her face. "I know," he said. "Every time you almost die, I almost die myself."

His words made her heart rattle in her chest as if she'd swallowed a mouthful of caffeine. "Jace. I came to tell you that—"

"Wait. Let me talk first." He held his hands up as if to ward off her next words. "Before you say anything, I wanted to apologize to you."

"Apologize? For what?"

"For not listening to you." He raked his hair back with both hands and she noticed a little scar, a tiny silver line, on the side of his throat. It hadn't been there before. "You kept telling me that I couldn't have what I wanted from you, and I kept pushing at you and pushing at you and not listening to you at all. I just wanted you and I didn't care what anybody else had to say about it. Not even you."

Her mouth went suddenly dry, but before she could say anything, Kaelie was back, with Jace's fries and a number of plates for Clary. Clary stared down at what she'd ordered. A green milk shake, what looked like raw hamburger steak, and a plate of chocolate-dipped crickets. Not that it mattered; her stomach was knotted up too much to even consider eating. "Jace," she said, as soon as the waitress was gone. "You didn't do anything wrong. You—"

"No. Let me finish." He was staring down at his fries as if they held the secrets of the universe. "Clary, I have to say it now or—or I won't say it." His words tumbled out in a rush: "I thought I'd lost my family. And I don't mean Valentine. I mean the Lightwoods. I thought they'd finished with me. I thought there was nothing left in my world but you. I—I was crazy with loss and I took it out on you and I'm sorry. You were right."

"No. I was stupid. I was cruel to you—"

"You had every right to be." He raised his eyes to look at her and she was suddenly and strangely reminded of being four years old at the beach, crying when the wind came up and blew away the castle she had made. Her mother had told her she could make another one if she liked, but it hadn't stopped her crying because what she had thought was permanent was not permanent after all, but only made out of sand that vanished at the touch of wind or water. "What you said was true. We don't live or love in a vacuum. There are people around us who care about us who would be hurt, maybe destroyed, if we let ourselves feel what we might want to feel. To be that selfish, it would mean—it would mean being like Valentine."

He spoke his father's name with such finality that Clary felt it like a door slamming in her face.

"I'll just be your brother from now on," he said, looking at her with a hopeful expectation that she would be pleased, which made her want to scream that he was smashing her heart into pieces and he had to stop. "That's what you wanted, isn't it?"

It took her a long time to answer, and when she did, her own voice sounded like an echo, coming from very far away. "Yes," she said, and she heard the rush of waves in her ears, and her eyes stung as if from sand or salt spray. "That's what I wanted."

Clary walked numbly up the wide steps that led up to Beth Israel's big glass front doors. In a way, she was glad she was here rather than anywhere else. What she wanted more than anything was to throw herself into her mother's arms and cry, even if she could never explain to her mother what she was crying about. Since she couldn't do that, sitting next to her mother's bed and crying seemed like the next best option.

She'd held it together pretty well at Taki's, even hugging Jace good-bye when she left. She hadn't started bawling till she'd gotten on the subway, and then she'd found herself crying about everything she hadn't cried about yet, Jace and Simon and Luke and her mother and even Valentine. She'd cried loudly enough that the man sitting across from her had offered her a tissue, and she'd screamed, *What do you think you're looking at, jerk?* at him, because that was what you did in New York. After that she felt a little better.

As she neared the top of the stairs, she realized there was a woman standing there. She was wearing a long dark cloak over a dress, not the sort of thing you usually saw on a Manhattan street. The cloak was made of a dark velvety material and had a wide hood, which was up, hiding her face. Glancing around, Clary saw that no one else on the hospital steps or standing by its doors seemed to notice the apparition. A glamour, then.

She reached the top step and paused, looking up at the woman. She still couldn't see her face. She said, "Look, if you're here to see me, just tell me what you want. I'm not really in the mood for all this glamour and secrecy stuff right now."

She noticed people around her stopping to stare at the crazy girl who was talking to no one. She fought the urge to stick out her tongue at them.

"All right." The voice was gentle, oddly familiar. The woman reached up and pushed back her hood. Silver hair spilled out over her shoulders in a flood. It was the woman Clary had seen staring at her in the courtyard of the Marble Cemetery, the same woman who'd saved them from Malik's knife at the Institute. Up close, Clary could see that she had the sort of face that was all angles, too sharp to be pretty, though her eyes were an intense and lovely hazel. "My name is Madeleine. Madeleine Bellefleur."

"And . . . ?" Clary said. "What do you want from me?"

The woman—Madeleine—hesitated. "I knew your mother, Jocelyn," she said. "We were friends in Idris."

"You can't see her," Clary said. "No visitors but family until she gets better."

"But she won't get better."

Clary felt as if she'd been slapped in the face. "*What?*"

"I'm sorry," Madeleine said. "I didn't mean to upset you. It's just that I know what's wrong with Jocelyn, and there's nothing a mundane hospital can do for her now. What happened to her—she did it to herself, Clarissa."

"No. You don't understand. Valentine—"

"She did it before Valentine got to her. So he couldn't get any information out of her. She planned it that way. It was a secret, a secret she shared with only one other person, and she told only one other person how the spell could be reversed. That person was me."

"You mean—"

"Yes," Madeleine said. "I mean I can show you how to wake your mother up."

CHECK OUT A SNEAK PEEK OF
BOOK THREE IN THE MORTAL INSTRUMENTS:

# City of Glass

# 1
# The Portal

**The cold snap of the previous week was over; the sun was** shining brightly as Clary hurried across Luke's dusty front yard, the hood of her jacket up to keep her hair from blowing across her face. The weather might have warmed up, but the wind off the East River could still be brutal. It carried with it a faint chemical smell, mixed with the Brooklyn smell of asphalt, gasoline, and burned sugar from the abandoned factory down the street.

Simon was waiting for her on the front porch, sprawled in a broken-springed armchair. He had his DS balanced on his blue-jeaned knees and was poking away at it industriously with the stylus. "Score," he said as she came up the steps. "I'm kicking butt at Mario Kart."

Clary pushed her hood back, shaking hair out of her eyes, and rummaged in her pocket for her keys. "Where have you been? I've been calling you all morning."

Simon got to his feet, shoving the blinking rectangle into his messenger bag. "I was at Eric's. Band practice."

Clary stopped jiggling the key in the lock—it always stuck—long enough to frown at him. "*Band* practice? You mean you're still—"

"In the band? Why wouldn't I be?" He reached around her. "Here, let me do it."

Clary stood still while Simon expertly twisted the key with just the right amount of pressure, making the stubborn old lock spring open. His hand brushed hers; his skin was cool, the temperature of the air outside. She shivered a little. They'd only called off their attempt at a romantic relationship last week, and she still felt confused whenever she saw him.

"Thanks." She took the key back without looking at him.

It was hot in the living room. Clary hung her jacket up on the peg inside the front hall and headed to the spare bedroom, Simon trailing in her wake. She frowned. Her suitcase was open like a clamshell on the bed, her clothes and sketchbooks strewn everywhere.

"I thought you were just going to be in Idris a couple of days," Simon said, taking in the mess with a look of faint dismay.

"I am, but I can't figure out what to pack. I hardly own any dresses or skirts, but what if I can't wear pants there?"

"Why wouldn't you be able to wear pants there? It's another country, not another century."

"But the Shadowhunters are so old-fashioned, and Isabelle

always wears dresses—" Clary broke off and sighed. "It's nothing. I'm just projecting all my anxiety about my mom onto my wardrobe. Let's talk about something else. How was practice? Still no band name?"

"It was fine." Simon hopped onto the desk, legs dangling over the side. "We're considering a new motto. Something ironic, like 'We've seen a million faces and rocked about eighty percent of them.'"

"Have you told Eric and the rest of them that—"

"That I'm a vampire? No. It isn't the sort of thing you just drop into casual conversation."

"Maybe not, but they're your *friends*. They should know. And besides, they'll just think it makes you more of a rock god, like that vampire Lester."

"Lestat," Simon said. "That would be the vampire Lestat. And he's fictional. Anyway, I don't see you running to tell all your friends that you're a Shadowhunter."

"What friends? You're my friend." She threw herself down onto the bed and looked up at Simon. "And I told you, didn't I?"

"Because you had no choice." Simon put his head to the side, studying her; the bedside light reflected off his eyes, turning them silver. "I'll miss you while you're gone."

"I'll miss you, too," Clary said, although her skin was prickling all over with a nervous anticipation that made it hard to concentrate. *I'm going to Idris!* her mind sang. *I'll see the Shadowhunter home country, the City of Glass. I'll save my mother.*

*And I'll be with Jace.*

Simon's eyes flashed as if he could hear her thoughts, but his voice was soft. "Tell me again—why do *you* have to go to Idris? Why can't Madeleine and Luke take care of this without you?"

"My mom got the spell that put her in this state from a warlock—Ragnor Fell. Madeleine says we need to track him down if we want to know how to reverse the spell. But he doesn't know Madeleine. He knew my mom, and Madeleine thinks he'll trust me because I look so much like her. And Luke can't come with me. He could come to Idris, but apparently he can't get into Alicante without permission from the Clave, and they won't give it. And don't say anything about it to him, *please*—he's really not happy about not going with me. If he hadn't known Madeleine before, I don't think he'd let me go at all."

"But the Lightwoods will be there too. And Jace. They'll be helping you. I mean, Jace did say he'd help you, didn't he? He doesn't mind you coming along?"

"Sure, he'll help me," Clary said. "And of course he doesn't mind. He's fine with it."

But that, she knew, was a lie.

Clary had gone straight to the Insititute after she'd talked to Madeleine at the hospital. Jace had been the first one she'd told her mother's secret to, before even Luke. And he'd stood there and stared at her, getting paler and paler as she spoke, as if she weren't so much telling him how she could save her mother as draining the blood out of him with cruel slowness.

"You're not going," he said as soon as she'd finished. "If I have to tie you up and sit on you until this insane whim of yours passes, you are not going to Idris."

Clary felt as if he'd slapped her. She had thought he'd be *pleased*. She'd run all the way from the hospital to the Institute to tell him, and here he was standing in the entryway glaring at her with a look of grim death. "But you're going."

"Yes, we're going. We *have* to go. The Clave's called every active Clave member who can be spared back to Idris for a massive Council meeting. They're going to vote on what to do about Valentine, and since we're the last people who've seen him—"

Clary brushed this aside. "So if you're going, why can't I go with you?"

The straightforwardness of the question seemed to make him even angrier. "Because it isn't safe for you there."

"Oh, and it's so safe here? I've nearly been killed a dozen times in the past month, and every time it's been right here in New York."

"That's because Valentine's been concentrating on the two Mortal Instruments that were here." Jace spoke through gritted teeth. "He's going to shift his focus to Idris now, we all know it—"

"We're hardly as certain of anything as all that," said Maryse Lightwood. She had been standing in the shadow of the corridor doorway, unseen by either of them; she moved forward now, into the harsh entryway lights. They illuminated the lines of exhaustion that seemed to draw her face down. Her husband, Robert Lightwood, had been injured by demon poison during the battle last week and had needed constant nursing since; Clary could only imagine how tired she must be. "And the Clave wants to meet Clarissa. You know that, Jace."

"The Clave can screw itself."

"Jace," Maryse said, sounding genuinely parental for a change. "Language."

"The Clave wants a lot of things," Jace amended. "It shouldn't necessarily get them all."

Maryse shot him a look, as if she knew exactly what he was talking about and didn't appreciate it. "The Clave is often right, Jace. It's not unreasonable for them to want to talk to Clary, after what she's been through. What she could tell them—"

"I'll tell them whatever they want to know," Jace said.

Maryse sighed and turned her blue eyes on Clary. "So you want to go to Idris, I take it?"

"Just for a few days. I won't be any trouble," Clary said, gazing entreatingly past Jace's white-hot glare at Maryse. "I swear."

"The question isn't whether you'll be any trouble; the question is whether you'll be willing to meet with the Clave while you're there. They want to talk to you. If you say no, I doubt we can get the authorization to bring you with us."

"No—," Jace began.

"I'll meet with the Clave," Clary interrupted, though the thought sent a ripple of cold down her spine. The only emissary of the Clave she'd known so far was the Inquisitor, who hadn't exactly been pleasant to be around.

Maryse rubbed at her temples with her fingertips. "Then it's settled." She didn't sound settled, though; she sounded as tense and fragile as an overtightened violin string. "Jace, show Clary out and then come see me in the library. I need to talk to you."

She disappeared back into the shadows without even a word of farewell. Clary stared after her, feeling as if she'd just been drenched with ice water. Alec and Isabelle seemed genuinely fond of their mother, and she was sure Maryse wasn't a bad person, really, but she wasn't exactly *warm*.

Jace's mouth was a hard line. "Now look what you've done."

"I need to go to Idris, even if you can't understand why," Clary said. "I need to do this for my mother."

"Maryse trusts the Clave too much," said Jace. "She has to believe they're perfect, and I can't tell her they aren't, because—" He stopped abruptly.

"Because that's something Valentine would say."

She expected an explosion, but "No one is perfect" was all he said. He reached out and stabbed at the elevator button with his index finger. "Not even the Clave."

Clary crossed her arms over her chest. "Is that really why you don't want me to come? Because it isn't safe?"

A flicker of surprise crossed his face. "What do you mean? Why else wouldn't I want you to come?"

She swallowed. "Because—" *Because you told me you don't have feelings for me anymore, and you see, that's very awkward, because I still have them for you. And I bet you know it.*

"Because I don't want my little sister following me everywhere?" There was a sharp note in his voice, half mockery, half something else.

The elevator arrived with a clatter. Pushing the gate aside, Clary stepped into it and turned to face Jace. "I'm not going because you'll be there. I'm going because I want to help my mother. *Our* mother. I have to help her. Don't you get it? If I don't do this, she might never wake up. You could at least pretend you care a little bit."

Jace put his hands on her shoulders, his fingertips brushing the bare skin at the edge of her collar, sending pointless, helpless shivers through her nerves. There were shadows below his eyes, Clary noticed without wanting to, and dark hollows under his cheekbones. The black sweater he was wearing only made his bruise-marked skin stand out more, and the dark lashes, too; he was a study in contrasts, something to be painted in shades of black, white, and gray, with splashes of gold here and there, like his eyes, for an accent color—

"Let me do it." His voice was soft, urgent. "I can help her for you. Tell me where to go, who to ask. I'll get what you need."

"Madeleine told the warlock I'd be the one coming. He'll be expecting Jocelyn's daughter, not Jocelyn's son."

Jace's hands tightened on her shoulders. "So tell her there was a change of plans. I'll be going, not you. *Not you.*"

"Jace—"

"I'll do whatever," he said. "Whatever you want, if you promise to stay here."

"I can't."

He let go of her, as if she'd pushed him away. "*Why not?*"

"Because," she said, "she's my mother, Jace."

"And mine." His voice was cold. "In fact, why didn't Madeleine approach both of us about this? Why just you?"

"You know why."

"Because," he said, and this time he sounded even colder, "to her you're Jocelyn's daughter. But I'll always be Valentine's son."

He slammed the gate shut between them. For a moment she stared at him through it—the mesh of the gate divided up his face into a series of diamond shapes, outlined in metal. A single golden eye stared at her through one diamond, furious anger flickering in its depths.

"Jace—," she began.

But with a jerk and a clatter, the elevator was already moving, carrying her down into the dark silence of the cathedral.

* * *

"Earth to Clary." Simon waved his hands at her. "You awake?"

"Yeah, sorry." She sat up, shaking her head to clear it of cobwebs. That had been the last time she'd seen Jace. He hadn't picked up the phone when she'd called him afterward, so she'd made all her plans to travel to Idris with the Lightwoods using Alec as reluctant and embarrassed point person. Poor Alec, stuck between Jace and his mother, always trying to do the right thing. "Did you say something?"

"Just that I think Luke is back," Simon said, and jumped off the desk just as the bedroom door opened. "And he is."

"Hey, Simon." Luke sounded calm, maybe a little tired—he was wearing a battered denim jacket, a flannel shirt, and old cords tucked into boots that looked like they'd seen their best days ten years ago. His glasses were pushed up into his brown hair, which seemed flecked with more gray now than Clary remembered. There was a square package under his arm, tied with a length of green ribbon. He held it out to Clary. "I got you something for your trip."

"You didn't have to do that!" Clary protested. "You've done so much. . . ." She thought of the clothes he'd bought her after everything she owned had been destroyed. He'd given her a new phone, new art supplies, without ever having to be asked. Almost everything she owned now was a gift from Luke. *And you don't even approve of the fact that I'm going.* That last thought hung unspoken between them.

"I know. But I saw it, and I thought of you." He handed over the box.

The object inside was swathed in layers of tissue paper. Clary tore through it, her hand seizing on something soft as kitten's fur. She gave a little gasp. It was a bottle-green velvet coat, old-fashioned, with a gold silk lining, brass buttons, and a wide hood. She drew it onto her lap, smoothing her hands lovingly down the soft material. "It looks like something Isabelle would wear," she exclaimed. "Like a Shadowhunter traveling cloak."

"Exactly. Now you'll be dressed more like one of them," Luke said. "When you're in Idris."

She looked up at him. "Do you want me to look like one of them?"

"Clary, you are one of them." His smile was tinged with sadness. "Besides, you know how they treat outsiders. Anything you can do to fit in . . ."

Simon made an odd noise, and Clary looked guiltily at him—she'd almost forgotten he was there. He was looking studiously at his watch. "I should go."

"But you just got here!" Clary protested. "I thought we could hang out, watch a movie or something—"

"*You* need to pack." Simon smiled, bright as sunshine after rain. She could almost believe there was nothing bothering him. "I'll come by later to say good-bye before you go."

"Oh, come on," Clary protested. "Stay—"

"I can't." His tone was final. "I'm meeting Maia."

"Oh. Great," Clary said. Maia, she told herself, was nice. She was smart. She was pretty. She was also a werewolf. A werewolf with a crush on Simon. But maybe that was as it should be. Maybe his new friend *should* be a Downworlder. After all, he was a Downworlder himself now. Technically, he shouldn't even be spending time with Shadowhunters like Clary. "I guess you'd better go, then."

"I guess I'd better." Simon's dark eyes were unreadable. This was new—she'd always been able to read Simon before. She wondered if it was a side effect of the vampirism, or something else entirely. "Good-bye," he said, and bent as if to kiss her on the cheek, sweeping her hair back with one of his hands. Then he paused and drew back, his expression uncertain. She frowned in surprise, but he was already gone, brushing past Luke in the doorway. She heard the front door bang in the distance.

"He's acting so *weird*," she exclaimed, hugging the velvet coat against herself for reassurance. "Do you think it's the whole vampire thing?"

"Probably not." Luke looked faintly amused. "Becoming a Downworlder doesn't change the way you feel about things. Or people. Give him time. You *did* break up with him."

"I did not. He broke up with me."

"Because you weren't in love with him. That's an iffy proposition, and I think he's handling it with grace. A lot of teenage boys would sulk, or lurk around under your window with a boom box."

"No one has a boom box anymore. That was the eighties." Clary scrambled off the bed, pulling the coat on. She buttoned it up to the neck, luxuriating in the soft feel of the velvet. "I just want Simon to go back to normal." She glanced at herself in the mirror and was pleasantly surprised—the green made her red hair stand out and brightened the color of her eyes. She turned to Luke. "What do you think?"

He was leaning in the doorway with his hands in his pockets; a shadow passed over his face as he looked at her. "Your mother had a coat just like that when she was your age," was all he said.

Clary clutched the cuffs of the coat, digging her fingers into the soft pile. The mention of her mother, mixed with the sadness in his expression, was making her want to cry. "We're going to see her later today, right?" she asked. "I want to say good-bye before I go, and tell her—tell her what I'm doing. That she's going to be okay."

Luke nodded. "We'll visit the hospital later today. And, Clary?"

"What?" She almost didn't want to look at him, but to her relief, when she did, the sadness was gone from his eyes.

He smiled. "Normal isn't all it's cracked up to be."

Simon glanced down at the paper in his hand and then at the cathedral, his eyes slitted against the afternoon sun. The Institute rose up against the high blue sky, a slab of granite windowed with pointed arches and surrounded by a high stone wall. Gargoyle faces leered down from its cornices, as if daring him to approach the front door. It didn't look anything like it had the first time he had ever seen it, disguised as a run-down ruin, but then glamours didn't work on Downworlders.

*You don't belong here.* The words were harsh, sharp as acid; Simon wasn't sure if it was the gargoyle speaking or the voice in his own mind. *This is a church, and you are damned.*

"Shut up," he muttered halfheartedly. "Besides, I don't care about churches. I'm Jewish."

There was a filigreed iron gate set into the stone wall. Simon put his hand to the latch, half-expecting his skin to sear with pain, but nothing happened. Apparently the gate itself wasn't particularly holy. He pushed it open and was halfway up the cracked stonework path to the front door when he heard voices—several of them, and familiar—nearby.

Or maybe not that nearby. He had nearly forgotten how much his hearing, like his sight, had sharpened since he'd been Turned. It sounded as if the voices were just over his shoulder, but as he followed a narrow path around the side of the Institute, he saw that the people were standing quite a distance away, at the far end of the grounds. The grass grew wild here, half-covering the branching paths that led among what had probably once been neatly arranged rosebushes. There was even a stone bench, webbed with green weeds; this had been a real church once, before the Shadowhunters had taken it over.

He saw Magnus first, leaning against a mossy stone wall. It was hard to miss Magnus—he was wearing a splash-painted white T-shirt over rainbow leather trousers. He stood out like a hothouse orchid, surrounded by the black-clad Shadowhunters: Alec, looking pale and uncomfortable; Isabelle, her long black hair twisted into braids tied with silver ribbons, standing beside a little boy who had to be Max, the youngest. Nearby was their mother, looking like a taller, bonier version of her daughter, with the same long black hair. Beside her was a woman Simon didn't know. At first Simon thought she was old, since her hair was nearly white, but then she turned to speak to Maryse and he saw that she probably wasn't more than thirty-five or forty.

And then there was Jace, standing off at a little distance, as if he didn't quite belong. He was all in Shadowhunter black like the others. When Simon wore all black, he looked like he was on his way to a funeral, but Jace just looked tough and dangerous. And *blonder*. Simon felt his shoulders tighten and wondered if anything—time, or forgetfulness—would ever dilute his resentment of Jace. He didn't *want* to feel it, but there it was, a stone weighting down his unbeating heart.

Something seemed odd about the gathering—but then Jace turned toward him, as if sensing he was there, and Simon saw, even from this distance, the thin white scar on his throat, just above his collar. The resentment in his chest faded into something else. Jace dropped a small nod in his direction. "I'll be right back," he said to Maryse, in the sort of voice Simon would never have used with his own mother. He sounded like an adult talking to another adult.

Maryse indicated her permission with a distracted wave. "I don't see why it's taking so long," she was saying to Magnus. "Is that normal?"

"What's not normal is the discount I'm giving you." Magnus tapped the heel of his boot against the wall. "Normally I charge twice this much."

"It's only a *temporary* Portal. It just has to get us to Idris. And then I expect you to close it back up again. That *is* our agreement." She turned to the woman at her side. "And you'll remain here to witness that he does it, Madeleine?"

*Madeleine*. So this was Jocelyn's friend. There was no time to stare, though—Jace already had Simon by the arm and was dragging him around the side of the church, out of view of the others. It was even more weedy and overgrown back here, the path snaked with ropes of undergrowth. Jace pushed Simon behind a large oak tree and let go of him, darting his eyes around as if to make sure they hadn't been followed. "It's okay. We can talk here."

It was quieter back here certainly, the rush of traffic from

York Avenue muffled behind the bulk of the Institute. "You're the one who asked me here," Simon pointed out. "I got your message stuck to my window when I woke up this morning. Don't you ever use the phone like normal people?"

"Not if I can avoid it, vampire," said Jace. He was studying Simon thoughtfully, as if he were reading the pages of a book. Mingled in his expression were two conflicting emotions: a faint amazement and what looked to Simon like disappointment. "So it's still true. You can walk in the sunlight. Even midday sun doesn't burn you."

"Yes," Simon said. "But you knew that—you were there." He didn't have to elaborate on what "there" meant; he could see in the other boy's face that he remembered the river, the back of the truck, the sun rising over the water, Clary crying out. He remembered it just as well as Simon did.

"I thought perhaps it might have worn off," Jace said, but he didn't sound as if he meant it.

"If I feel the urge to burst into flames, I'll let you know." Simon never had much patience with Jace. "Look, did you ask me to come all the way uptown just so you could stare at me like I was something in a petri dish? Next time I'll send you a photo."

"And I'll frame it and put it on my nightstand," said Jace, but he didn't sound as if his heart were in the sarcasm. "Look, I asked you here for a reason. Much as I hate to admit it, vampire, we have something in common."

"Totally awesome hair?" Simon suggested, but his heart wasn't really in it either. Something about the look on Jace's face was making him increasingly uneasy.

"Clary," Jace said.

Simon was caught off guard. "Clary?"

"Clary," Jace said again. "You know: short, redheaded, bad temper."

"I don't see how Clary is something we have in common," Simon said, although he did. Nevertheless, this wasn't a conversation he particularly wanted to have with Jace now, or, in fact, ever. Wasn't there some sort of manly code that precluded discussions like this—discussions about *feelings*?

Apparently not. "We both care about her," Jace stated, giving him a measured look. "She's important to both of us. Right?"

"You're asking me if I *care* about her?" "Caring" seemed like a pretty insufficient word for it. He wondered if Jace was making fun of him—which seemed unusually cruel, even for Jace. Had Jace brought him over here just to mock him because it hadn't worked out romantically between Clary and himself? Though Simon still had hope, at least a little, that things might change, that Jace and Clary would start to feel about each other the way they were supposed to, the way siblings were *meant* to feel about each other—

He met Jace's gaze and felt that little hope shrivel. The look on the other boy's face wasn't the look brothers got when they talked about their sisters. On the other hand, it was obvious Jace hadn't brought him over here to mock him for his feelings; the misery Simon knew must be plainly written across his own features was mirrored in Jace's eyes.

"Don't think I like asking you these questions," Jace snapped. "I need to know what you'd do for Clary. Would you lie for her?"

"Lie about what? What's going on, anyway?" Simon realized

what it was that had bothered him about the tableau of Shadowhunters in the garden. "Wait a second," he said. "You're leaving for Idris *right now*? Clary thinks you're going tonight."

"I know," Jace said. "And I need you to tell the others that Clary sent you here to say she wasn't coming. Tell them she doesn't want to go to Idris anymore." There was an edge to his voice—something Simon barely recognized, or perhaps it was simply so strange coming from Jace that he couldn't process it. Jace was *pleading* with him. "They'll believe you. They know how . . . how close you two are."

Simon shook his head. "I can't believe you. You act like you want me to do something for Clary, but actually you just want me to do something for *you*." He started to turn away. "No deal."

Jace caught his arm, spinning him back around. "This *is* for Clary. I'm trying to protect her. I thought you'd be at least a little interested in helping me do that."

Simon looked pointedly at Jace's hand where it clamped his upper arm. "How can I protect her if you don't tell me what I'm protecting her from?"

Jace didn't let go. "Can't you just trust me that this is important?"

"You don't understand how badly she wants to go to Idris," Simon said. "If I'm going to keep that from happening, there had better be a damn good reason."

Jace exhaled slowly, reluctantly—and let go his grip on Simon's arm. "What Clary did on Valentine's ship," he said, his voice low. "With the rune on the wall—the Rune of Opening—well, you saw what happened."

"She destroyed the ship," said Simon. "Saved all our lives."

"Keep your voice down." Jace glanced around anxiously.

"You're not saying no one else knows about that, are you?" Simon demanded in disbelief.

"I know. You know. Luke knows and Magnus knows. No one else."

"What do they all think happened? The ship just opportunely came apart?"

"I told them Valentine's Ritual of Conversion must have gone wrong."

"You lied to the Clave?" Simon wasn't sure whether to be impressed or dismayed.

"Yes, I lied to the Clave. Isabelle and Alec know Clary has some ability to create new runes, so I doubt I'll be able to keep that from the Clave or the new Inquisitor. But if they knew she could do what she does—amplify ordinary runes so they have incredible destructive power—they'd want her as a fighter, a weapon. And she's not equipped for that. She wasn't brought up for it—" He broke off, as Simon shook his head. "What?"

"You're Nephilim," Simon said slowly. "Shouldn't you want what's best for the Clave? If that's using Clary . . ."

"You want them to have her? To put her in the front lines, up against Valentine and whatever army he's raising?"

"No," said Simon. "I don't want that. But I'm not one of you. I don't have to ask myself who to put first, Clary or my family."

Jace flushed a slow, dark red. "It's not like that. If I thought it would help the Clave—but it won't. She'll just get hurt—"

"Even if you thought it would help the Clave," Simon said, "you'd never let them have her."

"What makes you say that, vampire?"

"Because no one can have her but you," said Simon.

The color left Jace's face. "So you won't help me," he said in disbelief. "You won't help *her*?"

Simon hesitated—and before he could respond, a noise split the silence between them. A high, shrieking cry, terrible in its desperation, and worse for the abruptness with which it was cut off. Jace whirled around. "What was that?"

The single shriek was joined by other cries, and a harsh clanging that scraped Simon's eardrums. "Something's happened—the others—"

But Jace was already gone, running along the path, dodging the undergrowth. After a moment's hesitation Simon followed. He had forgotten how fast he could run now—he was hard on Jace's heels as they rounded the corner of the church and burst out into the garden.

Before them was chaos. A white mist blanketed the garden, and there was a heavy smell in the air—the sharp tang of ozone and something else under it, sweet and unpleasant. Figures darted back and forth—Simon could see them only in fragments, as they appeared and disappeared through gaps in the fog. He glimpsed Isabelle, her hair snapping around her in black ropes as she swung her whip. It made a deadly fork of golden lightning through the shadows. She was fending off the advance of something lumbering and huge—a demon, Simon thought—but it was full daylight; that was impossible. As he stumbled forward, he saw that the creature was humanoid in shape, but humped and twisted, somehow *wrong*. It carried a thick wooden plank in one hand and was swinging at Isabelle almost blindly.

Only a short distance away, through a gap in the stone wall,

Simon could see the traffic on York Avenue rumbling placidly by. The sky beyond the Institute was clear.

"Forsaken," Jace whispered. His face was blazing as he drew one of his seraph blades from his belt. "Dozens of them." He pushed Simon to the side, almost roughly. "Stay here, do you understand? Stay here."

Simon stood frozen for a moment as Jace plunged forward into the mist. The light of the blade in his hand lit the fog around him to silver; dark figures dashed back and forth inside it, and Simon felt as if he were gazing through a pane of frosted glass, desperately trying to make out what was happening on the other side. Isabelle had vanished; he saw Alec, his arm bleeding, as he sliced through the chest of a Forsaken warrior and watched it crumple to the ground. Another reared up behind him, but Jace was there, now with a blade in each hand; he leaped into the air and brought them up and then down with a vicious scissoring movement—and the Forsaken's head tumbled free of its neck, black blood spurting. Simon's stomach wrenched—the blood smelled bitter, poisonous.

He could hear the Shadowhunters calling to one another out of the mist, though the Forsaken were utterly silent. Suddenly the mist cleared, and Simon saw Magnus, standing wild-eyed by the wall of the Institute. His hands were raised, blue lightning sparking between them, and against the wall where he stood, a square black hole seemed to be opening in the stone. It wasn't empty, or dark precisely, but shone like a mirror with whirling fire trapped within its glass. "The Portal!" he was shouting. "Go through the Portal!"

Several things happened at once. Maryse Lightwood appeared out of the mist, carrying the boy, Max, in her arms.

She paused to call something over her shoulder and then plunged toward the Portal and *through* it, vanishing into the wall. Alec followed, dragging Isabelle after him, her blood-spattered whip trailing on the ground. As he pulled her toward the Portal, something surged up out of the mist behind them—a Forsaken warrior, swinging a double-bladed knife.

Simon unfroze. Darting forward, he called out Isabelle's name—then stumbled and pitched forward, hitting the ground hard enough to knock the breath out of him, if he'd *had* any breath. He scrambled into a sitting position, turning to see what he'd tripped over.

It was a body. The body of a woman, her throat slit, her eyes wide and blue in death. Blood stained her pale hair. Madeleine.

"Simon, *move*!" It was Jace, shouting; Simon looked and saw the other boy running toward him out of the fog, bloody seraph blades in his hands. Then he looked up. The Forsaken warrior he'd seen chasing Isabelle loomed over him, its scarred face twisted into a rictus grin. Simon twisted away as the double-bladed knife swung down toward him, but even with his improved reflexes, he wasn't fast enough. A searing pain shot through him as everything went black.

**And now, a sneak peek of**
**the first book in Cassandra Clare's Infernal Devices trilogy,**
**the prequel to the Mortal Instruments series.**

**Travel back to Victorian London**
**with an earlier generation of Shadowhunters.**

*London. April, 1878.*

The demon exploded in a shower of ichor and guts.

William Herondale jerked back the dagger he was holding, but it was too late: The viscous acid of the demon's blood had already begun to eat away at the shining blade. He swore and tossed the weapon aside; it landed in a filthy puddle and commenced smoldering like a doused match. The demon itself, of course, had vanished—dispatched back to whatever hellish world it had come from, though not without leaving a mess behind.

"Jem!" Will called, turning around. "Where are you? Did you see that? Killed it with one blow! Not bad, eh?"

But there was no answer to Will's shout. Will was positive his hunting partner had been standing behind him in the damp and crooked street a few moments before, guarding his back, but now Will was alone in the shadows. He frowned in annoyance—it was much less fun showing off without Jem to show off *to.* Will glanced behind him, to where the street narrowed into a passage that gave onto the black, heaving water of the Thames in the distance. Through the gap he could see the dark outlines of docked ships, a forest of masts like a leafless orchard. No Jem there; perhaps he had gone back to Narrow Street in search of better illumination. With a shrug Will headed back the way he had come.

Narrow Street cut across Limehouse, between the docks beside the river and the cramped slums spreading west toward Whitechapel. It was as narrow as its name suggested, lined with warehouses and lopsided wooden buildings. At the moment it was deserted; even the drunks staggering home from the Grapes up the road had found somewhere to collapse for the night. Will liked Limehouse, liked the feeling of being on the edge of the world, where ships left each day for unimaginably far ports. That the area was a sailor's haunt, and consequently full of gambling hells, opium dens, and brothels, didn't hurt either. It was easy to lose yourself in a place like this. He didn't even mind the smell of it—smoke and dirt, rope and tar, foreign spices mixed with the river-water smell of the Thames.

Looking up and down the empty street, he scrubbed the sleeve of his coat across his face, trying to rub away the ichor that stung and burned his skin. The cloth came away stained green and black. There was a cut on the back of his hand too, a nasty one. He could use a healing rune. One of Charlotte's, preferably. She was particularly good at drawing *iratzes.*

A shape detached itself from the shadows and moved toward Will. He started forward, then paused. It wasn't Jem, but rather a mundane beat policeman wearing a bell-shaped helmet, a heavy overcoat, and a puzzled expression. He stared at Will, or rather *through* Will. However accustomed Will had become to glamour, it was always strange to be looked through as if he weren't there. Will was seized with the sudden urge to grab the policeman's truncheon and watch while the man flapped around, trying to figure out where it had gone; but Jem had scolded him the few times he'd done that before, and while Will never really could understand Jem's objections to the whole enterprise, it wasn't worth making him upset.

With a shrug and a blink, the policeman moved past Will, shaking his head and muttering something under his breath about swearing off the gin before he truly started seeing things. Will stepped aside to let the man pass, then raised his voice to a shout: "James Carstairs! Jem! Where *are* you, you disloyal bastard?"

This time a faint reply answered him. "Over here. Follow the witchlight."

Will moved toward the sound of Jem's voice. It seemed to be coming from a dark opening between two warehouses: A faint gleam was visible within the shadows, like the darting light of a will-o'-the-wisp. "Did you hear me before? That Shax demon thought it could get me with its bloody great pincers, but I cornered it in an alley—"

"Yes, I heard you." The young man who appeared at the mouth of the alley was pale in the lamplight—paler even than he usually was, which was quite pale indeed. He was bare-headed, which drew the eye immediately to his hair. It was an odd bright silver color, like an untarnished shilling. His eyes were the same silver, and his fine-boned face was angular, the slight curve of his eyes the only clue to his heritage.

There were dark stains across his white shirtfront, and his hands were thickly smeared with red.

Will tensed. "You're bleeding. What happened?"

Jem waved away Will's concern. "It's not my blood." He turned his head back toward the alley behind him. "It's hers."

Will glanced past his friend into the thicker shadows of the alley. In the far corner of it was a crumpled shape—only a shadow in the darkness, but when Will looked closely, he could make out the shape of a pale hand, and a wisp of fair hair.

"A dead woman?" Will asked. "A mundane?"

"A girl, really. Not more than fourteen."

At that, Will cursed with great volume and fluency. Jem waited patiently for him to be done.

"If we'd only happened along a little earlier," Will said finally. "That bloody demon—"

"That's the peculiar thing. I don't think this is the demon's work." Jem frowned. "Shax demons are parasites, brood parasites. It would have wanted to drag its victim back to its lair to lay eggs in her skin while she was still alive. But this girl—she was stabbed, repeatedly. And I don't think it was here, either. There simply isn't enough blood in the alley. I think she was attacked elsewhere, and she dragged herself here to die of her injuries."

Will's mouth tightened. "But the Shax demon—"

"I'm telling you, I don't think it *was* the Shax. I think the

Shax was pursuing her—hunting her down for something, or someone, else."

"Shaxes have a keen sense of scent," Will allowed. "I've heard of warlocks using them to follow the tracks of the missing. And it did seem to be moving with an odd sort of purpose." He looked past Jem, at the pitiful smallness of the crumpled shape in the alley. "You didn't find the weapon, did you?"

"Here." Jem drew something from inside his jacket—a knife, wrapped in white cloth. "It's a sort of misericord, or hunting dagger. Look how thin the blade is."

Will took it. The blade was indeed thin, ending in a handle made of polished bone. Both blade and hilt were stained with dried blood. With a frown he wiped the flat of the knife across the rough fabric of his sleeve, scraping it clean until a symbol, burned into the blade, became visible. Two serpents, each biting the other's tail, forming a perfect circle.

"*Ouroboros*," Jem said, leaning in close to stare at the knife. "A double one. Now, what do you think that means?"

"The end of the world," said Will, still looking at the dagger, a small smile playing about his mouth, "and the beginning."

Jem frowned. "I understand the symbology, William. I meant, what do you think its presence on the dagger signifies?"

The wind off the river was ruffling Will's hair; he brushed it out of his eyes with an impatient gesture and went back to studying the knife. "It's an alchemical symbol, not a warlock or Downworlder one. That usually means humans—the foolish mundane sort who think trafficking in magic is the ticket for gaining wealth and fame."

"The sort who usually end up a pile of bloody rags inside some pentagram." Jem sounded grim.

"The sort who like to lurk about the Downworld parts of our fair city." After wrapping the handkerchief around the blade carefully, Will slipped it into his jacket pocket. "D'you think Charlotte will let me handle the investigation?"

"Do *you* think you can be trusted in Downworld? The gambling hells, the dens of magical vice, the women of loose morals . . ."

Will smiled the way Lucifer might have smiled moments before he fell from Heaven. "Would tomorrow be too early to start looking, do you think?"

Jem sighed. "Do what you like, William. You always do."

*Southampton. May.*

Tessa could not remember a time when she had not loved the clockwork angel. It had belonged to her mother once, and her mother had been wearing it when she'd died. After that it had sat in her mother's jewelry box until her brother, Nathaniel, had taken it out one day to see if it was still in working order.

The angel was no bigger than Tessa's pinky finger, a tiny statuette made of brass, with folded bronze wings no larger than a cricket's. It had a delicate metal face with shut crescent eyelids, and hands crossed over a sword in front. A thin chain that looped beneath the wings allowed the angel to be worn around the neck like a locket.

Tessa knew the angel was made out of clockwork because if she lifted it to her ear, she could hear the sound of its machinery, like the sound of a watch. Nate had exclaimed in surprise that it was still working after so many years, and he had looked in vain for a knob or a screw, or some other method by which the angel might be wound. But there had been nothing to find. With a shrug he'd given the angel to Tessa. From that moment, she had never taken it off; even at night the angel lay against her chest as she slept, its constant *tick-tock, tick-tock* like the beating of a second heart.

She held it now, clutched between her fingers, as the *Main* nosed its way between other massive steamships to find a spot at the Southampton dock. Nate had insisted that she come to Southampton instead of Liverpool, where most transatlantic steamers arrived. He had claimed it was because Southampton was a much pleasanter place to arrive at, so Tessa couldn't help being a little disappointed by this, her first sight of England. It was drearily gray. Rain drummed down onto the spires of a distant church, while black smoke rose from the chimneys of ships and stained the already dull-colored sky. A crowd of people in dark clothes, holding umbrellas, stood on the docks. Tessa strained to see if her brother was among them, but the mist and spray from the ship were too thick for her to make out any individual in great detail.

Tessa shivered. The wind off the sea was chilly. All of Nate's letters had claimed that London was beautiful, the sun shining every day. Well, Tessa thought hopefully, the weather there was better than it was here, because she had no warm clothes with her, nothing more substantial than a woolen shawl that had belonged to Aunt Harriet and a pair of thin gloves. She had sold most of her clothes to pay for her aunt's funeral, secure in the knowledge that her brother would buy her more when she arrived in London to live with him.

A shout went up. The *Main*, its shining black-painted hull gleaming wet with rain, had anchored, and tugs were plowing their way through the heaving gray water, ready to carry baggage and passengers to the shore. Passengers streamed off the ship, clearly desperate to feel land under their feet. So different from their departure from New York, Tessa thought. The sky had been blue then, and a brass band had been playing. Though with no one there to wish her good-bye, it had not been a merry occasion.

Hunching her shoulders, Tessa joined the disembarking crowd. Drops of rain stung her unprotected head and neck like pinpricks from icy little needles, and her hands inside their insubstantial gloves were clammy and wet. Reaching the quay, she looked around eagerly, searching for a sight of Nate. It had been nearly two weeks since she'd spoken to a soul, having kept almost entirely to herself on board the *Main*. It would be wonderful to have her brother to talk to again.

He wasn't there. The wharves were heaped with stacks of luggage and all sorts of boxes and cargo, even mounds of fruit and vegetables that were wilting and dissolving in the rain. A steamer was departing for Le Havre nearby, and damp-looking sailors swarmed close by Tessa, shouting in French. She tried to move aside, only to be almost trampled by a throng of disembarking passengers hurrying for the shelter of the railway station.

But Nate was nowhere to be seen.

"You are Miss Gray?" The voice was guttural, heavily accented. A man had moved to stand in front of Tessa. He was tall, and was wearing a sweeping black coat and a tall hat, its brim collecting rainwater like a cistern. His eyes were peculiarly bulging, almost protuberant like a frog's, and his skin was as rough-looking as scar tissue. Tessa had to fight the urge to cringe away from him. But he knew her name. Who here would know her name except someone who knew Nate, too?

She nodded. "Yes?"

"Your brother sent me. Come with me."

"Where is Nate?" Tessa demanded, but the man was already walking away. His stride was uneven, as if he had a limp from an old injury. After a moment Tessa gathered up her skirts and hurried after him.

He wound through the crowd, moving ahead with purposeful speed. People jumped aside, muttering about his rudeness as he shouldered past, with Tessa nearly running to keep up. He turned abruptly around a pile of boxes and came to a halt in front of a large, gleaming black coach. Gold letters had been painted across its side, but the rain and mist were too thick for Tessa to read them clearly.

The door of the carriage opened, and a woman leaned out. She wore an enormous plumed hat that hid her face. "Miss Theresa Gray?"

Tessa nodded. The bulging-eyed man hurried to help the woman out of the carriage—and then another woman, following after her. Each of them immediately opened an umbrella and raised it, sheltering themselves from the rain. Then they fixed their eyes on Tessa.

They were an odd pair, the women. One was very tall and thin, with a bony, pinched face. Colorless hair was scraped into a chignon at the back of her head. She wore a dress of brilliant violet silk, already spattered here and there with splotches of rain, and matching violet gloves. The other woman was short and plump, with small eyes sunk deep into her head; the bright pink gloves stretched over her large hands made them look like colorful paws.

"Theresa Gray," said the shorter of the two. "What a delight to make your acquaintance at last. I am Mrs. Black, and this is my sister, Mrs. Dark. Your brother sent us to accompany you to London."

Tessa—damp, cold, and baffled—clutched her wet shawl tighter around herself. "I don't understand. Where's Nate? Why didn't he come himself?"

"He was unavoidably detained by business in London. Mortmain's couldn't spare him. He sent ahead a note for you, however." Mrs. Black held out a rolled-up bit of paper, already dampened with rain.

Tessa took it and turned away to read it. It was a short note from her brother apologizing for not being at the docks to meet her, and letting her know that he trusted Mrs. Black and Mrs. Dark—*I call them the Dark Sisters, Tessie, for obvious reasons, and they seem to find the name agreeable!*—to bring her safely to his house in London. They were, his note said, his landladies as well as trusted friends, and they had his highest recommendation.

That decided her. The letter was certainly from Nate. It was in his handwriting, and no one else ever called her Tessie. She swallowed hard and slipped the note into her sleeve, turning back to face the sisters. "Very well," she said, fighting down her lingering sense of disappointment—she had been so looking forward to seeing her brother. "Shall we call a porter to fetch my trunk?"

"No need, no need." Mrs. Dark's cheerful tone was at odds with her pinched gray features. "We've already arranged to have it sent on ahead. It would hardly fit in the carriage anyway." She snapped her fingers at the bulging-eyed man, who swung himself up into the driver's seat at the front of the carriage. She placed her hand on Tessa's shoulder. "Come along, child; let's get you out of the rain."

As Tessa moved toward the carriage, propelled by Mrs. Dark's bony grip, the mist cleared, revealing the gleaming golden image painted on the side of the door. The words "The Pandemonium Club" curled intricately around two snakes biting each other's tails, forming a circle. Tessa frowned. "What does that mean?"

"Nothing you need worry about," said Mrs. Black, who had already climbed inside and had her skirts spread out across one of the comfortable-looking seats. The inside of the carriage was richly decorated with plush purple velvet bench seats facing each other, and gold tasseled curtains hanging in the windows.

Mrs. Dark helped Tessa up into the carriage, then clambered in behind her. As Tessa settled herself on the bench seat, Mrs. Black reached to shut the carriage door behind her sister, closing out the gray sky. Her teeth gleamed in the dimness as if they were made out of metal. "Do settle in, Theresa. We've a long ride ahead of us."

Tessa put a hand to the clockwork angel at her throat, taking comfort in its steady ticking as the carriage lurched forward into the rain.

FROM THE *NEW YORK TIMES* BESTSELLING AUTHOR

# Ellen Hopkins

***CRANK***

"The poems are masterpieces of word, shape, and pacing . . . stunning." —*SLJ*

***BURNED***

"Troubling but beautifully written." —*Booklist*

***IMPULSE***

"A fast, jagged, hypnotic read." —*Kirkus Reviews*

***GLASS***

"Powerful, heart-wrenching, and all too real." —*Teensreadtoo.com*

***IDENTICAL***

★"Sharp and stunning . . . brilliant." —*Kirkus Reviews*, starred review

***TRICKS***

"Distinct and unmistakable."—*Kirkus Reviews*

***FALLOUT***

"*Fallout* is impossible to put down."—*VOYA*

***PERFECT***

"This page-turner pulls no emotional punches."—*Kirkus Reviews*

EBOOK EDITIONS AVAILABLE

From Margaret K. McElderry Books Published by Simon & Schuster

# ZOMBIES
# vs.
# UNICORNS:
## Which side are *you* on?

**These are zombies and unicorns**
**as you have never seen them before:**
**sexy, majestic, and seriously ruthless.**

---

EBOOK EDITION ALSO AVAILABLE
MARGARET K. McELDERRY BOOKS | Simon & Schuster Children's Publishing
TEEN.SimonandSchuster.com